A TIME FOR SWORDS

MATTHEW HARFFY

HEAD
ZEUS

An Aries Book

First published in 2020 by Head of Zeus Ltd
This edition first published in 2021 by Head of Zeus Ltd
An Aries book

9 7 5 3 1 2 4 6 8

A catalogue record for this book is available from
the British Library.

ISBN (HB): 9781838932855
ISBN (ANZTPB): 9781838932862
ISBN (E): 9781838932886

Printed and bound by CPI Group (UK) Ltd,
Croydon, CR0 4YY

Head of Zeus Ltd
First Floor East
5–8 Hardwick Street
London EC1R 4RG

WWW.HEADOFZEUS.COM

BY MATTHEW HARFFY

A Time for Swords series

A Time for Swords

Bernicia Chronicles

The Serpent Sword
The Cross and the Curse
Blood and Blade
Killer of Kings
Warrior of Woden
Storm of Steel
Fortress of Fury
For Lord and Land
Kin of Cain (short story)

Novels

Wolf of Wessex

A Time for Swords
is for Shane Smart.
Keep on reading, Big Shaner!

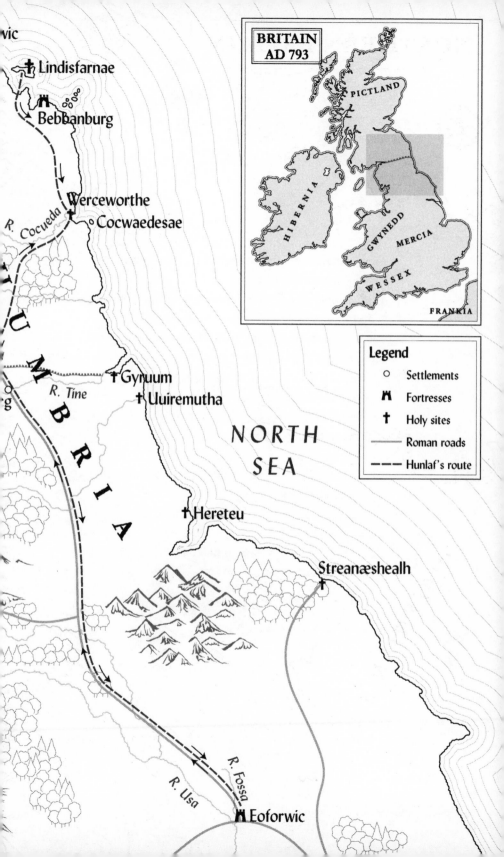

vic

† Lindisfarnae

Ħ
Bebbanburg

R. Cocueda

†Werceworthe
○ Cocwaedesae

NORTHUMBRIA

R. Tine

†Gyruum
†Uuiremutha

NORTH
SEA

†Hereteu

Streanæshealh

R. Fossa

R. Usa

Ħ Eoforwic

BRITAIN
AD 793

PICTLAND

HIBERNIA

GWYNEDD
MERCIA

WESSEX

FRANKIA

Legend

○   Settlements
Ħ   Fortresses
†   Holy sites
─── Roman roads
- - - Hunlaf's route

To every thing there is a season, and a time to every
purpose under the heaven:
A time to be born, and a time to die; a time to plant,
and a time to pluck up that which is planted;
A time to kill, and a time to heal; a time to break down,
and a time to build up;
A time to weep, and a time to laugh; a time to mourn,
and a time to dance;
A time to cast away stones, and a time to gather stones
together; a time to embrace, and a time to refrain from
embracing;
A time to get, and a time to lose; a time to keep, and a
time to cast away;
A time to rend, and a time to sew; a time to keep silence,
and a time to speak;
A time to love, and a time to hate; a time of war, and a
time of peace.

Ecclesiastes 3, verses 1-8

Place Names

Place names in early medieval Britain vary according to time, language, dialect and the scribe who was writing. I have not followed a strict convention when choosing the spelling to use for a given place. In most cases, I have chosen the name I believe to be the closest to that used in the late eighth century, but like the scribes of all those centuries ago, I have taken artistic licence at times, and, when unsure, merely selected the one I liked most.

Some of the place names also occur in my Bernicia Chronicles novels with different spellings. This is intentional to denote that this is not part of that series and also to indicate the passage of time and the changes to language that occur over the centuries.

Bebbanburg	Bamburgh
Berewic	Berwick upon Tweed
Byzantion	Constantinople (Istanbul)
Cocueda, River	River Coquet
Cocwaedesae	Coquet Island
Cordova	Córdoba, Spain
Corebricg	Corbridge
Duiblinn	Dublin
Eoforwic	York

Fossa, River	River Foss
Gwynedd	early medieval kingdom, now a county, situated in the north-west of modern-day Wales.
Gyruum	Jarrow
Hereteu	Hartlepool
Ifriqiya	area comprising what is today Tunisia, western Libya and eastern Algeria.
Lindisfarnae	Lindisfarne
Loch Cuan	Strangford Lough, Northern Ireland
Magilros	Melrose
Oguz il	(Oguz Land) Turkic state located in an area between the coasts of the Caspian and Aral Seas.
Powys	early medieval kingdom, now a county, situated in central modern-day Wales.
Roma	Rome
Rygjafylki	Rogaland, Norway
Streanæshealh	Whitby
Tine, River	River Tyne
Tuede, River	River Tweed
Ubbanford	Norham
Usa, River	River Ouse
Uuiremutha	Monkwearmouth
Vestfold	Vestfold, eastern Norway
Werceworthe	Warkworth

One

I am dying.

For months I have denied the signs, but this morning there was blood in my shit and a hollow ache has settled deep into the pit of my stomach. It feels as though there is a demon inside me, gnawing on my guts. Perhaps there is. Maybe the Devil has been given my body to do with as he wishes before I succumb to the cold embrace of death. I would not blame God if He has abandoned me. I have done my best these last years to do His bidding. With prayer and labour I have worshipped and honoured Him, but perhaps a man can sin too much in his lifetime for forgiveness. I know the Scriptures say otherwise, but I cannot but wonder whether the things I have done have made even the Almighty turn His back on me.

I have often awoken, in the cold stillness of my cell, my nose bitten by the chill, the world dark and silent, and I have lain on my pallet, thin blanket clutched tightly to my throat, terrified that I will not be brought unto my Heavenly Father on my death. Could Jesu truly forgive a man such as me?

Well, I am dying now, so I will know soon enough. Death is coming for me just as sure as the snow is thawing outside, turning the fields into a clinging quagmire that cakes the feet of the ceorls who toil there. The days are filled with the constant

3

dripping from the melting ice and, every now and then, the growl and thump of snow sloughing down the sloping shingled roofs of the monastery. As the land warms, I can feel my strength leaching away. It feels as if, as the winter recedes, so its frost settles within my bones.

For the longest time I believed I was immortal, as all young men do, I suppose. When I was young I would have scoffed if someone had told me that I would grow old and weak, unable to walk more than a few unsteady strides, hands gnarled and painful, eyes dimming and blurring so that it is difficult to see the letters I scribe, except on the brightest of days. But time, like wyrd, is inexorable, and slowly, without cease, it has taken those I cared for from me and it has withered my frame until I am a miserable, wheezing husk; a shade of the young, vital man who once thought he would live forever. That young man was defiant and headstrong.

And yet despite the ravages of time on my body, that impulsive youth resides within me still. For what I am about to do is rebellious and disobedient.

I have pondered for many days now whether I should undertake to write this story down. Vellum, ink and quills are all costly and Abbot Criba will be furious when he discovers that I have not been working on a copy of the *Vita Sancti Wilfrithi* as he instructed. His ire will do him little good though, I fear. For he does not enjoy my company and he will not visit me until the book is finished. He likes me not, but he trusts in my abilities as a scribe, even though it takes me longer than it once did to fill each stretched calf hide sheet with my scratchings. As likely as not, I shall be buried before he discovers the truth of what I have done. The thought of this deception sends a thrill down my spine.

Yes, the young man is still in there somewhere, still wilful and filled with pride.

Another sin to add to the list.

4

And yet, perhaps this is not such a thing of evil that I do. The life of Saint Wilfrid, blessed as it was, has already been written, but my life is known to nobody. The lives of saints and kings are piled high in the scriptoria of the world, and that is good. But what of my life? I've seen things that people wouldn't believe. A Turkic ship on fire off the shore of Odessa. I've watched sunbeams glitter in the dark eyes of the Empress of Roma, as we passed beneath Byzantion's Golden Gate. I do not want all those moments to be lost in time like the winter snow when the rains of spring come.

For years I have copied countless books on history, from Tacitus to Bede. Each of those tomes is filled with accounts of illustrious emperors, kings and queens; lords and ladies. But what of the men who served them? Their lives are forgotten after their deaths. Few of those who have died over the centuries have had the knowledge to commit their thoughts to writing, but my letters are yet clear when I scratch them onto a page and my memory is sharp. It seems that, as I have the opportunity and the skill, perhaps it would be sinful for me not to pen the history of my life. For I am now a writer and if not me, then who will record the history of my times?

Nobody else remains to speak of the secrets I have borne all these years. These stories are too important to vanish, buried along with my frail mortal form. But there is danger in my tale, mysteries that I have been too afraid to speak of before. Now all I fear is death, and I would have my secrets set down for those who come after. I have at times been accused of hubris, and perhaps this desire to record my life for posterity stems from that overbearing pride. Such judgement can be reserved for the readers of this work and for the Almighty Himself.

Time is passing quickly. I can all but feel the breath of Death on the nape of my neck. So I will begin with no further preamble. But where to start? I could tell of my childhood in a small village on the banks of the Tuede, but there is little remarkable to speak of there. No, I should commence with the day that my world changed forever. The day that blood, fear, fire and death descended on our once peaceful shores.

On that momentous morning my mind was teeming with images of a thing of wonder and beauty. A treasure that would prove to be an undying passion; the mistress I would turn to throughout my life. I have cherished her, fought and spilt blood for her. Even killed for her. And now, before my death, I aim to finally, truly entwine my story with hers.

This tale begins long ago when I was still a young man, heart swollen with pride. My sharp-witted mind overflowed with thoughts of knowledge and learning, of the perfection of words, philosophy and theology, and I had no inkling of the horrors that would befall Lindisfarnae on that fateful June day in the Year of Our Lord Jesus Christ 793.

The day the northern devils came.

Two

I can still recall the wonder of walking northward towards the holy isle of Lindisfarnae. The mule, cantankerous at times, but biddable enough, plodded along beside me. Brother Leofstan, long-legged and slender, strode ahead of us, as if he was keen to be away from my chatter. I walked with a spring to my step, tugging the laden beast to greater speed, more often using a softly spoken word of encouragement than a stroke of the hazel switch I carried. My heart soared at the feeling of freedom from being outside the minster of Werceworthe after so many months of inclement weather through the winter and spring.

I could still barely believe that Leofstan had chosen me, above all of the other novice monks, to accompany him. He was to bring a stack of freshly dried, stretched and scraped lamb skins to be used by the brothers at Lindisfarnae's scriptorium. When I had heard, I begged to be taken with him.

"You would do better to apply yourself to your studies than trudging north with me," he said.

"I have already finished committing to memory chapters eight to nineteen of the *Regula*," I told him.

Leofstan raised an eyebrow.

"What about the Latin exercises?" he asked, squinting down his thin nose at me.

"I copied out all of the declensions and I have learnt those pronouns that deviate from the normal order."

I proffered a wax-covered boxwood tablet to him. He took it, glancing down at my scratched letters in the thin veneer of beeswax. I have always had a natural ability with the learning of languages, both written and spoken, and I knew my Latin was all correct. His thin fingers traced the words as he read and he grunted, whether with approval or annoyance, I could not tell.

He stared at me for a long while.

"What is it that so draws you to Lindisfarnae?" he asked.

I longed to be free of the oppression of the minster, to travel further than the boundaries of the small parcel of land around Werceworthe. But I chose a different reply for Leofstan.

"You often tell us that the scribes of Lindisfarnae are the best in the whole of Christendom," I said. "Now that I have begun to learn the finer arts of writing, I would like to see the finest writing in the world." He stared at me, his thin, wrinkled face expressionless. Was there a slight creasing of his brows? I pressed on regardless, forcing myself to stare into his eyes with what I hoped was an open and eager mien. "I think I would learn much from watching the scribes at Lindisfarnae work and," I said, adding what I hoped would be the winning argument to my cause, "I would also welcome the chance to see the head of Saint Oswald and the bones of Saint Cuthbert; to offer up a prayer to that splendorous king and to the most sacred of holy men. I would pray for my dear mother's immortal soul. May she rest in the eternal peace of the Almighty's bosom."

I felt a pang of guilt at using my mother's memory to get my way. She had died when I was but a small boy, and my recollection of her was nebulous. And yet my words were not a lie. I would pray for her soul to the saints of Lindisfarnae, if Leofstan took me with him.

My teacher frowned and was silent. I was often as lazy as I was talented at languages and scribing and he clearly had his doubts as to my sincerity. For several heartbeats I was certain that he would reject my request, but after a time, he nodded.

"Very well," he said. "You will attend me on the journey. You might learn much from the brothers at Lindisfarnae. The mule will be your responsibility. Do not make me regret my decision."

I am quite sure he regretted his decision more than once as we headed north on the old crumbling road of Deira Stræt. I was poor company and the closer we got to our goal the harder I found it to suppress my excitement. I pointed out a tiny tan-coloured warbler, flitting in and out of a tangle of gorse. Leofstan glanced at the small bird, nodding absently. Free of the rule of silence imposed in the minster, I talked incessantly and, looking back, I see that Leofstan was indulgent to my whims. I thought nothing of it then. I was genuinely excited to see the monks' work in the scriptorium that supplied Gospels, missals and psalters to bishops and kings all across the world, from distant Roma in the south, to far-away Duiblinn in the west. I was already fascinated with the art of creating books and I was sure that I would indeed learn from the masters of the craft; the best scribes in the land. I was also intrigued about what the head of Saint Oswald would look like. And what about the remains of the saintly Cuthbert, the bishop whose name was now forever intertwined with Lindisfarnae? Would I feel the power resonating from his tomb? Would I sense the holy energy throbbing from the reliquary that held Oswald's wizened skull?

These were exciting questions for a young man who had not yet lived twenty summers. Little did I know then, as we walked north through the long warm summer days, that I would soon lay eyes on something of such exquisite beauty and dark mystery that my life would never be the same again. Leofstan had wanted me to learn from the trip, but I cannot believe he had any idea of how deep and vast that learning would prove, or what an impact that journey would have on both of our lives.

When we reached the crossing to the island we had to wait for the tide. We rested and I watched the terns and gulls swooping and wheeling in the cloud-streaked sky. A few cormorants swam in the dark waters to the south where the heads of seals bobbed above the surface. We sat in quiet for the most part. Now that we had almost reached our destination, with the fortress of Bebbanburg looming on the horizon to our right, my excited talk had been replaced by a tense anticipation of setting foot on the holy isle. Leofstan seemed content with the peace and surveyed the land, sea and sky in silence.

Eventually, the tide rolled out exposing the safe track across the mudflats to Lindisfarnae. The path, used by pilgrims and travellers, was marked with long staves that jutted from the dark sand.

Leofstan led the way and I pulled the mule behind me. It unnerved me to walk on land so recently covered by the sea, and the mule, perhaps sensing my unease, refused to walk at first. I tugged at his halter and cooed low soothing words and eventually he begrudgingly trudged down through the dunes and onto the flat sands that separated the holy island from the mainland of Britain. Despite the bright sun, the air was cool here; the blustery wind redolent of the sea.

"The way is safe enough," said Leofstan, "but to stray from the path can see a walker stumble into deep mud." He looked out over the mudflats to where oystercatchers strutted between pools that reflected the bright sky. "Out there you will find a quagmire that would suck at your limbs, holding you fast until the waters rush back with the next tide to claim another victim."

I shuddered and dragged the mule onward so that I did not fall too far behind Leofstan.

I was glad when we reached the dry land of the island where I knew the waters of the sea would not engulf me come the next high tide. It was early afternoon and we passed the cluster of buildings that were the homes and workshops of the lay people who served the holy men and women of the minster. Men and women looked at us, but they were used to seeing tonsured monks passing through their settlement and they quickly went back about their business. A couple of children ran beside us for a time, excited to see new faces. A dog barked at the mule and chased after us until its owner, a broad man with the shoulders of one used to heavy labour, stepped out from the shade of a hut and whistled. The dog scampered back and the man raised a hand in welcome.

Leaving the settlement behind, we crossed the vallum, the ditch that encircled the monastery buildings, and walked the final steps of our journey. The brethren were filing into the chapel and, looking at the sun, I realised it must be time for the office of None, the ninth hour. I thought Leofstan, who was never one to miss a prayer, would have me tether the mule and follow the others into the church. But before we arrived at the building, a figure hurried towards us.

It was a young monk, maybe two or three years my senior, with hooded eyes peering out from a face ravaged by some childhood disease.

"Brother Leofstan?" he asked, breathless. Leofstan nodded. "You are well met. Brother Oslac sent me to meet you."

Leofstan raised an eyebrow.

"And you are?"

"Tidraed, brother."

Leofstan gestured in my direction.

"This is Hunlaf."

Tidraed nodded absently, while turning and beckoning for us to follow him. He was heading towards the largest building in the monastery.

"Why the urgency?" Leofstan asked. "We have not even had a chance to unload the mule or to slake our thirst."

"We saw you coming across the pilgrim's path," Tidraed said. "Oslac has found something he wants you to see." He halted and turned to face us. His eyes flicked to the chapel from where now echoed the familiar sounds of voices chanting the liturgy of None. "He thinks it best you see it now while the rest of the brothers are at prayer."

Leofstan scratched at the back of his head. He glanced at me, but I could not decipher his expression. With a shrug, he said, "Lead on then, Tidraed."

When we reached the large building, an elderly man was standing in the doorway. His pale face was lined with age and the little hair that remained about his ears was white and floated in the breeze like gossamer.

"It is good to see you, Brother Oslac," said Leofstan, stepping forward and holding out a hand.

"There is no time for that," said the old monk. Turning, he hurried into the gloom of the building. Frowning, Leofstan followed. I left the mule cropping at the straggly grass that clung to the sandy soil and rushed inside. I had no idea what I was about to witness, but Oslac exuded a nervous sense of expectation that kindled my imagination.

Inside the long hall, the afternoon light slanted in through the unshuttered windows. Motes of dust danced in the sunlight. It was cool and still. I blinked after the bright daylight. But the smells that pervaded the air told me the story of the place before my eyes grew accustomed to the gloom. The acrid bite of the vinegar, copperas and oak galls used to make the encaustum, the faintly animal tang of the vellum, the liberal dusting of pounce, the oily sweet scent of feathers. As my eyes adjusted I saw the writing desks, the scattered quills, and the stacks of books and scrolls, but I already knew I was inside the fabled scriptorium of Lindisfarnae.

I breathed in deep of the familiar smells and gazed about me. The room was easily twice the size of the scriptorium back at Werceworthe where I spent most of my days. The number of books dazzled me. I wanted to reach out and touch them all, to leaf through their pages and drink in their wisdom. I stepped towards the nearest writing desk to peer at the finely styled writing on the smooth calfskin vellum. But before I could begin to engross myself with what looked like a new rendition of the *Calendar of Saint Willibrord*, I saw that Leofstan, Tidraed and Oslac had reached the far corner of the room.

"Can the boy be trusted?" asked the old man, peering back at me.

"Of course," replied Leofstan without hesitation. "And he is as sharp as any student I have ever had. I would not have brought him with me otherwise."

Oslac beckoned to me impatiently. I hurried over, my heart swelling with pride at my teacher's words. The three of them were looking down at an object on a table. As I approached, Oslac pulled away a cloth that had been covering it and their faces were lit in a warm glow, as from a fire's embers.

Leofstan crossed himself. I could not see what they were gazing at and had to lean over Tidraed's shoulder to get a glimpse. I gasped and for a time I was unable to breathe or speak, such was the beauty of what lay before me.

It was a book, but a book unlike any I had ever seen before. All books are of great value, of course. They are made from the hides of many animals, be they calves or lambs, the letters are painstakingly scratched onto the parchment and the ink is expensive. The best books have coloured pictures and patterns on their pages, and sometimes even a thin layer of gold is applied to highlight certain characters or images. The covers are likewise decorated and adorned with patterns and in rare cases even gemstones and precious metals. At Werceworthe, Leofstan had allowed me to read a copy of the Gospels. It was the most precious of all the books in the minster, richly decorated inside and out; a tome of staggering beauty and value. But nothing I had ever seen before had prepared me for the book that Oslac had uncovered.

The light spearing through the dark of the scriptorium from the nearest shutter fell upon the closed book, reflecting from myriad gems and the finest golden scroll work. The distant sound of the brethren singing in the chapel drifted through the open window, as if they sang in praise of what we gazed upon. We stood in silence for a time, all seemingly unable to speak, or perhaps unwilling to break the spell cast by the masterful craftsmanship of the cover's decorations. I drank in the swirling images, picking out details of what looked like letters that formed no words I recognised. The twists and turns of gold swarmed over the cover in designs so complex I was sure they had a meaning that eluded me. Such was the elaborate detail of the ornamentation, I felt stupid to stand in its presence. The book was about the length of a man's arm and perhaps half as wide. It was encrusted with jewels dotted over the cover. They glimmered in the dust-swirled light from the window, like animal eyes staring out from a thicket of golden branches. At the centre of the tome nestled the largest gem of all, a brilliant blood-red stone, held in an intricate nest of golden threads that flowed away like roots of a tree to join a solid band of gold that spanned the middle of the book's cover.

Leofstan broke the awed hush.

"Where in all of God's earth did you find this marvel?"

"How it came to be here is unimportant," whispered Oslac, his tone tense. "It is what we do with it, that must be decided."

"You mean…" Leofstan's voice trailed off.

By way of answer, Oslac took a deep breath and, trembling as if the book might burn his fingers, he swung open the cover.

The first page was almost as elaborate as the cover. It was entirely taken up by a convoluted diagram. I peered at it for a moment, marvelling at the draughtsmanship, but making no sense of what seemed to be interlocking streams and paths. Close to the centre there was what looked like a great tree, around which water flowed. Above this were several curved lines that reminded me of the rings you see within a tree's trunk when it has been felled. All over the picture were symbols and the images of people and animals.

Leofstan frowned and turned the page. This was filled with words and I pushed Tidraed aside so that I might get a better look. I quickly saw that the words were written in Latin. They had been formed by a master scribe. Despite the fine penmanship and brilliant colours of the inks, the book exuded a sensation of great age.

"The Treasure of Life," I read aloud.

Oslac looked at me sharply and made the sign of the cross.

"I told you he was clever," said Leofstan.

"What is it?" I asked.

Leofstan, as interested as me to know the answer, looked at Oslac, but the old monk shook his head. He held up a hand to his ear. I noticed that the sound of singing had vanished. The monks in the chapel would be finished soon.

"It is the teachings of a prophet named Mani," Oslac said, "but there is no time to talk now." Reaching over, he slammed the book shut and began wrapping it in the dusty cloth.

"Mani?" Leofstan whispered, his eyes bright. "Heresy then?"

Oslac finished hiding the tome's lustre beneath the linen. He nodded to Tidraed, who picked it up and carried it to one of the many cabinets that lined the rear wall.

"It is knowledge and a thing of great beauty and worth," he said. "It must not be destroyed."

Leofstan's face was sombre as he nodded in agreement.

"Destroyed?" I hissed, horrified at the thought.

Oslac smiled wearily.

"Alas, not all are as open to learning as you seem to be, young Hunlaf. There are those here that would burn any work they deem to stray too far from the established doctrine. They fear such heretical writings would pollute otherwise pure minds, leading them into temptation. Even damnation."

I shivered.

"Is it the work of the Devil then?" I asked. Was the lavish binding, with its gems and gold, designed to entrap the unwary and doom them to hell for opening the pages and allowing the accursed words into their minds? I took a step back, making the sign of the cross.

Leofstan placed a calming hand on my shoulder.

"It is but a book," he said. "Words and images on parchment. The work of men. Nothing more."

"But what if it is evil?" I shuddered, imagining the flames of hell licking at my ankles. "Perhaps it should be destroyed."

"No, Hunlaf!" Leofstan snapped. "Do not speak thus. I know you. You love books as much as I. They are a window into the past, into the minds of men long dead. Never speak of destroying them. Such is not God's will."

I nodded uncertainly. It was true that I loved books, but this talk of heresy had filled me with fear.

"You must speak to nobody of what you have seen here," continued Leofstan, his voice earnest and stern. "Not until I have had time to study the contents at least." He sighed. "Even if the words within the book are evil, they are but words. God is all powerful and fears nothing from words on pages in a book."

Outside, we could hear the approach of the monks who had finished their prayers. Leofstan stared into my eyes and saw my unease.

"Remember how you felt when I told you the tale of the library of the Mouseion at Alexandria. You would not see this book burnt like all of those, would you?"

The story of the destruction of so much learning had appalled me. Such was my dismay, I had later dreamt of the great conflagration. In my dream, I had been trying to enter the flames to rescue the scrolls, but the intense heat had kept me outside, watching with tears streaming down my face at the terrible loss of such vast quantities of knowledge.

"No," I said.

"Good. Then speak to nobody of what you have seen until we have had time to investigate more fully and decide what is best."

He held my gaze, a fervent glow in his eyes I had never seen before. I nodded again.

The first of the monks was entering the scriptorium now and Leofstan relaxed and turned at the sound of a new voice.

"Brother Leofstan," said an old man, who wore a large golden cross on his chest, which indicated he must be Hygebald, leader of the brethren here. Despite his age, Hygebald walked purposefully forward with arms outstretched. "What a delight to see you again. Who have we here?"

"Hunlaf, your Excellency."

The bishop appraised me with a glance and I noted he had kindly eyes.

"Welcome, Hunlaf," he said, then continued to Leofstan. "Have young Tidraed here and Hunlaf unload the mule. You must come with me and tell me tidings from the south."

And with that he led Leofstan away.

All about the scriptorium, the scribes were seating themselves, sharpening quills, adjusting the pages before them, stirring encaustum and setting to the laborious task of copying whatever text they were working on. I wished that I could join them and fill my mind with the painstaking job of transcribing a document. Such work would have consumed me, occupied my hands and my mind, leaving no room for my troubled thoughts of heresy and cursed books.

But as I followed Tidraed outside, I could not push aside the vision of the book, blazing in the sunlight, gems gleaming. I wondered at the words I had read within the book. *The Treasure of Life*. What could it mean? Who was Mani and what could the detailed images I'd seen signify?

As I helped Tidraed to lift the reams of vellum from the mule and carry them into the gloom of the scriptorium, my eyes strayed to the far cabinet where the wondrous book was hidden and I knew I would not be able to rest until I had seen it again and deciphered its secrets.

Three

I didn't see Leofstan for the rest of the day. I joined in with the office of Vespers and then sat with the brethren in silence at the evening meal. Tidraed sat across from me and only offered me a single brief signal with his hands that I recognised as a perfunctory welcome to the refectory. He glowered at me for a time and in the end I looked away, unsure of what had provoked his evident dislike of me.

After Compline, when it grew dark, I was shown to a small cell for visitors. There was no sign of Leofstan as I lay down to sleep on the small pallet. I noted that he was still not there when I awoke in the darkest part of the night for Vigils. My mind was in turmoil, but the rhythms of the minster were comforting to me and I rose again before dawn with the rest of the monks to walk over the dew-wet grass to the chapel for Matins.

After Hygebald gave the blessing, the brethren dispersed each to their own tasks and I found myself with the unusual situation of having nothing to do. So I wandered away from the minster, the sun tinging the east with golden light that reminded me of the cover of the heretical book Oslac had shown us.

I wanted time to think and I had a vague idea that, should I be berated for not attending Prime, I would say I had become lost. I crossed the vallum, and headed towards the cluster of huts occupied by the lay people. The scent of woodsmoke and fish was strong in the air as mackerel was being smoked on timber frames over fires on the beach. A mist lingered over the waves that whispered on the sand and stones. The smoke from the fires hazed the air, mingling with the mist. When I looked back towards the thatched roof of the church, I realised I could no longer make out the shapes of the buildings. A scratch of worry ran down my spine as I thought of the punishment I might face if I was found to have left the monastery. But the fear was only a dull nagging, easy to ignore. It was as nothing to the anguish I felt at keeping secret the existence of *The Treasure of Life*, which was how I had come to think of the book. I told myself I would speak to Leofstan at the earliest opportunity and demand answers. But in truth I knew I would do no such thing. He was my teacher and I feared him. And, I realised, as I walked onto the sand, I respected him. If he'd told me to keep this secret, it must be for the best. He would not wish me, or anyone, harm. I was sure of that. He was a firm master, but he was fair and just. And if what he'd said about people wishing to destroy the book was true, we had to proceed with caution.

My footfalls made little sound, as I stepped onto the strand, muted by the smoky haze in the cool morning air.

That was when I heard it: a lilting singing that rose and fell as though with the waves rolling up the beach. It was the voice of a young woman and she sang with effortless abandon, her mind clearly focused on something else. The song entranced me. There was something haunting and familiar about it, as if perhaps I had once heard it in a dream. Hesitating, I listened for a while before moving forward more slowly, not wanting to interrupt the creature that made such beautiful music, but also needing to glimpse the face of one whose voice was so sweet.

The shapes of the wooden frames that covered the flaking fish began to become clearer as I approached. The rising sun caused the fog to glow with a golden light. The mist was already thinning and I could make out the shadowy shape of the singing girl. She was moving from one fire to the next, pulling aside the frames, adding fuel as necessary, checking the fish and turning them when she deemed they needed it. She hummed and sang all the while, oblivious of my presence.

Again I felt a strange sense of familiarity. I shuffled a few steps closer, my emotions roiling. I wanted her to notice me, but I also wished to continue to watch her unseen. She was clearly poor. Her peplos and dress were threadbare and she was barefoot. Her hair was the russet brown of autumn leaves and it hung down her slender back in a single braid. She moved with the grace of a cat, no gesture out of place. She was lithe and strong, and her clothes, old and shabby as they were, still managed to accentuate the feminine curves of her hips and breasts.

"What are you staring at?" she asked without warning. She turned quickly to face me. Her plait swished and curled behind her.

"I... I..." I stammered. My mouth was as dry as if I had been hung over the smoke fires to cure along with the fish.

Her eyes blazed at me with a sudden anger and I thought she might pick up one of the sticks from the fires and strike me. I took a step back, mouth working but no words coming to me.

She stepped toward me and I flinched. Without warning, her expression changed from one of anger to amazement.

"Hunlaf?" she said. "Is that you?"

And just like that, I recognised her. I knew those eyes that glittered in the early morning sunlight. How many times before had I seen that same slight smile on her lips? With the golden dawn limning her features, I saw that her face was as beautiful as her singing. My heart jumped and pounded. She had always had a pretty face, but age had made her blossom.

"Aelfwyn?" I replied. "What are you doing here?"

She grinned.

"I could ask you the same, cousin," she said with a broad smile. In an instant she had closed the gap between us and embraced me. I felt the warm curves of her body against me and squirmed uncomfortably. Pushing me to arm's length so that she could get a better look at me, she shook her head, still smiling. "I thought you were yet at Magilros."

"I left there two years ago."

"Are you to live here?" she asked, her tone tinged with excitement. "On the island?"

"No." I shook my head to clear it. I still couldn't quite believe Aelfwyn was there on the beach in the smoky haze of the dawn. "I live at Werceworthe. To the south. We brought vellum for the brethren here." The mention of vellum brought with it thoughts of *The Treasure of Life* and its secrets, but just as quickly, I pushed the anxiety away.

"How long has it been?" she said, turning back to the fish and the fires.

"Six years since you left." She was my mother's sister's youngest daughter and we had been inseparable as children; more like siblings than cousins.

She glanced back at me.

"Six years," she said, looking me up and down. "I suppose it must be!"

I imagined myself as she saw me and felt my cheeks redden. I was as young as she, but where she moved with youthful grace, her lustrous hair shimmering like a serpent down her back, the crown of my head was shaved in a tonsure, making me look much older than I was. She was supple, with skin tanned by the sun and wind. I was pallid from days spent inside praying and reading, studying the ways of the Scriptures and learning how to copy letters from ancient manuscripts.

"It is wonderful to see you again, Hunlaf," she said with a grin. "Are you able to stay here?"

"I think we will be returning to Werceworthe tomorrow, or maybe the next day."

She laughed and the sound brought back a flood of memories.

"I meant here on the beach," she said. "I am busy and I need to tend to these fish. But I would hear your tidings."

I blushed.

"I think my master has forgotten I am here," I admitted. "I shouldn't really be outside of the minster, but I had no chores."

"Good," she said. "Then we can talk while you help me."

"I don't really know much about smoking fish."

"It shouldn't prove too complicated for one as clever as you," she said. "*Ora et labora*, isn't that right? Pray and work. Well, you are not praying, so get working."

Her use of Latin stunned me into silence and I found myself staring at the way her hands moved the spits of wood. She had always had nimble fingers and I remembered how she would sit with my aunt and weave, twisting the tablets and intertwining the numerous threads as she chattered with her sisters and mother.

"How do you come to be here?" I asked after a while. "I heard a few years ago from a wool trader that you had wed a man from Berewic."

"I did," she replied with a quick smile. A strand of hair slipped from her braid and fell in front of her eyes and she flicked her head in a way I had seen her do countless times before as we had roamed the woods and hills around our home. "With eight sisters there were never going to be enough men closer to home." She paused and turned to face me with a wink. "What with the best ones becoming monks."

I lowered my eyes at her words and went to fetch some of the cut logs from the pile. She threw her head back and laughed. The peals of her mirth followed me. I walked back and handed her a log, which she placed carefully on one of the fires. The smoke was pungent and hot and stung my eyes until they streamed as if I was crying.

"So if your husband was from Berewic, how is it that you are on Lindisfarnae?" I could see she was not prosperous from her clothing and worried she might be a widow.

"He is a fisherman." She shrugged. "We follow the fish," she said, as if that explained it. "Besides, he has family here. They needed extra hands and we needed a home of our own."

"You have children?"

Her hands hesitated as she turned one of the sticks that held the skewered fish. For the first time I saw her smile slip.

"We have not been blessed with children."

"You are yet young," I muttered, embarrassed and unsure of what to say.

"My husband's uncle says they have lived here since before the time of Saint Cuthbert," she said, changing the subject, cheery again. "They have always fished." She gestured at the smoking mackerel.

"And smoked their catch," I replied. A ridiculous grin stretched my mouth. Happiness pervaded my spirit the way the smoke permeated the mackerel flesh. I was awash with joy at meeting someone I had believed lost from my childhood.

She laughed, happy again. How could I have almost forgotten that laugh? Now that I heard it again, it felt as if we had been apart for days, not years.

"Nothing slips past you."

She laughed again as she moved along the beach to the other smoke fires and I followed along behind her.

"Remember how we used to wade into the river to catch salmon and trout with our hands?" I asked.

She smiled at the memory.

"How could I forget? More often than not we never caught anything."

"Well, you did catch a fever!" I said, remembering with

the softening that comes with the passing of time, the feeling of terror when I had learnt Aelfwyn was ill. My mother had died, elf-shot with a fever and when I heard that my cousin had become sick after falling into the Tuede, I had been distraught.

"By Christ's teeth," Aelfwyn said. I crossed myself at her blasphemy and it was her turn to blush. "I have never been so cold as that day. I think that was the last time we ever went fishing." She pushed an errant strand of hair behind her ear. "The memory was so bad that when Eadwine came with the bride-price for me, I told my parents I would never be wed to a fisherman."

"Do you regret changing your mind?"

"No, Hunlaf. I don't." She looked me in the eye and I saw the truth there. I was happy for her.

As we progressed down the strand we spoke of our life in the small village beside the Tuede. And with each passing moment the years that had separated us fell away, replaced with the vivid memories of our shared experiences.

I had all but forgotten my previous worries about secrets and heresy until Tidraed came looking for me. I heard his voice in the distance, but ignored it for a time. But the mist had already cleared and I could hear his calls coming closer.

"I must go," I said to Aelfwyn.

She nodded.

"I hope you are better at praying than you are at working," she teased.

I didn't know what to answer to that, so I said nothing.

"Hunlaf!" Tidraed had seen me now, and was hurrying towards the beach. "Where have you been? Brother Leofstan has been looking for you since Terce."

I did not want Tidraed to see Aelfwyn. I felt stupidly possessive of her. Sadly, already feeling bereft at being parted from her, I turned towards Tidraed.

"I am here most mornings, Hunlaf," Aelfwyn said. I flashed her a smile and hurried to intercept Tidraed further up the beach.

For the rest of that day my thoughts were filled with memories of Aelfwyn and worries about the book. I spoke to nobody. Tidraed had sullenly ignored my requests for information as we had walked back to the minster and, despite saying that my teacher had been looking for me, Leofstan was nowhere to be found. I longed to talk to him about meeting my cousin, but more than that, I wished to unburden my anxieties about *The Treasure of Life*, to hear from him what he had ascertained and what should be done with the book.

As I recited the offices of Sext and None along with the rest of the congregation, my mind was constantly wandering back to the bejewelled book, to the forbidden secrets and dark knowledge that might lurk within its pages. As I collapsed into my bed that night, I pondered the possibility of telling Aelfwyn about the book when I saw her in the morning. If I saw her, I thought, rolling over, trying to get comfortable on the thin straw mattress. Leofstan had sent Tidraed for me when I had gone missing the day before. If he put me to work in the morning, I would not be able to sneak down to the beach.

When I woke for Vigils, Leofstan's bed was still empty and I wondered at his prolonged absence. There was still no sign of him when I returned, bleary-eyed from the nocturnal prayers. But when I opened my eyes in the grey pre-dawn light before Matins, I heard snoring from his bed. I did not wake him, but on my return from reciting the liturgy, he was sitting in the cell waiting for me.

His eyes gleamed in the gloom and he fidgeted with nervous energy.

"You must be wondering where I have been hiding, Hunlaf," he said.

"Reading the book?"

"Yes." He lowered his voice to the barest of whispers. "I need more time to fully decipher what I have read there." He let out a long breath. "But it is incredible."

"Is it heresy?" I asked in a quiet voice.

He hesitated, then nodded in the dark.

"There are those who would say so." He sighed. "They cannot be allowed to destroy it. By all the saints, if what I have understood is correct, the text provides directions. A map, if you will."

"A map to what?"

"To answers. To the very centre of our faith." He grew silent, as if the words he spoke unnerved him. "I cannot yet be certain." He hesitated. "Your keen eyes and sharp mind will be useful to help me study it, to unlock the secrets contained within the book."

I felt a surge of pride that Leofstan would want me to aid him with something so important.

"You mean to take it back to Werceworthe?"

"It is for the best," he said, nodding. "Oslac agrees." He rubbed at his eyes. "Hygebald too."

"You have told the bishop about *The Treasure of Life*?"

He raised his eyebrows at my use of the tome's title.

"Of course. I could not keep it from our spiritual father. He agrees that we should not mention it to the others here and that we should carry it back to Werceworthe. There, you and I will unravel its mysteries."

"Tell me more of what you have read?"

He shook his head.

"Now is not the time." He looked about him at the lightening cell that was lit by the dawn filtering beneath the door and around the ill-fitting shutter that covered the small window.

"Or the place." He gestured vaguely to encompass the minster beyond the walls of our small room.

Without warning he yawned and lay back on his bed.

"You are exhausted," I said. His eyes were already closed. Such was his obvious fatigue, I decided not to mention my encounter with Aelfwyn. That could keep for later.

"The flesh is weak," he whispered drowsily.

"Sleep now," I said. "I will fetch you some shellfish to restore you." Leofstan loved shellfish and I had hoped that my offer to find some would provide me with an excuse to venture down to the beach once more to see Aelfwyn.

Leofstan grunted and moments later he was snoring once more.

It seemed I needn't have bothered with an excuse; I would once again be free to do what I pleased.

I slipped away from the minster just as I had the previous morning, crossing the vallum and making my way down to the beach.

My heart sank when I did not find Aelfwyn on the beach. I had expected her to be there, surrounded by fish and smoking fires and I had looked forward to being able to once again talk with her as easily as if we had never been parted. Following the conversation with Leofstan, I had decided I would not mention *The Treasure of Life*. I was confused about the book and feared she would not understand my teacher's motives. The truth was I did not fully comprehend Leofstan's plans and the thought of the book still filled me with anxiety. But I cherished the memory of the chance encounter of the previous dawn, and longed to spend time once again with my cousin and childhood friend. For a time at least I would be able to cast off my worries and reminisce about those endless summer days when Aelfwyn and I would rove all along the vale of the Tuede.

But there were no smoking fires and the strand was empty of people. So I half-heartedly plucked whelks and winkles from the sand and used a stone to knock limpets from their rocky perches before the tide came in and drowned the mudflats once more.

For a time I watched the birds and that lifted my spirits somewhat, though it did not provide the relief from my concerns that I had hoped to find in Aelfwyn's company.

I spotted a couple of black and white oystercatchers, their beaks as bright as flames in the morning gloom. There were also many dunlins, sporting their black summer bellies and darting this way and that over the sand and shingle in search of food. I even saw a long-legged redshank. It stopped its probing of the mud to stare right at me, before deciding I was too distant to be a threat.

When the first screams came on the light breeze, my initial thought was to look for a new species of bird. Maybe the sounds came from a bird I was not familiar with; perhaps one of the waders that dotted the beach and would teem over the mudflats when the sea rolled away at low tide to expose the land between the holy island and Northumbria. I loved watching birds diving into the slate-dark waters of the North Sea and I knew the calls of all those that frequented the skies and waters around Werceworthe, but I did not recognise these high-pitched ululating screams. Mayhap there were birds here in Lindisfarnae that I had not seen or heard before. The thought excited me, briefly shaking me out of my dark humour. But I could see no birds save the usual gulls and terns out to sea and the waders on the beach. The acrid scent of smoke stung my nose and for the briefest of moments I thought that Aelfwyn must be further along the shore, tending her fires to preserve the latest catch of mackerel.

But there was something different about this smoke. It was thick, cloying, somehow unpleasant. Fresh shrieks echoed in the morning air and I suddenly felt as though I had been plunged into the cold sea. Those were not the cries of some unusual bird, those were the screams of people. Men and women in fear for their very lives.

Four

It seems hard to believe now, but there was a time when we did not look to the seas with fear. When I was a boy we would hear the wolves howling their sadness in winter, and we were fearful, as we huddled around our fires, that the beasts might come down into the village and worry the sheep. We did not travel alone, as there were brigands in the hills, and we all knew of people who had gone missing, never to be seen again. The old greybeards spoke of the battles against the Picts when Eadberht had been king of Northumbria. But those were distant memories, tales to be told around the crackling hearth-flames on long dark nights.

There were dangers in the land, of course, and the Picts still fought on the borders from time to time, but that was far away. The kings of Northumbria came and went, plotting, fighting and murdering one another in their great halls, but their dynastic struggles had no impact on my life or the world where I grew up. On the banks of the River Tuede, life was quiet and peaceful, cloaked in a sense of calm and order.

So it came as a great shock to me to hear the screams of the dying on that warm June morning.

The early morning mist had begun to dissipate as the day warmed and the breeze from the seaward side of the island picked up. The damp sack in my hand was heavy with the limpets and winkles I had harvested from the sands and rocks before the tide had rushed back to cut off the island home of Saint Cuthbert once again from the mainland. I should not have tarried when I'd discovered Aelfwyn was not on the beach, but my head had been filled with swirling thoughts that eddied and fretted in my mind like storm-tossed seas.

I listened and now the noises were clear. Shouts and howls of terror. And there were other sounds on the breeze: the clash of metal and thudding crashes such as would be made by an axe chopping into timber. The jagged scrape of a man's laughter, evil and full of hatred, was carried to me on that bitter breeze. And then the terrifyingly piercing scream of a woman in agony sliced into my senses.

I sometimes wonder what would have become of my life if I had chosen another path in that moment. If I had listened to the horrific sounds of slaughter and done that which most men would have thought sensible and run in the opposite direction.

Of course, I will never know. But the mind does like to play such games, imagining a life unlived, wrongs righted and decisions overturned.

And yet, on the beach of Lindisfarnae, as the stench of burning became stronger and the screams of the dying grew louder, the thought of fleeing did not enter my mind. Before I was even aware of my own decision, I was sprinting over the thin grass that grows on the sandy soil, not away from the danger, but towards it.

My feet pounded the soft earth as I sped back towards the dwellings of the ceorls. A green plover, startled by my passing, burst from the long grass that brushed against my bare legs as I ran. I stumbled in shock and surprise at the bird's screeching call, so like that of the screams of the people dying in the minster and the huts of the villagers. I rushed on, my lungs burning and the thickening smoke stinging my eyes.

I came up over the low rise from the beach to a scene of chaos. When I had left the minster at dawn, its buildings had rested peacefully, close to the natural harbour and overlooked by the mound of rock at the island's tip. A few small fishing boats had been canted in the shallows of low tide, and the morning had been still and quiet. Now the brightening day was filled with noise, fire and smoke.

And death.

In the harbour were three huge ships, sleek and menacing with terrifying carven serpent head prows. Around the ships were congregated several men. The land all around was full of movement. Dozens of armed warriors had poured from the ships and had made their way into the grounds of the minster. Three of the monastery buildings were burning, great pillars of flame and smoke smudging the sky. My heart lurched as I realised one of the fires was the scriptorium. I imagined the gold cover of *The Treasure of Life* melting, the parchment leaves curling, smouldering and then bursting into flames. Leofstan and I would never unpick the secrets within its pages now. I felt tears prickle my eyes as I thought of so many books being consumed, just like in my nightmare of Alexandria. Countless days of painstaking work and skill gone in an instant. So much knowledge snuffed out and lost. I was a long way off, but as I crested the rise I could feel the heat from the fires on my face.

The screams of the brethren came to me on the hot wind of the conflagration. It was not only books that were being destroyed that day. A deep rage, as hot as the flames, began to kindle within me, replacing the concerns that had plagued me since we had arrived on the island.

Who were these warriors? Where had they come from in their dragon-prowed ships?

Someway off, a tall, red-bearded brute, in a crimson cloak and a helm that covered his eyes, pointed to the collection of buildings where Aelfwyn and the other villagers lived. His voice was loud and guttural. I could not make out all of his words, but the tongue was familiar to me as that of the traders from the north who would sometimes sail along the Tuede, inland from Berewic. With my ease at picking up languages, I had learnt how to converse in the Norse tongue during my childhood meetings with those merchants who sold amber, beaver pelts and fox furs, whalebone, walrus ivory, and many other wondrous items, from beside their broad-bellied boats on the shingle beach of the river. But even if I had not been able to understand any of his words, the red-bearded man's meaning was clear. Several other warriors, armed with spears, huge axes, swords and vicious-looking knives followed the red-cloaked leader's order and ran away from the minster and towards the village.

I was gripped by indecision. As I watched, I saw two of the heathen devils dragging one of the brethren from the church. Dark shapes dotted the ground and I realised with a twist of my stomach that they were corpses. The two warriors pulled the monk away from the burning buildings. I recognised him. It was Tidraed. He screamed and struggled until one of the raiders struck him hard across his pock-marked face. Tidraed collapsed to the ground and they laughed. One of them rolled him onto his front and the other pulled up Tidraed's habit, exposing his pale buttocks. The warriors laughed again and began to loosen their belts.

I turned away, my gorge rising.

A shout of command cut through the screams and tumult. The massive leader, in his bright cloak and polished helm strode towards the two men abusing the young monk. He shouted at them again and, reluctantly, the warriors released their captive. Tidraed sprawled on the ground, sobbing with relief. The leader said something to the two men and pushed them away. Their faces were dark with anger at their interrupted sport, but they clearly feared the tall leader and did not argue. Shaking their heads and grumbling, they wandered off towards the beach, where the raiders were piling up the riches they had pilfered from the minster.

The leader scanned the burning buildings, impassively taking in the destruction that his men had wrought. He began to turn and fear lanced through me. If he saw me, he would surely send men to kill me, or worse. I knew I should run, but I could not move. The Norse leader shifted his balance as something caught his attention. Tidraed, still on his hands and knees, was scrabbling away through the grass. For a heartbeat, the red-cloaked raider watched him and I thought he was going to allow Tidraed to escape. But then, with three swift strides, the leader closed the gap, pulling a long knife from his belt. Taking hold of the monk's habit, he hauled Tidraed back and, without pause, plunged his knife into the young monk's right eye. The blade went in up to the handle and Tidraed flopped onto the earth, motionless.

I could not breathe. The Norseman had killed Tidraed with no more emotion than a ceorl slaughtering a sheep at the arrival of winter.

All about the minster, other monks were already dead or were being abused. A small group, their faces pallid with fear, were being goaded with spears by laughing warriors down towards the harbour. Fleetingly, I wondered whether Leofstan yet lived. There were so many bodies littering the ground between the monastery buildings, it seemed most of the brethren had already been slain.

Countless bearded warriors swarmed the smoke-swirled enclosure. Surely none of the monks could survive against them. As I stood there, unsure of what to do, the roof of the scriptorium collapsed in a great crumping *whoosh*, sending up a huge shower of sparks into the heavens. This was the funeral pyre of the minster, and the sight of it snapped me out of my daze.

I glanced about me. So far, none of the heathens had seen me standing alone on the slope rising from the beach. To my right lay the burning minster, the dying monks and the savage warriors returning to their ships in the harbour laden with reliquaries and ornaments from the church. To my left I could see the backs of the raiders who were loping like wolves towards the village.

Towards Aelfwyn.

Looking back towards the burning minster, my gaze met that of the Norse leader. His face was partially covered by his helm, but his eyes gleamed bright as he stared at me. His were the eyes of a hunter. A predator; the eyes of Death.

I knew then I had no choice. If I should die that day, and it seemed certain I would, I would die trying to save Aelfwyn from these men of evil and violence. I spun away from the staring leader and his cold eyes and sprinted after the hulking figures of the seamen. He did not seek to pursue me, or to call a warning to his men. I was no threat to them in his eyes. I was but a scrawny, unarmed monk in a thin robe. The men I followed hefted long-hafted axes, their iron-bossed circular shields slapped against their backs. Most had simple helms of iron and some wore long byrnies of metal rings. These were formidable warriors, men who lived and breathed fighting and killing as I lived and breathed reading and writing and illuminating sheets of vellum. They were as different from me, as a wolf is to a lamb.

I should have been terrified, but the strangest thing happened. As I ran behind them, my habit swishing against my bare calves, a cold calmness settled on me, replacing the searing ire. I was empty-handed and had no protection. I had no plan and no weapon, but I raced after the raiders, allowing this unusual coldness to envelop me. I had never felt anything like it before, but over my long years I have come to recognise and to embrace the calm that comes over me in battle. It sets me apart from most others. Most men are born to raise families, to plough their fields, or, in the case of monks and priests, to pray and spread the word of God. But there are some who are born different. When these men are tempered in the fires of battle, they do not break, but become sharp and hard like the best steel. I found out on that morning of chaos that, despite having been cloistered away with holy men for much of my life, I was such a man. I was born to battle.

I heard shouts from behind me, but I did not turn. I could not chance one of the warriors I was pursuing turning and spotting me. I watched their backs and followed. None of them glanced behind. They were fully focused on the buildings and what further plunder they could find. Beyond the buildings, some of the villagers were running away, fleeing inland, perhaps in the hope that the raiders would not follow them. As they reached the settlement, one of the band shouted a command and they split into different groups. They unslung their shields and without delay made their way between the huts in search of defenders and prey.

I did not pause. Offering up a silent prayer to Saint Cuthbert to watch over me, I hurried between two buildings after the smallest group that numbered but five warriors.

It was madness. What could I do against five armed killers? But thoughts of my own safety had fled with the wanton destruction and murder that had ripped through the peace of that morning. I rushed on.

A sudden wailing shriek filled the air and as I rounded the corner I saw one of the warriors step from a doorway with an infant in his hand. He held it upside down by the feet. The child's mother was screaming and clawing at the man, but he seemed barely to notice her. The babe's cries were loud and terrible. The man shook the tiny creature, but its cries intensified. Seemingly disgusted with the noise, he swung it hard into the lintel of the door, dashing its brains out. The mother's screams raised in pitch as she scratched and tore at the warrior's face. Turning, he punched her in the stomach and shoved her back inside the hut. Two other men followed him into the dark interior of the house.

The last two men seemed about to join them when something caught their attention. I followed their gaze and saw a flash of movement. I gasped to see it was Aelfwyn, her youthful beauty and slender curves evident for the briefest of moments before she disappeared behind a long squat building. The two raiders let out a roar and sped after her.

I sprinted in their wake.

The moment I skittered around the corner hot blood splattered my face. For a heartbeat I stood there, shocked into inaction; uncertain what had happened. The warrior that was furthest from me tumbled backwards, his face a gore-slick mess. One of the villagers, a young, broad-shouldered man, had buried a wood-axe into the raider's head and now, as the dead attacker collapsed, the weapon was pulled from the man's hands. Faster than thought, the second sea-wolf leapt forward and plunged his own sharp axe-head into the defender's shoulder. The man clutched at the oak shaft, his eyes wide and filled with terror.

"Eadwine!" screamed Aelfwyn, who stood just behind the dying man.

"Run, Aelfwyn," he said, his voice wavering with the pain and horror of his approaching death.

The warrior yanked his axe free with a grunt. Eadwine fell to his knees. Despite his command to run, Aelfwyn stood as if rooted to the ground. Her mouth opened and closed as though she could not find air to breathe.

She stared aghast as the invader slammed his blood-drenched axe down once more into her husband. Eadwine fell, his body slumping on top of the man he had killed. The axe-wielding warrior licked his lips and stepped over the corpses towards Aelfwyn. Such was her fear she did not move. Her mouth was open wide but she did not shout. She would face her end in silence.

The warrior reached for her. She flinched, shying away from him, finally spurred to action. But it was too late. As fast as a striking serpent he grasped her wrist and pulled her towards him. He growled something in his foreign tongue and, dropping his shield to the ground, he reached up with his left hand to squeeze her breast. Aelfwyn whimpered in terror and closed her eyes to shut out the evil that was about to befall her.

Within all the horror that surrounded us, the stench of blood and smoke, and the screams of the infant's mother coming from the nearby hut, Aelfwyn was like a shining piece of gold in a field of churned mud; a ray of sunshine through a dark storm cloud. And she was my kin. I would not allow any harm to come to her.

With the icy calm that had engulfed me I glanced down at the two bodies entangled on the ground. Eadwine was still twitching. He gasped for breath. But his skin was the colour of new cheese and his blood pumped ever more slowly from the cavernous wound in his shoulder. Without hesitation, I pushed him aside, to reveal the dead warrior beneath. Eadwine moaned. I ignored him. Sheathed at the heathen's belt was a long-bladed knife. I wrapped my scribe's fingers around its antler handle and pulled it forth from the finely-tooled leather scabbard. The seax was heavier than I had anticipated, but I was strong with the need to protect Aelfwyn; powerful with my fury at these savages who had rent our peaceful existence asunder.

I stepped quickly behind the man who was now lifting Aelfwyn's skirts, thrusting his dirty hand between her pale thighs. Aelfwyn's eyes were still clamped shut and she was shaking her head, as if she could negate what was happening.

Something must have warned the foul heathen of my presence, for in the instant before I struck, he lifted his head and spun towards me. His eyes widened in shock as he saw me approaching, wicked knife held high. He pushed Aelfwyn away at the same moment that I lunged. He raised his hand to parry my clumsy blow, but I had all the force of my horror and righteous hatred behind that thrust. He partially deflected it, but the keen edge found his throat, opening up a deep gash that instantly welled with blood. He howled with anger and pain, clutching at my arm and grinding my thin wrist in his meaty fist. I threw myself into him and we crashed to the earth, everything forgotten now apart from the enemy we each grappled with.

He was much stronger than me, muscled arms as thick as my legs. And yet the cut was deep and I had the advantage of landing atop him. He tried to push me off and for a moment he lifted me in the air. He would have thrown me clear of him too, had I not punched down again with the blood-smeared knife. The blade scraped across the rings of his byrnie, and perhaps Saint Cuthbert had listened to my prayers, for the sharp steel skittered upward and plunged into the open wound in the man's throat. This time it found a pulsing artery and hot blood spurted, drenching us both. His strength quickly left him then, and his grip on me loosened. Soon his hands flopped at his side. He snarled and gurgled at me as blood filled his throat, but I could not make out the meaning of his words. At the last, his eyes widened in terror and I believed death had claimed him. But then, in a final convulsive effort of will he reached to the side and his grip found the haft of the axe he had dropped. I readied myself to withstand a renewed attack, unbelieving that he had enough strength left to fight as his blood soaked the earth around us, turning it to mud.

But as his fingers wrapped about the axe, the horror left his eyes and he grinned savagely. A heartbeat later, he trembled and then was still, eyes unseeing and glazing even as I looked down.

I stared into those dead eyes for what seemed a long time but must have only been moments. My breath came ragged and burning. My vision blurred and darkened. I had slain a man, his blood even now cooled on my skin. I panted and shook my head. I had been concerned about heresy and now I was a murderer. I had broken God's sixth commandment. And yet I felt no shame, only a surging tide of hatred for this man and the others who were slaying and defiling all who stood in their path.

I heaved myself to my feet with a grunt and looked about me. Aelfwyn had gone, no doubt taking the opportunity to flee. If any of the raiders should see her, she would be doomed. I staggered after her, leaving the three corpses behind. The cries of the mother who had been taken into the hut had diminished over time. No sound came now from the house. Her attackers would soon step out into the daylight and I would be no match for the three of them. I shuddered to think of what had happened to the woman and her child, but hurried away, placing a barn between me and them.

I was in a narrow alley, shaded from the rising sun that was still low in the sky. Was it still truly so close to dawn? How had so much changed in so little time? Such a glut of death and suffering in an eye-blink.

I stumbled down the alleyway. My face was cold and tight; the mask of dead men's blood cooling in the shadows. My back felt exposed and I was certain that any moment the woman's attackers would suddenly block out the light between the buildings behind me. I pressed on. Nobody followed me.

I slowed as I approached the end of the alley. The taking of the raider's life had sobered me, reminding me how readily death lurked round every corner, at the end of every path.

Pressing myself against the timber of the barn, I peered around the corner. There was no sign of Aelfwyn and I wondered where she could have gone. Perhaps she had taken refuge in one of the buildings.

The space between the huts was empty. The people of the settlement had all fled and I imagined that the raiders would soon tire of pillaging the hovels of peasants when there were riches to be had back at the minster. Of course, as I had seen, there was also a different kind of treasure that these men sought. They sated their lusts on the island's inhabitants and, as evidenced by the monks being led to the harbour, they would surely also make thralls of those they thought would fetch a good price.

I stepped into the sunlight, unsure of where to go next. Should I run and join the villagers that had vanished into the island's broad expanse of moorland and shrubs? But what if Aelfwyn were yet in danger?

A shrill scream cut through my thoughts. I turned towards the sound and saw three of the seamen stepping from one of the smaller huts. They had their backs to me and were all focused on a fourth man, one of their own, who stepped through the doorway and faced them. He was a giant of a man, his shoulders broad enough to touch the door beams and so tall that his red-tinged fair, braided hair would snag in splinters from the lintel if he did not stoop. He wore an iron-knit shirt and in his hand he held a massive axe as if it weighed no more than an eating knife.

The three men shouted at him. They were too far away for me to hear clearly, but I made out the Norse word for "children". The man did not reply, but shook his head. He half-turned and gestured in a shockingly gentle manner to someone behind him, holding his huge hand out to signal not to move.

In the gloom of the hut's interior I could just make out two small figures.

Again one of the three warriors shouted something, his anger clear. Once more, the giant shook his head and this time said something quietly, his tone too soft for me to pick out the sounds. He waved his axe, as if shooing sheep away and spoke more forcefully. The men before him growled, clearly unhappy with his words.

I did not know what to make of this. It was obvious that the huge warrior was telling the others to leave these children alone. I could not make out his words, but when he next spoke, from his tone and stance, I could imagine he was saying, "There are plenty of others you can take as slaves. Leave these two."

What was the meaning of this? Surrounded by so much killing, for this man to defend these children made no sense. And yet that is exactly what he appeared to be doing.

Before I had time to try and decipher any of their words or to fully comprehend what was happening, the three men leapt forward as one, their blades glinting in the rising sun's rays.

The speed of the big man amazed me. Without seeming to move, he swayed to the side, parried one swinging sword and hacked his axe into the wielder's bicep. Before the other two could press their attack, he shoved the injured man into their path and moved back to block the darkened doorway. The wounded man let out a roar of pain and rage and stumbled back from the fight, clutching his ruined arm.

Without even being aware of it, I had begun running towards the fray. I don't know what compelled me to react in that way. I later told myself it was because one man was defending the children and needed help, but the reality of it is that, for all I knew, he might well have been saying to the others that he wanted them for himself. But in that moment, my body took the decision for me and my feet carried me towards the backs of the two remaining warriors. As I ran, the giant saw me, his pale gaze piercing mine. No words were spoken, but in that instant, some form of communication passed between us. We had decided to become allies in this fight. He made no acknowledgement of me and so his attackers were oblivious of my presence until I attacked.

I was brave and I was foolhardy. The calm of battle had wrapped its cool cloak about me and I seemed impervious to fear. But back then, I was still just a monk. I was not trained in the art of weapon-play. Still, I made up for my lack of skill and experience with determination and foolishness. Some might call it courage, but it was stupidity. And it almost got me killed.

I clattered into the rearmost warrior from an angle that took him out of the fight and knocked him into the injured man. I had thought to stab him with the heavy seax in my hand, but the knife blade was turned by the iron links of his armour and all I managed to do was to cut my own fingers badly as my fist slipped down the handle and slid along the cutting edge. To this day, the fingers on my right hand ache when the weather turns and the scarred skin pulls when I stretch my fingers.

I was not as bulky as my enemy, but I hit him at a run and he was taken by surprise. Despite not injuring him, he stumbled into his wounded comrade and tripped. We both collapsed heavily onto the hard rutted earth. He grunted as we hit the ground, winded, I hoped. The relative ease with which I had slain my first enemy had bolstered my belief in my abilities. I imagined I would take another swing with the knife and finish him readily enough. But no man will allow himself to be killed easily and to underestimate an opponent spells almost certain defeat. The man was as lithe as he was strong and in an instant, he had flipped me off of him and was already on his feet. Above us, I saw the great axe of the giant swipe down and blood fountained in the morning air, dousing us in a hot crimson rain as he slew one of the men facing him.

My assailant had dropped his shield, and his sword had been knocked from his hand in the collision and fall. But it seemed he needed no weapon to best me in combat. He clutched my habit in his fists and hauled me up. I flailed ineffectually at his arms, certain that I would soon be meeting my maker.

The warrior's eyes blazed at me from the eye sockets of his iron helm and he spat insults at me. His breath was strangely sweet and I noticed with a vivid clarity that his teeth were white and clean. And then he smashed his armoured forehead into my face.

I was dimly aware of the crunching sound of my nose breaking, loud and echoing inside my skull. Warm blood flowed into my mouth and down my chin and then, mercifully, the day darkened about me and I felt nothing more.

Five

When I awoke I was not sure where I was. My thoughts were
a buzzing confusion in a head that felt as if it were twice its
natural size. I opened my swollen eyes with difficulty and moved
my head to look towards the sounds of whispered conversation
I could hear. Gasping at the pain that shot through my neck
and head, I found my nose to be blocked. The metallic taste of
blood was thick in my throat.

The flicker of rush lights and candles lit the darkened
room. My vision swam and blurred and for a time I could not
make out where I was, but then I noted the stone wall near
my head. Looking up, I saw an arched window and through
it the dark night sky, clear and pricked with the cold light
of stars. I shivered. Beneath me lay the unyielding slabs of a
flagstone floor. I was inside the church building. A blanket
had been placed over me and someone had rested my head on
a folded cloak.

I groaned as the memories of the morning flooded back to
me. How did I yet live? How long had I been insensate?

Hearing me, a figure peeled away from a group who were
huddled together in deep hushed conversation. The kindly
face looked down at me, the shaved tonsure from his thinning
grey hair marking him out as a monk. He carried a candle

and the dancing light from its flame picked out his sharp features and narrow nose as he gazed at me with a concerned expression.

It was Leofstan. Such relief washed through me that my sight once again blurred as tears filled my eyes.

"Hunlaf, my boy," the older man said, patting my shoulder. "Praise be to God. I have been praying for you."

I pushed myself up onto my elbow. Leofstan held me still with a firm hand.

"Easy now. Do not rise. You have been badly beaten."

My face ached and my head throbbed, but I could not remain lying on the cold floor of the church while my mind swarmed with the events of the attack on the minster.

Pushing his restraining hand away, I sat. I noticed that my hand had been bound with a strip of linen. My fingers pulsed with pain and I recalled with a shiver of dread how I had stabbed the man and ended up gripping the sharp blade of the seax.

"You need rest," he said.

The thought of inaction terrified me. It was as if, by fighting against the raiders, I had unleashed a beast that now paced and snarled within me. It longed to lash out again, to fight. To kill. I shuddered and held out my left hand for Leofstan to hold.

He hesitated, frowning.

"I cannot lie here thinking of what happened," I croaked.

He nodded, gripped my proffered hand, and pulled me to my feet. I grimaced at the lancing pain in my head and staggered dizzily. Leofstan put a steadying hand on my shoulder.

"You must not overexert yourself," he said. "We have lost many good men this day. I do not want you adding yourself to their number with your stubbornness." His words stung as if he had slapped me. They felt like a reproach, as if he held me somehow responsible for the deaths. Perhaps seeing my expression, he squeezed my shoulder and said, "Come, eat and drink something. Your body needs nourishment to heal itself. Just as your soul needs the love of Christ."

I thought of the screams of the dying, the Norse leader ramming his knife into Tidraed's eye, the babe's brains splattering the ground before its mother's horrified eyes, the woman's wails as she was pushed into the darkness from which she never returned.

Where had the love of Christ been then? Where was God when His flock had been violated and murdered?

I allowed Leofstan to lead me towards the end of the church. I was unsteady on my feet and clung to him for support. All about the small church lay men and women. Some slept, but many were awake, their pale faces tight with remembered terror. Their eyes glimmered in the candlelight as we passed. Many of the people had the tonsured pates of monks, but there were several faces I had not seen before. Villagers, I assumed. I scanned the features of all of them, but there was no sign of Aelfwyn.

Upon the small altar was some bread and a meagre amount of hard cheese. There was also a large earthenware jug from which Leofstan poured ale into a mug.

I took a long draught and sighed with the sensation of the liquid soothing my dry throat. Leofstan cut off a piece of the loaf and handed it to me with a thin slice of cheese.

"I saved you some. The devils took much of the food from the stores."

It had been a bad summer so far, with terrible storms that had battered the crops. The loss of stored provisions would be a terrible blow.

"That is not the worst of what they took from us," I said, around the bread I chewed.

Leofstan's face clouded.

"No. They killed many and destroyed much."

I gestured about me at the shadowed people within the church.

"Is this everyone that remains?" I asked in a whisper. I did not want to believe it, and yet I had seen the numerous corpses that had littered the earth in the morning light.

With sorrow etching deep lines in his brow, Leofstan nodded.

"How did this come to pass?" I asked, the anger inside me kindling once more at the horror of what I had witnessed. "Why would God allow this to happen?"

Leofstan sighed.

"I cannot answer that," he whispered. "The Lord alone knows the reason for our tribulations on this earth. He sends them to try us. We must learn from them and become better servants of His word."

I chewed the bread and cheese, but it had become a hard ball in my throat, as difficult to swallow as the idea that God had wished this upon His faithful. A darker thought surfaced from the pool of my despair: was this God's way of destroying that which Leofstan and Oslac had sought to protect and to study?

"What I saw today looked more like a punishment than a test of our faith," I said, looking at him pointedly. "What good can come of slaying the holiest men in Northumbria? How can allowing the violation and murder of the best scribes in Christendom be anything but evil?" My voice grew louder as my anger increased.

Leofstan placed a hand upon my arm.

"Hush, Hunlaf," he said. "You will upset those who seek peace after this terrible day."

I drew in a long shuddering breath and finished my food in silence. Despite the fury that smouldered within me, I could feel the strength returning to my body.

"You are not the only one to believe this is a punishment from God. Brothers Eadgar and Godwig have said the same today; that the Almighty sent the heathen raiders to show His displeasure. They say that this is the outcome of the sins of those who live here. That it has not happened by chance, but is the sign of a great guilt."

"What guilt?" I asked. "Do they know of the book?"

Leofstan looked about furtively to see if I had been overheard. He pulled me close.

"No," he hissed, his voice a sibilant whisper. "And you must not speak of it." He scanned the shadowed church again, but nobody seemed interested in us. "There was much consternation at Bishop Hygebald for permitting the burial here, at this holiest of places, of Lord Sicga, after what he had done."

Some years before, Sicga had led a plot against King Ælfwald, which led to his murder. I recalled the gossip that had reached us at Werceworthe in the cold of winter. It was said that Lord Sicga had taken his own life, but there was much speculation as to whether one of Ælfwald's followers had finally managed to exact vengeance. However he had died, many had been outraged when the bishop of Lindisfarnae had allowed Sicga's body to be carried to the holy island and interred there with the kind of ceremony saved for the most pious of benefactors. But Sicga had been a wealthy man, and men whispered that gold could buy forgiveness for any sin.

"What do you think?" I asked, my voice harsh. I had grown to respect Leofstan's opinion above any other and I hoped he would provide me with an answer, a piece of flotsam to cling to in the raging seas of my own uncertainty and doubt. Something to allay my fears that the raid had been God's punishment on a brethren who housed heretical books. Leofstan shook his head and lowered his gaze. His eyes were shadowed, but the guttering flames glimmered in the tears that welled there. I knew in that moment that he had the same doubts and was no more certain of what had occurred than I. The thought filled me with despair.

"If you wish to talk," he said, "let us step outside and leave these good people to rest in peace."

"Is it safe?" I asked and immediately felt foolish. If I had learnt anything it was that safety was an illusion.

"The raiders have long gone," replied Leofstan, his tone sombre. "I do not think they will return."

Not soon, perhaps, I thought. But like the fox that kills hens in a coop, now that they have tasted blood, they would be back. But I said nothing of my fears and merely nodded and followed him from the church and out into the dark.

Leofstan inclined his head to one of the other monks as we passed, and I realised with a start that it was Oslac. The old monk's lined face was soot-stained and his tonsured head was blistered and red. I wanted to stop and speak to the old monk, but Leofstan ushered me through the door. The sound of a woman's quiet sobbing followed us into the night.

Outside there was no light save from the stars and the moon. We walked away from the church and, glancing back, the dim flickering flame light that shone from its arched windows and doorway gave the building the aspect of some monstrous night creature's face. I shuddered. There was a chill in the breeze that blew in from the sea.

The night was redolent of smoke and ashes and I was glad of the darkness that cloaked the extent of the destruction. I recalled the smoke and sparks flying up from the collapsed roof of the scriptorium and my breath caught in my throat. The loss of so many books pained me almost as much as the dead. The moment the thought crossed my mind, I regretted it. Books were mere objects, not children of God. My thoughts threatened to turn to those I had seen slain and I shied away from those memories, as a man would run away from a wolf in a dark forest. But before I could flee from my thoughts, the image of Aelfwyn, pale and terrified, filled my mind's eye. Unbidden, tears trickled down my cheeks.

I cuffed at them. The brush of my hand brought a flash of acute agony. I gasped with the pain.

Leofstan halted and turned to me in dismay.

"Should we return? You need to rest."

I shook my head in the darkness.

"No. I just made the mistake of touching my nose." I hawked and spat out some of the dried blood that caked my throat. "How bad is it?"

He paused, as if contemplating his answer.

"It is broken and badly swollen," he said at last. "I doubt you will ever be handsome now."

Despite myself, I smiled at his attempt at humour.

"Perhaps it will improve my looks," I replied.

He snorted, but said nothing more. For a time we stood there in the dark, staring out into the night, lost in our thoughts. The sigh of the waves washing the harbour beach reached me and I knew it must be high tide.

"Oslac went into the burning scriptorium, you know?" said Leofstan, breaking the silence that had descended between us. "He went back more than once, saving as many of the works there as he could."

Perhaps I was not the only monk who was somewhere in between foolhardy and brave.

"How many did he rescue?" I asked.

"Not many."

"*The Treasure of Life?*"

Leofstan sighed.

"No. That book is lost, along with so many others. Oslac is old and not the strongest of men. But he did manage to carry to safety the Ceolfrith pandect, Jerome's *Martyrology* and the most beautifully illuminated copy of Primasius's *Commentarius in Apocalypsin.*"

"Praise be to the Lord," I said, but I was thinking how it had been futile for one man to attempt to save all the books in the building. I smiled without humour. Hadn't I thrown myself into combat against battle-hardened Norsemen? I'd had no real hope of succeeding to save anyone, and yet I could no more have turned away from that fight than I could have pulled the moon from the sky. Mayhap Oslac felt the same way about the books he had worked on for the best part of his long life. It is true what people say about moments of crisis. I have seen it many times. You truly never know how any man or woman will react when faced with an impossible decision. Some freeze. Others run. But a few find themselves grasping the painful nettle and confronting the danger head on. It seemed that Oslac and I had that in common. Not that it had done either of us much good.

"Do you think God sent the Norsemen to destroy the book?" I could not shake the feeling that we were to blame for the bloodshed and chaos that had descended upon the island.

"I will not lie to you, Hunlaf. Such thoughts have crossed my mind." He drew in a deep breath, letting it out slowly. "But I cannot believe that the Almighty would smite so many of his faithful for the sins of a few."

"Did He not send a great flood that swept away all but Noah and his kin?"

"But it was God's covenant to us that He would never again call down such a flood on the earth."

I spat into the darkness.

"Was it also His promise not to send Norsemen?"

Leofstan was silent. He turned away from me, shoulders slumped, and stared out into the darkness. Gone was the man of that dawn, full of energy and the excitement of discovery.

I sucked in a deep breath of the cool, smoke- and salt-tinged air and finally turned the conversation away from the book and in the direction I had been dreading since I had awoken.

"How is it that I survived?"

"I do not rightly know," replied Leofstan. "I had hoped you would be able to tell me something of how you came to be found in a heap of dead Norsemen." He hesitated, perhaps thinking carefully of his words. "I know you as a studious, inquisitive boy, quick to learn and always questioning. I would not have thought you capable of such violence."

"It was not I who brought violence to the holy island," I snapped, bridling at the accusation in his words.

He placed his hand upon my shoulder.

"Forgive me, Hunlaf. I know your heart is true. You are a man of peace. Nobody can know how they will react in such a situation." His words echoed my thoughts, but I was not so sure of my peaceful nature. I had not brought the violence, it was true, but I had embraced it with relish.

"I did not think about whether what I did was right or wrong," I said, my tone flat and hushed. "I saw what was happening and I was so full of rage." The sensation of running after the Northmen, the rushing excitement I felt when plunging the knife into the man's throat, the warm blood splattering my face. I should have been horrified, but I had revelled in the joy of it, as though I had been waiting for release all my life.

"The Lord moves in mysterious ways," Leofstan said, and I could hear the uncertainty in his voice. "You were trying to defend your brethren and our flock." He hesitated again. "Why were you in the village? When those Norse devils left, I first looked for you on the beach and then the minster. When I did not find you, I thought they had taken you with them, or that you had been pushed into the sea and drowned, like so many others..." His voice trailed off as he relived the horrors he had seen.

"Why did they leave?" I asked, choosing to ignore his question. "They seemed intent on killing everyone and destroying everything, but they did not complete their task."

"I do not know, but I suspect they had not expected to face

any resistance. When they had lost a few of their number, they seemed to lose interest. They rounded up the last of the villagers they could find, those who had not fled, and they forced them into the barn." His voice cracked and a sudden scratching dread ran down my spine.

"What did they do then?" I asked, but I did not wish to hear the answer.

He sighed and I sensed that he made the sign of the cross over himself in the darkness.

"They barred the doors," he said, his voice barely more than a whisper. "And then torched it."

I did not speak for a long while. The night air stank of smoke. Was that the sweet scent of cooked meat? My stomach recoiled.

"Did any…" I choked on the words. "Did any survive?"

"Of those who did not flee, only two."

My heart skipped. Perhaps Aelfwyn was one of the lucky ones.

"But none of those in the barn," Leofstan went on, his voice as desolate as the star-strewn sky above us. "Just the two children you were protecting."

My mind span. I did not understand.

"Children?"

"Yes," Leofstan said, his voice gentle. "A little boy and girl. Poor things. Both of their parents were slain and the Lord alone knows what horrors they witnessed. But you must tell me how it is that you came to be helping them and how you convinced that giant heathen to aid you?"

I frowned.

"I helped them, because I could not turn away and see them hurt. And the Norse giant did not aid me. I helped him. He was already fighting his companions."

"Of all the things that happened this day, this is one of the strangest," said Leofstan.

"So, you see it must have been the huge warrior who slew the men around me," I said. "I tried to protect the innocent, but as you said, I am a scholar not a warrior." My failure to save Aelfwyn or the children stabbed me like a seax in my guts. But something Leofstan had said made me turn towards him suddenly. His face was a pale smudge in the faint moonlight.

"How did you know of the Norse warrior who fought to save the children?" I asked.

"As I said, this is the strangest thing of all. And the Almighty must surely have a plan of His own that we cannot fathom."

"Why? What happened?"

"After the raiders had returned to their ships and set sail, we watched until they were a long way to the horizon. We were frightened that they might come back to finish what they'd started. But once they were small in the distance, we were sure they had truly left and it was then that we made our way down to the village. The barn still burnt and the smell..." His words choked him and he hesitated, taking a long steadying breath before continuing. "There were several slain in the alleys, left where they had fallen. We found the first dead raiders there, killed by Eadwine it seems. A young man of the villagers, as he was there too. Then we discovered you, with a mound of the dead around you, like a great warrior in the tales of our forefathers. You were so covered in blood I believed you to be dead too, but that giant Norseman pointed to you and made it clear you yet lived."

"That warrior did not leave with the ships?" I could scarcely believe what I was hearing.

"No. We found him sitting with the two children. He cradled them in his huge arms and they seemed content to be with him. The few villagers who had fled wanted to kill the man and I thought they would rip him asunder like so many mad dogs."

I imagined the giant warrior surrounded by angry villagers.

He would have been able to overcome a dozen such men with his bulk, speed and obvious battle-skill.

"What happened?" I asked.

"Well, nothing really. Hygebald spoke to the people, reminding them of Christ's words. The warrior pushed the children towards us and held up his hands to show they were empty and he meant no harm to us. The bishop's words and the man's actions calmed the people somewhat. It was then that he pointed to the heap of corpses and we found you."

"So where is he now?"

"He is locked inside one of the prayer cells."

"He is still on the island?" The idea of the massive Norse warrior being close filled me with dread. I had seen him fight. Should he decide he did not wish to remain captive, we would be no match for him.

"Yes. We sent a messenger to Bebbanburg at low tide and tomorrow the king's reeve should come. He should know what to do with the Norseman."

I remembered the silent communication that had passed between us in the instant before I threw myself into the fight. My hand throbbed and my face ached. I could not wait for the next turn of the tide for the reeve to arrive.

"Take me to him," I said.

Six

The room was unlit and shadowed. The thick timber door, studded with trenails, closed behind me with a grating crunch. I couldn't make out any form or movement within the cell, but my nostrils were filled with the sharp scent of sour sweat, cured leather and a lingering hint of sweetness that I could not place. It was silent and no hint of a breeze reached the floor of the room. I forced myself not to shiver as the cool darkness swallowed me.

Looking up, I stared at the spray of stars that covered the night sky. Where beams and thatch or shingles would normally protect a hut from the elements this prayer cell had no roof. Instead, it was open to the sky, and its walls had no windows. Its inhabitant would face no distractions from the earthly realm and would be able to focus all of their prayers to the heavens. It was one of a handful of such cells built in the style originally created by Saint Cuthbert. They usually housed the most pious and devout followers of Christ. On this night the cell was home to a huge heathen. And he was now accompanied by a young monk who, after the bloody events of the day, was already beginning to question everything he had ever known about God and piety.

This was hardly what Cuthbert had envisaged when he had

designed these cells, but as Leofstan said, the Lord truly was mysterious.

I peered into the darkness, willing my eyes to penetrate the gloom, yet still I could see nothing. I cursed myself inwardly for asking to come here. What did I hope to achieve?

Leofstan had refused to allow me entrance at first, but I had told him that I spoke some words of the Norse tongue and I might be able to learn something useful. The older monk had argued against me and where I might have pleaded with him only days earlier, now I merely stood my ground and repeated my reasoning calmly and resolutely, adding that God had spoken to me. Who were we to ignore the Lord's word? As he looked at my bruised and battered face I could see from the way he stared at me that I was not the only one to have been changed that day. I doubted he truly believed my tale of hearing the voice of God, but my relationship with Leofstan had shifted somehow and after only a short discussion, he had acquiesced to my visit.

"This is madness," he had muttered, as we approached the prayer cell where the Norseman was being held.

I did not refute Leofstan's summation of the situation. My throat was tight and it was all I could do not to pant with anxiety. And yet I could not turn away. I had to speak to the prisoner. Perhaps if I could get him to talk, I could find some answers to make sense of my world again.

"He's a beast," said one of the men guarding the door. He was old, perhaps forty, with thinning hair and a full beard. But he was broad-shouldered and had a pugnacious face. He looked like a man who had seen his share of fights and could like as not hold his own in a brawl. I wondered with a flash of anger where he had been when the raiders had struck. If more men had stood against them, maybe things would have ended differently.

Maybe Aelfwyn would yet live.

"You'll not be wanting to go in there," he said, oblivious of my sudden rage. "Wait for the reeve. He'll bring spear-men tomorrow. Let them deal with the Norse brute."

"I would speak with him now," I said, surprised at the steadiness and strength of my voice. The slightly nasal quality of my tone, caused by my broken nose, made my words deeper and more commanding.

The two men stared at me. Leofstan nodded and the man who had spoken turned to the door. I could see where somebody had fashioned a crude locking bracket to the door and the frame for the purpose of securing the captive. Before lifting the bar, he hesitated.

"He's been quiet ever since we put him in there, but he could snap you like a twig, boy." He turned to Leofstan. "Brother, you should not allow this. It is folly."

Leofstan nodded and I wondered if he would agree with the guard. But then he sighed and shook his head.

"You are not wrong," he said. "I have told Hunlaf as much, but, rightly or wrongly, he believes the Lord has called him to speak with the prisoner. And, as he pointed out, if the stranger had wished to kill him, he had ample chance to do so while he waited with the children for us to arrive. Go on, open the door."

"Wait," I said, suddenly fearful that when they slid back the bar from the door, the massive man inside might rush out and slay us.

The guard halted, looking at me askance.

"Ready your spear," I said to the second guard; a shorter man who held a hunting spear loosely in his left hand. He looked at me quizzically, his eyes glimmering in the moonlight.

"He did not kill me when he had the chance," I said, "but some time in captivity might have changed his mind."

The man lowered his spear, pointing it at the closed door.

"Now wait a moment," said the first guard.

"Just open the door," I repeated, my voice sounding calm to my own ears. "I will enter quickly and you can bar it behind me."

"Too right I'll lock it behind you," he grumbled. He fixed me with a dark stare and let out a pent-up breath. "Ready?"

I nodded, then, realising he might not see the movement, I said, "Yes."

He slid back the locking bar and I sensed the other man bracing his spear for a rushing attack from within the cell. None came. The door swung open. I took a deep breath and slipped inside.

I was plunged into darkness and the still hush was nearly absolute after the wind-whisper and the sigh of the waves. I heard the guards speaking outside and I strained to hear their words, but the thick door and the wall made it impossible to even be sure I could hear them, let alone make out what they said.

The loud sound of a man clearing his throat made me gasp. I cursed my fear and my own stupidity. I had not thought to bring a light and so here I was, locked into a chamber with a giant killer, and I could see nothing.

A rumbling voice spoke from the darkness. It took me a few moments to understand the words. I was unused to the tongue of the Norse, but quickly I remembered the words I knew and the meaning of others was often evident from how they were used and sometimes by the similar shape of sound to the words in my native Englisc.

As well as I could tell, the voice said, "Well, little priest man. Why come you here to wake me?"

It was a simple question, but I had no good answer for him. My mind spun with all that had occurred since the previous dawn. My body ached and screamed at me for rest. My skin prickled with cold and fear. The guard had been right, I was a fool for entering here.

"I..." I said, struggling to form words the man might understand. "I am not a priest. I am a..." But then I realised I did not know the word for monk. "I am Hunlaf," I said.

He did not reply. But now that I had heard him speak and my eyes had become accustomed to the shadowed cell, I could just make out his bulky form, dimly silvered by the moon and stars that looked down into the roofless chamber. He was sitting with his back to the wall, long legs outstretched before him.

"You are?" I enquired, hoping that my words were well formed and that he would understand me.

"I am Runolf Ragnarsson," he said.

I shuffled forward, careful not to trip. I did not know how well he could see me, but I held a small sack of hemp cloth, offering it to him. He did not move. I took another step closer. Still, he remained unmoving.

"Here," I said. "Take it."

Before I was aware he was moving he had reached out a meaty hand and snatched the bag from my grasp. I staggered back, certain that he would leap up and lunge at me. But he did not rise.

I moved away until I touched the wall farthest from him. I lowered myself down until I was sitting with my back to the cold wall, a feeble mirror image of the Norseman's muscular frame. He sniffed at the contents of the bag.

"Food," I said. Thinking of the words and translating them into his tongue one by one, I continued: "Bread. Cheese. Water." I had collected small quantities of the scant provisions before we had come to the cell. Leofstan had protested, but without much conviction.

"We should save the provender for God's faithful," he'd said.

"Would Christ refuse to feed a hungry man?" I had asked. "Surely even our enemies are God's children."

Leofstan always liked to quote the Gospels to the younger monks whenever they were in danger of behaving in a way he saw as less than Christian. It was my turn to chastise him. "Did not Jesu tell us 'Thou shalt love thy neighbour as thyself'?"

Again, I'd felt the shift in our relationship. Just days before, I would never have dared to answer him in this way, and he would never have responded as he did, with a sigh and a small nod of the head.

Runolf pulled out the contents of the bag and I heard sounds of him chewing and swallowing. When the food was gone, he lifted the leather flask I had brought and drank several mouthfuls of water. I did not speak until he had finished. He stoppered the skin and settled back, seemingly content to sit in silence.

"Why did you come here?" I asked. I'd had plenty of time to think of the correct words, and my voice was loud and clear in the stillness.

"Why think you?" he replied, his voice rumbling like distant thunder. "For gold. Silver. Slaves." He spoke with the tone he might use for a stupid child.

"But why here? There are many places with treasure. Why Lindisfarnae?" I did not know how to fully convey the outrage I felt that such violence had come to this peaceful place of worship and contemplation. "It is a sacred place," I said at last, not fully pleased with my words, unsure he would understand.

He sniffed.

"Sacred?" he asked.

I wrestled with the words I knew of his tongue. Eventually, I said, "It is a holy place, a heilagr place. Helgistaðr."

"You worship Óðinn?" he said. "Þórr? Frigg?"

"No, we worship Christ, the one true God." I tried to keep my voice steady.

"This place is not heilagr to us. You are weak and your god is weak."

I thought of the Norsemen hacking down the brethren with impunity. Tidraed's pleading pock-marked face as the laughing bearded warriors forced themselves on him and then the horror as their leader slew him with the ease of a butcher. I shuddered in the dark. I could not argue against his claims of weakness.

As if feeling sorry for me, he softened his tone.

"Jarl Skorri had heard tell of your island and its riches. He could not believe there were no spear-men or sword-men to protect such wealth, so he sent men to check." My memory of the Norse tongue was coming back to me now, and I was finding it increasingly easy to make out the meaning of Runolf's words. He seemed happy to continue speaking and I did not interrupt.

"Skorri sent traders in a knarr here in the spring. They were men he trusted and they told him of what they had seen with their own eyes. Gold and silver ornaments in your stone building. Books bound with gems and precious metals. And many young men and women who could be sold as good slaves in the east and south."

My stomach churned at his words, thinking of the fate of those who had been taken away in the serpent-headed ships.

"Tell me," he said, "why do you not have warriors?" He sounded truly incredulous and interested in the answer. "Are you all mad?"

"God protects us," I answered. The words sounded hollow as they echoed up through the chamber and out into the night sky above us.

The big man snorted with grim laughter.

"He does not do a good job, your god."

I bit my lip. I did not like his tone or his words. His apparent humour at the murder of my people and the desecration of the holy island stirred the embers of my anger. Taking a deep breath to calm myself, I changed the path of the conversation.

"Why did you fight your own?" I asked, my voice clipped and as sharp as the seax I had used to kill a man.

Runolf drew in a long breath and took a swig of water from the skin. Perhaps he was less inclined to speak of himself than he was of his leader and the men and women they had slain. He pushed the stopper firmly into the neck of the flask.

"I came for gold." He hesitated. "I did not come for this." He fell silent, and I could sense his own rage building, brooding in the gloom.

"But you knew why you came. Why come here on Skorri's ships if not to fight?"

"I am Runolf Ragnarsson. You have seen me deal the slaughter to my foe-men. You think I do not wish to fight?"

I thought of him looming in the doorway of the hut, the speed of his axe, the splash of hot blood as he hacked into his enemies with seeming ease.

"Then why?" I pushed him for an answer.

He sighed.

"No battle-fame comes from fighting women and killing dress-wearing priest men. I did not come to wage war on children."

"Did you not think there would be womenfolk and children on the island?" I could scarcely believe what I was hearing. Of all the Norsemen I had witnessed, Runolf had seemed the most imposing, the deadliest. And I had seen the others committing atrocities that would live in my nightmares for the rest of my days.

Runolf bridled and he let out a growl. I flattened my back against the wall, readying myself for the inevitable attack.

"I will not slay children," he said. His words caught in his throat, giving me pause. I chose not to press him further for his reasons.

"You are a good man," I said. "You saved those children."
He let out a barking laugh. It sounded like a sob.
"I am not good," he said.
"Perhaps God sent you to us."
He snorted, but did not speak for some time. I pondered his
words, allowing the silence to gather about us like a cloak.
"Is it true?" he asked, his voice cracking before he coughed
to clear it.
I was startled and realised I had been close to sleep, dozing
in the darkness. The thought of my recklessness filled me with
dismay. I could not relax in the presence of this man. I would
need to seek rest soon.
"What?" I replied.
"That there are many more such places? Holy places along
the coast. All filled with gold and silver."
I was suddenly fully awake. I shivered as the meaning behind
his question became clear to me. I imagined lying to him, but
then smiled at my own foolishness. What did it matter what
he knew? He was a captive, with no chance of escape. And
tomorrow the reeve would come and surely seek to take the
blood-price from him for what his companions had done here.
"There are others," I said, my voice unsteady and tentative.
I thought of the brethren at Gyruum and Uuiremutha on
their secluded, windswept locations overlooking river mouths
and the cold expanse of the North Sea. Then I pictured the
place I had called home these last months. Werceworthe stood
far removed from any aid, on a tongue of land surrounded
by the river Cocueda on three sides. Like all of the minsters it
had been established away from distractions. Perfect for quiet
prayer and contemplation. They were places of peace. None
was as rich as Lindisfarnae, with its noble history, pilgrims and
links to the royal house of Northumbria, but all of the minsters
had reliquaries and valuable books. Gold and silver adorned
the altars of all these places of worship. And all of them housed

many healthy men and women. I shivered. Men and women who would sell for a good price in the slave markets of the south and the east.

And none of the minsters had any form of defence.

As if he could hear my thoughts, Runolf hoomed in the back of his throat.

"Jarl Skorri is a greedy man. He loves gold as much as the dragon, Fáfnir. He would sleep on a mound of treasure, if he could." For a time, Runolf was silent and I imagined Skorri, so full of lust for riches that he would sail across the North Sea to rip asunder the bones of saints, defile Christ's most holy of houses, violate and murder. I wondered if he had been the man in the red cloak I had seen orchestrating the raiders as they'd poured from the beached ships. I recalled the knife blade plunging into Tidraed. And in my memories, I saw again the killer's cold eyes. I shuddered.

"Do you think he will return?" I asked. The thought filled me with foreboding.

Runolf did not hesitate.

"Yes, little priest man, Skorri will return, as sure as snow comes in winter. He will come back now that he has tasted the blood of your people and seen how weak you are."

I heard the truth in his words and shuddered.

"And there are many more greedy jarls," he said.

I imagined more ships sailing out of the early morning sea fret that often cloaked the slate grey North Sea. I saw in my mind swarms of howling Norsemen and I could already hear the screams of the dying and the cries of anguish from the men and women they despoiled.

And then recalled Leofstan's words. The Lord truly was mysterious. Surely it had been the Almighty who had filled me with righteous anger. It was God who had brought me to this place and it was He who had seen to it that Runolf Ragnarsson, this giant of a Norseman, should be here in this prayer cell. It could be no whim of wyrd, no accident of fate that we should be here, in the open-topped chamber, with nothing between us and heaven.

"Tomorrow, the reeve will come for you," I said.

"Reeve? What is this?"

I did not know the Norse word, so replied, "The king's man. He will come for you from Bebbanburg and he will bring spearmen. They will want to kill you."

Runolf said nothing.

"Are you Skorri's man?" I asked. "Does he have your oath? Your..." I searched in my memory for the right word. "Your eiðr?"

"Skorri is nothing to me," Runolf said with a vehemence that surprised me. He spat in the darkness.

"When Skorri returns to these lands for treasure, his men will slay more of my people. Men, women." I paused. "Children."

Runolf growled quietly.

"I would not see you killed by the reeve," I said.

"Why? I am your foe."

"I believe Christ sent you to aid us."

"Aid you? Against Skorri?"

"Yes," I said, eagerness entering my tone. "You know the ways of the Norse. The way they fight. With your help, we can defeat them."

He was silent for a time, perhaps mulling over my words.

"I am but one man," he said at last.

"But you are Runolf Ragnarsson," I said, and he laughed mirthlessly at my attempt to flatter him.

"We will not be able to defeat Skorri when he returns," he said, his voice flat and low. Disappointment washed over me. "But perhaps," he went on, "we could make him think twice about attacking you. He is no fool and a wolf will always seek out the weakest prey."

"Truly? You think he could be made to turn away?"

"Anything is possible," Runolf rumbled in the dark.

I could feel hope and a new purpose welling within me. God was mysterious indeed.

"Come then, Runolf," I said, "tell me how we give ourselves teeth that will make this wolf think twice."

Seven

The next day dawned wet and grey. Clouds had gathered in the latter part of the night and in the first dim light of day a constant drizzle washed the land.

"It is as if God himself is weeping," whispered Godwig in between prayers at Prime, his wispy grey hair floating about his ears like smoke. Usually, he would have been chastised for speaking during offices, but on this day neither Hygebald nor any of the other older monks seemed inclined to offer punishments or harsh words. Perhaps they agreed with Godwig. The destruction all about us was such that several of the monks murmured about prophecies and the end of days.

Leofstan met my gaze on hearing Godwig's doom-laden words. He did not speak or make any sign, but I believe we both pondered whether the book that had somehow come into Oslac's possession might have been the cause of God's wrath.

Despite the battering my body had taken, I had barely slept. My sinews felt as taut as the sheep guts strung on a lyre and my mind was a tangle of thoughts and worries, each jostling and vying for my attention like a pack of hungry hounds after a hunt, yapping and snarling for a morsel of meat.

The rain smudged and smeared the world and, when coupled with the sight of the blackened bones of buildings that had stood whole the previous morning, the day had the feeling of a bad dream. But the sour stink of burnt flesh hung in the damp air, and the sombre task of burying the dead was all too real. Most of the brethren were involved in the grim work as soon as we had finished our morning worship.

Nobody spoke of what to do about those who had perished in the blazing barn and I noticed that everyone kept as far from the charred, steaming place as possible.

The rain softened the earth, making it easier to dig with the wooden shovels that were normally used for turning the loam to cultivate the land. Leofstan told me to rest, but I stubbornly refused to sit in the church while others toiled under the louring sky. Each corpse had been cleaned and dressed and made to look as at peace and whole as possible. When they were ready, they were carried individually to the burial place and laid to rest in the earth alongside their loved ones. Hygebald led the prayers over the deceased. There were so many dead that I estimated that the number of stone markers jutting from the earth would double. My first attempts to dig had made me gasp as the bandaged wounds of my fingers screamed in agony. Fresh blood flowed and the clean wrap that Leofstan had bound about my hand that morning was soon soaked crimson.

"Enough," he said. "You cannot help like this. If you wish to be useful, make a note of where we are burying each person so that later we can properly mark their resting place."

This was a good idea. With so many burials, it would be easy to forget where each one would rest until called up to Christ's side in heaven. I busied myself preparing small wooden stakes which I marked with a numeral. After each burial, I would place the stake in the freshly turned mound of earth and then write the name of the person who had been buried on a piece of vellum. This I left inside the church. It made for a lot of walking back and forth, but even though the drizzle stopped falling as the sun rose into the watery sky, I could not risk the vellum and the ink getting wet. Besides, those involved with the hard work of digging and transporting the corpses were doing much more arduous work than I. And walking between the chapel and the graves gave me time to think of the conversation with Runolf and my growing certitude that he had been sent by God to help us.

The tide was lowering throughout the morning and with each trip I looked landward expectantly. The sun was almost at its zenith when the tide reached its lowest point, leaving the broad expanse of puddles and mud that allowed firm enough footing for people to cross without the aid of a vessel. I peered out, shielding my eyes against the glare and haze caused by the now warm sun reflecting on the slick surface of the mudflats and glistening from the pools and plashes like so much silver.

Was that movement I saw, far off in the distance?

I halted, staring westward. Sunlight glinted, possibly from a helm or a polished spear-tip. I watched until I was sure. Yes, some two dozen horsemen were riding slowly across the flat surface of the mud. They rode in single file, tentatively following the path that the brethren and pilgrims used. I remembered what Leofstan had told me about the clinging mud that could entrap the unwary who strayed from the path. Only a fool would tempt fate and head away from the markers. The reeve led his men from one staff to the next with purpose but without undue speed. He was clearly no fool. I offered up a silent prayer that he would be wise enough to listen to me about Runolf.

Some of the other monks gathered around me to watch the approaching riders. Hygebald strode up to where we stared, his step firm and his shoulders resolute, despite his advanced years. That morning I had thought he looked old, bent-backed and feeble; face drawn, eyes haunted by what he had witnessed. I did not judge him harshly for it. The attack had been horrific and the men and women slain and captured had been in his care. Any man would feel the weight of such a thing. But with the arrival of the reeve from the mainland of Northumbria, Hygebald's strength seemed to return.

"It is not yet time to rest, brothers," he said. His tone was soft, but all the monks knew not to disobey him. "Return to your work. There is yet much to do."

Without reply, the men obediently trudged back to the toil of digging the earth, preparing it to accept the mortal remains of their friends.

Hygebald came and stood beside me. I fidgeted, tugging at a loose thread of my sleeve. I was nervous in Hygebald's presence. Both of us stood in silence, watching as the horses' hooves churned up the sodden sand. The lead rider wore a deep blue cloak and the sun shone from silver fittings on his horse's harness. Behind him came over a score of armed men. Many bore spears and some of those at the head of the column also wore byrnies and had baldrics slung over their shoulders from which dangled swords.

"So, Hunlaf," Hygebald said without turning to face me. "Leofstan tells me you think the heathen should be spared from judgement." I had not expected him to converse with me and the sound of his voice startled me. I could not recall the bishop addressing me directly before.

I took a deep breath and swallowed my nervousness. If I could run towards savage heathen raiders armed with nothing but my faith, my rage and a seax, I could speak to my bishop. Still, my throat was dry and my voice rasped when I spoke.

"Nobody should be spared the Lord's judgement, your Excellency," I said. "Indeed, we will all be judged by the Almighty when we stand before His throne."

Hygebald nodded slowly. I glanced at him. He seemed content with my answer.

"But what of the judgement of man?" he asked. "You spoke to this Norseman for some time in the night. Do you believe he should be spared punishment?"

"I think he is a good man." I hesitated. "Or at least a man capable of being good."

"All men are capable of good and evil," Hygebald replied.

"Yes, but it is also true that all men are fallible. Perhaps Runolf set out with the rest of the pagans to despoil the sacred isle, to steal and to kill." I could sense the bishop stiffening beside me at my words. I hurried on. "But I believe that God spoke to him when he was surrounded by the evil that descended upon us yesterday. Most men ignore Christ's voice, but whether he knows it or not, I think Runolf listened. For if not, why fight against his own to protect the innocent children?"

For a while, Hygebald said nothing. An afternoon breeze had picked up, tugging at our woollen habits. A flock of dunlin flapped in a coruscating white and grey cloud into the sky out of the path of the reeve and his band of horsemen. The riders would reach us soon. Hygebald turned towards me and I found myself staring into his thoughtful hazel eyes.

"Did you hear Christ yesterday, young Hunlaf?" he asked. "For I do not recall anywhere in His teachings where He says to snatch up a knife and fight those who oppress you."

He did not await a reply. Instead, he strode down the slight slope towards the horsemen. The reeve's fine grey steed was cantering up the rise. It tossed its head, shaking its long white mane, evidently pleased to be free of the clinging mud. Its hooves and fetlocks were smeared with the stuff, giving the impression that its legs were wrapped in dark bindings of grime.

The man astride the pale horse was stocky of build, with florid skin and quick, darting eyes. He swung a leg over his mount's saddle and leapt to the ground. He threw his reins to the next man who had pulled up beside him. Strutting quickly to where Hygebald waited, his gaze swept across the remains of the settlement and the minster buildings.

"Your Excellency," he said, "these are grave times indeed. Please forgive me for taking so long to reach you, but by the time your man came to us, the tide had turned." He spoke in quick spurts, every now and then jerking and pausing, as if tugging on the reins of wayward words. All the while his eyes shifted, his gaze roving ceaselessly, never settling in one spot for long, but missing nothing.

It seemed strange to me that nobody had thought to come when they had seen the fires, for the smoke had risen high and black in the clear sky of the previous day, but I held my tongue and watched in silence.

"There is nothing to forgive, Lord Uhtric," said Hygebald with a dip of his head. I had believed they would send the reeve, instead, the lord of Bebbanburg had ridden to the island. "There would have been nothing more for you to do if you had come earlier. The dead are going nowhere and we are tending to their spiritual and bodily needs now."

Uhtric recoiled as if he had been slapped by the bishop. Frowning, he said, "I see that your man did not embellish his tale. I had hoped that he had allowed his youthful imagination to get the better of him."

"Alas," said Hygebald, "if yesterday had been any worse, you would find only corpses here."

In the distance a small group of monks pushed a handcart towards the burial ground. In the bed of the cart lay a linen-wrapped shape that could have been a small woman or a child.

"What in the name of all that is holy happened here?" Uhtric's voice trembled as he began to take in the scale of the destruction.

"Come," said Hygebald with a sigh, "I will show you."

Uhtric ordered a few of his men to tend to the horses. I noticed that these men wore no armour. Their clothes were simple kirtles and breeches and while they carried shields and spears, they bore no other symbols of wealth or battle. Surely, these were men called from the nearby villages to bolster the number of Uhtric's guard, I thought.

The rest of the men were dour-faced, with long moustaches and the swaggering gait of warriors. The leather scabbards at their belts were tooled with patterns and symbols; the hilts of their swords gleamed with gold and garnets. These were Lord Uhtric's personal hearth-warriors and they fell into step behind him as he walked alongside the grey-haired bishop. As nobody had objected to my presence, I followed along in their wake.

Hygebald led them first past the remains of the settlement where Aelfwyn had lived. Uhtric shook his head. He asked questions about what time of day the raiders had landed their ships, how many vessels there had been and how many men. Hygebald answered his queries in his calm, quiet voice.

When we neared the shattered, blackened husk of the barn, Uhtric enquired why the Norsemen had burnt such a large building, leaving some other, smaller huts within the settlement, untouched. Hygebald paused. Sighing, he told the tale of the last of the villagers and how they had been rounded up and burnt alive.

Uhtric and several of his warband crossed themselves. Their faces were pale, their mouths down-turned in scowls as we trudged past the building where I had found Runolf. I could feel their mood souring with each passing moment. The wall near the doorway was smeared with a dark brown smudge. Uhtric's ever-moving eyes fixed on the stain.

"And this is where the captured man fought?" he asked. "And you say he saved two children from the slaughter?"

"Yes," replied Hygebald, "with the help of Brother Hunlaf here." He gestured in my direction. I felt my face grow hot beneath the bruises as all of the men turned to look at me with expressions of incredulity.

"Indeed?" said Uhtric, his tone making it clear he thought that the bishop must be mistaken. "And how did you help save the children?" he asked me.

"It looks like he put his face in the way," retorted one of the men. A few of the others began to laugh, pleased that somebody had broken the darkening sombre mood. Uhtric rounded on the man who had spoken.

"This is not a thing to make light of," he barked. The men fell silent once more. Turning back to me, he said, "Well?"

I swallowed against the lump that had formed in my throat.

"I don't rightly know, lord," I said at last, my voice quiet and crackling from dryness. I coughed. The lord stared at me, clearly expecting more, so I added: "I just saw the children and the big man defending them, and I could not turn away." I hesitated, unsure what more to say.

"What else?" he prompted me to continue.

"I—" I stammered. I didn't want to speak about it, but there was something in Uhtric's eyes that would not allow me to remain silent. "I almost felt as though the hand of God was pushing me forward," I blurted out in a rush.

Uhtric stared at me for several heartbeats.

"And did you fight? Did you slay any of these heathen bastards?"

I shook my head.

"Not any of those here," I said. "I attacked one, but his armour turned my blade. The last thing I remember he was doing this to my face." I raised a hand and waved it before my features.

"Not any of these, you say. But you did kill then?" asked Uhtric, his eyes narrowing.

I had told nobody of how I had buried the seax into the throat of the Norseman, but standing there before the piercing gaze of Uhtric, with Bishop Hygebald looking on, I knew I could not lie. And so I merely nodded.

I don't know what I had been expecting, but I was startled when Uhtric grinned and slapped me on the shoulder.

"Good man," he said. "We might have to take this one from your side, bishop. I am always in need of men who don't shy away from danger in a fight."

Hygebald said nothing, but he looked at me with an unreadable expression. I knew that the lord was jesting, but I could not help myself feeling a thin rush of pride at his words.

We continued to survey the damage and soon we were walking towards the chapel and the burnt-out shell of the scriptorium. After the brief exchange at the hut, Uhtric had ignored me. As the men from the mainland took in each new affront to the island, their mood darkened, like clouds gathering over the North Sea before a storm struck.

A solitary birch, twisted and bent from the prevailing winds on the island, rose from the flat land at the edge of the minster. The wind whispered through its leafy boughs and it swayed gently, creaking in the stiffening breeze. The tree seemed to catch Uhtric's attention.

"That looks as good a spot as any," he said to one of his warband. "Don't you think, Hereward?"

"Aye, lord," the man replied, sizing up the tree. "High enough. And stout branches to survive in the wind that comes in from the sea here."

I was confused. Hygebald seemed at a loss too, for he said, "Of what do you speak? That birch is one of the few things to have survived yesterday's attack without damage."

"Little enough worth stealing from a tree, eh?" said Uhtric, with a mirthless smile.

"Indeed," replied Hygebald, clearly still confused as to his reason for mentioning the tree.

"We have seen and heard enough of what these foul heathens did here," said Uhtric, his tone brisk and matter of fact. "We shall have to see what our lord king, Æthelred, decides to do about the attack. Perhaps, he will send men to raid the kingdom from whence these Norsemen came."

Hygebald crossed himself, perhaps imagining such bloodshed perpetrated in the name of retribution. The bishop composed himself, smoothing his robes over his thighs with his slender hands. He was a thoughtful man, learned and wise, and he rarely spoke without considering his words at length.

But Uhtric was clearly a man of action and he did not wait for Hygebald to order his thoughts.

"But those are matters for the king to ponder with the Witan," Uhtric said. "For now, I have my own work to do, and I think this birch will do nicely."

Hygebald frowned, still unsure of Uhtric's meaning. I caught the hard glint in the lord of Bebbanburg's eye, and with a sinking feeling, I knew exactly what use he had planned for the tree.

"As you said, your Excellency," said Uhtric, "there is little we can do here now, except to mourn and bury the dead, and to pray for their souls. That is not work for me or my warriors. In time, I will send some of my men to help you with the rebuilding. But for now, the only thing I can do is mete out justice to the one heathen killer we have within reach. Let us bring out this Norseman you have in custody. This tree is perfect for a hanging."

Eight

A raven croaked angrily and flapped into the grey sky as one of Uhtric's men threw a length of hemp rope over the thick trunk of the birch where it leaned to one side, bent by years of winds from the sea.

Runolf looked up at the sound of the bird and his face paled. He had not spoken since he had been led from the cell by four of Uhtric's hearth-men. They had taken the precaution of binding his hands behind his back and they had clearly already exacted some small vengeance upon him while doing so. His cheek was bruised and swollen, and blood trickled from his split lip, soaking into his beard. I winced at the sight of the huge Norseman's face when he arrived in the shadow of the towering tree. He had met my gaze and offered me a small nod. He had seemed unfrightened by the fate that awaited him until he had seen the black-winged raven.

While the warrior secured the rope and tied a noose, Uhtric addressed Runolf.

"Who led you here and why did you come?" he asked.

Runolf tracked the raven's flight until it vanished into the distance. Then, turning to Uhtric, he shook his head.

"Is the man stupid?" Uhtric asked. "Moon-touched?"

"No, lord," I said. "He does not speak our tongue."

"But you can speak with him?"

"Yes, I know some of his words. Norse traders used to come to my home on the Tuede, and—"

"Very well," he interrupted me. "Ask him my questions. I would take what knowledge I can from him before he swings."

I nodded and asked Runolf about his leader and why they had come to Lindisfarnae.

"You know this," he growled.

I nodded.

"But he is a lord. You must answer him."

Runolf spat a gobbet of bloody spittle into the grass. He glowered at Uhtric from beneath his heavy brows and for a time I thought he would not respond to the questions.

"Jarl Skorri led the raiding party," he said at last, his voice deep and flat. "We sailed west for silver, gold and thralls."

I patiently translated Runolf's taciturn, terse answers.

Uhtric stared out to sea without acknowledging Runolf's reply.

The warrior with the rope finished tying the noose and signalled to Uhtric, who seemed already bored of the interrogation. The noose was well-fashioned. Uhtric's man was clearly experienced in executions. The lord let out a long breath, as if what he was about to do pained him. He gestured to his man, who looped the noose about Runolf's neck.

"Tell him this," Uhtric said. "With the power vested in me as the lord of this shire by his majesty the king, Æthelred of Northumbria, I sentence him to death for the wilful murder and defilement of the king's subjects. May God have mercy on his heathen soul."

"But lord," I said, "perhaps this is not the best way…"

Surely I had not been so wrong. God must have brought Runolf here for a reason.

Uhtric glared at me.

I had become convinced that God had sent Runolf to me. He could not be there simply to be dangled at the end of a rope.

"Tell him," Uhtric said, "or he will face his maker without hearing my sentence. It makes no difference to me. He clearly knows the wrong he has done." He nodded to his man, who took up the slack on the rope. Two other warriors joined him and picked up the coils of hemp, ready to hoist Runolf off the ground. He would strangle slowly then, slain by his own weight pulling against his throat.

"Wait," I said, unsure what to say to convince Uhtric. "He is more valuable to you alive than dead."

Uhtric held up his hand. His eyes flickered towards Runolf, who stood still, patiently awaiting his demise, then back to me.

"Explain," he said.

"If you kill him, what he knows dies with him," I said, struggling to make him understand.

"I care nothing for what this man knows," sniffed Uhtric. "I would rather see him hanged and know that I have meted out some justice for those slain here, than to keep him alive and maybe hear some morsel of information from him. And to what end anyway? He is a brute of a man. Such is plain to see. He knows nothing of import. He is no leader of men, no lord or reeve. No. He dies now, and we shall see what Æthelred King wishes to do about a possible retaliation for what has occurred here."

He waved a hand at his men, and they tugged on the rope, pulling Runolf first onto his toes and then clear of the ground. They grunted with the effort and as the rope tightened about his neck Runolf began to gag and thrash at the bonds that held him. His body flapped and swung like a fish on a hook. His eyes grew wide with the terror of impending death and his tongue protruded from his mouth.

I dashed forwards, but had no hope of stopping the burly warriors from carrying out the punishment Uhtric had decreed.

"No!" I shouted, but they all ignored me. I could feel tears stinging my eyes. This could not be what God intended. Surely there was some hidden method in Runolf's presence. There had to be, for the alternative was unthinkable. "No," I repeated, despair in my voice. Nobody paid me heed. Runolf's gaze met mine and I felt an immense emptiness. I was powerless and of no import to these armed men.

Runolf would die now. Just one more corpse to bury in the sandy soil. Another meaningless death.

And then a new voice joined my protests.

"Wait," said Hygebald, his tone quieter than mine, but carrying with it the heft of authority. "Lower him down." The bishop's intervention surprised me as much as it did Uhtric and his men. But the sight of the old man's set jaw and his unwavering stare, filled me with a sudden respect and love for him. I thought of our brief conversation while waiting for Uhtric and his men. It seemed he had listened to my words.

The three warriors who were straining on the rope, looked from the bishop to their leader. For the first time, Uhtric seemed uncertain.

"Let him live a moment longer," Hygebald said. "Hear me out, and then decide. But if the man is already dead, you will lose possible favour with the king."

For an agonisingly long time the only movements came from Runolf's struggles, his feet kicking, body jerking. The only sounds were his gurgling cries, the sough of the wind through the birch's branches and the distant sigh of the waves in the harbour.

At last, Uhtric nodded and made a cutting motion with his hand.

"Let him down," he said. His warriors released the rope and Runolf fell to the earth. His legs buckled beneath him and he collapsed in a sprawling heap, gasping, coughing and retching.

MATTHEW HARFFY

Uhtric turned to Hygebald, ignoring the rest of us. His gaze did not rove now, but was fixed on the eyes of the bishop.

"Why should I not have this man killed, your Excellency?" he asked, his voice clipped with suppressed anger at having been made to look weak before his men.

"The reasons are many," replied Hygebald, his tone calm and confident. "Firstly, I believe that every man has the right to seek forgiveness for his sins."

"He can ask God for forgiveness when he sees Him," Uhtric growled. "I am no man of God and I will not stay my hand so that you can present the other cheek for him to slap."

"It is true, that you are no man of God," replied Hygebald, and the reproach was clear. "But you understand that all men can be led astray by others, do you not?"

"Of course," Uhtric sputtered. "But that is no excuse for a man's actions. His deeds are his own."

"Ah, yes. And a man should try to fight against his own wickedness and his mistakes, is that not so?"

Uhtric nodded slowly, grudgingly.

"And you have heard how this man did just that," the bishop went on. "He fought against his own companions to save two helpless children. If he had not done so, those orphans would now be dead or carried away, and he could have fled with the rest of his people aboard their dragon ships."

Uhtric frowned.

"Those children's parents were only killed because this man and his kind came here in their ships and murdered them!"

Hygebald nodded sadly.

"This is true, but as the good Lord said, 'He that is without sin among you, let him first cast a stone'. I see in this man's actions that he heard the word of God and turned against his own to protect the innocent. If he had not been here, and if he had not heeded the whispered word of Christ, those children would no longer be with us."

Uhtric pursed his lips and shook his head as if to clear it of confusion.

"I care nought for the man's immortal soul. I do not know if you truly believe that this brute heard the word of God," he crossed himself, clearly uncomfortable with the path the conversation was treading, "but you spoke of favour at court?"

"Indeed," said Hygebald, rubbing his thin fingers over his chin. "Indeed, I did. Have you not considered that the king himself might like the opportunity to question the only captive from this terrible attack on his lands?"

A loud squawk from high above made us all pause and look up. The raven, all sleek blackness and sharp beak had returned to settle in one of the highest boughs. It peered down with its beady eyes and I felt a sliver of unease scratch a finger down my spine. I shivered and made the sign of the cross. Hygebald did likewise and a few of the warriors copied us.

Uhtric bristled, seemingly oblivious of the effect the dire bird had on the rest of us.

"I have questioned the Norseman already," he said.

"Yes, that is so," replied Hygebald, his tone placatory and soothing. "But do you presume you can have anticipated all of the king's questions?"

Uhtric knitted his brows.

"What else could our king wish to ask him?"

"Who can tell what the king might wish to know?" said Hygebald. "Would you second guess him? A wise man such as yourself would provide his king with the ability to fully interrogate such an important prisoner and give him the option of deciding the man's fate. Would you deny your king these things? Would it not profit you more to take the whole cow to him rather than a few drops of its milk in the hope that is enough to slake his thirst?"

Uhtric pondered for a time, looking first at Hygebald and then Runolf, who had pushed himself up onto his knees. The

Norseman glared back at the lord of Bebbanburg. There was no hint of fear in his eyes, merely a glowering defiance.

With a sigh, Uhtric finally nodded. From its high perch in the tree, the raven croaked once more.

"Very well," Uhtric said. "I will not go against the will of one as holy and wise as yourself, your Excellency. I will take the Norseman to Eoforwic where the king can question him and decide his wyrd." One of the warriors spat at hearing these words and a few others murmured their disapproval. But Uhtric had made up his mind and his men's disappointment at being cheated out of a hanging was nothing to him. "Remove the rope," he snapped, "and get him up on a horse. We will leave immediately. I do not wish to miss the tide and be stuck here on the island."

Grumbling, his men went about doing their lord's bidding.

I stepped towards Uhtric. He turned, a disdainful sneer on his features. My blood pounded in my ears. My throat was dry, but I forced myself to speak. I was surprised at how steady my voice was.

"Lord Uhtric," I said, "with his Excellency's leave, I would accompany you to Eoforwic."

Nine

I looked about me, trying to take in everything within the hall at once. I could scarcely believe where I stood. This was the great hall of Bebbanburg, the impregnable fortress that loomed over the North Sea on its huge fist of rock. I had gazed up at its palisades and buildings before when travelling past. On clear days, you could see the citadel in the distance from the minster on Lindisfarnae. But I had never set foot inside the fabled fortress before. I must have looked foolish, mouth agog, as I stared at the sumptuous wall hangings with their golden threads. Weapons and shields from past foes or fallen heroes adorned the walls and stout columns. And all of the exposed timber I could see was finely carved with interlacing animals and figures from legend. I wondered whether Beowulf, the slayer of Grendel, was depicted on one of the lintels or pillars. There was so much detail and colour, I could not make sense of all that I saw. My head swam with the assault of sights and sounds of the massive building.

I had heard tell of Bebbanburg all my life in tales of sieges and battles. As we had entered through the palisade's great gate, the door wardens staring grimly down at us from their platforms, I could picture in my mind's eye the famous battle before the gates where the great hero, Beobrand, and his black-shielded warband had rushed through the flames and sparks to defeat Penda of Mercia. My father would tell tales of Beobrand when I was a boy, claiming he was a distant forebear of ours. I never truly believed him, or the tales he told. Who knew if the stories of Bebbanburg and its battles were true, or merely fantasies spun by scops? I am sure now, as an old man, that all such yarns have been embellished, for is that not the way of the storyteller, to make the tale more exciting than the simple truth? But as a child, I had revelled in the sagas of shieldwalls, of warriors soaking the earth with slaughter-sweat and feeding the crows with the bloody harvest of scything blades.

And now, here I was in the hall of the greatest, most famous fortress in my small world. At that time I had yet to travel beyond our shores. I had not then stood in the shadow of the great walls of Byzantion or walked amongst the columned majesty of the soaring buildings of Roma, and the huge hall of Bebbanburg, with its colourful decorations, carved and painted pillars, blazing hearth fire and the cacophony of sound from the gathered warriors and nobles, was the most magnificent thing I had ever witnessed. My breath caught in my throat as we walked to the bench at the side of the room where we were to sit for the meal.

"You look like a child who has been given a whole pot of honey," said Leofstan, shaking his head. "I cannot believe you are enjoying this."

I swallowed back the laughter that had been bubbling up within me. It was true. I felt gleeful at seeing this place that I had often dreamt of as a boy. And I could not deny that I was exhilarated by the outcome of my actions on the holy island. My nose was blocked and painful, my face bruised. And my bandaged hand stung when I forgot about my wound and tried to grip something, but those things seemed unimportant. When I thought of all those who had been killed just the day before I felt a wave of sorrow. And yet, even the atrocities I had witnessed seemed distant, less raw than they should rightly be. I'd wondered at my seeming inability to feel sorrow, as we had walked across the sands from Lindisfarnae. If it was indeed true that it was God who had given me the rage to fight, and it was He who had sent Runolf to help us in our time of need, then surely it must also be the Lord who made me this way. I would be no use to anyone if I was weeping like a child. I mused that if I felt the destruction and killings of my brethren as keenly as others, I would be unable to function, and so I embraced what seemed to be a God-given ability to push my sadness aside.

And yet I saw the expression on Leofstan's face as he looked at me in the heat of the hall. His was not the look of a teacher who sees his pupil growing in ability and independence. No, his expression was one of confusion. And something else: disappointment.

I reached for a cup that had been filled by a young serving maid. Her hair reminded me of Aelfwyn. I imagined her then, her terrible last moments in the searing heat of the burning barn and my throat thickened. Tears stung my eyes. I forced those dark thoughts away and nodded my thanks to the servant.

My hands shook as I drank deeply. It was cool, fresh ale and it began to refresh me.

"I am pleased to see this place," I said to Leofstan. "I have oft wondered what it would be like to dine in this great hall." Leofstan frowned and I continued quickly. "But I would rather we had come here under better circumstances."

The older monk nodded, seemingly mollified by my words.

"When we have eaten," he said, "we will go to the church of Saint Peter, see the relics there and pray for the souls of the fallen." He paused. "We can pray for your cousin too."

I focused on the food on the board, blinking back the tears that threatened to fall. I had told him of my chance meeting with Aelfwyn as we had followed Uhtric and his men over the pilgrims' path. I took up a piece of bread and bit off a chunk. The loss of Aelfwyn and the brethren had left me feeling empty. I could not fill the yawning hollow left by so much death, but my body still needed fuel and the ale had opened up my appetite. It was only in that moment that I realised how hungry I was. We had not eaten since the morning. There had been no time to tarry after Uhtric had made his decision to allow us to accompany him.

At first he had been sceptical.

"Why would you come with us to Eoforwic?" he asked.

"You will need someone to interpret the prisoner's words," I said, keeping my expression neutral. "There might be others there who can speak his tongue, and the king is surely clever enough to make himself understood," I acknowledged, "but would you risk confusion? The king will surely be pleased of your forethought in bringing someone who can help him communicate with the Norseman."

Uhtric stroked his moustache and surveyed me for a while before nodding.

"Come then," he said, his mind made up. "We leave right away to avoid missing the tide. I will find you a mount at Bebbanburg, but till then, you will have to walk."

Leofstan had not been pleased when he heard the news that I was leaving. But Bishop Hygebald had given his consent, so there was not much he could do apart from nod. Hygebald, perhaps sensing his discomfort, told him he must accompany me. I was pleased to have Leofstan's company and guidance. The thought of travelling with Uhtric and his warriors filled me with a mixture of anticipation and trepidation. And I was all too aware that I had been partly responsible for Uhtric's decision not to execute Runolf and then to take him to Eoforwic to see the king. If things got difficult, I feared I would be blamed. If such came to pass, I would be glad of Leofstan's calming presence.

And so it was that we trudged across the wet sand, following the pilgrims' path behind the mounted warriors. Runolf, noose tight about his neck and hands yet tied at his back, stumbled along in the wake of the riders. The noose rope was looped about the high saddle pommel and on more than one occasion Runolf fell and was dragged, choking and gagging through the dark muck. When this happened, I called out, halting the rider for long enough to allow me to heave Runolf to his feet.

As we crossed the sand and then walked along the shore southward the short distance to Bebbanburg, Uhtric's mood soured. I saw him looking back at the three of us walking at the rear of the column. The disapproval was clear on his face and I could imagine what he was thinking. He was questioning his decision to take Runolf south to Eoforwic. And he wondered whether he should have rejected my request to join him on the journey. But just as soon as these thoughts came to him, so they were dispelled. He had told his Excellency the Bishop of Lindisfarnae that he would take us, and the idea to transport the huge Norseman had come from Hygebald himself. Uhtric balanced up the value of his prisoner to the king and also the benefit to be had from pleasing one of the most powerful holy men of the land. The balance must have come out in his favour, for by the time we reached the slope leading up to the fortress gates, he was at peace once more with his decisions. As we crossed the threshold between the stout oaken doors he even smiled, perhaps gladdened to be safe within his rocky domain once more.

"Welcome to my humble home," he said. "Within the church yonder rests the uncorrupted arm of Saint Oswald and you are welcome to see it and pray within the chapel, of course. My steward will find you somewhere to sleep and in the morning my hostler will provide you with horses. Tomorrow we will ride south, but tonight you will dine as my guests in the great hall. The hall where kings and queens have feasted for centuries."

Runolf, begrimed and staggering, gazed about him. His eyes gleamed as he took in the expanse of open ground surrounded by the high palisade and the thatched barns, stables, guard houses and halls that made up the citadel of Bebbanburg. Uhtric noticed the Norseman's hungry look and frowned, his good humour gone in an instant like so much smoke on the wind.

"Take that heathen bastard and see that he is locked in a room with no window," he said to one of his warriors. "One of the storerooms should do."

Runolf had been dragged away and I had thought little of him until I had sated my thirst on Uhtric's fine ale and filled my belly with roast venison and a thick vegetable pottage. There was smoked herring too, but the sight of the shiny yellow flesh conjured memories of Aelfwyn and my eyes brimmed with tears. I pushed away the proffered platter.

Only when I was replete did I wonder if Runolf had been given any sustenance. I cut a thick hunk of the gritty bread and on top of it I scooped a piece of meat, and a sliver of herring. I filled a cup with ale and stood.

"Do you plan to eat another meal in the church?" asked Leofstan; and I was pleased to hear the familiar tinge of humour in his tone. It seemed the food and drink had done much to restore both of us.

"Let us take this to Runolf first," I said. "Then we can go and pray."

We walked along the edge of the hall, swerving to avoid the servants who hurried by with large pitchers of wine, ale and mead. The noise now was deafening. Most of the diners had drunk too much already and the feast seemed to have no end in sight. Close to our host at the high table, a dwarf capered and gambolled and a slender man, who was stripped bare apart from a loin cloth, bent himself into all manner of seemingly impossible knots. His bones looked set to pop out of his skin and the sight of him turned my stomach. The onlookers cheered and yelled encouragement. Neither I nor Leofstan spoke until we had left the building as we knew our voices would be drowned by the debauchery.

Stepping into the cool darkness outside, I felt a sudden pang of desperate sadness. The sounds from the hall subsided as we walked into the night and I let out a long breath. All my earlier joy at seeing the location of so many childhood tales had evaporated like mead spilt onto a hearthstone.

Beside me, Leofstan sighed too.

"I am glad of the food," he said, "but I miss the simple ways of the minster."

"How can they laugh and gorge themselves as if at a Crístesmæsse feast?" I asked. "Not two days ago dozens of Christian men and women, innocent people all, were abused, murdered and enthralled, not even a day's walk away."

"To be able to ignore that which is right before them, is both a strength and a weakness of mankind," Leofstan said. "If we allowed all the horrors of the world to assail us without respite, we would surely be consumed with grief, unable to do anything save cry and pray to the Almighty for salvation."

We walked in silence for a time towards the storerooms where Runolf had been taken. A light drizzle began to fall. It was cooling after the sweltering heat of the hall.

"You say it is a weakness too?" I said.

"Men who commit the worst sins are often those who are able to push away their emotions completely. If a man feels no sorrow for others' suffering, there is nothing to stop him inflicting pain with abandon."

My hands were full with the food, but I felt an almost overwhelming urge to cross myself and pray. Was my own ability to suppress my woe and sadness a blessing or a curse?

"What if a man is able to lie about a forbidden book?" I said, my tone sharp. I hated being made to confront my actions, and so I forced Leofstan to face his own.

He sighed.

"No man is without sin, it is true, Hunlaf," he said. "But a man's sin is between him and the Lord. I spoke to the bishop about the book. I tried my best to do what was right. But whatever the correct course of action, it matters not now. The book is destroyed. And you cannot believe that the loss of such knowledge, perhaps the last copy in existence of the works of a great mind, should have been burnt."

"I know not what I think anymore," I replied. But in truth, the thought of *The Treasure of Life*, with its elaborate decorations and perfectly executed words and diagrams being turned to ash filled me with sorrow.

I glanced over at Leofstan and he smiled at me sadly. He knew my mind well enough. I loved learning as much as he did.

We spoke no further until we reached the building where Runolf was being held. Two men lounged outside the door, their faces lit from below by the dancing flames of a brazier. As we approached, one murmured something I could not hear and the two of them laughed. The red fire-glow gave their faces a demonic air.

"Have you fed the prisoner?" I snapped, suddenly angry. The two guards jerked upright at the harsh sound of my voice, undoubtedly surprised to hear the tone from a young man bearing the tonsure.

I struggled to keep my ire in check. Leofstan placed a hand on my shoulder.

"We have brought some food and drink for him," he said in a calming tone.

"Well," said the shorter of the two, "leave it with us and we will see that he gets it." He leaned forward so that his broad face caught the light of the flames. His eyes were deep set and close together. I had an urge to strike him and had to whisper the paternoster under my breath to control myself.

"Hunlaf, give the man the provender," said Leofstan quietly.

I glared at the guard and he returned my gaze, seemingly amused at my obvious anger. With an effort, I let out my breath and handed him the cup of ale and the bread topped with fish and meat.

"This looks tasty indeed," the man said, with a sidelong glance at his companion.

"Very tasty," the other man replied, smacking his lips. The two men chuckled and I bunched my hands into fists at my side. My right hand throbbed terribly where I'd once again split the scab on the wounds across my fingers.

"You will give the food and ale to the prisoner?" asked Leofstan, his voice still soft and soothing, despite the crackle of confrontation between the men and me.

"Of course, brother," replied the short warrior, offering an ingratiating grin. The other guard giggled.

"Good," said Leofstan. "I will tell Uhtric that you have followed his orders faithfully. I pray that the rest of your evening is without incident."

The guard frowned at the mention of the lord of Bebbanburg, but Leofstan did not wait for his reply. Turning me with his grip on my shoulder, he pushed me away. I could barely breathe, such was my anger, and the force of it frightened me.

When we had walked some distance from the storeroom and the guards, Leofstan spoke again in his gentle tone.

"You must learn to control that anger of yours. Ire and violence are seldom the best way to get the outcome you desire in life."

I nodded glumly, scared of what had been unleashed within me by the events on Lindisfarnae.

"Let us go now to Saint Peter's," Leofstan said. "I would see the remains of the arm of the saintly Oswald, and I believe we are both in need of prayer and guidance from the Almighty."

Ten

We rode south the next day with a column of a dozen of Uhtric's hearth-warriors. He sent messengers on ahead with news of our coming so that halls along the way could prepare to house us for each night of our journey. As we travelled, we left the clouds and drizzle behind us in the north, a memory like the terrible storms that had ravaged the land in the spring and early summer. Stores had been ruined by rot and flooding, and the winter crops of wheat and rye had been crushed and destroyed in the dreadful winds and torrential rains. Either side of the crumbling, rutted Roman road were signs of the famine that yet gripped the land. Dirty, emaciated children followed us whenever we passed a dwelling. They trotted alongside the horses for as long as they were able, holding out their hands and pleading for food. I wanted to halt, to see whether there was anything we could do to alleviate their struggle, but Uhtric would not countenance the idea.

"You convinced me that taking this man south to the king was important," he said, gesturing with his chin towards Runolf, who now sat astride a mule that was led by one of Uhtric's men. "You cannot now tell me that it is important to pause at every sign of a hungry mouth. The whole land is hungry, as well you know. All we can do is pray for a good harvest and that God will spare us from any pestilence this year."

I made the sign of the cross, feeling an impotent anger growing within me, twisted and strangling, like the weeds in the fields. What did Uhtric know of hunger and hardship? His belly was not shrivelled with starvation, his muscles would not wither on his frame from lack of nourishment.

I swallowed down my fury and nodded, saying no more.

Leofstan caught my eye and offered a thin smile. I thought I saw a glimmer of the pleasure he used to show so often when I proved that I had listened to one of his lectures.

Kicking my heels into my horse's flanks I rode on, away from the impoverished and starving children with their brimming eyes and gaunt cheeks.

Uhtric's hostler had picked out a mud-brown mare for me. She was broad-backed and slow, but she was also peaceful and biddable. The hostler had clearly marked me out as someone not used to riding. It was true that the brethren usually travelled on foot, and by midday my thighs were raw and chafed. When we dismounted to rest and to eat some of the bread and cheese we had been given by the steward of Bebbanburg, I could barely walk. I staggered over to Runolf, who had slid down from the mule seemingly without any ill effects from the ride. The bruises on his face were turning a greenish yellow and I wondered how my own face must look. I touched my nose gingerly and winced. The pain was less acute now, but it was certainly not healed.

"It is still there," Runolf said, with a grin.

I returned his smile and offered him half of my bread.

"Did they give you food last night?" I asked.

"Yes," he said, sliding down the trunk of a beech tree to sit with his back to its bark. "Thank you."

"For what?" I asked.

"I heard you talking to the guards outside. They gave me the food shortly after. And some good ale."

I glanced over to where Leofstan sat nibbling at his own crust of bread. He raised his eyebrows as if to say, "See, I told you so."

I shrugged and sat down beside the Norseman. We ate in silence for some time. I did not know what to say. Praying in the cool dark of the church the night before had brought me some peace. I still did not know what God wanted from me or Runolf, but as I had knelt on the hard cold flagstones of the chapel, the only light coming from the single beeswax candle that dimly illuminated the bejewelled reliquary that housed Saint Oswald's arm, I had felt a calmness wash over me. I had hoped for a clear sign, an answer from on high that would show me the path I must take, but all I received was this sense of tranquillity.

Afterwards, lying wrapped in a thin blanket on the lumpy straw mattress that the steward had given me, I realised that this calm was an answer in itself. I must learn to let God lead me without dissent or anger. His wisdom was infinite and I must accept that He knew how best to put me to use. For now, the Lord had ensured that I was at Lindisfarnae when the attack occurred and that I would be the one to see Runolf defending the children. Surely it could not be chance that I was the only person on the island who could converse with him. The seed of a thought had been sown when I spoke to the Norseman in the prayer cell that night. I tried not to nurture it, hoping that it might wither and die. But now I knew that if God wished me to act on that idea, He would make His will clear to me. If He wished the seed to take root and to grow, God would see that it was given the water of hope.

We had finished our food and one of the warriors wandered over to us and handed me a water skin. I took a long draught, allowing some of the liquid to drip onto my left palm. This I splashed on my face. It was cool and refreshing. The day was now hot and sultry. I passed the skin to Runolf, who accepted it and drank deeply.

"Thank you too for what you said at the tree," he said. His voice was roughened from where the noose had tightened around his throat.

"You understood?" I asked.

"Some of the words. Our languages are not so different, it seems. And you are not the only one with quick wits, Hunlaf," he said with a lopsided smirk.

I paused then, staring at him. He was a huge giant of a man, with legs like tree trunks and arms bulky with knotted muscle. I imagined that he was often mistaken for being stupid.

I nodded and offered him my left hand. He hesitated for the merest instant and in that moment I was sure that he would pull me to him and snap my neck, or perhaps seek to use me as a hostage, enabling him to escape. If he used his strength against me there would be nothing I could do to prevent him. I looked into his eyes and saw the sharp intelligence there. I gasped, my skin cold, despite the warm day. I was going to snatch my hand away when he gripped it in both of his as they were still bound together. His meaty hands enveloped mine and I tensed. But he did not attack me. He merely stood, allowing me to pull him to his feet.

Once standing, he towered over me.

"Your words have kept me alive, Hunlaf," he said. "I will not forget that." He held my gaze for a time, before turning to his mule. "Now, where are we heading?"

I let out a ragged breath.

All around us, the riders were mounting again. I groaned at the thought of having to endure the long hot afternoon in the saddle.

"We are going to Eoforwic, to speak to the king," I said, "but first, we will stop at Werceworthe."

"Werceworthe?" he enquired.

"The minster, where I live." Wincing against the pain in my bandaged hand and the soreness in my thighs and rump, I pulled myself onto my mare's back. "It is on the way," I added.

Eleven

The sun was low in the sky when we finally reached Werce-worthe. The minster buildings, the church and the settlement all nestled in a loop of the river Cocueda. The monastery cells, refectory and scriptorium were at the northernmost end of the tongue of land that was partially encircled by the wide waters of the Cocueda. The minster was thus surrounded by water on the north, east and west, and to the south, beyond a hill that overlooked the settlement, a thick wood of oak and beech grew. As we approached, weary and dusty from the long day's ride, I welcomed the sight of the minster, buildings partly hidden by the alders that bordered the banks of the wide river.

Uhtric's messengers must have done their job, because when we rode down to the sandy shore of the river, the ferry was already waiting for us. It was a wide, shallow raft that four ferrymen pushed through the water using long poles of ash. When the river was in spate, it was impossible to cross at this point and we would have needed to ride far to the west before fording the river and heading eastward again to approach Werceworthe from the south.

Mossy, mouldering timbers jutted from the river at regular intervals. The people of Werceworthe said that there used to be a bridge across the water, but no living soul could recall actually having seen it.

"Well met," called the oldest of the ferrymen, a cheery man with a wrinkled and weathered face that made him seem to be made from leather. His features were partially shaded by a wide-brimmed hat woven out of straw. The bright sun shone through the gaps in the hat, dappling his face in light and shade. The man's name was Copel and I knew him to be an affable sort, always polite and willing to lend a hand at harvest time. He nodded to Leofstan and me, having recognised us. He tugged his forelock to Uhtric. "God be with you all this afternoon."

Uhtric was impatient and nudged his stallion forward.

"How many horses and men can you take at once?" he asked.

Copel rubbed his hand across his bald pate and sucked his teeth.

"Four horses and four men, along with us, I reckon," he said after careful consideration.

Uhtric sighed.

"Very well," he said. "Let's get moving."

"Right you are," said Copel with a raised eyebrow and a sidelong glance at the lord of Bebbanburg. "We will be as quick as we can be, but it is not easy to steer this old barge when fully laden, and you won't want to be swimming before your supper, I reckon."

"Can you get us all across or not?" barked Uhtric.

"Oh aye, lord. The river is low and the tide is on the ebb. We'll get it done. But it will take a few trips and we'll be right tired afore the sun sets." He sniffed, raised a thumb to one nostril and snorted out from the other a stream of snot into the river.

Uhtric turned away, disgusted by the man.

"Just get us across."

Despite the ferryman's words, the process of shuttling the men and their mounts across the Cocueda did not take very long. The only disruption came when one of the warriors was pushed from the ferry by his horse, much to the amusement of the rest of Uhtric's hearth-men. Luckily the man was not wearing his byrnie and so was able to cling to an outstretched hand before being heaved back onto the boat. He cursed and shouted abuse at his laughing comrades. His annoyance only made them laugh harder. When they stepped from the raft onto the sandy shingle of the beach the bedraggled warrior was shaking with anger. He yanked hard at his horse's reins and when the beast refused to do his bidding, he punched it hard on the snout. The animal whinnied, eyes white-rimmed. Tugging the reins from the warrior's grip, the horse reared up, pawing the air. The man shied away from the enraged animal, lost his footing and stumbled backwards into the river once more, splashing and tottering before ending up sitting in water that lapped about his chest.

This sent the rest of the men into ecstatic paroxysms of laughter and more than one seemed incapable of drawing breath for a time, such was their mirth. I laughed with the rest of them. Leofstan and I had travelled across the river on the first trip with Uhtric and now we waited the arrival of the second ferry-load which included Runolf. As they finished disembarking, the wet warrior came sploshing from the shallows. The huge Norseman looked down at him, then tipped his head back, his long beard jutting, and laughed. This set the men off again, but the sound of their laughter drove the warrior into a rage. He surged out of the river and swung a fist at Runolf. The Norseman did not stop laughing, but swayed back, allowing the strike to miss him.

"Hereward!" snapped Uhtric. "Enough of this foolishness. Whatever crimes the Norseman has committed, it is not his fault you are a clumsy oaf. And a man who mistreats his horse deserves a dunking."

The other warriors, sensing that the time had passed for merriment, bit their lips and pretended to see to their own mounts. Hereward glowered first at Runolf, then at Uhtric and lastly, for some reason, at me, as if I had somehow been responsible for his fall. I saw then that it was the same man who had helped Uhtric choose a tree from which to hang Runolf. Something in the man's defiant glare kindled the spark of anger that had lingered within me since the attack on Lindisfarnae, but before I could put words to my feelings, a cry came from the village that nestled beyond the alders to the south.

Everyone turned in the direction of the sound. A young monk I recognised as Osfrith was sprinting towards us. His habit flapped about his thin, pale legs and he waved his hands in the air as he ran.

"Come!" he shouted. "Come quickly!"

He arrived moments later, breathless and gasping.

"You are well come, Lord Uhtric," he panted, bending over with his hands on his knees, trying to regain his breath.

"Who are you, and what is the meaning of this?" asked Uhtric, staring down at the young monk from where he sat astride his stallion.

"I am Osfrith," he said. "The abbot sent me to bring you at once. Please, lord. Something terrible has happened."

Twelve

"And you say the brigand is in there?" asked Uhtric. His face was flushed from the rush into the settlement of Werceworthe.

"Yes, lord," Osfrith replied. He slipped down from the horse's back and seemed relieved to once more be on his own feet. After he had delivered his garbled message at the ferry, Uhtric had ordered one of his men to pull the monk up onto his mount with him. It was clear Osfrith would not have been able to keep up on foot.

The wailing scream of an infant came from the small, thatched hut that was the object of our interest. Some way from the hut, near Garulf's forge, a large group of people had assembled. From a quick glance, I calculated that most of the villagers, and not a few of the monks, were there. We dismounted and Uhtric strode over to the gathering.

"Ah, Abbot Beonna," he said, spotting the leader of the brethren of Werceworthe amongst the frightened people. "What is going on here?" We moved close to hear the abbot's answer. Osfrith's explanation had been jumbled and confused.

The baby screamed again from the gloom of the hut and a young woman I knew as Wulfwaru let out a moaning cry of her own. Tears streamed down her face and her husband, the tanner, Aethelwig, held her tight, whispering to her to be calm.

His face was pallid and taut as he stroked her head and stared over her shoulder at the darkened doorway.

"May God give you good health and long life," said the abbot, a man of some fifty years, with honest eyes and dark hair that was silvering at the temples beneath his shaven tonsure.

"Yes, yes, waes hael, to you," Uhtric said, waving his hand to be done with the niceties of greetings. "What is happening? Your boy here spoke of a thief?"

Beonna nodded, his expression sad.

"Alas, I fear this thief was a good lad once, but his hunger has let the Devil into his soul."

"Speak plainly, man!" said Uhtric. "The sound of that child's crying is enough to drive a man mad."

Beonna made the sign of the cross and took a deep breath to compose himself. I knew he was a man of contemplation and wisdom, not one prone to make hasty decisions. The clamour and excitement of the afternoon must have been sorely testing his usual calm demeanour.

"The man inside the hut is a young ceorl, called Framric," the abbot said at last. "He was caught stealing grain from the village store. As far as I can make out, when one of the other men threatened to take him before the reeve at the next moot, Framric flew into a terrible rage. He ran off and snatched poor Wulfwaru and Aethelwig's son, Aethelwulf. Framric has hidden himself in their house and has threatened to kill the babe if anyone should approach."

As if to highlight the abbot's words, the captive child let out a piercing howl, as if in pain. Tears flowed down the tanner's face now as Wulfwaru seemed to swoon, collapsing into his arms.

I turned to look at the hut where Framric was menacing Aethelwulf. The afternoon was warm, the sun sliding slowly downward, where it would be lost soon behind the hut's roof.

With a start I realised that one man stood in the open space before the hut.

Runolf, hands still bound before him, was staring fixedly at the building. The infant screamed again and the Norseman winced. Turning, he strode towards me.

"Tell me," he said, his meaning clear.

I stammered over a few words, but soon enough I had explained to him what had happened.

"Hungry, you say?" he asked. "All this for food?"

I nodded.

"What is the prisoner saying?" asked Uhtric, an edge of frustrated anger in his voice.

"He merely asks what has happened," I replied.

"It is no concern of his."

Aethelwulf howled again and Mildrith, one of the women in the group, said, "It is hungry. The poor mite must be fed soon."

"By God," said Uhtric, "we cannot go on like this. It will be dark soon. And that man will either escape then or kill that baby. I will not have it." He looked about him with his roving gaze, but evidently found no solution for he did not move.

"I will rescue the child," said Runolf.

"What is he saying now?" snarled Uhtric.

"He says he will save the babe."

"How?" Uhtric scowled at Runolf. He clearly wanted to dismiss the Norseman outright, and yet Runolf had caught his attention. Uhtric narrowed his eyes and stared at him. "How?" he repeated. The setting sun made the giant's beard and hair glow like molten gold.

To my surprise, Runolf answered in the Englisc tongue.

"Knife. Water. Food." His accent was thick, but the words clear enough. "And this." He reached out with his bound hands and took hold of the edge of my habit.

Uhtric was taken aback. I thought he was going to shout at Runolf, to tell him not to waste his time. But Runolf stared back at him with a steady gaze and something in his bearing gave Uhtric pause.

"What will you do with those things?" he asked. "And how can I trust you?"

Runolf looked at me quizzically. Clearly his new-found language skills did not stretch that far. I repeated Uhtric's questions to him in his own tongue.

Runolf nodded as he listened.

"I have a plan," he said.

"What is it?" I asked, after translating his words for Uhtric.

The giant Norseman nodded and told us.

Thirteen

"Are you sure?" I asked Runolf, dipping the freshly stropped blade of the knife into the bucket of water beside me.

He nodded.

"It is only hair," he said. "It will grow back."

He knelt, placidly waiting for me to begin. I lifted the knife from the cold water and pinched some of the long golden-red hair at the top of his head between my fingers. I had already moistened his scalp, ladling water from the bucket with a small wooden cup. I was just about to cut into the hair when his voice made me halt.

"It will grow." He chuckled. "If I live that long." I shook my head at his composure and began to shave the damp hair from his head.

From the hut in the distance, the baby's cries had dropped to a whimper. It was quieter here. We had retreated, taking the horses and all of Uhtric's men away from the trampled earth before the tanner's hut. I offered up a prayer that Framric, the thief holding the child, had not been peering out of the darkened building. If he had seen us arrive, witnessed Runolf and his hulking presence, the ruse would have no chance of success.

I scraped the sharpened blade across the crown of Runolf's head. The knife's edge was keen and I was well practised in the ritual of maintaining the tonsure. I still could not quite believe that Uhtric had consented to Runolf's plan. For a time, he had seemed ready to dismiss it, but Aethelwulf's wailing had grown in intensity and the sun was moving inexorably towards the fiery western horizon. For the plan to work, Runolf would need to be unbound, and this is what rankled most with Uhtric.

"What is to stop him running off?" he asked.

When I translated the lord of Bebbanburg's words to Runolf, he smiled and held up his hands so that everyone could see clearly the hemp cords tied about his wrists. His hands were as huge as shovels and his forearms were knotted with bunched muscles.

"Does the lord Uhtric truly believe these bonds could hold me?" Runolf asked. He raised an eyebrow, awaiting an answer while I interpreted.

Uhtric frowned, but said nothing. It was obvious to us all that the ropes did not make Runolf a defenceless captive.

"Tell him," Runolf said, "that whether I fail or succeed to rescue that poor babe, I will return to his custody immediately."

I told Uhtric his words and for a long while he held Runolf's gaze. Eventually, he nodded.

"Very well," he said. "Get what he needs and hurry. We must finish this before dark."

On hearing this, some of Uhtric's men spoke out against the decision.

"This is madness, lord," said Hereward. "The Norseman will as likely slay us all as do your bidding."

Uhtric rounded on the man.

"Do you question my judgement, Hereward? I know you to be a brave man, which is why I yet tolerate you. But you would do well to remember who is your hlaford. There are a dozen of you here. Surely you do not fear one Norseman so much."

Hereward grumbled, but said no more. I could feel his angry glare burning into me now as I shaved the last of the tonsure into Runolf's hair. I set about shortening his long locks quickly, sawing away at his plaits. On top of Hereward's glower, I could feel the pressure of the setting sun. Uhtric was right. If this was not resolved before darkness enveloped the land, I feared the worst for Aethelwulf. Of course, if the child should die, Framric had nothing more to bargain with. Then he would flee as quickly as he was able, or face certain death for his crimes.

From the tanner's hut came yelling. A man was shouting angrily. He was answered by the calming tone of the abbot, whom Uhtric had convinced to go along with the plan. I could not make out the words from this distance, but I knew he would be promising the thief that someone would be bringing food for him soon. Beonna was a devout, holy man who would never knowingly lie and there was truth in his words. I wondered what the abbot thought would happen to the ceorl when the food was delivered. Perhaps he chose not to think that far ahead. Or maybe he had weighed up the value of an infant's life against that of a starving ceorl who had been driven to thieving and threatening babes in arms.

I looked at Runolf appraisingly. The tonsure was clearly freshly cut, the skin white where it had never been touched by the sun's rays and there were a couple of beads of bright blood where I had nicked his scalp in my hurry. Perhaps the gloaming of the twilight would help to cover the signs of Runolf's rapid conversion. Looking westward I saw that the red orb of the sun now touched the tops of the alders in the distance. I had planned to shave Runolf's cheeks and chin too, but there was no time. I gripped the braids that dangled from his thick thatch of beard and with one deft cut of the knife, I severed them. With a few quick cuts I shortened the beard, but it would be dark if I tarried long enough to shave his face. And, I thought, looking at the pallid, cut skin of his tonsure, perhaps it would only serve to make him stand out more.

"Up," I said. "Let me take a look at you."

He pushed himself to his feet and looked down at me. I smiled without humour. I was suddenly certain that this ploy would not work. Whatever I did, or didn't do, to his hair, surely nobody would believe that Runolf was a monk, a man of God. The habit we had found him was owned by Brother Eoten, the tallest of the monks of Werceworthe, but still it hung about the Norseman's calves, and the sleeves barely reached halfway down his massive forearms.

His beard was raggedly cut, his tonsure rushed, and his face still bore the bruises from his ill treatment at the hands of the warriors on Lindisfarnae. I shook my head.

"Is he ready?" asked Uhtric. "There is no more time."

"As ready as he'll ever be," I said. "But I'm not sure this will work. Look at him."

Hereward added his own voice to my concerns.

"It is true, lord," he said. "He looks like a father dressed in his son's clothes. We should think of another way." He hesitated. "Perhaps I should go."

"There is no time now," snapped Uhtric. "Perhaps you should have offered your own head for shaving before the sun had set."

Hereward fell silent.

Runolf opened his hands palms upward. He gave me a lopsided smile. From the far side of the smithy, Framric screamed again. The infant wailed. Abbot Beonna offered him quiet placatory words of solace.

Without speaking, Leofstan stepped forward, pulling the wooden cross he wore over his head. He held out the pendant in two hands towards Runolf, stretching the leather thong wide. The Norseman stared for a long moment at the crucifix that dangled between Leofstan's outstretched hands. Frowning, Runolf at last dipped his head and allowed the monk to place the cross around his neck. The symbol of Christ was tiny against Runolf's broad chest.

"Give him the food," said Uhtric, snapping his fingers with impatience. One of his men scooped up the basket that the monks had brought down from the monastery. The smell of freshly-baked bread wafted from beneath the cloth that covered the contents. Inside there was also a hunk of ham and a triangle of goat's cheese cut from one of the round wheels that Gewis made.

Runolf rolled his head around, working out the kinks in his neck from inactivity. He stretched both arms high above his head and then took the proffered basket.

None of us spoke now, and we followed him in silence as he walked back around the buildings to where the people were gathered before Aethelwig and Wulfwaru's house. Abbot Beonna stood in the middle of the open ground. His shadow streamed out behind him, dark and solid on the packed earth. The individual threads of the wool of his cassock were picked out starkly by the last golden rays of the setting sun. The villagers hushed as they saw Runolf. Several of them crossed themselves and Uhtric hissed, "Do not give the riddle up. The thief must believe that this man is one of the brethren here. If he does not, all will be lost."

They quietened and Uhtric indicated to his men to hang back out of sight. Runolf did not hesitate, but strode forward, the basket held in his left hand as if it weighed nothing. The wicker basket, so small in his meaty hand, made his manner of dress even more comical and I was again sure that Framric would see through the disguise in an instant. But since then I have learnt much about men and the nature of lies and belief. Most men will believe exactly what they want to believe, rather than what is evidenced by their own eyes and knowledge. They do not need much encouragement to make the improbable seem plausible, the ridiculous, sensible.

I walked ahead in Runolf's shadow with Uhtric at my side. The lord of Bebbanburg seemed ready to draw his sword and rush into the open doorway in the shaded side of the hut. He twitched and looked this way and that, his hand clutching into a fist at one moment and then, a heartbeat later, resting on the pommel of his blade.

"Wish him luck," he said without warning.

"He offers you luck," I relayed to Runolf.

Runolf looked at Uhtric over his shoulder and his smile was cold now, unyielding.

"I am not the one who needs luck," he said, and without another word, he walked past Beonna towards the tanner's hut.

The abbot called out after him: "You see, Framric? I told you someone would bring you food. Here he comes now."

"Don't come any closer," shrieked the voice from inside the building.

Runolf walked on, either not understanding, or ignoring the man. He hefted the basket before him, lifting the cloth to show the food inside.

"No closer!" screamed Framric, but still Runolf approached. "I will kill the baby!"

At last, close to the entrance, shaded now from the setting sun, Runolf halted.

The baby howled and I could see in the gloom of the hut momentarily, the figure of a man holding an infant swaddled in a pale blanket. Runolf stood very still, holding out the basket.

"Food," he said, his tone soft and barely audible from where we watched. "I bring you food. Are not you hungry?" I winced as he stumbled over the Englisc words. We had practised what he would say. Now was the moment that Framric would see through the thin disguise.

I held my breath.

The infant squealed again.

"Food," Runolf repeated, raising the basket and taking a step forward. Then, with the terrible speed I had witnessed as he had battled three men on Lindisfarnae, he sprang forward and disappeared through the darkened doorway. All of the villagers gasped as one. I squinted into the darkness, taking an involuntary step forward. Uhtric half drew his sword, also moving towards the hut.

The baby's screams rose in pitch and then were cut off.

There was no sound and no movement in the settlement of Werceworthe then. It was as if even animals held their breath, waiting to see the outcome of events. The sparrows and finches that had been wittering in the alders were silent and the honey bees that constantly droned over the clovers and comfrey that grew in the hedgerow appeared to hush their buzzing.

My mouth was dry and my right hand stung where I had dug my nails into my bandaged palm.

Then, with a sudden explosion of movement, a figure flew out of the hut. It was a skinny, dirt-smeared man, not much more than a boy. His cheeks were as sharp as knives and his eyes were sunken and dark-rimmed with exhaustion and deprivation. He stared about him, seemingly unsure of where he was. Then I noticed the crimson bloom on his grubby kirtle. The stain spread quickly and the wound where the blood came from must have been terrible indeed, for within moments, his chest was dark and slick with his lifeblood. He fell to his knees and, already dead, he collapsed face-first into the hard earth.

Still nobody spoke. The shadowed entrance to the hut yawned dark and unnervingly silent. Was it possible that Runolf had somehow slain the ceorl, only to be killed himself? I could feel my mind spiralling into bleak fears. Mayhap the babe had been killed in the struggle and Runolf was slumped inside the building, cradling the tiny corpse in his huge hands. Or maybe...

Beside me, Uhtric seemed to awaken as if from a dream. He rushed forward.

"By God," he shouted, "that Norseman must have run for it through the back of the hut."

I sensed Uhtric's warriors surging forward behind me.

Could it be true? Had Runolf broken through the wattle and daub wall of the tanner's house and fled?

But even as the thought formed, so Runolf's massive form stepped from the hut. The sky above him was blood red and his face was dark and shaded. A thin mewling cry filled the late afternoon air and as Runolf walked into the light, everybody could see that he was carrying a small bundle in one hand.

Uhtric pulled up short, allowing his sword to slide back into its scabbard. At the sight of her child, Wulfwaru let out a sobbing cry and sped towards Runolf. Tenderly, he handed Aethelwulf to her, gently prising his callused finger from the infant's hungry mouth.

Grinning through his raggedly cut beard and rubbing his hand over his poorly shaved scalp, Runolf walked over to where I waited. I drew in a breath, suddenly aware I had not breathed for a long time.

Uhtric joined us and to my amazement, he slapped the Norseman on the back.

"See," said Runolf, smiling broadly, "I told you I did not need luck."

Fourteen

That evening, the minster refectory reverberated with sound. Gone was the usual hush.

The brethren often housed travellers on their journeys, and pilgrims would sometimes come to see the finger of Saint Edwin in its ivory cask in the church, and to petition the once powerful king of Northumbria to heal their illnesses. But it was certainly not common for so many grizzled warriors to be entertained by the monks. The monastery was usually a quiet place of reflection where speech was frowned upon, but Uhtric's men, and even the monks who had witnessed Runolf's rescue of the child, were abuzz with what they had seen.

When we had first sat to eat, the refectory had been hushed and subdued. Beonna prayed for those of our brethren who had fallen at Lindisfarnae and gave thanks for delivering Aethelwig and Wulfwaru's son alive from his ordeal.

"The child's redemption has been as a moment of light in the darkest of days," he said. He chose not to mention Runolf, perhaps unsure how to speak of a heathen who had brought both life and death to Werceworthe. But he did go on to speak of Leofstan and me. "We must also offer up our sincerest thanks to the Almighty, His Holy Mother and the saints for the safe return of brothers Leofstan and Hunlaf." I looked up at the mention of my name and found more than one of the monks staring at me. I wondered what they thought. Did they see something had changed within me? Did they think I believed myself somehow better than them? Did I? Perhaps so. How many of them knew I had killed a man? Did they pity me, thinking me lost and damned?

"And before we nourish our bodies with this fine food and drink," the abbot went on, "let us not forget to commend the soul of Framric to the Lord. He was a sinner, as are we all. But his death came too soon for him to repent. Let us pray for his unshriven soul."

It had taken some time for the mood in the hall to lift. The monks were naturally restrained, and the tidings from Lindisfarnae and the slaying of Framric had shocked them and left them reeling. But they were still but men, and soon, as they drank more ale than was habitually allowed, their voices too were raised to be heard over the hubbub. Now the room was awash with the raucous sound of voices retelling the story of Framric's death and from time to time warriors would stand and make their way to where Runolf sat. They slapped him on the back and he grinned, looking strange and unnerving with his tonsured head and shaggy beard. His cup was kept filled and the huge man seemed to have no limit to how much ale he could consume.

I noticed that Uhtric had not ordered Runolf's wrists to be bound again. Instead he had promoted the prisoner to the position of guest, allowing the Norseman to sit at the board alongside him and the abbot. Beonna picked at his food. He appeared distracted and annoyed by the noise and the presence of so many men of violence.

Hereward had glowered at Runolf for a time, clearly envious and angry at his elevation to sit beside his lord. But as the ale flowed, Hereward relaxed. Now, with an acclamation, he stood, swaying for balance atop the bench, and began to tell riddles of the most bawdy nature.

"I am a joy to women all!" he shouted. "I stand up high and steep over the bed; underneath I'm shaggy."

"Your shrivelled cock!" one of the men shouted. Everyone knew the correct answer was 'onion', but they all cheered and jeered, guffawing with laughter as Hereward clutched his groin and thrust it towards his fellows before continuing.

"Sometimes a young and pretty wench, a maiden proud, lays a hold on me," he said, leering and lascivious. "She seizes me, red, plunders my head, fixes on me fast, feels straightway what meeting me means. That eye is wet indeed."

The men roared with laughter at his performance. At last he shouted out, "It is an onion, you filthy pigs! An onion." More laughter.

I scanned the faces of the monks. Most were sombre and unsmiling. Old Hildulfr crossed himself and shook his head. Only Leofstan, it seemed, was comfortable with these rough men.

Hereward was telling another riddle now, and I could barely hear him over the noise of his audience.

"It is stiff and hard," he said to more jeers. "When the young man lifts his tunic over his knee, he wishes to visit the familiar hole he has often filled with its equal length."

"It is a key," said Leofstan.

The men turned at the sound of the monk's voice, silenced for an instant in shock, but then howling with renewed hilarity, rocking back and wiping their eyes.

"A key it is," shouted Hereward.

I was not sure how much Runolf could understand of what was being said, but he was laughing as loudly as the rest. As his laughter receded, he took a great gulp of ale. Beside him Uhtric seemed oblivious to the unseemly noise his men were making. He leaned in close to Beonna, who listened absently. But the abbot did not turn his full attention to him. Instead he was staring directly at me, a disconcerted frown on his face.

Unable to hold his gaze, I looked down at the food before me and ate in silence. The abbot had only spoken to Leofstan and I briefly in the village, but it was clear that events of the afternoon had shocked him to the core. When he asked us who the man who had killed Framric and rescued Aethelwulf was, we told him of what had occurred at Lindisfarnae. He had made the sign of the cross and paled. I had feared that he would swoon, but he had gathered strength from deep within himself, or perhaps from God, and had led us to the refectory where he had welcomed us all, dispensing with Vespers, given the special circumstances.

I took a mouthful of the thin vegetable pottage. It was simple fare, but there was plenty of bread and the food was welcome after the long day. I noted that none of the men complained at the lack of meat. The brethren brewed exceptional ale and that seemed to make up for any shortcomings of the provender in the eyes of the warriors. I chewed on a hunk of bread I had moistened in the thin stew and looked up again.

Beonna still stared at me, as though he were gazing into my very thoughts. Earlier, in the glow of the setting sun, I had spoken little. I did not wish to draw attention to myself or my involvement in the fighting on the holy island. But of course, the bruises on my face told some of the story for me and Beonna enquired after my health and asked how I had come to be so beaten. Under his scrutiny, I was suddenly embarrassed by what I had done, of the idea that I might become something other than a monk who had a steady writing hand and a keen mind. I mumbled something about being knocked senseless by one of the Norsemen in the raid. I was surprised, and dismayed, when Leofstan began to describe how I had taken up a weapon and defended some helpless children. I knew immediately that Beonna would judge my actions to be at best folly and at worst sin, probably both. He would most likely think me touched by the Devil.

His eyes had widened at the telling of how I had fought, but he had not chastised me. He had shaken his head, scratching a hand against his shaved pate. It had been hard to read his expression. With each new revelation he had seemed to shrink into himself, becoming smaller, paler and somehow weaker. He said nothing more as we trudged towards the minster buildings, but I could feel the weight of his sadness and disapproval radiating from him like the last red light from the dying sun.

I mopped up the last of my stew, looking into my bowl. But I could feel Beonna's reproachful gaze upon me. All about me was the riotous sound of conversations, laughter, riddles and the clatter of knives and platters on the boards, and I thought how strange it was that with our arrival, the minster's refectory, normally so peaceful and tranquil, had become transformed into a mead hall full of debauchery.

The thought seemed to strike the abbot at the same moment, for he stood up and raised his hands in a gesture that all the brethren knew well. He was calling for silence, and obediently every monk in the refectory ceased speaking immediately. For a short time, Uhtric's men continued to laugh and talk loudly, but the sudden hush from all the monks made them soon falter. Faces turned towards Beonna and a few heartbeats later, everybody was silent.

"Friends and brothers," he said, his voice soft but carrying to everyone in the room. "It is fitting that we eat together and celebrate the rescue of the infant this afternoon. This is good and worthy of celebration. But we must not forget that a man was also killed today. A man driven mad by hunger and want. And many more have been horribly murdered just days ago by treacherous agents of Satan, heathens from the north who swept down upon the peaceful brethren on the holy island. So let us enjoy each other's company, think about those who have gone to sit by the right hand of God, but let us not forget that this is a sombre place. A place of worship and contemplation."

All around the room monks were nodding, faces grave and serious. Several of Uhtric's men cast their gaze downward, chastened by the abbot's words. Runolf saw me glancing about the hall and raised his cup in my direction. He smiled broadly before draining the contents. Beonna noticed the movement out of the corner of his vision. Turning, he saw the giant finishing his ale and then slamming the empty cup onto the rough oak timber of the board. Beonna's face grew pale, with colour flushing high on his cheeks.

"This is not a place for buffoonery or japes," Beonna continued. "Not somewhere to tell riddles or to drink to excess. You are our guests," he nodded to Uhtric, "and you are, of course, welcome. But please remember that this is a place of God. I implore you all to remember that and to behave as though Christ Himself were beside you." He indicated to the seated monks. "We will leave you now to pray for the immortal souls of the departed. May you rest well."

He turned to lead the brethren from the refectory. The room was quiet save for the scrape of benches as they were pushed back and the shuffle of robed monks filing out after their abbot. I sat where I was and watched them.

"Not coming?" hissed Leofstan, who stood by my side. I looked up, cheeks flushed with embarrassment. I could see in his expression that he knew exactly what had occurred. For the briefest of times I had not seen myself as one of the monks of Werceworthe. I stood quickly, knocking over my half-filled cup in my haste. I cast a quick glance about the room and my eyes met Runolf's. He was smiling at me. I did not acknowledge him or make a sound as I followed the rest of the monks from the hall.

While I walked out, there was but one thought playing in my mind. If I did not consider myself to be a monk, who did I think I was?

Fifteen

The prayers droned on and on. My mind wandered.

It was late and the chapel was dark, lit only by the thin flames from a smattering of candles. The singed-meat smell of the tallow was masked somewhat by the heady aroma of the incense that Beonna had ordered to be burnt in the large bronze censer that hung from the ceiling of the building from a lengthy iron chain. Clouds of rich, sweet-smelling smoke wafted over us as we intoned prayers and sang the psalms.

It had been a long and eventful day and my body yearned for sleep. I had only consumed a couple of cups of ale, but more than once I found myself swaying on the spot, unable to keep my balance. Glancing about the shadowed figures in the church I noticed a few others who looked as though they wished they had not imbibed so much of the strong drink.

When we paused between prayers, muffled sounds of raucous laughter and conversation drifted through the uncovered windows. It sounded to me as though Uhtric's men were trying to be quiet, but too much drink had flowed for total silence. That would not come until the men were wrapped in their cloaks and snoring. Each time we heard the merrymaking, Beonna would tense almost imperceptibly and I wondered at how this day, with its shocks and revelations, must have affected him.

The prayers and homilies merged together into a purring constant noise, familiar and comforting. My exhaustion enveloped me like a cloud and I drifted into a state of almost-sleep; on my feet, but with my thoughts far away. Perhaps this was how God spoke to His own, I mused.

I saw again the horrors I had witnessed at Lindisfarnae, the splashes of blood and the pleading faces. I heard once more the screams of terror of the dying. And then I remembered what it was to allow my righteous rage to wash through me like a summer storm, shaking all in its path, destroying my fear and allowing me to fight back against our aggressors. I saw Runolf, his hair aglow in the early morning light, towering over the other Norsemen like an avenging angel, smiting them with the huge axe he wielded. The final vision that came to me in my weariness was that of Runolf stepping from the tanner's house, the swaddled infant lying peacefully in the crook of his arm. Runolf walked out of the shadows and into the light of the setting sun, where the last rays shone on his tonsured scalp. My mind's eye focused on his stubbled head and then I found my attention drawn down towards the child. On Runolf's chest, dangling from its leather thong, was the simple wooden crucifix Leofstan had given him to complete his disguise as a monk.

"Brother Hunlaf," someone said, penetrating my fogged senses. I recognised the speaker's voice, but for a time I knew not where I was. I opened my eyes, blinking at the piercing glimmer of the candle flames in the gloom. Had I been sleeping on my feet? I shook my head and took in the faces of the men before me. Leofstan placed a hand upon my shoulder and peered at me, clearly concerned for my wellbeing.

"Brother Hunlaf," came the voice again, and I saw it belonged to Beonna. With a start I realised that all of the other monks had left the chapel and only the three of us remained. "Are you quite well?"

"Sorry," I stammered. "I was praying, but then..." I shook my head to clear it. "It was as if I slept... I am tired. Sorry."

Beonna stared at me for what seemed a long while before eventually nodding.

"There is no need to apologise, young man," he said. "It has been a trying few days for you. Did you see anything as you slept now?"

I felt foolish. Sure that he would not believe me, or that he would merely dismiss my visions as youthful imaginings. Sensing my reticence to speak, he said, "Do not fear. Perhaps we should retire to my chamber where the three of us can talk. Maybe you will tell us what you saw then."

All I wanted was to sleep, but I obediently followed the two older men out into the night. We walked through the darkness and I noted that the sounds from the refectory had quietened now. The night felt still and strangely safe. As if the cloak of night could protect us from the vicious men I knew to exist. Leofstan had lifted one of the candles and placed it within a lantern made of thin horn. The dim glow of the flame through the horn walls of the lantern did little to light our path. But we knew the way well enough and soon we were in the room where Beonna slept and conducted the monastery's business. It was a sparsely furnished room, with a simple writing desk beneath the window, a narrow sleeping pallet, a chair and a few stools. On one wall hung a depiction of Christ on the cross. I gazed up at it, taking in the carving of the crown of thorns that had been cruelly pushed onto his head before he had been lifted onto the tree that would see him die. It was carved from a single piece of dark wood and the workmanship was astounding. Every detail was cunningly scratched into the wood and the sculptor had managed to capture a deep sadness in Jesu's eyes.

"Sit," said Beonna, waving a hand at the stools by the desk.

Leofstan pushed one towards me and seated himself on another. I sat, facing the abbot's chair. The cross was behind me and I could imagine Christ looking down with those sorrowful eyes, judging me, weighing up my resolve and my faith. Would he find me wanting?

Beonna bustled over to a small chest. Opening it, he produced a flask and three small wooden cups. Returning to his chair, he unstoppered the flask and filled the cups, handing one each to Leofstan and me. He finally filled his own, rammed the stopper back into the neck of the vessel and placed the flask by his feet. He raised his cup to his face, closed his eyes and sniffed slowly.

With a sigh, he took a sip and leaned back in his chair. Opening his eyes, he indicated for us to drink. I let some of the liquid trickle into my mouth and was surprised to find it was mead. Strong, sweet mead. I could feel its warmth wash down inside me.

"It has been a very difficult day," said Beonna, "and I feel the Lord would forgive us this small indulgence." Neither Leofstan nor I replied. We drank in silence for a while before Beonna continued. "So, why is it that the two of you are going to Eoforwic with Lord Uhtric?" he asked.

I did not know what to say, so was pleased when Leofstan answered.

"Uhtric is taking the Norseman to the king. Hunlaf can converse with Runolf and so he offered his services to both Uhtric and King Æthelred."

"Do you truly believe that nobody in the great city of Eoforwic can act as interpreter for the heathen's words? His language is not so different from our own in any case." Beonna reached for the flask again and refilled his cup. He did not offer more to us.

"We cannot be certain," said Leofstan, "and so we thought it best to accompany Lord Uhtric. It does us good to keep the lord of Bebbanburg content and in good standing with the king."

Beonna fixed Leofstan with an unblinking gaze.

"There is nothing else?" he asked at last.

Leofstan hesitated.

"Well?" pressed Beonna.

"Hunlaf believes that Runolf has been sent to us."

"Does he indeed? Sent by whom and to do what? Slaughter us? As his people did to those poor souls at Lindisfarnae?"

"No, father," I said, finding my voice in a sudden rush of words. "You saw how he saved Aethelwulf today. And you heard how he saved two other children at Lindisfarnae. Runolf is a good man."

"A good man?" Beonna frowned. "I saw him slay a defenceless wretch today!"

I felt my anger swelling within me.

"A wretch who was using an innocent babe to protect himself from punishment for his crimes," I said, forcing myself to keep my tone even.

"To kill is wrong." Beonna's words were final, brooking no challenge.

"Can there never be a time when it is right to fight? Would you rather Runolf had done nothing today and allowed that child to die?"

"I would prefer for nobody to have died," snapped the abbot. "We cannot know what might have happened if that pagan had not killed Framric."

I let out a long breath, willing myself to calm, but I could feel my anger simmering within me.

"No," I said, my words clipped and precise, "nobody but God can ever know what might have happened if we trod a path unseen. But I cannot believe that the Almighty has sent this man to us for no reason. I trust in God's infinite wisdom."

Beonna drank more mead and pondered my words.

"What has the foreigner told you?" he asked.

"The Norsemen will come again." I took a sip of the mead to calm my nerves. My hand shook. "They will come here."

The abbot frowned.

"He is sure of that? How?"

I recalled our long conversation beneath the stars in the prayer cell.

"Traders have told them of all the minsters along the coast. They plan to move southward, pillaging each one as they come. Runolf did not know the names of all of the places, but he spoke to me of the minster surrounded by the river's bend, inland from the island we call Cocwaedesae."

Beonna's face was pale in the flickering glow of the single candle.

"But why?" he whispered. "Why profane these holy places? We are men of peace and prayer."

"That is why they come," I said, my voice harsh as a slap in the quiet room. "We are not warriors. We are weak. And yet we have riches here. The bones of saints in fine boxes. Think of the golden cross in the chapel. The jewels on the books." I remembered the awe I had felt at seeing the dazzling bindings of *The Treasure of Life*. I glanced at Leofstan and thought I noted the slightest shake of his head. I hesitated, but Leofstan sipped his mead and did not meet my gaze. Perhaps I had been mistaken and the movement I had seen had been a trick of the candlelight. I turned back to the abbot.

"These things can be sold for silver. And more than that," I said, the anger at what I had witnessed on Lindisfarnae colouring my voice, "there are many young men and women who would fetch a good price in the slave markets of far-off Roma or Byzantion."

Beonna took a long draught of his mead and then made the sign of the cross.

"And what is it that you think God has called you to do, young Hunlaf?"

"I believe we can stop them."

"Who? You and this Runolf? You are but two. The foreigner is a killer, for sure, but even though you seem to have found an unholy love of killing, you are no fighter."

I bit back the angry words that threatened to tumble from my lips.

"I do not love killing," I said. My voice hitched as I thought of the corpses at Lindisfarnae. "But I would rather my enemies were dead than my friends; my family."

"Your enemies?" Beonna asked, raising an eyebrow.

"Very well," I spat. "Enemies of us all. Enemies of God." Trembling with emotion, I drank the last of my mead. "You were not there," I said at last, my voice hushed as if I was scared to hear my own words. "You did not see what they did to the brethren there."

"If these raiders do come, Hunlaf," Beonna said softly, "you cannot protect us. God will protect his own. He is good and mighty."

My ire flashed into burning life.

"Well, He did not protect His faithful at Lindisfarnae!" I shouted. With a great effort I swallowed back my rage. "Forgive me. I am sure that God has provided us with the means to protect ourselves."

For a time, Beonna was silent. I looked at Leofstan, but I could not discern from his expression what he thought of my outburst. I expected the abbot to send me away with a punishment for speaking to him in such a way and I sat in sullen silence awaiting his judgement.

"What did you see?" Beonna asked after a pause.

"When?"

"While we prayed in the chapel. You had a vision, didn't you?"

"I do not know if it was a vision from God," I said, uncertain and scared of being ridiculed.

"You are a follower of Christ," Beonna said, not unkindly. "Who else would send a vision to you?"

I took a long calming breath.

"I saw the dead on the holy isle," I said, shuddering at the vividness of the memory. "And I saw Runolf saving them. And then I saw him, tonsured and wearing the robes and crucifix, with the rescued infant in his arms." I chose not to mention the sensation of my own surging wrath and the feeling of power that had filled me. "A white dove landed on his head," I added, though I had seen no such vision. I could feel the graven eyes of the Christ on his cross behind me boring into my back.

Why I lied, I will never know. I felt a sliver of excitement down my spine as I spoke the words and my face flushed. Beonna stared at me and I was certain that he was going to call me out on my untruth.

"You saw a white dove in your vision?" he asked. His eyes were wide. They glimmered in the candlelight.

"I did," I replied, keeping my voice steady. "Its feathers were pure as snow," I elaborated.

"Perhaps you are right," he said, rubbing his hand against the greying stubble on his cheeks. "Mayhap God has sent you a sign. It is not for us to question His ways. I will pray on this for guidance. But you have already given your word that you will travel to the king and this was agreed with his Excellency, Bishop Hygebald, was it not?"

"Yes, father," interjected Leofstan. "His Excellency said I should accompany the lad too."

"Indeed. Yes." Beonna seemed resigned to his decision now. "Then it must be so. Now, you must get some rest before leaving tomorrow. I give you dispensation to miss Compline."

"Thank you, father," Leofstan mumbled.

A sudden thought gripped me as we rose to leave.

"I will ask the king for men to come and guard us from the raiders."

Beonna looked up from where he sat with tired, red-rimmed eyes. He held my gaze and I worried I had overstepped, that he would forbid me from petitioning the king. My father had always said to me, "it is better to beg for forgiveness than to ask for permission". By mentioning my intentions, I had unwittingly asked the abbot for his approval.

I needn't have worried, for after a moment, he merely nodded.

"I am sure you will, Hunlaf," he said, his tone flat. "If the good king sees fit to fulfil your request of him, so be it. I will not turn away good Christian warriors. We are nestled within his dominion, after all. The lands of Werceworthe belong to the Church, gifted to us by King Ceolwulf nearly a century ago, but we are an island in a sea of Northumbria and it is right for the king to offer us protection from threats, as we pray to protect his soul and those of his people from spiritual attacks."

I did not wait for him to say more and followed Leofstan out into the dark. We had left the single candle burning in the abbot's room and the night engulfed us as the door scraped closed behind us.

"A snow-white dove?" said Leofstan in a quiet voice. "Really?"

I did not reply, but my cheeks were hot in the gloom. We walked without speaking towards the cells where we monks slept. The night was cool and I shivered. But I knew it was not from the cold that I trembled, but from excitement. In the morning we would set out for Eoforwic and I would see the king.

Sixteen

We travelled south, riding faster and for longer than I had ever endured before. My thighs were agony and whenever we dismounted, I hobbled about like a cripple. The warriors laughed at my discomfort. At the end of the first day, when we stopped at the hall of one Gleadwine at a place called Corebricg, I practically crawled out of the stables. I moaned with each step, legs wide apart to avoid them chafing together.

"You look like you have been fucked by the Norseman," Hereward called out. He was rewarded by guffaws from his companions. I was too tired and sore to think of a clever retort, though several came to me later that night and I berated myself for not being more quick-witted.

Runolf was riding unbound now. He dismounted, seemingly as agile and full of energy as when he had departed from Werceworthe shortly after dawn. He asked me what Hereward had said. I interpreted and had dark hopes of the Norseman taking umbrage at the slur on his manliness and beating Hereward with his massive fists. Instead, Runolf put his hands on his hips, threw his head back and roared with laughter.

"Yes," he said, when he was finally able to breathe, "you do! Like you have been fucked right up the arse!"

I blushed and hurried into the hall as quickly as I could go on my aching limbs. The sounds of laughter followed me inside. I was grumpy and quiet that night and, not for the first time, I questioned my decision to offer to travel to Eoforwic.

But in the morning, the men seemed to take pity on me and one of them, a sallow-faced, thick-browed man named Grimcytel, gave me a small pot of rendered pig fat to rub into my inner thighs and buttocks. "It will make the riding easier," he said with a smile.

I worried that this was some kind of joke at my expense, that after I performed the embarrassing task of wiping the foul-smelling unguent on my bare legs and arse, all of the warriors would laugh at what a gullible fool I was. Despite this fear, I was desperate for relief and so I followed his advice and smeared the fat liberally over the area that came into contact with the saddle. To my surprise, not only did none of the men make fun of me, but the treatment seemed to work. Perhaps coupled with growing more accustomed to the riding, but that night, after crossing the Tine and riding through the hot, cloudless day between fields of swaying green barley and scrubby patches of vetch, my body hurt much less than before and I was able to dismount and walk into the hall that we stopped at without too much groaning.

The world seemed new and different to me as we rode. On the first couple of days I could focus on nothing but my pain, but as I became more used to riding, and thanks to the fat I had rubbed into my skin, by the third and final day of the journey I was able to appreciate how strange everything felt. My horse was docile, following placidly the animal in front, so I held the reins loosely and looked about me, trying to understand what was causing this feeling. I probed my thoughts and memories of the violence at Lindisfarnae and my reaction to it, and whilst I could not deny that something had shifted fundamentally within me, this sensation I had was different.

We splashed through a shallow ford, sending up great sprays of water that hung in the air in a coruscation of rainbow colours. The day was hot and the few droplets that reached my face were soothing after the heat and dust of travel. Beside the stream huddled some huts, their moss-draped roofs crooked and dipping, as if with the weight of the years of their existence. At the sound of our passing, figures emerged from the gloom within. Women, wiping their hands on their aprons, with skinny children standing beside them, upturned faces full of awe at the sight of so many armed horsemen.

In the fields, far off, I could make out men running towards the houses. But they were distant and would not reach their families before we had passed by.

The women did not speak. One of the children, a boy with a mop of dark hair and a mischievous smirk, made to run off after us, perhaps meaning to race us, or to ask us for food. His mother angrily pulled him back, placing a protective hand on his shoulder. The boy struggled, but the woman said something that I could not hear and shook him. He pouted, but the mother held him firmly and watched us pass. I turned back in my saddle and her gaze met mine.

It was then that I understood what was different. It was there in the woman's face. I was used to entering a settlement on foot, with a few of my brethren. At such times we were met with friendly acceptance, for the people knew we would work and we would help them to cure their ills, as well as administering to their souls. But what I saw now, as I rode surrounded by grim-faced warriors, byrnies, helms and spear-tips gleaming, was a different expression. There was no welcome for us. As we rode past without halting, the woman's features shifted from one of awed fear to one of relief. Horsemen bearing weapons and armour were never harbingers of glad tidings. Such men only brought sorrow and bloodshed. Life was hard enough for these people. That year's storms had wreaked their havoc and the harvest would be poor again. Hunger was etched into every line of their weather-beaten faces. But that hardship was one they knew how to deal with. They would toil throughout the long days and, with luck and God's grace, they would survive.

The last thing they wanted was to have to contend with entitled noblemen and their rowdy hearth-warriors.

We rode away, the bouncing gait of the horse's movement now strangely familiar and comforting to me. I stared back at the cluster of houses until we had ridden out of sight over the next rise. I watched as the men arrived from the village and had hurried conversations with their wives.

I could imagine their conversations.

"Are you well? Did the warriors halt here? Are you hurt?"

And then I understood what had been eluding me. The difference I felt came from the riding, but was not the soreness of my body, it stemmed from the change in my perspective. Where I normally looked people in the eye as I walked amongst them, now I looked down on everyone who crossed my path. And it was not merely my perspective that had altered, of course. People we passed no longer looked at me with warmth in their eyes, now they gazed up at me with a mixture of jealous longing and fear.

I pondered this as we rode towards Eoforwic. Uhtric and the warriors would be oblivious of the effect they had on the ceorls we passed.

I rode close to Leofstan and told him of my observation. Though I had never seen him ride before this journey, he sat astride his mount naturally and did not complain. I wondered then at his past. I knew nothing of where he came from or his family. Now, he nudged his horse nearer with effortless skill.

He nodded and said, "Even if they were aware of how others looked upon them, do you think they would care?"

I looked at the stern faces of the warriors and Uhtric's straight back and haughty air from where he rode at the head of the column. There was a man utterly assured of his position.

"No," I said. "I think they would consider it their right."

For a time, Leofstan said nothing. The thrum of the hooves and the jangle of the horses' harness were the only sounds.

At last, he turned in his saddle. I could not read his expression.

"I think you have the right of it," he said. "They look down on everyone else because they always have and they have always ridden." He gave me a sidelong look and raised an eyebrow. "And for how long do you think you would need to ride before you too began to consider yourself more than those who walked and worked in the dust beneath you?"

His words surprised me, and I wanted to blurt out that I would never think of myself as more important than others merely because I had a horse. But Leofstan, with a skill I could only dream of, spurred his horse forward into a gallop and headed along the line to where Uhtric rode. Dust clouded the air behind him, mingling with that of the other horses.

Was his implication right? Would I, or anyone, feel superior in time, due to a perception of their standing in the world, their wealth and their power? But what power did I possess? I looked down at my bandaged hand. It hurt much less now and was healing well. But it was a vivid reminder of how I had taken a man's life. I had plunged the seax into the Norseman and I had felt him die beneath me.

I rode on in silence, jostling atop my horse, lost in my thoughts.

The people did not fear these men because they were rich and rode horses. Their very real fear was that the warriors would harm them in some way. These men, the hearth-warriors of a lord, had the strength and weapons to kill. And they had the righteous belief in their own ability and worth.

As we rode, I remembered the rushing feeling of ecstatic joy as the Norseman's hot blood had coated my hand and I wondered about Leofstan's question. How long would I need to ride with these men to fully shed the habit of my old life and to become something new? Holy men were respected too, and I had never thought anything of it before. But now I wondered whether I wanted more than mere respect.

Perhaps, I thought, as my horse carried me ever closer to the great city of Eoforwic, I also wanted to be feared.

Seventeen

The sun was low in the sky when we finally saw Eoforwic in the distance. The land about was green, and lush; well-watered by the seasonal flooding of the rivers Usa and Fossa. The city itself appeared more vibrant and alive than the land we had ridden through. Colourful flags and pennants fluttered above the old Roman walls, and the gate we rode up to was thronged with a multitude of people and beasts. Ox-drawn carts and waggons harnessed to donkeys blocked the road, while drovers shouted at their lowing cattle that had spilled from the path. An old woman, presumably the owner of the small plot of land now being trampled by the errant cows was screaming and slapping at the animals with a hazel switch.

Half a dozen door wardens were trying their best to control the situation, but without much success it seemed to me.

We arrived at the rear of the press before the gates in a clatter of hooves and shouts from Uhtric and his warriors. Leofstan caught my eye as Uhtric barged his horse through the people, causing shouts and curses of protest. Men and women were shouldered away by the lord of Bebbanburg's steed and more than one tumbled over and was in danger of being crushed by the horsemen or the gathered folk and animals.

Uhtric seemed oblivious to the distress he left in his wake and I could hear him shouting over the cries of anger caused by his passing.

"You, man," he snapped. "I am Uhtric, lord of Bebbanburg, and I bring important tidings and a prisoner to our lord king, Æthelred."

The guard at the gate looked confused and uncertain.

"Wait your own turn," shouted someone from the crowd.

Uhtric ignored the yelling.

"Have your men order the crowd to move aside and allow us passage," he said in a tone that demanded instant compliance.

The warden said something. I could not hear the words, but I could see from his posture that he was still unsure what he should do.

Uhtric leaned down from his saddle and hissed something only the man could hear. The guard paled, but shook his head, raising his hands as if to say there was nothing he could do. The colour rose in Uhtric's cheeks and I thought he was about to strike the man. My horse shied as someone in the crowd roared and threw something. I listed in the saddle precariously and almost lost my seat. A dark shape flashed through the sunlight and smacked into Uhtric's uncovered head. The object splattered wetly, leaving a damp stain on his hair and his tunic, where it slid away to be lost in the rabble pressing about his horse. It was a lump of manure. Uhtric, face suddenly grim with rage, surveyed the crowd, but he could not see who had thrown the turd.

"Men," he bellowed. "Disperse this crowd." He cast his gaze about the traders, farmers and ceorls, as if he expected the one who had assaulted him to step forward. "Now!"

My horse sidestepped again and I clung to the reins. All of Uhtric's warriors slid from their saddles and with practised speed hefted shields that had been slung on their backs. Where the day had been hot and dusty, there was a sudden chill of death in the air. Hereward drew his sword and cracked it against the rim of his shield. The rest of the men did likewise and in moments, the dozen warriors, shields overlapping and rhythmically beating their blades against the linden boards, had formed a shieldwall and were stepping menacingly towards the crowd. I was shocked at how quickly the threat of violence had come to this place and again I understood why the ceorls were scared of lords and their warbands.

I saw defiance in the eyes of some of the local men, but then Hereward and the others crashed their blades against their shields again and took a deliberate step forward. With the approach of the warriors, naked steel glimmering in the late afternoon sun, the rabble seemed to deflate. First one, and then another retreated to make way for Uhtric and his retinue. In a few heartbeats, they had moved back sufficiently to grant us passage. Anger rolled off them like the stink from the manure underfoot, but they did not move as Hereward and the others, seemingly confident that the men and women of Eoforwic had been cowed, climbed back onto their mounts and rode slowly after their hlaford.

Suddenly fearful that I would be left behind, I heeled my horse and followed the others. Runolf nudged his own mount forward and slipped into step beside me. He seemed unperturbed by the crowd, but I detected a lopsided smile on his face as if he had enjoyed the crackling tension in the air. He saw me watching him and his smile broadened. The flash of his teeth was feral and his eyes seemed to glow in the golden afternoon sunlight.

I shivered, despite the warmth, and quickly rode past him. I could hear him chuckling as I passed.

We clattered through the gates and into Eoforwic. I had heard many tales of the city, of course, but I had never before visited the largest settlement in the north of Britain. The sounds and smells of so many people instantly assailed my senses and left me reeling. I knew not where to look and I soon felt giddy with trying to take in so many things at once.

There were traders with open-fronted shops displaying all manner of wares from plain earthenware pots to cunningly crafted colourful glass beads. There were butchers and fishmongers, leather workers and wood turners. All shouted for our attention and the sound was an assault on our senses after riding through the calm of the countryside. We rode now along streets thick with mud and refuse. The stench was terrible and I wondered how so many people could survive in such close proximity. Surely the stink would bring the pestilence. I made the sign of the cross and offered a silent prayer to protect us from the miasmas of the city.

The clanging of a smith at work made me twist in my saddle in time to see the soot-smeared man in his leather apron plunging something into a barrel of water with a hiss of steam. My horse snorted but plodded on, following the others.

Two men stumbled out of a darkened doorway, cursing and shouting something about cheating at dice. The first man staggered backwards, into Hereward's horse. Hereward kicked him and the man swung around, raising his fists aggressively. Hereward placed his hand on his sword hilt and half drew the weapon from its scabbard. The man was not drunk enough to fight an armed warrior and so, shaking his head he turned away, only to receive a solid punch in the face from his original opponent. He fell to the quagmire of the street and soon the two men were gouging and punching, snarling like animals as they rolled in the muck.

We rode on.

Turning a corner past a dilapidated shed with mildewed walls and a great rent in its mouldering thatch, the smell of fish struck me. Grey and red guts slimed the ground, but all of the day's catch must have already been sold for I could see no fresh fish. A great rack of hanging smoked mackerel stood before one of the houses. The sight of it made me think of Aelfwyn and, unbidden, tears pricked my eyes. I cuffed them away, hoping that nobody had witnessed my weakness.

"It is quite something, is it not?" said Leofstan. "I am always surprised at the number of people who live here."

Even Runolf, usually so calm and undaunted by anything, looked about him with a sense of wonder. There could be no doubt from his face that, like me, he had never seen the like of Eoforwic before.

Hereward had dropped back to ride near us and now he laughed at our expressions.

"Impressive, isn't it?" We were passing a sizeable stone church which I assumed was the building originally erected by Bishop Paulinus centuries before. "But don't let the church fool you," Hereward went on. "You will never find a more wretched hive of scum and villainy."

"Is it always like this?" I asked.

"Always busy, but this is the week leading up to Saint Peter's day. People have journeyed from far and wide to take part in the feast day. It is a good time to come here. There are many entertainments to be enjoyed, if you understand my meaning." He laughed at his own comment. "But before we can partake of the pleasures offered to us within the walls of the city, we must first follow my lord to the king's hall. And then, perhaps we will be able to finish what we started back on the holy island." He indicated Runolf with a nod and mimicked placing a noose around his neck and tugging on an invisible rope. He made a squawking sound and stuck his tongue out. Laughing, he kicked his mount forward, joining Uhtric once again at the head of the column.

No interpretation was needed from me for Runolf to understand Hereward's meaning.

"You think they plan to hang me?" he asked, his tone seemingly unconcerned.

"I will not lie," I replied. "Your future is uncertain."

He nodded, but said nothing. Leofstan was also silent. I could feel the weight of both men's gaze on me; their expectation like a great stone upon my shoulders.

"But I truly believe that the good Lord brought you here for a reason."

"I know nothing of your god," Runolf said. "Just that his worshippers trust him perhaps too much." He hawked and spat a gobbet of phlegm into the mire of the street.

I could think of nothing to say to that. Runolf had come to Lindisfarnae and found riches and treasure unguarded, supposedly safe because men feared God's damnation. Without that fear, what power did God truly have?

I shuddered at the direction my thoughts were taking me. Christ was loving and forgiving. Did that make him weak? In the face of heathen ferocity love would do nothing to protect the faithful. Surely even a shepherd had a dog to protect his flock from wolves.

We rode on in silence, my disquiet building as we finally approached our destination.

The open ground before the church was a jumble of tents and awnings. The sound of pipes and a lyre danced briefly over the noises of laughter and shouts from where two men were battling each other, surrounded by a dense mass of people. From my vantage point atop my horse, I could see over the heads of the baying spectators watching the men who were stripped to the waist. As I looked, the taller of the two, a brute of a man with fists like hams, grabbed his opponent behind the neck with his left hand and proceeded to pummel his right fist repeatedly into the man's face. Blood splattered. The onlookers cheered. The smaller man went limp and slumped to the churned earth. A great roar went up from the crowd. I turned away, wondering what kind of man would stand and fight like that, toe to toe, blow for blow, blood-spattered and yet still grinning. And then I glanced at Runolf, taking in his massive shoulders and shovel-like hands and I knew the answer. His eyes glimmered with excitement at what he had witnessed and he craned his neck to see more as we left the expanse of ground with its chaos of festivities behind us.

Eighteen

"You have brought these tidings from your fortress in the north very slowly it seems to me, Uhtric." Æthelred glowered at the lord of Bebbanburg. The king was not an old man, but grey frosted his hair and moustache and his eyes were pinched and shadowed. I had never seen him before, but I knew of the intrigues, plots and rumours that surrounded him. Watching Æthelred now, I could sense the suspicion in him. Here was a man who trusted nobody. Such a life, constantly in fear of an assassin's blade or poison in your food, must be a poor one indeed, no matter how filled with power and riches it might be.

Uhtric shifted uncomfortably under the king's stern gaze.

"I apologise, my lord king," he said, and I could hear how much he hated the taste of the words in his mouth. But the king's suspicion often led to violence and many of his closest retinue had been slain over the last few years since his return from exile. I did not blame Uhtric for treading with care. "The tides kept us from reaching the island for a day, but we have ridden with all haste."

"Indeed? Your messenger said you had halted at Werceworthe. Why waste time there?" The king's eyes narrowed and he sniffed, as if he could detect a lie.

"We only stayed for the night. I thought to inform the abbot there of what had occurred to his brethren."

"And he sent these two with you?" Æthelred indicated Leofstan and me. We stood a few paces behind Uhtric and I squirmed to feel the eyes of the king and his nobles on me. The hall was grander even than the great hall of Bebbanburg, taller, longer and with more ornate carvings on the timber pillars. The walls were hung with tapestries which glistened with gold and silver threads. Ornaments and fine weapons were displayed from the beams, columns and every spare piece of wall. No space was wasted, instead each area was used to show the power of the owner of this hall. Æthelred, plagued by doubts and suspicions, was still one of the most powerful men on the island of Britain, second only perhaps to Offa of Mercia, and he did not want his guests forgetting it.

When we had reached the royal grounds, leaving the festival atmosphere of the city behind us, we had not been required to wait long for an audience with the king. Our horses had been led away by servants and, moments later, we were ushered into the hall. It was laid out for a feast, with benches and boards lining the length of the building, but only the king and his most trusted advisors were present at the high table. Uhtric had left his men outside guarding Runolf, but had told Leofstan and me to accompany him before the king. It was warm in the hall and sweat trickled down the back of my neck as all eyes turned to us. I had no right to be here. I was nobody. I wished then that I had stayed back at Werceworthe. The monks would be preparing for Vespers now. Why had I been so keen to come to Eoforwic?

"Not exactly, lord king," said Uhtric in reply to Æthelred's question. "These monks were present at Lindisfarnae when the attack took place."

This seemed to awaken the king's interest and he leaned forward, placing his hands on the board before him.

"Indeed? So perhaps they can tell me more than the vague tales I have heard."

The only instruction Uhtric had hissed at us on entering the king's presence was not to speak unless asked a direct question. And yet now, I found myself suddenly speaking, though I had not been addressed.

"We saw what happened on that fateful sixth day before the ides of June, my lord king," I said.

Uhtric gave me a hard stare, as if willing me to be silent. But if the king took issue with my lack of protocol, he did not let it show.

"And your name is?" he asked.

"Hunlaf, lord." I indicated Leofstan. "This is Brother Leofstan."

"So, Hunlaf of Lindisfarnae," said Æthelred, "what did you see on that terrible day?"

"Werceworthe, lord."

"What?" the king asked, confused.

"We do not dwell on the holy island. We were visiting from Werceworthe."

"Oh." The king frowned and I wished I had not corrected him on what was an unimportant distinction. "And what did you see, Hunlaf of *Werceworthe*?" He emphasised the last word, twisting it with sarcasm and I swallowed against the lump in my throat. My mouth was suddenly dry. I cursed inwardly my foolishness in pointing out the king's error.

"They came with the tide just after sunrise," I said. My voice came out as a croak and I coughed to clear my throat. "There were three of them."

"Only three?"

"Three huge longships, lord. With prows like serpents and great banks of oars like the wings of a giant bird. I do not know how many men there were, but they knew what they were about. They were well armed and came with a purpose."

"To destroy that most Christian of sites." His voice was reverent and he hesitated, as if lost in thought, before taking a sip from a silver cup.

I did not wish to contradict the king again, but I shook my head.

"No?" He raised his eyebrows and placed the cup back on the board before him. "Did the heathens not put the place to flame then? That is what I had heard."

"Yes, lord king," I said, lowering my gaze and wincing. If half of what I had heard about Æthelred were true, to appear in defiance of the king might be more dangerous than facing armed Norsemen. "They burnt several of the minster buildings and some of the settlement of the lay people too."

"But you think their goal was other than destruction? Do you not believe these pagans to be sent by God to punish us for our sins?"

I swallowed against the parched dryness of my throat. Æthelred stared at me and would not let me go from the grip of his glare. There were many in the land who believed the king's actions – the betrayals and murders of opponents and erstwhile friends alike – to have led to the portents that had been seen in the sky that year. People muttered that it was the king's sins that had seen God send the terrible storms to flatten the crops and usher in famine. The brutal attack from the sea could easily be seen as another of God's chastisements for the transgressions of the king and the people of Northumbria, just as Eadgar and Godwig had said.

"I cannot know the way of the Almighty," I said at last. "But the men who attacked Lindisfarnae caused untold devastation. They slew many, and razed the great scriptorium, where priceless works of learning were consumed by the flames and turned to ash. And yet, they were careful enough to take gold and silver from the church. And they carried away many thralls."

Æthelred stroked his moustache.

"So, more than a holy punishment, you think this was akin to a cattle raid."

I recalled the huge Norse leader ramming his knife blade into Tidraed's eye with as little remorse as a farmer slaughtering a lamb. With a shudder I remembered vividly the infant's wailing cries cut off as its head was smashed against a door post. My pulse quickened and my bandaged hand throbbed as I clenched it. Closing my eyes, I willed myself to breathe deeply, to calm my nerves, but more images flashed in the darkness of my mind's eye. Brothers in Christ, faces tear-streaked and pale, rounded up and led towards the waiting ships. Bearded Norsemen, arms filled with loot, silver coins spilling from a chest that proved too cumbersome to carry, shouting and jeering as another warrior pleasured himself with a helpless monk he had bent over a small hand cart. I opened my eyes to escape the nightmare scenes that somehow I had no recollection of until my memory conjured them up now like malevolent spirits.

I met Æthelred's brooding gaze. Had it been like a cattle raid for the Norsemen? Was that all the brethren had been to them? Nothing more than beasts, to be driven before them, exploited and sold?

"Well?" he asked, clearly impatient for my answer.

"The Norsemen came for plunder; for treasure and loot," I said. "They destroyed what they did not want or could not easily bear with them. Many of the holy men were slain." I swallowed down the bile that burnt the back of my throat as the horrific memories fought once again to resurface. "The raiders seemed to revel in the slaughter. But they came for the riches they knew the brethren possessed. It is no secret that the minster is unguarded."

As he'd heard of the devastation and the atrocities perpetrated on the brethren, the king's face had darkened.

"Which kingdom did they come from, these Norsemen?" he said, tugging at his moustache. "Were they sent by a rival king?"

"They came from a land of islands and mountains called Rygjafylki," I replied. "It is far across the North Sea."

Æthelred raised his eyebrows at this. He had been voicing the question for himself and had clearly not expected an answer.

"How can you know that for certain?" he asked.

I realised then that he had not been informed of Runolf's presence with us. As the huge Norseman was no longer bound, there was nothing to make him stand out from the other warriors in Uhtric's band, apart from his lack of weapons.

"One of them told me," I said. The king looked at me dubiously. "I questioned him," I added, by way of explanation.

"You spoke to one of these heathens?" Æthelred's incredulity was obvious.

"I did, lord." I hesitated, unsure how to proceed. "I have."

"Explain," he snapped. There was a sharp edge in his tone now.

I took a steadying breath, wishing I had never travelled to Eoforwic, never entered this hall.

"One of their number turned on the heathens and fought in defence of two children."

Æthelred's eyes widened in surprise.

"He fought against his own?"

"He did, lord," I replied. I chose to omit my own part in the fight. "He slew several of the Norsemen."

"Astonishing! And the children lived?"

"Yes. They are both hale."

Æthelred shook his head, obviously amazed at the tale he was hearing.

"Can this be true?" he said.

Before I could answer, Uhtric took a step forward and said, "It is all as Hunlaf says, lord king."

"And you say you spoke to this heathen?" Æthelred said, ignoring Uhtric.

"Yes, lord," I said. "After the Norsemen had sailed away."

"He was left behind when they sailed?" Æthelred asked.

"Yes, lord," I repeated.

"And you speak the Norse tongue?"

"A little. Enough to communicate."

The king nodded and pulled at his moustache.

"And where is this Norseman now?"

He turned to Uhtric, who twitched as the king fixed him with a questioning look.

"He is outside, lord king," Uhtric said. "With my men."

"He is here?" Æthelred said, clearly amazed at this news. "Bring him in. I would see him."

Uhtric hurried to the hall's doors to do as he was bidden. Æthelred turned back to me.

"You can interpret his words for me? And mine for him to understand?"

"I can, lord," I replied. "There will be no confusion."

"Good." His eyes flicked towards a movement behind me. I turned and watched as Uhtric, along with Hereward and two other warriors, led Runolf down the length of the hall.

The tall Norseman's gaze roved hungrily about the treasures on display. I suddenly wondered whether I had been wrong about this man all along. Was it possible to train a wolf to protect the shepherd's flock?

The men halted near me and Runolf gave me a small nod by way of greeting.

"Tell him who I am," said Æthelred.

I nodded.

"This is Æthelred, son of Æthelwald Moll, lord and king of Northumbria."

Runolf inclined his head.

"My lord king," I said, "this is Runolf Ragnarsson."

For several heartbeats the two men stared at each other. I could not comprehend the communication that passed between them, but after a time Æthelred, seeming to have taken measure of the prisoner, began to ask questions. These I translated. Runolf replied, truthfully, as far as I could tell, and I passed on his meaning to the king. This went on for some time. There were no surprises for me, as Æthelred raised most of the same questions I had already asked.

When he questioned the Norsemen's motivation and was met with Runolf's customary dismissive response about treasure and slaves and the weakness of the monks, there was a distinct shift in the atmosphere of the hall. It felt the same as when a cloud flitted before the sun, or the way the day cools and coils in anticipation before lightning strikes and the heavens open.

"And so," Æthelred said, his tone now as sharp as an unsheathed blade, "you admit that you prey on the weak and helpless?"

I interpreted.

Runolf seemed puzzled. He spoke in his rumbling voice. I hesitated, knowing that his words would stir up anger. The king stared at me impatiently so with a sigh I translated the words for Æthelred and the other listeners.

"Would a fox not take a hen? Does a wolf not kill the lambs in the field? If the farmer does not protect his livestock, the cunning and strong beasts will fill their bellies with their flesh."

At these words, Æthelred's face clouded with rage. For the first time, one of the other men at the high table spoke. A slender man, garbed in the dark robes of a priest, stood up quickly. On his chest hung an ornate crucifix of gold.

"This is an outrage!" he spluttered. "The heathen has admitted his crimes and must pay the penalty. Death is the only punishment for his evil."

The king held up a hand for peace and let out a long breath. He did not turn to look at the priest.

"Be seated, Daegmund," Æthelred said. "I hear your ire at what this man and his people have done and I am mindful of your words. But a king should never be hasty. I must glean as much as possible from this fruit before casting aside its husk."

I chose not to translate these words for Runolf. I wondered how much he understood of what was said. His grasp of Englisc was improving daily.

The priest sat down, making the sign of the cross as he did so. His face was twisted and thunderous and he muttered under his breath.

The king took a steadying sip from the silver cup and stared at Runolf.

"So you accuse me of being responsible for the deaths of these monks?"

Æthelred paused and nodded at me to speak the words in the Norse tongue.

Runolf listened and then replied with a shrug.

"As the master of these lands, it is your duty to protect your people."

For several heartbeats nobody spoke. The king glowered at Runolf and the Norseman, seemingly undaunted, stared back.

"My lord king," stammered Uhtric at last, unable to bear the weight of the silence any longer, "what would you have me do with the prisoner? What is your will?"

"It is not a matter of what I would like to do, or my will," said Æthelred. "If it were, I would be minded to have the skin flayed from him until he begged for mercy." His gaze had not moved from the Norseman as he spoke. "And then, if it were up to me, I would deny him that mercy, as his kind denied clemency to those they violated and murdered on the holy isle of Lindisfarnae!" With these last words, he raised his voice to a shout and slammed his fist into the board before him. The silver cup wobbled and he quickly reached out a hand to stop it from toppling over. He stared at it for a moment and then sighed.

"But a king cannot always do what he wishes. He must do that which is right for his people." He lifted the goblet and took a gulp of its contents. "He says there will be more attacks?"

It was unclear to whom the king was addressing the question and so, after a brief hesitation, I responded.

"He does, lord king. He told me that there are plans to attack the other minsters that are situated along the coast. He says the next attack will probably be at Werceworthe."

Æthelred nodded.

"More hens and sheep for the foxes and wolves," he said. He shook his head slowly. "Do you believe him?"

Surprised by the question, I faltered.

"Yes, lord king, I do," I said at last. I flicked a glance at the massive warrior beside me and realised it was true. "Runolf came to these shores with murder in his heart," I continued, "following this Jarl Skorri. But since I first saw him, he has done nothing to make me doubt his word and he has risked his life to save three children from death."

"Three, you say?" replied the king. "I thought you said there were two."

I told him of how he had saved the child and slain Framric at Werceworthe.

"He is a curious man indeed," Æthelred said. "And now I understand the strange cut of his hair. I had thought it unusual that a murderous Norseman should wear the tonsure."

"Perhaps the hair is not so strange," I said.

The king raised his eyebrows.

"You think he is become a monk?" he asked with a frown. One of the men at the table sniggered.

"No. He is yet no Christian. But I believe that he has been touched by God."

"Truly? Why do you think this?"

I looked at the expectant faces of the men of worth gathered along the length of the high table. I could feel the tension in Leofstan from where he stood close to me. My mouth was as dry as dust. What was I thinking? I was talking to the king. He did not wish to hear the opinions of the likes of me. And yet he was waiting patiently for an answer to his question. Surely, if God had truly chosen Runolf to help defend His brethren from the scourge of Norse attacks, as I believed, then it was also He who had given me the courage and rage to fight on Lindisfarnae. And it must also be the Almighty's plan to have brought me here before the king of Northumbria.

"I—" My voice cracked. I started again. "I believe God has brought Runolf to us, so that he might help us fight against the heathens who will surely come from the sea once more."

"This is ridiculous," said Daegmund, the priest, raising his voice and half-standing in his anger. "This boy is speaking nonsense. Sentence the heathen to death and then dispatch some of your warhost to protect the minsters at Hereteu, Streanæshealh, Gyruum and Werceworthe."

Æthelred held up his hand once more for quiet and turned slowly to face the priest. Daegmund withered beneath the monarch's stare.

"Do not presume to tell me how to run my kingdom, priest. And I will not tell you how to pray." The king scowled at Daegmund. When he was finally sure the priest would speak no more, he continued. "Ever since Uhtric's messenger arrived with the grave tidings of the attack on Lindisfarnae, I have pondered what I should do. If the Norsemen plan to attack again, surely it is my duty as king to send warriors to guard the monasteries. And yet I do not even have the men to defend all of my borders. The Welsh of Powys and the Mercians are threatening the south and west. I cannot send men to stand idle for weeks or months just in case the Norse should come once more. There are real battles I will need to fight this year, I cannot spare the men to protect against raids that may never take place. Besides, you do not need a host to fight against pirates and brigands."

"But lord," said Daegmund, "you would leave the minsters unprotected. If the Norse return, the men and women will be slaughtered."

Æthelred closed his eyes and pinched the bridge of his nose.

"I had thought, Daegmund, that men of God would pray for their protection. Will not the Lord protect His own?"

Daegmund, clearly enraged, began to respond, but I cut off his surly reply.

"A wise man once told me," I said, "that God leads us down mysterious paths. You do not have the warriors available to protect the minsters, but the Lord has sent us one who knows the ways of the Norsemen. One who can fight and help us to defend ourselves."

Æthelred frowned.

"Surely you cannot be suggesting that I send this heathen back with you to Werceworthe."

"Lord, I—" blurted out Daegmund, but the king silenced him with a cutting gesture of his hand.

"I am speaking, Daegmund," he said.

"But—" replied the priest.

"Silence." Again Æthelred sliced the air with his hand and this time Daegmund ceased talking. "I am speaking to Hunlaf of Werceworthe. Well," he asked, staring into my eyes, "is that what you are proposing?"

I could not breathe, but I managed to answer.

"It is, lord king."

For a long while, Æthelred was silent. He stared at me, as if weighing up my worth. I wanted to flee, but I stood my ground and met his gaze.

"No," he said at last. "This thing you ask for cannot be.

Look at him. He said it himself. It would be like the fox sent to guard the chickens."

I sighed. Of course I had known that the king would reject the idea. What had I been thinking? I would return to Werceworthe and await the imminent attack from the Norsemen myself. Perhaps I could convince Beonna to move the brethren, or we could build defences.

"If I may, my lord." Uhtric's voice broke me out of my dejection. The king nodded to the lord of Bebbanburg, giving his consent for the man to talk.

"I know this is unusual," Uhtric said, "but I agree with the monk. When first I laid eyes on this man," he nodded towards Runolf, who stood in rigid silence, "I wished to see him dead for his sins and those of the men he had travelled with. We even had a rope about his neck and had lifted him from the ground. But it was the bishop of Lindisfarnae who bade us cut him down." He shook his head as if he could scarcely believe his own words. "And since then, I have seen a man who would put his life at risk to rescue a child from a crazed thief. He has made no attempt to escape, despite knowing we were taking him to what was probably certain death. He gave me his word that he would not flee and I believed him. And so it was. And here he is before you, at your mercy. And I cannot believe that the Lord has seen fit for him to come here only to be killed. There must be more purpose in his being here than that."

I was amazed that Uhtric was speaking out for my idea and for Runolf. It must be the workings of the Almighty for his mind to have changed so drastically.

"Mayhap the Good Lord spared him on Lindisfarnae so that he could save the child in Werceworthe," mused the king. "Perhaps there is nothing more for him to do."

"Maybe," replied Uhtric. "But I think the monk has read the signs correctly."

"It is true, lord king." The new voice startled me. It was Leofstan, who had until this moment remained silent.

The king raised one eyebrow.

"Speak, brother monk," he said.

"Not only has Christ spared the life of Runolf and brought him here to us with knowledge and ability to fight against the heathens, but the Lord also sent Hunlaf a vision."

"A vision?" asked the king, leaning forward.

"Yes, on the night after the events at Werceworthe. The Holy Spirit came upon him and he was filled with the certainty that Runolf was sent to aid us."

"What did you see, Hunlaf?" Æthelred asked, his eyes narrowing.

"I saw Runolf fighting against the heathens. They fell before him like wheat under a scythe. And above his head there fluttered a white dove."

The king made the sign of the cross and glanced over at Daegmund.

"This changes everything," he said, and there was awe in his voice. I felt a twinge of guilt at my embellishment of the truth.

Leofstan inclined his head to me in acknowledgement. If he knew I had lied, he showed no sign.

"But the man is a pagan," said Daegmund, his voice dripping with disdain. "He cannot be trusted."

"The vision shows that Christ has chosen him," said the king. "And so he must be baptised. Can you do that without delay?"

"Well," the priest said, "that would be most irregular. He should learn the catechism, and then—"

Æthelred interrupted him.

"Can it be done today?"

Daegmund's face grew red, but he bit his lip and said, "Tomorrow morning would be possible, my lord king."

"Good." Æthelred clapped his hands and grinned. He seemed pleased to have made up his mind. "Tell him." He looked at me, and I explained to Runolf as best I could, what had been decided. I did not know the word for baptism, so I described the process to him.

"I am to be washed?" he growled, confusion furrowing his brow. "Not killed?"

"Washed clean of your sins," I said.

"And then what? Will I have to shave my head like this forever?" He rasped one of his massive hands over the stubble on the crown of his head. "If I have to do that, I would rather they hang me and be done with it."

I chuckled, relief washing through me.

"No, only monks wear the tonsure."

He grinned.

"That is good then. I like my hair long, but I do not mind a bath. I am stinking like a pig anyway!"

Runolf's smile was infectious and the mood in the hall lifted.

"So it is settled then," said Æthelred. "The Norseman will be baptised on the morrow."

One of the nobles, a portly man with quivering jowls and a bulbous nose, coughed and whispered something that I was unable to hear.

Æthelred looked sombre once more.

"Is the Norseman oath-sworn?" he asked. "Does a lord have his oath?"

I posed the question to Runolf and he replied with a gruff shake of his head and a few terse words.

"He says he is sworn to no man."

The king stroked his long moustache.

"A lordless man is dangerous. If I am to allow him to keep his life and to remain within my kingdom, he must prove his fealty. Uhtric, you have vouched for this man, so you will hear his oath. Tomorrow he will be baptised into the one faith and he will swear loyalty to you. He will be your man, and your responsibility."

Uhtric paled at these words, but there was no way for him to back out now.

"Now go and prepare yourself for the feast, man," Æthelred said. "You must find yourself some clean clothes, for you will sit at the high table and I would hear more of what has occurred in the north under your watch."

Æthelred's dismissal was clear.

Uhtric bowed and we made to leave the hall. As we turned, the king spoke again.

"And Uhtric." We halted and faced the king once more.

"My lord king?" Uhtric said, keeping his voice low and devoid of emotion.

"You will see to it that this new man of yours, Runolf Ragnarsson, ensures that the minster at Werceworthe is safe from the heathen pirates. The monk's vision was of the Norseman protecting the brethren. He is your man now, so it is on your shoulders to see that he delivers on the promise of the lad's dream."

Nineteen

When we left the hall, the enormity of what had transpired within seemed to hit us all at once, as if we had been plunged from the dry deck of a ship into the freezing waters of the North Sea, and we were left breathless and struggling.

Uhtric was furious and would not speak to anyone as a bondsman led us across the courtyard to another building that was considerably smaller than the great hall, but still a large structure with a freshly thatched roof and recently painted walls. The sun was setting and the promise of darkness hung over the land and in the shadows around the hall where we would spend the night.

Behind us, guests were arriving at the king's hall and the sounds of merriment drifted from the open doors. As we had left, servants and thralls were hurrying to light all the candles and lamps needed to illuminate such a majestic building.

The servant opened the door to the small hall that had been appointed as our lodging and Uhtric strutted inside, dismissing the man with a click of his fingers. We followed the lord in silence. The doorway was carved with interlocking creatures and patterns in much the same way as the columns of the great hall, and I marvelled at the skill of the craftsman who had fashioned such ornate figures in the timber. The interior of the hall was gloomy, but one rush light had been lit, allowing a couple of Uhtric's men to use the flame to light the others. Soon the smell of burning tallow pervaded the place and the flickering lights filled the dwelling with a ruddy glow.

"What has happened?" murmured Runolf. Uhtric's displeasure was clear, but of course, the Norseman had missed most of the words spoken in the great hall before we left.

I whispered an explanation of the king's final commands and Runolf's face darkened.

"I do not wish to swear an oath to Uhtric or to any man," he grumbled. "An eiðr is not something given lightly."

As if he could understand Runolf's words, Uhtric rounded on him.

"Tell him I would rather not accept the oath of a heathen. But I cannot defy my king."

"Well, lord," said Hereward with a twisted grin, "by midday he will be baptised and no longer a heathen."

Uhtric glowered at him before tugging off his travel-stained kirtle and flinging it onto one of the pallets that had been set up for us.

"Fetch me clean clothes, Hereward," he snapped. "And if you know what is good for you, you will keep your idea of wit to yourself."

Hereward, seeming to realise he had overstepped his mark, nodded and silently began to rummage through the saddle bags that servants had carried in from the stabled horses.

"What if I do not swear?" asked Runolf.

Uhtric had picked up the dirty kirtle once more and, having dipped it into a pail of water, was rubbing it over first his face and then his torso, wiping away the sweat and grime from the journey.

"What is he saying?" he growled.

I told him.

"Well, Runolf," Uhtric said, taking a clean blue kirtle from Hereward and pulling it over his head, "if you do not swear your oath to me on the morrow, I will be in disfavour with Æthelred. That is something I truly do not want." He sat and used the damp kirtle to wipe the dust of the journey from his shoes. "If that happens, I will finish what I started at that tree on Lindisfarnae." He glanced up at Runolf. "And that, I imagine, is something that you do not want."

He spoke in a deadly earnest tone. I relayed his words to Runolf, who sat silent for a long while, watching as Uhtric rose and replaced his belt that Hereward had cleaned without being asked.

"And what is the price for me being washed by the priest and giving my oath to you?" Runolf asked.

Uhtric listened to my translation.

"Apart from keeping your life?" he said.

Clearly understanding the words or the meaning, Runolf nodded.

"Yes," he said in his heavily accented Englisc. "More than that."

"Well, you will be my oath-sworn man, so you will obey me. And first of all, you will go to Werceworthe and prepare its defence against your friends."

On hearing this Hereward could keep silent no longer.

"But, lord," he said. "Surely you cannot be saying you will allow the heathen to lead the defence of the monastery!"

Uhtric smiled, but there was no mirth in the expression.

"But, Hereward," he said, mocking the warrior's tone, "after midday tomorrow he will be a heathen no longer." Some of the other men laughed as Hereward blustered at having his own jest flung back into his face. "Besides," continued the lord of Bebbanburg, "I do not wish for Runolf to lead the defence. The king has made me responsible for the minster, so I will need someone I can trust. A good Christian Northumbrian man, not a Norseman still wet from his baptism."

Hereward frowned, his lord's meaning becoming clear.

"But, lord—" he began, but Uhtric held up his hand for quiet.

"Yes, Hereward," he said, his grin broadening. "You are to return to Werceworthe and you will organise the defence. Make good use of Runolf's knowledge and his battle-skill, but you will lead."

"But—"

"Enough!" snapped Uhtric. "My decision is made. You will lead the defence and speak with my voice. And I will be glad of the peace from your chatter and complaining." Again the other warriors laughed. Hereward scowled. "You are a brave warrior," Uhtric said, taking his cloak from one of the men who had been brushing it, "but you do harp on like a fisher woman."

The use of the term made me think of Aelfwyn and the joy I had felt at the turn of events was dampened.

Uhtric swung the cloak about his shoulders. Fixing the fine golden brooch at his neck, he stepped towards the door.

"I will see that food and drink are sent to you," he said. At the doorway, he turned. "So, Runolf," he fixed the great Norseman with his gaze, "what say you? Will you give me your oath tomorrow? Or shall I have your neck stretched."

Runolf loured back at him for several heartbeats. Nobody made a sound.

"Oath," Runolf rumbled at last.

Uhtric nodded.

"Very well," he said. "Till the morn then."

Just as he was about to leave the hall, Hereward called after him.

"Lord, how many men may I lead to Werceworthe?"

Uhtric leaned against the carved door jamb. I noticed that where he had placed his hand gave the impression that a carven image of a raven rested on his fingers.

"You heard the king," he said. "It is madness to garrison a monastery and just wait for an attack that may never occur."

"Lord?" Hereward's voice had lost its bluster now. It sounded small and uncertain.

"I am not sending any men with you. You will have to fend for yourselves. Or maybe," he said, with an unkind gleam in his eye, "you and the Norseman can teach the monks and ceorls to fight."

He did not wait for a reply from Hereward, but swept out and into the night. From across the courtyard came the sound of revelry and laughter from the feast.

As I stood there in the dimly lit hall staring after the form of the lord of Bebbanburg, I couldn't help but wonder if the guests in the great hall were laughing at me.

Twenty

I slept poorly despite the tiredness of my body from the long days of riding. My head was a-swirl with worries and fears like a flock of sparrows flitting about a hedgerow, never settling, always in flight, impossible to grasp.

Runolf appeared unconcerned by his decisions and when I tried to speak to him of what it meant to be baptised, he waved me away.

"Unlike you Northumbrians, I have been washed before, Hunlaf," he said with a grin.

I told Leofstan what he'd said and the monk simply smiled.

"You cannot control everything," he said. "Allow the Lord to lead Runolf where He will."

"You believe this is all part of God's plan?" I asked.

"Do you believe it is not? I thought that was why we had come here."

I had no answer to that and so I wrapped myself in a blanket and flopped onto the pallet farthest from the door. I closed my eyes but sleep was a long time coming.

The next day, servants arrived when the sun was yet low in the sky to lead us to the church of Saint Peter where Daegmund was awaiting us. The air was still cool and the dew-encrusted shadows were long on the ground.

Accustomed as I was to rising for the different offices, I came awake quickly. Uhtric's warriors grumbled and groaned at being asked to rise so early, but they were well trained and drilled to be ready for combat whenever called upon and so, soon enough, we were all up and following the servants through the awakening streets of the city towards the church.

Lord Uhtric had been the last to climb from his pallet. He had clearly imbibed copious amounts of the king's ale and wine and was now feeling the after-effects. He staggered blinking into the bright morning, holding his head and shouting for water.

Eoforwic was already awake and by the time we reached the stone edifice of the church, the streets were beginning to grow crowded. We fell into step behind clusters of people heading to the festival ground before Saint Peter's.

Smoke and the scent of cooking meat hung over the tents and shelters in the early morning air. There was no wind and the banners, flags and pennants hung limp, dew-dampened and flaccid in the still air. But already the mood of the place was ebullient. Like a pot set on a smouldering fire, I had the sense that like the day before, as the day warmed, so would the festival and soon the place would be a cacophony of music and merriment. Men and women would hawk their wares and others would scream and bet on their favourites to win contests of chance and skill.

Stepping out of the bright morning sunshine into the church of Saint Peter, I was struck by how dark and chill it was inside. I shivered. At the far end of the building stood Daegmund, waiting impatiently for our arrival. His reception was as cool and gloomy as the church's interior.

"We have been waiting," he said, his acerbic tone scratching at my nerves. "The baptismal font was not ready and we had to be awake at dawn in order to fill it. There is already so much to do with the Feast of Saint Peter approaching." He looked about him as if seeking something else to complain about.

"I am sure God will be pleased that you have laboured and risen early to bring a new soul to the fold," said Uhtric. Daegmund glowered at him. I expected him to respond to the obvious jibe, but something in Uhtric's demeanour checked him.

"Quite," he said at last. "Is the Norseman ready?"

"He is," said Uhtric. "Runolf," he clicked his fingers and the sound echoed within the stone chamber, "it is time."

Before the altar there was a large recess hewn into the ground. It was stone-lined and shaped like a cross. Water lapped over the steps that led down into the font. To one side, resting against the southern wall was the timber framework that would cover the font when not in use.

I had never seen such a baptismal pool before and all the while we had walked towards the church I had wondered how they meant to baptise Runolf within the building. I had thought that perhaps they would pour the water over his head rather than submerge him three times as was the traditional way. But the sacrament of the baptism could only be given in this way if someone was unable to enter the water fully. And, while Runolf's great height might make it difficult for him to fully submerge, there was no real impediment to him wading into a river, which is where I had expected the baptism to take place. I stared at the close-fitting stones and wondered how the water did not seep away. The water was dark, as if it were very deep and I leaned forward to get a closer look. Then I understood. The apparent darkness was not from the shadows of a deep well, it was from the grey-coloured lining of lead that covered the bottom of the font.

A movement caught my attention and I turned at the same moment that Daegmund let out a cry of dismay.

"What in all that is holy is he doing?" he squawked.

For a heartbeat, I could not make out what had so upset the priest. Runolf bent down and stood and I gasped to see his pale, muscled body. He was completely naked, having removed all of his clothing and left it in a pile on the flagstones. There were scars and bruises on his pallid flesh. His physical presence was overpowering in the gloom of the church as he stared at the priest with a quizzical expression.

Hereward laughed, a loud, harsh sound that reverberated from the stone walls.

"What are you doing?" I hissed.

"I am not going to walk around all day in wet clothes," he replied in a tone that implied I was simple to ask such a question.

I stood silent, mouth agape and unsure how to answer.

"There is a robe for him and a place to change behind the screen," said Daegmund, his voice rasping like fingernails being scratched across slate.

He studiously ignored Runolf's naked form and I glanced to where he was looking. I realised then that the font's wooden cover was propped up in such a way as to provide space behind it.

"You are meant to disrobe behind that," I said, pointing at the wooden partition. "There is a robe for you there."

"I have no need of a robe," replied Runolf. "It is cold in here. Let's get this over with."

Without waiting for a response, the huge Norseman strode past the spluttering Daegmund and splashed into the font.

"By Óðinn's cock," Runolf said, "this water is chill enough to freeze a man." I chose not to translate his words. His pale skin prickled with the cold like that of a plucked goose. He took a deep breath and stepped down further into the font until the water reached his waist. "Come on, man," he said in Englisc to Daegmund.

For a moment, the priest merely looked down at Runolf. His

mouth worked as if chewing over words he wished to say. In the end, he apparently found none suitable, for he hitched up his robe and stepped into the cold water with a sharp intake of breath. Standing shivering beside Runolf, Daegmund turned to us.

"Which of you is to be this man's Godfather?"

Uhtric grunted.

"If I am to take his oath, I might as well be his sponsor in this too," he said.

Daegmund nodded.

"Very well. Step into the water and place your hand upon his shoulder."

Uhtric recoiled at the suggestion.

"By Christ's bones, no!" he said.

Unbidden, I found myself making the sign of the cross at Uhtric's blasphemy, along with Daegmund, Leofstan and the other clergy who stood observing in the shadowed church.

"Someone must be the man's Godfather as he accepts the true faith."

Nobody spoke, but Uhtric shook his head vigorously. Slowly, all eyes turned to me. I looked at the cold water, imagining its icy embrace.

"Well, boy? What are you waiting for?" snapped Daegmund. "Do not tarry. There is much to do today."

It was clear that nobody else was going to offer themselves for the role and so, with a sigh, I began to quickly untie my shoes. The stone floor of the church was cold.

"Hurry, boy," said Daegmund.

"Come on, Hunlaf," rumbled Runolf. "My balls are shrivelled with the cold."

I had the sudden urge to piss and bit my lip not to giggle at the thought of emptying my bladder into the font. Tentatively, I stepped down into the water and joined the two men. To be someone's sponsor was not something to be taken lightly, but the water was icy and I could think of little else save for getting out. I placed my hand on Runolf's shoulder to symbolise that I was offering him support and guidance as he accepted Christ as his saviour. At first I cared little for the words that Daegmund uttered. He was clearly unhappy to be performing this rite, wanting nothing more than to be done with it and able to go about the day he had planned. But as he posed the questions to Runolf about faith and everlasting life, and I interpreted for him, telling him how to reply, I felt an unlikely serenity. I was unsure whether anyone else felt it, but I was suddenly gripped once more by the certainty that this was all part of God's plan.

When he had to repudiate and reject all other gods, Runolf hesitated, a distant look in his eye. The silence drew on uncomfortably. The water leached the warmth from my body and I shivered. Eventually, I repeated the words that Daegmund had spoken and told Runolf once again what he must say in reply.

As if brought out of a dream, Runolf's eyes snapped back to the present. There were tears there and a terrible sorrow pulled his face into a scowl.

"I reject them all," he growled and I was surprised at the anger in his voice.

At the culmination of the Holy sacrament, Runolf's eyes seemed to glow in the gloom and he did not resist as Daegmund and I lowered him into the water. The moment he was completely submerged, we pulled him out, and then, after he had taken a breath, we pushed him under again. One final time, he was submerged; the three soakings a reminder of the Holy Trinity.

As soon as he came up the third time, Daegmund, his work done, stepped from the font. A servant waited for him with a cloth to dry himself. The servant also held out cloths for Runolf and me.

"I feel no different," murmured Runolf, as he passed a hand

over his eyes and then proceeded to squeeze moisture from his thick beard.

My habit was wet to the waist and clung clammily to my legs. I sat on the cold flagstones and wiped my feet and calves as dry as possible.

"What did you expect?" I asked.

He shrugged, rubbing the linen cloth against his scarred, pale body.

"Tell him to go behind the screen," said Daegmund. "I have seen quite enough of his nakedness."

I told Runolf, and with another shrug of his massive shoulders, he scooped up his kirtle and breeches and slipped behind the upright font cover.

I pulled on my shoes, tying the leather laces. Standing, I shuddered at the cold touch of my sodden robe against my calves.

"Now, if there is nothing else," said Daegmund, "I must change and attend to the rest of my flock on this busy day."

"There is one more thing," said Uhtric as the priest turned to leave.

Daegmund halted.

"Yes?" he asked, his tone wary.

"I would have you witness Runolf's oath to me."

"God is your witness," Daegmund replied. "You have no need of me now."

"That is as may be," said Uhtric, rubbing his knuckles into his eyes and then passing his hands across his stubbled cheeks. "But Runolf is now a child of Christ and I would have you observe his oath-giving."

Daegmund spun about and I thought he would shout his objection at Uhtric, but the lord of Bebbanburg simply smiled a tired smile and said, "Thank you."

Daegmund swallowed and I bit back a chortle of laughter that threatened to come bubbling up. It was plain to see that

Uhtric was toying with Daegmund. The priest's attitude had annoyed him and he aimed to make him pay in whatever small way possible. I disliked Daegmund too, and I felt a thin sliver of pleasure at Uhtric's meaningless victory. And yet I could not deny that part of me was saddened by it. A lord should be above such pettiness.

I watched the two of them as we all waited for Runolf to return from where he was dressing. Daegmund, furious and impatient, breathed deeply. Uhtric closed his eyes and leaned against the cold wall of the church, seemingly ignorant of the anger he had stirred in the priest. Perhaps there was something to be learnt from this dance, this song without words. Uhtric had flexed his muscles with the cleric and in doing so, he had not only learnt where he was perceived to be in the rank of the king's followers, but he had let Daegmund know that he was in command here.

Uhtric yawned and belched. He was clearly tired and I believed he would rush through the oath. I was wrong. Whether because he wished to show Daegmund his power over him, or because he believed an oath between a warrior and his lord was more important than that between man and God, Uhtric spoke to Runolf slowly and clearly about his responsibilities as an oath-sworn man. He had me interpret every word and would not proceed until he was convinced that Runolf had understood.

For his part, the Norseman took the oath-giving in total earnest. Both men gave the other their full attention and neither smiled. This was a solemn vow and there was no doubt to any who witnessed the oath that it was not taken lightly. When both men were satisfied with the other's replies to their questions, Runolf knelt before Uhtric and spoke the words of the plight in his heavily accented Englisc.

I had never before been present at such a moment and I felt a squirming excitement in my belly at the power in the words.

"By the Lord before whom this sanctuary is holy," Runolf said, haltingly repeating the words that Hereward whispered to him, "I will to Uhtric be true and faithful. Love all which he loves and shun all which he shuns, according to the laws of God and the order of the world. Nor will I ever with will or action, through word or deed, do anything which is unpleasing to him, on condition that he will hold to me as I shall deserve it, and that he will perform everything as it was in our agreement when I submitted myself to him and chose his will."

I wondered what it would feel like to swear such allegiance to a leader of men rather than to God. Of course, I had given myself to Christ and to my brethren, but something about this oath sent a shiver down my spine. My hand throbbed and I imagined clutching the seax, the weight of the metal in my grip, the surge of power and rage that had washed through me.

Uhtric pulled Runolf to his feet and embraced him, dispelling the serious mood that had fallen over us.

With a slap on the huge man's back, Uhtric said, "It is done."

Daegmund fidgeted, but seemed strangely quiet and subdued. Again I marvelled at Uhtric's power over the small man.

"Thank you for your blessing, Daegmund," Uhtric said, as if just remembering that the priest was present. "You may leave us."

Daegmund frowned and opened his mouth to speak. He then snapped it closed again, thinking better of it.

"Have a good day," he said, and stalked away down the length of the gloom-laden church, followed by his acolytes. As he opened the doors, the noise of revelry from outside was loud. Bright sunlight lanced into the church, cutting through the sombre atmosphere inside.

"I am tired," Uhtric said. "I'm going back to the hall. I need to rest my head. Tomorrow we head north, into the lands of Causantín mac Fergusa. The king has ordered that I join forces with Lord Lanferth there, to defend the northern border."

He began to walk away, towards the warm day. His men trailed after him, leaving just Runolf, Hereward, Leofstan and me standing by the font. The servants of the church were already replacing the cover. With an echoing clatter they dropped it into place. I started at the noise and Uhtric turned.

"What about us, lord?" Hereward asked.

"What about you?" Uhtric replied. "You are to go to Werceworthe, with my new Christian warrior."

"But what are we to do?" Hereward replied. His voice held a pleading note. "We have no fighting men."

Uhtric sighed.

"No fighting men? The two of you are worth ten normal men." He saw that his words did nothing to settle Hereward's concerns. "Think," he said, "did the abbot not say you could bring back good Christian men to fight for the minster?"

"Yes, but what men? The king can spare none and neither can you."

"There are men who fight for other things besides their king or their sworn lord. Men who may not have a master, but are good Christians, I'm sure. Those men can still fight."

He made his way to the doors and pushed them open. Again, the sound of the crowds rolled in with the brilliant sunshine. We walked down the length of the church and joined Uhtric at the open doors.

"You mean men who would fight for silver?" asked Hereward.

"Perhaps," Uhtric replied, staring out at the mass of tents and people.

"I have none," said Hereward. "Would you give me some silver to pay for men, lord?"

Uhtric glanced at him. A slight smile played on his lips.

"No," he said.

The scent of cooking made me suddenly ravenous.

"What are we to do then?" Hereward asked.

Uhtric said nothing. I followed his gaze and saw that he was looking at a throng of people. Like the day before a crowd had congregated around a bare-knuckle fight.

I recalled the pinched faces of the people we had passed as we'd travelled south, the poor crops following the storms of the spring.

"We should search for men there," I said, pointing at the jostling people gathered about the fight. "It looks to me that most of Deira has come to Eoforwic for the festival. Surely we can find some good Christians there who can fight."

"But we have nothing to offer them," said Hereward, shaking his head.

"We have no silver," I replied, "but there has been famine in the land and people are starving."

"You mean…" his voice trailed off.

"Yes," I said. "There is food at the minster. We cannot offer riches, but we can offer sustenance."

His face twisted into a humourless smile.

"So," he said, rubbing a hand over his beard, "what you are saying is that we must find hungry warriors."

Twenty-One

"I can't see what is happening," I moaned.

The crowd before me swayed like an ocean. A great roaring cheer went up as one of the combatants landed a blow. We had left the cool quiet of the church of Saint Peter and headed towards the heated excitement of the fight, but by the time we arrived, the wagers had been placed and the brutal combat with fists had commenced. The two fighters were standing on an area of grass the size of a laid-out cloak and even if either should wish to run from his opponent, they were surrounded by such a dense pack of baying onlookers, that flight would have been impossible.

Just as it was impossible for me to see anything of the action taking place just a few paces away. Even Runolf with his extra height could make out little. He stood up on his toes and peered over the heads of the crowd.

Another cry from the audience spoke of excitement in the contest, but all I could see were people's backs. The sun was warm on my tonsured head but my legs were cold. My habit was still soaked and it had flapped like a chill hand against my calves as we had walked. Unable to see anything of interest, I looked up and saw there was not a cloud in the sky. The day would be hot and my robe would dry soon enough.

The crowd gasped at some unseen event and I sighed.

"I cannot see a thing," I said again. Leofstan shook his head. I knew he disapproved of such violent activities, but I longed to watch the two fighters trading blows. Besides, I told myself, perhaps one of them, or even both, might join our band. Men who would allow themselves to be beaten in such a manner must be desperate indeed.

With a sudden growl, Runolf began pushing people aside with his huge bulk.

"Follow me," he said.

After an instant of hesitation, I moved in close behind him and allowed him to lead me through the tightly packed throng. Hereward and Leofstan fell in behind me and the four of us made our way through the surging sea of people like Moses traversing the Red Sea. But instead of God's power parting the waves, Runolf used brute strength and his size. Men yelled abuse at him as he barged them out of the way. A few turned, ready to fight, until they saw the giant of a Norseman, bristling beard jutting from a square jaw, arms knotted with muscles and legs like tree trunks. When they saw him, they backed away, allowing him free passage through the crowd. I knew it was not only his strength and size that made men change their mind. There was a coldness to Runolf's eyes that spoke of a past of bloodletting and death. And few men want to become part of the future of a man with such a dark history behind him. Fewer still are brave enough to confront him.

As we reached the edge of the mass of humanity, Runolf grasped my shoulder in one of his huge hands and shoved me in front of him. I felt like a child whose father helps him to better see the entertainment. My cheeks flushed in embarrassment, but the truth was, I was pleased to be able to see and happy that Runolf had brought me to the front.

I shifted my attention from the Norseman and the crowd, to the two figures in the small rectangle of space before us. The smaller of them grunted and staggered as the other landed a crunching punch to his jaw. His head snapped back and blood fountained from his mouth and splattered across my face like a slap. I gasped and tasted the metallic warm liquid on my tongue. The audience jeered and screamed, the noise terrible now that we were at its centre.

I spat and wiped my hand across my face. The back of my bandage came away red.

I stared at the combatants and my world narrowed, so that all I could see were the two men, fists up, stripped bare to the waist. Each wore plain breeches and I noted that neither man had shoes on his feet.

They were both clearly skilled in the art of fist fighting, for the two of them were smeared in blood, but they still moved quickly, alert and ready to attack or defend.

One of them was a massive monster of a man. His shoulders and neck were clumped with slabs of muscle and sinew and I was instantly reminded of a bull. He was bald and his features were pudgy and swollen, his ears great lumps of meat as if not a day went by without someone battering him about the head and face. His knuckles were covered in blood, and I could not be sure if from his own wounds or his opponents. Then I noted that both men's fists were bound in rags, presumably to stop their skin from splitting.

As I watched, he threw out a jab. His arms were very long and his reach almost caught his opponent off guard. But the smaller of the two was fast and he rolled his head to one side, allowing the giant's fist to glance harmlessly off his shoulder.

The crowd screamed and shouted. They wanted more blood. I could feel myself pulled in by the energy of the fight, like jetsam dragged along on a swelling sea.

The smaller fighter was a full head shorter than his adversary and I could not imagine how he could hope to stand against such a mighty foe. This second fighter was like nobody I had ever seen before. His hair was dark, oiled and tied in a plait down his back. His torso, arms and face were painted in whorls and swirls of dark blue. I had heard of such men. They lived far away in the north, in the lands of Causantín mac Fergusa, beyond the realms of King Æthelred. The tattooed fighter was one of the painted men; a Pict. I was fascinated by the patterns on his skin, but it was difficult to make sense of them for he never stopped moving. His feet danced in the muddy grass and his fists flew almost too quickly to see. The massive bald warrior was struggling to make contact with the nimble Pictish fighter until, with a feint followed up with an uppercut to his midriff, he connected one of his boulder-like fists with the Pict's lean, tattooed body. The Pict was lifted from his feet and fell to one knee, panting. I expected the huge warrior to finish him. But he stepped back, raising his hands to the crowd and accepting their cheer of approval for letting the fight run on. On his knee, the Pict stared up at him, struggling to regain his breath. I thought of Runolf towering over me. Like me, the smaller man looked like a child when compared to the hulking bald warrior before him. But there was no denying he was brave and well-skilled.

"The big man is a fool," Hereward said and I glanced at him incredulously.

"Why?"

"He should have finished the Pict while he had the chance. He was lucky to hit him then. But such is the way with some men, they seek glory from the crowd more than success. Never lose sight of the prize, Hunlaf."

"What is he saying?" rumbled Runolf. I told him and he nodded. The Pict was now pushing himself up and standing unsteadily before the massive bald fighter.

"He has the truth of it," Runolf said. I frowned. Were they watching the same fight? "Watch," he said, perhaps sensing my disbelief.

Beside me, Hereward was speaking to someone, shouting over the noise to place a wager on the Pictish warrior winning. I could scarcely believe it. Hereward must be mad, I thought. But of course, then, like most men, I was no warrior. I had not stood in a shieldwall. I had not seen countless men meet their deaths at the hands of those faster, stronger or luckier than them. And having done none of those things, I could not see beyond the obvious. I saw a stronger man, with a longer reach. He had skill and power and a seemingly endless amount of confidence. Runolf and Hereward measured the two fighters with the eyes of seasoned warriors. They noted the scars beneath the tattoos, denoting where the Pict had survived injury in battle. There were no scars on his back, only on his arms and chest. They took in the fleetness of his feet and the speed of his fists. They recognised a man who will not allow himself to be beaten. Someone who will kill or be killed in the attempt.

They saw one of their own kind.

The crowd quietened somewhat as the two men circled each other. They exchanged a few punches, but nothing decisive. There was a flurry of blows and then the men parted. The Pict lowered his head, seemingly exhausted.

"Kill the fucking Pictish bastard," came a shout over the general hubbub.

The bald giant turned towards the shout with a grin. And without warning the tattooed Pict flew into action. He leapt forward and the onlookers let out a collective gasp as his right fist smashed into the giant's nose. The Pict was smaller than the bald fighter, but he was not a small man and his blows carried a warrior's strength. Anticipating the larger man's response to the crunching right hook that broke his nose and sent blood streaming over his chin and chest, the Pict danced back, easily avoiding the wild swings. The giant roared and surged forward, but the Pict ducked and weaved before him, dodging and deflecting his attacks. Gone was his apparent tiredness of moments before, replaced with a vibrant energy and savage ruthlessness.

The hugely muscled fighter stumbled forward, bloodied and raging. The Pict skipped out of his reach and then, the instant he saw an opening, he sprang forward, driving a jab into his opponent's ear, which sent him reeling. The Pict followed this up with a solid punch to the man's exposed throat. Gurgling and gasping for air, the huge fighter staggered backwards, clutching at his neck, but the Pict did not stop raining blows on his enemy. Again and again the bald man's head was snapped back as the Pict hammered his fists into the bleeding face. In moments, the giant was a bloody mess and he soon fell to the earth, insensate.

There was so much blood smearing the big man's face that he looked like a slab of butchered meat. My mind spun at the speed of the change in his fortune. There was a pause, as if the crowd held its breath, and then everybody was talking and shouting at once. Those who had backed the Pict were overjoyed, but the majority had placed their bets on the giant and many of the shouts were filled with anger. Men rushed to the fallen form of the fighter and I wondered whether he would live.

"You see?" said Runolf. "There is more to fighting than strength." He grinned, clearly having enjoyed the spectacle. "Though that helps too."

The crowd was thinning already as the people went to find other forms of entertainment. That was another lesson I learnt that day. There are few who care for the warriors once a fight is over.

Leofstan was pale next to me. I wondered if I looked as shocked. I thought not. I felt exhilarated and breathless; stunned at the violence, but excited by the skill and power I had witnessed. Leofstan reached out as if to touch my face, then snatched back his hand.

"There is blood," he said.

I wiped at my cheek with my bandaged hand, but could not be sure if I had removed all of the offending fluid.

"I told you," said Hereward, returning from collecting his winnings. "I wish I had wagered more now. Perhaps then we would have had enough silver to pay for men."

"Perhaps," said Leofstan, "a man willing to withstand having his face battered for the chance of making enough to live, might also be interested in joining us."

"Perhaps," said Hereward with a broad smile. "There's only one way to find out."

We walked through the dispersing crowd to where the Pict sat with another couple of men beside a cart. One of the men held a wooden bucket and the other was using a cloth to wipe the blood from the Pict's wounds. The tattooed man was unwrapping the blood-soaked rags that had protected his knuckles. Beneath the dirty bandages, his hands were red and swollen. He plunged them into the cold water of the bucket and held them there.

Looking up from where he sat on a chest, the Pict said, "If you lost money on the fight, do not blame me." His accent was thick and strange, but the words were clear enough.

He took our small group in with a glance, lingering a heartbeat longer on Runolf.

"No, no, it is nothing like that," said Hereward. "I could see you were the better fighter from the first blow I witnessed." The Pict said nothing. "I bet on you." The Pict nodded.

The older of the two men with him, the one cleaning his cuts, turned to Hereward.

"We thank you for your praise and hope you enjoyed the fight, but now, Drosten must rest."

"We have a proposition for you," Hereward said.

"What kind of proposition," asked the old man, narrowing his eyes appraisingly.

"Not for you, old man," replied Hereward, dismissing the man and fixing the Pict with a cold stare. "This is an offer for you, Drosten," he stumbled over the name slightly, but it sounded close enough to my ears.

"What offer?" asked Drosten.

Hereward told him that we were looking for warriors to fight against Norsemen.

"And I would be paid only in food?" Drosten asked, shaking his head in disbelief.

"And a roof over your head," added Hereward.

"And the blessing of the Abbot of Werceworthe and the Bishop of Lindisfarnae," said Leofstan. Judging from the frown on his face, the offered rewards for his service were not doing much to convince Drosten.

"So what say you?" Hereward asked. "Will you join us?"

Drosten stared at each of us in turn as if we were all mad. Pulling his hands from the bucket, he held them out for the old man to dry.

"No," he said, shaking his head.

Twenty-Two

We walked despondently through the jumble of stalls and tents that were set up all over the open ground before the church.

Hereward nudged me to get my attention and handed me one of the four small pies he had bought with his winnings.

"Here. Eat this. It will take your mind off the fact that we are doomed to die at the hands of marauding Norsemen." He gave me a lopsided smile, but I could not be sure if he was jesting or not. I had been there on Lindisfarnae and I could find no humour in his words. "You didn't truly believe men would offer their services for a crust of bread and a roof over their heads, did you?" he asked.

I looked at my hands and my stomach grumbled. The pastry was warm and the rich scent of meat and vegetables that oozed from within was delectable. I did not know how to respond to Hereward's words so I took a bite of the pie, regretting it instantly as hot juices ran over my chin and scalded my fingers. I breathed quickly through my mouth in an effort to avoid burning my tongue.

Hereward snorted at my predicament and shook his head. He nibbled on the crust of his own pie. He spoke lightly, but I could see the tension in his eyes and the set of his shoulders.

We walked on. Runolf alone amongst us seemed relaxed and

unfrightened by what would happen when we returned to the minster. He gazed about him at the hawkers, jugglers, livestock, acrobats and scops with a broad grin on his face.

"You do not worry?" I asked him in Norse.

"Worry? About what?"

"The future."

He laughed, without much mirth it seemed to me. He looked about him with wide eyes.

"Days ago I was hanging from my neck. A few more heart-beats and I would be dead. Everything since then is a gift, Hunlaf." He bit into his pie, licked his lips and closed his eyes, relishing the flavour. The pies were delicious, but my mouth was now burnt and painful, making it difficult for me to enjoy mine. "Look about you," Runolf said. "The day is warm, and for now, we are safe. There are things to see and food to eat. There is little else in this life of value."

I thought of the Scriptures I had copied onto vellum, of the word of God I had learnt and the offices that Leofstan and I had missed since leaving the monastery. Surely hard work and a devotion to God were important. Surely such things had worth.

"You want nothing more then?" I asked.

He turned to me and his face clouded.

"I have had more," he said, then looked away as a boy ran past whooping with glee as a younger girl chased him, screaming and laughing. Runolf watched them as they dashed between two stalls and were lost to view. "Nothing lasts. This is all there is." He swallowed the rest of his pie and walked on.

"Why would a warrior join us?" said Hereward, bringing me back to the problem we faced. "He would be offering to die for strangers, and for what?"

I shook my head. I had been certain that this was God's plan for me; that He had brought me and the others here so that we could take warriors back to Werceworthe. And yet the more time that passed, the more futile my idea seemed and the less sure I was that it was the Lord who spoke to me and not my own wishful imaginings.

I wanted to say to Hereward that God would provide us with men, but Drosten's terse rejection was still fresh in our minds. After speaking to the Pict, we had sought out his defeated opponent. Despite the battering he had sustained, the huge man had been sitting up and drinking ale when we'd found him. He had cleaned some of the blood from his face, but there was still enough on him to make him look like an animal who had escaped the butcher's blade halfway through being slaughtered.

Hereward had bought him a cup of ale and praised him on his fighting, his strength and his bravery. The bald man had seemed accustomed to such sentiments being expressed after a bout and he only really appeared to listen when the Northumbrian warrior explained our offer.

The giant listened patiently, then guffawed with laughter, showing off his blood-stained teeth. I noticed that two of his front teeth were missing, whether lost in the most recent fight or from a previous brawl, I could not tell.

When he had his laughter under control, he said, "I do not make a lot of silver in these fights, but I make enough to get by. And when I lose, I get to pick myself up and have a drink, like now." He raised his cup to his swollen lips and took a long draught to illustrate his point. "I will fight again later, or tomorrow. If this had been with blades, I would be feeding the crows now. So no. I am a fighter with these," he held up his massive, gnarled and scabbed fists, "not with an axe or a sword. May God grant you victory over these Norsemen you speak of, but I will not be joining you."

I don't know what I had expected, but I hadn't thought we would be dismissed so quickly by the warriors we were drawn to.

Leofstan placed a hand on my shoulder.

"God spoke to you, didn't He?" he asked.

"I thought so," I replied. I had been so certain, but Hereward was right, this was folly.

"Then have faith," said Leofstan. "Put your trust in Christ."

I frowned. I was not sure that faith would be enough. Who was I to think that God would work through me? But before I could reply, a loud shout drew my attention.

A man was bellowing in anger, or perhaps pain. We all heard it and Runolf turned in the direction of the commotion, following several others who were moving towards the sound to find out the cause. The source of the shouting soon became apparent.

A burly man with a full beard and ruddy, sweaty cheeks stood before a younger, slender man. The slim man was unmoving, despite the tirade of abuse and invective that the bearded man was spouting at him. The older man leaned in close so that his spittle flecked the other's face. The slim man blinked.

"You did not win, I say!" screamed the stocky, bearded man, swaying slightly with the force of his anger and with just enough drunkenness to make him brave and foolish.

"Come on, Rilberht," called an onlooker. "Leave it now. Let's go and get another ale. It is too hot to be standing here arguing over a couple of peningas."

The angry man spun around and almost lost his balance.

"You go then," he slurred. "I will beat this Welsh bastard first."

"He was better than you," said the man in the crowd. "We all saw it. Come now, you lost, but we'll still buy you that drink." Several other men nodded, clearly wishing to dampen the flames of the man's ire.

"Maybe we can come back later," said one, with a placatory smile. "You can try again then."

"No!" bellowed Rilberht. "I will show him," he jabbed a finger towards the slim man, who calmly took a step back, "and you all!"

For the first time, the thin man spoke. His voice was cool and clear, but with the musical lilt of the inhabitants of the western kingdoms, from Powys or Gwynedd; the men known as the Welsh.

"I have beaten you once. I can do so again, if that will make you accept defeat."

"Defeat, is it?" spluttered Rilberht. "You did not defeat me before and you will not do so now."

The Welshman shook his head and sighed.

"If I win this time, you will pay me the two peningas we agreed?"

"I will not have to pay you anything because I will win."

One of the drunk man's friends called out, "We'll see he pays you what he owes."

"I'll show you," said the drunk. "I'll show all of you." His eyes narrowed. "But I do not trust your thrower. You are in league with him."

"The man who threw the wood was not known to me," replied the Welshman with a shake of the head. "Choose another. I care not."

The drunk scanned the crowd until his gaze settled on me.

"You," he said. "Monk, come here. A monk won't cheat." I thought of Leofstan's words. Was this God's plan? I should have faith in Him. I turned to the older monk and he shrugged.

"Be careful," he whispered.

"What is it you would have me do?" I asked, stepping forward.

The Welshman picked up a round slice of timber, a cross section of elm, by the look of it. He handed it to me and I noted that it was scored and pitted, as if gouged by knives or a butcher's cleaver.

190

"Stand there," he said, pointing to a spot a few paces away. "When we are ready, toss it up and away from you as high as you are able." He picked up another slab of wood and mimed swinging it underarm. "Understand?" I nodded.

"And what will you be doing?" I asked, suddenly nervous for my own safety. "Throwing knives?"

"Not knives," he replied, with a thin smile. "These."

He turned and scooped up two short handled axes. The heads were sharp and shone in the sun.

"The same as before," said the Welshman, addressing the crowd as much as the surly man who had been shouting at him and who had picked me out of the audience. "We will each have two axes to throw. The most axes that stick win. If there is a draw, we will repeat until there is a winner."

"Throw it high and be careful of his axes," the Welshman whispered to me. He nodded for me to go to the place he had indicated. The crowd grew quiet and people moved away from where the axes would land if they missed. I could feel everybody watching me and I wished I had not stepped forward and accepted the timber target.

The Welshman held out his axes to his opponent. The angry man snatched them from him.

"Get on with it," he shouted at me. "I would be done with this."

I looked back, weighing the piece of wood in my hand. It was not heavy, but the scabs on my bandaged fingers stung, so I changed to my left hand.

"Ready?" I called out.

"Throw it," growled the man.

I looked up at the pale blue of the sky. There was no breeze and the air was warm. A hush fell on the crowd as I started to swing the piece of wood with my arm straight. I swung it once, twice, three times and on the fourth swing, I shouted out, "Now!" and let the circle of wood soar into the sky, upwards

191

and away from me. As it left my hand, I turned to watch the burly man, mindful of the Welshman's warning. I needn't have worried. Despite obviously suffering from the effects of too much drink, the man could throw. He stepped forward and let fly both axes, one from each hand. They glinted and glittered as they spun through the air. I was amazed at the skill to even attempt such a throw, and was astounded when one axe clattered into the spinning wood. The other missed it by less than a hand's breadth.

The wood fell to the ground, along with both blades, but neither axe had bitten into the timber.

The man cursed loudly.

The Welshman said nothing, but walked slowly to retrieve the weapons. I followed him to pick up the wooden target.

"That throw was perfect," he said in a quiet voice as he stooped to pick up the axes from the grass. "Just like that again, please."

"What are you two whispering about?" shouted Rilberht.

The Welshman ignored him, returning to his side.

"Ready?" I asked when he had reached his original spot and had turned towards me. He nodded.

Again I swung my arm, building up momentum and letting fly with a shout of "Now!" on the fourth swing.

If I had been impressed with the drunk man's throws, the Welshman's skill was almost beyond belief. The axes flicked from his hands with a flash of reflected sunlight. They spun through the warm air and both of them hit the disc of wood blade-first. The timber flipped over from the impact and dropped to the grass. As it hit the earth, one of the axes was dislodged, leaving one sticking out of the scored flat side of the target and the other lying atop it.

The crowd gasped at the skill and then erupted in applause and shouts of praise.

Marvelling at what I had witnessed, I walked slowly back

to where Hereward, Runolf and Leofstan watched. As I passed Rilberht, he grabbed at my habit. I pulled away, and felt a spark of the rage that had filled me on Lindisfarnae.

"Do not touch me," I hissed.

The Welshman stepped forward in my defence, placing a hand on the sweaty man's arm.

"I do not know this monk," he said in his musical voice. "Leave him be."

Rilberht, seeming to forget about me, spun about to face his adversary. He staggered briefly before regaining his balance and snarled, "You would say that, wouldn't you? You are all in this together. You are a cheat and a braggart."

The crowd had grown hushed now, watching the confrontation. This was an entertainment in its own right.

"Be careful of your tongue," said the Welshman quietly. He was still calm, but a sudden chill had entered his voice, as if we had stepped out of the sunshine and into shade. "You are drunk, so I will ignore your insults, but I am running out of patience." He fixed Rilberht in an unflinching gaze. "Now, pay me what you owe and begone."

"I will pay you nothing!" spluttered Rilberht.

His friends stepped forward from the mass of onlookers. One held out a small pouch from which he produced a couple of thin silver coins.

"Here," he said, offering them to the Welshman.

Another of his friends made to pull Rilberht away, but he shrugged him off and lunged, knocking the coins from the other's hand before the Welshman could take them.

"You will not have my money. You won by deception."

The Welshman shook his head.

"I won by dint of skill," he said. "Perhaps if you had not partaken of so much ale you would have bested me. You have skill." This was gracious when all he had received were insults and abuse, but rather than mollifying Rilberht, his words seemed to have the opposite effect.

"Skill, is it?" he growled. "I have more skill in one hand than any Welshman has in his whole body." He rushed forward and shoved the slim man hard in the chest, sending him backward a couple of paces. "If we had an axe each, I'd show you. I would best you in a duel."

The Welshman steadied himself.

"I do not wish to duel with you," he said.

"No," sneered Rilberht, "of course you don't. Because you know I would slay you in a fight."

"I do not wish to fight you, friend." The Welshman's tone was soft and soothing, like one talking to an angry child or a wild animal.

"You're not my friend, you Welsh cunt," roared Rilberht. "You are a cheating, lying, sheep-swiving pig!"

"Come on, Rilberht," implored one of his friends. He bent to retrieve the coins. "It's not worth it."

"I will say if it is worth it," he said. "I will fight this Welsh weasel and you'll all see who has more skill." He raged at his friends to let him go and reluctantly, they stepped back.

The crowd watched on in hushed anticipation. Where there had been the promise of seeing skilled men throwing axes into wooden targets, now there was the prospect of blood and death. Forgotten now by both men, I backed away.

The Welshman sighed. He walked over to where the target and axes lay on the grass. Without taking his eyes off of Rilberht, he bent and picked up the axes. As if to taunt the drunk, the wooden target came up with one of the weapons and it took some effort to pry the blade free. The Welshman let the wooden disc fall back and walked towards Rilberht.

"My name is Gwawrddur ap Mynyddog," he said, his voice now as cold and sharp as the axes in his hands. "I will let no man speak to me as you have. I have given you chance enough to walk away, but it seems you are determined to fight."

Gwawrddur turned to the onlookers.

"Do you bear witness that I have not sought this? That this man is provoking me to fight?"

A rumble of agreement from the crowd.

"I do not wish to be hauled before the reeve for murder when I kill him," Gwawrddur said to Rilberht's friends. They shook their heads, holding up their hands.

"It is a duel of his making," one said.

"Stop your talking," slurred Rilberht. "Give me one of those axes and it will be you who dies."

Gwawrddur smiled sadly and tossed one of the weapons to Rilberht, haft-first. Rilberht fumbled the catch and dropped the weapon. Someone in the crowd sniggered and Rilberht glared in the direction of the sound. Snatching up the weapon, he stood, legs apart, and faced Gwawrddur.

The Welshman walked back to where I had stood when throwing the targets. Rilberht swivelled to follow him, turning his back to us. The crowd shuffled backwards, suddenly fearful of an errant blade hurtling towards them. I too followed their example and stepped to one side.

"We have nothing to worry about," muttered Hereward. "That Welsh bastard is not going to miss. I'd place silver on it."

But there was no time for wagers now. The two men stared at each other, Rilberht swaying slightly, holding his axe in his right hand by his side. Gwawrddur also held his axe at his right side, but I noted that he held it with the blade pointed forward.

Sounds of music and laughter drifted from other parts of the festival where people were celebrating in the warm summer's day. But here, in this cleared piece of grass, there was no cheer, only imminent violence. Nobody spoke as the two men faced each other.

For a long time, it seemed that neither would move. And then, with a speed that belied his drunkenness, Rilberht stepped forward, lifted his axe above his head and threw it unerringly towards Gwawrddur. In the same instant, the Welshman seemed to flinch, stepping forward and letting fly his own axe while also raising his left hand. I could not make sense of what I had seen at first, but then Rilberht grunted, falling to his knees. With a shudder, he slumped onto his back, his legs bent awkwardly beneath him. Gwawrddur's axe was buried deep in his face, blade sunk between his bushy eyebrows, the haft sticking upward.

And then I understood. The Welshman had thrown underarm, giving him the edge when it came to speed.

My gaze shifted to where Gwawrddur stood some distance away. As I watched, he rose up to stand straight and lowered his left hand. The hot sun glittered off the axe he held there. He had caught Rilberht's axe!

The crowd did not seem to know how to react to what it had seen. There was no cheer of excitement and no applause. It was something to watch a man beaten in a fight, it was something quite different to see a man's life taken from him in an eye-blink.

Rilberht's friends stumbled forward and dropped beside the dead man. I noticed that his hands were twitching as though searching for something in the grass, but there could surely be no way that he could survive such an injury.

Gwawrddur walked over and pulled his axe unceremoniously from Rilberht's skull. He needed to tug a couple of times to free it from the grip of bone and flesh. Blood pumped slowly from the gash, pooling in Rilberht's staring eyes.

One of his friends, the one who had offered the peningas surged to his feet.

"You didn't need to kill him, you Welsh bastard," he yelled. His face was red and his eyes filled with tears.

"Take him away," Gwawrddur said. "He only found what he was looking for."

The other men pulled back their weeping friend and together they lifted Rilberht and carried his corpse away.

Gwawrddur watched them leave. Then he bent and picked up something from the ground. He blew on the two coins and secreted them in a small leather pouch he wore on his belt. He shook his head and then walked quickly to retrieve his wooden targets.

We followed him.

Sensing our approach, he spun about, an axe in each hand.

"Easy, friend," said Hereward. "We mean you no harm."

Gwawrddur narrowed his eyes, looking beyond us, scanning the thinning crowd.

"What do you want?" he asked.

"Men who know how to fight."

Gwawrddur turned his gaze to Hereward, sizing him up.

"Who are you fighting?"

Hereward drew in a deep breath. I could sense he was concerned about how his offer would be received.

"Norsemen," he said. "They've attacked once. At Lindisfar-nae." He seemed intent on getting the words out as quickly as possible and rushed on, perhaps not wanting to give the Welsh-man a chance to stop him. "They are going to strike again," he went on. "Another minster. South of the holy island, but north of here. Werceworthe."

"Never heard of it," Gwawrddur said, placing his targets into a sack and swinging it over his shoulder. "What is at Werceworthe?"

"Monks." Hereward shrugged. "Lay people."

"And books," I added. "And the sacred finger of Saint Edwin."

Gwawrddur glanced at me.

"How many Norse are you expecting?" he asked, with a shake of his head as if he could not quite believe he was still engaged in this conversation.

Hereward hesitated for a heartbeat before answering.

"Three shiploads."

Gwawrddur looked at him sidelong with a raised eyebrow.

"How many warriors have you recruited to your cause?"

Hereward held out his hands.

"We are hoping for more than we currently have."

The Welshman looked at each of us in turn. His gaze lingered on Runolf. He shook his head again when he took in mine and Leofstan's habits.

"So you want me to fight against a much larger force of Norsemen to save a monastery and some ceorls?" He turned to me. "And some books and a saint's finger."

I felt my cheeks grow hot.

Hereward nodded.

"That's about the sum of it," he said.

"And what will you pay for my services in such a foolhardy endeavour?"

Hereward sighed.

"Food and shelter," he said. "We can offer no more, apart from our gratitude and that of the brethren of Werceworthe."

Gwawrddur thought for a moment, his gaze still roving over the crowd.

"Very well," he said. "I like a challenge."

Hereward laughed and clapped him on the back. I could scarcely believe it.

"And this would have nothing to do with wanting our company in case that drunken fool's friends come seeking vengeance?"

"They will drink more now," Gwawrddur said. "And drunk men are brave, especially when surrounded by their friends. Hopefully, if I travel with you, they will be less likely to summon up enough courage to attack. There needn't be more blood spilt."

Hereward nodded.

"But if you join us now, you are giving your word to come with us to the minster?"

"I give you my word," said the Welshman, "and that is not something I give lightly."

Hereward held his gaze and they grasped each other's forearms in the warrior grip.

"Come then, Gwawrddur ap Mynyddog," said Hereward, "let us leave here."

And so our number had grown by one.

"Do you believe me now that this is God's plan?" I asked Leofstan.

He made the sign of the cross and sighed.

"Who can say? A man has died here today. Was that what the Lord wants? Christ says that God is love." He bit his lip, clearly torn and unable to express how he felt.

"Do not doubt His plan," I said, thinking of Gwawrddur's uncanny speed. I remembered Leofstan's words to me only a short while before. "You see what happens when we have faith?"

He shuddered and walked away.

Walking past the trampled earth where Rilberht had fallen, I saw that blood had stained the grass.

A large hand on my shoulder made me start. I turned and looked up into the bearded face of Runolf.

"You see?" he said, pointing with his chin at the blood-soaked earth. "Savour every moment. There is nothing to be gained from worrying about tomorrow."

Twenty-Three

We returned to the hall shortly after midday. It seemed unlikely we would find any more men to join our small band and Gwawrddur wished to leave before Rilberht's friends drank so much ale that their bravery would be bolstered enough for them to confront him. As we walked away from the tents and flags, the cacophony of noises and the wafting scents of food, I watched the slender Welshman. He walked with the grace of a dancer, seemingly without haste. The only thing that spoke of his disquiet were his eyes. He never stopped scanning the crowds for threats.

"Well," said Hereward, "at least we have one more fighting man to aid us, even if he is Welsh." This last comment he said in a hushed tone. He smirked at me, but I did not return his smile.

He frowned.

"I thought you would be pleased. It is no easy thing to find one with such skill who has no lord and is happy to offer his services for nothing."

"Skill is not everything," I said.

He looked at me askance.

"Skill will make the difference between life and death," he said. "If the Norsemen return, we will not only need men to carry spears, but skilled warriors to train them. And in a battle, a true warrior is worth a dozen untrained peasants with sticks."

Hereward was silent, and I wondered if he was picturing the fight that would come. After a moment, he whistled softly.

"I do not believe I have ever seen a faster man than Gwawrddur," he said. "And those throws! Now that is skill that might truly help win a battle."

"But for that, there needs to be a battle," I said. A slow anger twisted in my gut and I was filled with resentment. I had not truly admitted it to myself, but I had expected us to attract men easily to our cause.

"No man should ever want there to be a battle, Hunlaf," Hereward said, his eyes narrowing at my pained expression. "If God smiles on us, there will be no fighting and everyone will live."

We walked on for a way. My habit had dried, but the summer warmth did not lift my mood. Could it be possible that the Norsemen might not return to the coast? What if they sailed by? Perhaps it would be as Hereward said and there would be no fighting. Surely that would be the best outcome of all. But I could not dispel my sense of disappointment at the prospect. It was madness, I knew, but part of me longed for the return of the sea wolves in their dragon ships. Was it revenge I sought? Perhaps. Or did I simply wish to feel that swelling rage and freedom that had engulfed me on Lindisfarnae?

What a fool I was. But I was young and death seemed like a distant thing, something that would surely never happen to me.

"Is that what we seek then?" I asked. "That there might be no battle?"

Hereward rubbed his chin.

"I believe it is what a good lord or king seeks," he said at last. "We all know there are times that war cannot be avoided, but surely peace is better than fighting." He glanced at Gwawrddur.

"Better to turn away from a fight if you can do so without putting your own at risk or losing face."

"But is that not the mark of a craven?" I asked, lowering my voice. I had seen what had happened to the last man who had insulted Gwawrddur. "Was it not cowardly to run away from Rilberht's friends?"

Hereward stared at me, frowning in consternation.

I held up my hands and said, "I understand that it would have been foolish to stand and fight against them. He is but one man and they were many. But I would have expected a true warrior to fight. If he cannot fight a group of drunks, how will he fare against Norsemen?"

Hereward let out a barking laugh.

"You have twisted things around in your mind, young Hunlaf," he said, still chuckling. "You have seen things with the eyes of a monk and not of a warrior."

I bridled at his tone. Of course he was right, but even then, I already longed for him and the other fighting men to think of me as one of them.

"I saw things clearly enough," I replied.

"Did you not see how quick Gwawrddur is? How he was able to slay Rilberht from a distance of several paces with barely a movement, and snatch his enemy's axe out of the air while doing so?"

"I have eyes," I said, unable to hide my anger.

Hereward smiled.

"Yes, but you must learn to use them better. Gwawrddur was not frightened that Rilberht's friends would kill him. He was worried that they would become emboldened enough with drink to attack him. And then he would be forced to kill more of them."

I watched Gwawrddur's lithe movements. As well as the two axes that he had used to such devastating effect, a long-bladed sword hung from a baldric he had slung over his

shoulder. Was Hereward right? Had the Welshman sought
to avoid killing men whose actions did not truly warrant
death? Did any man deserve death? I thought of the grim-
faced killers who had slain my brothers and sisters in Christ
on Lindisfarnae. Did those savage Norsemen deserve death
in revenge for what they had done? I could not shake from
my mind the feeling of carrying the heavy seax in my hand
and the elation that had filled me as I'd taken the life of the
raider. Part of me, a dark secret part, hoped that I would have
the chance to face the Norsemen again and, when I did, that
I would be able to make them pay for what they had done.
Perhaps all of this was not God speaking to me after all,
but the work of the Devil. I shuddered and spoke no more,
brooding on the events of the morning and wondering at the
change within me.

We passed through the bustling streets, leaving the buzz of
the festival behind us. The smells of meat and oatcakes cooking
were replaced by the acrid stench of nightsoil that had been
tossed into the gaps between buildings. We were careful to
watch our step. As we approached the entrance to the grounds
of the king's enclosure, the sound of running footsteps made us
turn. Gwawrddur spun around and I noted both his axes had
somehow found themselves in his hands. My heart hammered
and I could hear the rushing of my blood. If those friends of
Rilberht had come for vengeance, they would regret it. Would
Gwawrddur need to use his sword or would the axes suffice
to kill his enemies, I wondered? Would Hereward and Runolf
help the Welshman, if it came to a fight?

What would I do? I suddenly wished I was not wearing the
woollen habit. I clenched my bandaged hand and longed for a
weapon to hold. I could not bear the thought of standing by
defenceless while others fought.

But there was no fight. The figure sprinting towards us was
alone and did not appear intent on mischief. The man splashed

through a filthy puddle, past the shadow of a large house and then into the bright sunshine beyond. He was only some twenty paces from us when I saw the flash of blue tattoos on his face.

Drosten, the Pictish brawler.

His chest was now covered in a plain kirtle and on his feet he wore simple leather shoes. A sack was slung over one shoulder. From his belt hung a large knife and in his left hand he carried a stout spear. He showed no sign of slowing and Gwawrddur tensed.

"Easy, Welshman," said Hereward. "We know this man. I do not think he means us harm."

Gwawrddur appeared to relax, but his axes still hung in his hands loosely by his sides, ready for action.

Drosten slid to a halt before us. He appraised Gwawrddur and nodded. Gwawrddur responded with a nod of his own.

Turning his attention to Hereward, the Pict said, "You still seek men?"

"We do," replied Hereward. "My offer remains open to you."

The Pict's eyes glittered above his painted cheeks.

"I will come with you," Drosten said.

"Indeed?" said Hereward. "Why the change of heart?"

Drosten's face clouded.

"The men I was with. They took my money."

Hereward's hand fell to his pouch, checking that his coins were safe.

"The ones helping to tend your wounds?"

Drosten nodded and spat into the mud of the street.

"We saw you fight," said Hereward, "and we saw those two. I do not think they'd pose you much of a problem, if you want your money back."

Drosten sighed. It sounded more like a growl.

"Not just my money. They took it all. All the wagers too. And they have spread the lie that it was I who stole it. There are many men here who have placed bets. Some powerful men. I cannot fight them all."

"And you did not take the money?"

Drosten squared his shoulders.

"I am no thief," he said. His eyes blazed with barely contained fury.

"Then why not tell the truth to the men who have lost bets?"

The Pict scowled.

"I can settle disputes with my fists or a blade, but look at me." He raised his tattooed face defiantly. "My word will not be believed when pitted against a Northumbrian's."

Hereward stared at him for a time, clearly considering Drosten's story.

"Well, this Northumbrian believes you," he said at last. "You are welcome to join us. But if you do, the terms are as I said before."

"Food and shelter in exchange for my spear and knife and my fists?"

"Yes. And nothing more. If the Norsemen come, it will be dangerous."

"Life is dangerous," said Drosten. "I am done with Eoforwic. I like the idea of travelling northward once more."

"If you come with us now, you will come to Werceworthe. I have your word?"

"You have my word."

Hereward squinted at him.

"But can I trust the word of a heathen?"

Drosten stepped back and slammed the haft of his spear into the ground.

"I am no heathen," he said. His cheeks were flushed beneath the swirling lines of his tattoos. "I worship Jesu Christ. My people have followed the teachings of Christ since before the Englisc ever did. It was the great Saint Colm Cille who brought

the true faith to the Pictish lands and we have praised the Lord
ever since."

"So you are a good Christian then?" enquired Hereward.

"Yes," Drosten replied, angry at the question, "like my father
and my father's father."

"Good," replied Hereward with a grin, "for the Abbot of
Werceworthe said we could only return with good Christian
men."

He winked at me and I swallowed, thinking about my dark
desires for more bloodshed. Perhaps I was the one who the
abbot should be concerned about.

Twenty-Four

That evening there was another feast in the king's hall, but once again, we were not invited. Resting in the small hall during the day had improved Uhtric's mood somewhat, and he had been grudgingly impressed with the two men we had recruited.

"Hardly a warhost," he said, "but better than I had expected."

"Thank you for your confidence in me," Hereward replied, with a twisted smile. "Remember, lord, that you ride on the morrow."

Uhtric had glowered at him as he prepared to head for the great hall. A heartbeat later his expression softened and he shrugged.

"You are right," he said. "I should be cautious with the king's hospitality tonight. I cannot imagine riding if my head feels like it did today. You will head back to Werceworthe tomorrow too?"

"Perhaps," Hereward said. "We might look for more men to join us first. We'll have a warband soon enough."

Uhtric nodded and left the hall to us. Servants had already brought us a barrel of ale. They had assured us that food would follow.

Runolf asked me what Uhtric and Hereward had been speaking of. He sipped his ale and I noted that he was drinking more sparingly than I had seen on earlier occasions. I translated the conversation and Runolf stroked his beard absently, lost in thought. Picking up his cup of ale, he refilled it from the barrel and then stepped outside. After a moment's hesitation, I followed him.

The sun was setting and the sky was tinged with the hue of hot iron. Runolf was staring up at the dusting of clouds on the horizon. The pale orb of the moon hung in the sky above us, somehow unnerving in the bright sky.

Neither of us spoke for a long time. My mind turned inward, prodding and probing my thoughts the way someone will scratch at a scab until it bleeds. When we had returned to the hall I had sat by myself and prayed for guidance, but no matter how much I prayed to the Lord, my mind was no less clouded. I fretted over my motivations. I had said this was the will of God, and perhaps I believed that myself. But had I not pushed for this outcome? Was I driven to do so by the Holy Ghost or was there some other dark force propelling me to seek out violence and blood? Was I still a monk worthy of the brethren to whom I belonged?

And then, the most frightening thought of all; so shocking that I barely dared to contemplate it. But like a distant whisper in darkness, I could still hear the question hissing in my mind. Did I truly still wish to be one of that brethren?

Leofstan had sensed my unease and asked if he could pray with me. I'd welcomed his support and we had gone through Vespers together, taking comfort in the familiarity, despite the strangeness of our situation. But despite the sense of wellbeing at the repetitive liturgy that I knew so well, my soul remained restless.

Runolf still gazed up into the heavens and I felt a stab of guilt. I was not the only one to have been through upheavals. This huge man was surrounded by strangers, abandoned by his erstwhile friends. He had nearly been hanged and now he had taken a solemn oath to serve a lord whom he did not know and who surely despised him. And beyond all of that, he had accepted Christ as his saviour when he had been baptised that morning.

"It has been a day of much excitement," I said. "Many changes."

He grunted.

"Are you well?" I asked.

"The ale is good," he replied absently. "But I am hungry."

A gust of wind whispered through the lindens that grew on the southern side of the royal vill Runolf turned to stare at the swaying trees. He seemed lost in thought.

"Do you wish to talk?" I said.

"Hmmm?" he looked confused and gazed down at me.

"We are talking," he said.

I tried again.

"I mean, do you wish to unburden your..." I could not think of the Norse for "soul", and so, I tapped my chest and said, "Your inside."

Runolf raised his eyebrows.

"I had a shit just now," he said.

"No, no!" I held up my hands. "You do not understand me."

He smiled.

"That is true. You are a strange one. Are you ill?"

"No, I am not unwell," I said. "But I am worried."

"So am I," Runolf replied. I was pleased that my words had reached him.

"Would you like to pray with me?" I asked, hopeful now that he had opened to me about his uncertainty.

He furrowed his brow.

"Pray?"

"To speak to God," I said.

"Why would I want to do that?"

"To ask for His guidance."

He shook his head.

"No. I do not much like speaking to most men, and at least I can see their faces when I do. The gods do not listen to the likes of me. You, perhaps." He raised his cup in mock salute and took a sip. "You are a holy man, but not me."

"You are baptised now," I said, persevering. "The Lord will listen to you."

"But will He answer me?"

"If you listen in return," I countered, "He will."

Runolf reached up to his neck and I thought the bruising there troubled him. But to my horror, he pulled out a small amulet in the shape of a hammer.

"It is Þórr I need to listen to me now," he said.

I made the sign of the cross.

"Do not say such things," I said. "You are a Christian now."

"But if we are to have time to ready ourselves, we need Þórr to send a storm. To smite the sky with Mjǫllnir," he lifted the amulet up, shaking it to emphasise his words. "To ride across the heavens in his great chariot."

As if in answer to Runolf's words, the lindens shook and rattled in a stiffening breeze. I shivered.

"The one true God controls all things," I said. "He commands the wind and the storms." Runolf seemed unconvinced. I was about to continue, explaining how God is all powerful, how every earthly thing bows to his word, but instead, I hesitated. Something Runolf had said snagged at my mind.

"What worries you?" I asked. "And why do you want there to be a storm?"

He looked up at the reddening sky again.

"The weather has been fine these past days," he said.

I said nothing, unsure where he was leading the conversation. Sighing at my clear lack of comprehension, he continued.

"Good sailing weather."

At last I grasped his meaning.

"You mean…"

"Yes," he nodded. "Jarl Skorri will have reached home by now. He will be feasting and boasting, much as Uhtric and your king." He pointed with the hand holding the cup of ale at the great hall. Its timbers were picked out in the golden light of sunset, its shadows stark and crisp. The sounds of merriment within reached us clearly on the warm breeze.

"Your king too now," I corrected.

Runolf snorted.

"Yes, my king." He shrugged. "Soon Skorri will have had his fill of mead and slave girls and he will get to thinking about all of the riches he has taken from your island minster. And he will look at the sky and see that the weather is ripe for sailing."

"You think he will return before the harvest?"

"Who can say? Perhaps you can ask your God?"

"Your God," I murmured and he chuckled.

"But I think he will surely plan another raid before the autumn storms. I can think of nothing that would keep him on land apart from seas that are too rough for the crossing. This is why we need to ask Þórr for his help."

"Þórr is not your god any longer," I replied, my tone made harsh by fear. And, if I am honest, with a tinge of excitement.

"He would not listen anyway," he said. "Not without a blood sacrifice."

I shuddered, and again made the sign of the rood over my chest. I looked up at him for a signal that he spoke in jest in an attempt to unnerve me. His bearded face was ruddy and hard in the warm light of the sunset. There was no hint of a smile on his lips.

"Will my new god answer us if we ask for a storm?" Runolf asked.

I thought of all the times I had petitioned the lord with prayer. How many times had He responded?

"I do not know," I replied, my voice small next to Runolf's booming echoing tone. "He might."

"Perhaps you ask Him then," he said. "But I think we should not tarry here any longer."

"But we need more men," I said. "We cannot hope to defeat three shiploads of Norsemen as we are."

He stared down at me with a grin.

"You speak of 'we' as if you plan to fight."

"Perhaps I do," I said.

"That is good," he said and turned away from me so that I could not see his face. "A man should defend his land. And his family."

"But we will not be able to defend the minster with the men we have."

"We have two more men now," Runolf said. "And there is no need to protect corpses. If we are not there when Skorri comes, all of this will be for nothing."

I reached a trembling hand out for the wooden cup. Runolf handed it to me.

"We can build defences and train the men of Werceworthe to fight," he said. "We can train you, eh?"

He slapped me on the back. A sudden peal of laughter from the great hall made me start and for an instant it was as if I was back on Lindisfarnae, surrounded by death, fire and blood. How could I wish to witness such a thing again? What madness was this? But I could not ignore the excitement that rippled through me. I drained the contents of the cup and grimaced at the bitter taste of the ale.

Two servants were crossing the ground from the great hall, bearing large platters. One plate was filled with what looked like steaming whole roach, the fishes' silver scales glistening like treasure. The other tray was piled high with fresh bread.

"Ah," said Runolf with a broad grin. "Perhaps our God listens after all, Hunlaf. For I have been praying for food for a long time."

He laughed and followed the servants into the hall where the rest of the men let out a cheer at the sight of provender.

Twenty-Five

That night I explained Runolf's concerns to Hereward, and, after some thought and deliberation, the Northumbrian warrior was in agreement. So, as the morning dawned still and dry once more, we set off through the streets of Eoforwic to retrace our steps northward.

"It is just as well we decided to leave now," grumbled Hereward, as we walked past the open ground near the church that was yet cluttered with tents. "It will take close to a sennight to reach Werceworthe." He leaned from his saddle and spat into the tangle of nettles that grew on the verge of the path.

He had gone to Uhtric that morning with a request for mounts, or the silver to buy them. Uhtric denied him both animals and coin. We had the steeds we rode south on, but Drosten and Gwawrddur would have to walk. All Hereward had returned with was Runolf's great axe. He'd handed it to the Norseman with a warning not to make him regret returning it to him. Runolf nodded and grunted, and a grin played on his features as he held the axe once more in his massive hands.

The festival was still ongoing and there would yet be much debauchery, gambling and games of chance in the coming days. Both Drosten and Gwawrddur were ever vigilant as we travelled through the streets that were mired with the waste and detritus of the city dwellers and the numerous people who had flocked to Eoforwic to celebrate the festival of Saint Peter.

The tense watchfulness of the two newcomers to our small band made us nervous. As we progressed towards the gate, I expected an angry mob to descend upon us at every turn. When a goodwife screeched at someone out of sight, we all tensed. I clenched my hands and again wished for a weapon and the knowledge and skill to use one. To my surprise, and to the evident relief of the others, we reached the city gate without incident.

The day was warming already and people were beginning to congregate around the entrance to the city, but the door wards waved us through. Beyond the confines of the walls the early morning sun gleamed from the waters of the Fossa and Usa. I had thought about walking with Gwawrddur and Drosten, but in the end I had decided to ride. If I truly wished to bear a blade and to be thought of as a warrior, I must learn to ride naturally, as if it were my right. Before leaving, I had covered my thighs and arse in the greasy unguent Grimcytel had given me. The thought of the suffering I had endured on the journey south filled me with more dread than the coming of the Norsemen.

I shifted in the saddle, in an effort to get comfortable. Further northward, hills rose and beech and oak skirted the road. The day would be hot and we would be glad of the shade of the woodland by the time we reached the wooded slopes.

It was midday when we finally entered the shadows beneath the towering trees. All of us were hot and tired and I almost moaned with pleasure when Hereward called a halt beside a small stream that burbled near the road. I dismounted and was pleased to find that the greasy concoction had worked, or perhaps I was now an accomplished rider. Whatever the reason, my nether parts no longer smarted and ached as they had only a week or so previously. I watched as Drosten and Gwawrddur caught up with us. Neither man complained at having to walk, but I felt a pang of guilt that I had not offered my mount to either of them. Turning to retrieve bread and ham from my saddle bags, I frowned at my own weakness. What sort of warrior would I be, if I could not even ride a horse without feeling remorse while others walked?

I nibbled at the food and approached Gwawrddur. He looked up from where he sat on a moss-covered rock.

"Yes, monk?" he said.

"Hunlaf," I said, and squared my shoulders. Gwawrddur waited patiently for me to say something else. I could sense the others looking at me and my face felt flushed as the Welshman said nothing. "Would you teach me?" I blurted out.

"Teach you what?" he asked.

"How to fight," I said.

He sighed.

"I cannot teach you that," he said.

My shoulders sagged and I felt my cheeks redden with embarrassment. Everybody was watching the exchange. I turned to leave, feeling deflated and foolish.

"It is impossible to teach any man how to fight," he said. "But I can teach you how to use a blade. The skill to parry and attack can be taught to any with the use of their limbs and a head on their shoulders. I see you have your arms and legs. Do you have any sense in there?" He tapped his forehead.

"Yes. I am no fool," I said, feeling more foolish than ever before beneath his calculating gaze.

He stared at me for a few heartbeats before turning to Leofstan who sat scowling in our direction.

"What say you, Brother Leofstan?" Gwawrddur asked. "Is Hunlaf here a fool?"

For a moment Leofstan said nothing.

"He may be," he said at last. Gwawrddur and everyone else laughed. A sudden anger borne of shame boiled within me. Sensing my ire at his reply, Leofstan smiled. "But no more a fool than any other young man," he said with a shake of his tonsured head. "He is strong and clever, and keen to learn. He will be a good student to you, as he always has been to me." I now felt a rush of warm affection and fresh shame at my doubt of the older monk. He was troubled by the change in me, I knew. He must have been dismayed at my desire to learn the ways of the warrior, but to his credit, he did not confront me or seek to alter my course. He did what he always advised me to do and placed his faith in God.

"Very well," said Gwawrddur, appraising me. "You look strong enough. Lean, like me, but there are more ways to best an opponent than with brutish force. Those of us who are not born with a body the size of a bear," he looked pointedly at Runolf, "must learn to be fast and skilful. When we camp tonight I will give you your first lesson. Only time will tell if you can fight and kill."

"I have already killed," I said, wishing to prove myself worthy in the Welshman's grey eyes.

Gwawrddur raised his eyebrows.

"Well then," he said with a sardonic smirk, "I will be careful."

When we prepared to continue our journey I offered Gwawrddur my horse. He smiled, but declined.

"You will need all your strength later," he said. "You ride."

So I clambered up into the saddle and we headed northward once more as we had in the morning, with Gwawrddur and Drosten following on foot.

The afternoon passed slowly and without excitement. I wanted to ride back to where Gwawrddur walked, but I sensed that to do so would make me look foolish, too eager, like a child who wished to play at being a warrior. Was that how I looked to these hard men? Probably. I was not much more than a boy, and a monk no less. They must think me ridiculous.

"So, you want the thin one to teach you to fight," said Runolf, who had moved his mount close to mine. "I am not good enough?" He spoke in Norse, but he understood more Englisc daily and conversed haltingly with the others directly now, only turning to me for help when he could not comprehend a particular phrase or when he failed to make himself understood.

"He says he cannot teach a man to fight, only how to wield weapons," I replied.

Runolf grunted.

"He is right," he said. "A man cannot make a fighter of someone. That is something that comes from within." We rode on in silence for a time, the only sound the thud of the horses' hooves on the cracked stones of the road. "Gwawrddur is skilled," he said at last. "He will train you well, I think. But I have seen you fight, Hunlaf. I alone of all these men have seen the warrior inside you. When you are done with Gwawrddur's lessons, come to me and I will show you the Norse ways of killing."

He patted the huge axe that was strapped to his saddle and grinned.

The long summer day dragged on. It was hot, with little shade after we passed out of the woodland. I could feel my tonsured head burning red in the sun and wished for a hat. I willed Hereward to call a halt for the evening camp, but he wanted to cover as much distance as possible and so we trudged on until the sun was dipping low in the sky to the west.

Finally, Hereward pointed to a copse of aspens, shimmering in the breeze on a rise overlooking the road.

"We will camp there tonight," he said.

I cantered my horse up the slope and dismounted quickly. I was pleased to note that, although my limbs were stiff from the riding, I was not in pain. Unbuckling the horse's girth, I heaved the saddle from the beast and set it beside the bole of a tree. Then I pulled up a great handful of long grass and proceeded to rub the sweat and grime from the animal's back and flanks. It had been a long day, but I was full of nervous energy. Gwawrddur was still in the distance and I wanted the camp to be ready when he arrived. I clenched and unclenched my bandaged hand. It did not really hurt now and I would be able to hold a weapon well enough.

Hereward, Leofstan and Runolf arrived at the stand of trees, having approached at a more leisurely pace.

"If you are so eager to work," said Hereward, sliding down from the saddle, "you can tend to all the horses." He tossed me his reins. "I'll get a fire lit."

I thought about complaining, but that would only waste time, so I went about unsaddling the horses, currying them, and then leading them down the other side of the hill to where a small brook flowed. There was not much water in the stream, but enough trickled down from the hills to the north-west, that in places the burn opened out into small pools. I tethered the mounts to a stunted bush and then dipped our leather skins into the murky water, holding the hem of my habit over the mouth of each vessel to keep out insects and other items that might be floating in the pond. Once the last flask was full, I let the horses drink.

I made my way back up towards the aspens. The trees were brightly lit by the setting sun, their leaves glimmering like jewels. The comforting smell of woodsmoke welcomed me. I threw down the water skins and secured the horses. There was ample fodder on the hill for them to forage and they dropped their muzzles and began to contentedly rip up and chew the grass, clover and fīcwyrt that grew there.

Hereward was feeding twigs to the first flames of the fire. It would be some time yet before it burnt hot enough for him to be able to cook the mutton he had brought from Æthelred's hall. He would wait for glowing embers before placing the meat on a spit, to avoid charring it.

Gwawrddur was lounging near the saddles, his back to a tree, gazing down at the road, the way we had come. The low sun picked out every fold and ripple in the land, striping it with shadows. Beside the road grew several ash trees. Their canopy was dense and it was already dark beneath their branches.

"You wish to begin your training," he said without looking at me. It was not a question.

"Yes," I said. Beside him lay his two axes and he had unbuckled his sword belt, leaning the blade up against the trunk of an aspen. I wondered which of his weapons we would train with first. I assumed it would be the axes, but I longed to hold the finely crafted sword. That was the weapon of a true warrior.

Without warning he sprang to his feet, making me start and take a step backward.

"Very well, Killer," he said, "we will begin."

I said nothing, ignoring the name he had given me and awaiting his instruction. Leofstan had taught me how to be a good student, but I remembered the many times he had rebuked me for interrupting when he was teaching me about the Scriptures. I vowed I would not make that mistake with Gwawrddur. He did not look like the sort of man to forgive as readily as Leofstan.

Turning, he picked up his sword. I moved closer, expecting him to hand it to me, but instead, he slung the belt over his shoulder.

"The first weapons any warrior has are his speed and his resilience. So you can stop eyeing up my sword. You will not be touching that today." I could not hide my disappointment and he chuckled at my frown. "The time for swords will come soon enough, but before that, you must prove yourself to be fast."

"And how do I do that?" I asked, cringing inwardly at how petulant my voice sounded.

"You see that stand of trees there?" Gwawrddur pointed to the copse of ash near the road.

I nodded.

"Beat me to them," he said, and without a pause, he sprinted off down the hill. His sword slapped against his back as his legs pumped and his feet pounded the earth. He followed the track through the long grass and flowers that we had trodden and crushed as we'd come up to the campsite. He was easily ten years my senior, but he was quick. Watching him run, it appeared impossible to catch him, but one thing was for certain: if I stood there I would never prove my speed and fitness to him and would never move on to learn the ways of the sword. Hitching up my habit, I ran as fast as I was able after him.

"Come on, Hunlaf," bellowed Runolf. Hereward laughed and I could imagine the two of them placing wagers on who would win the contest. The thought of losing a race against a much older man spurred me on and I bounded down the slope. Gwawrddur was tall and slender and fast. But I was perhaps a hand's breadth taller and I had youth on my side. I had always been a fast runner and now I ran as fast as I ever had before. Throwing aside all caution I almost flew down the incline. One misstep now, placing my foot in a depression hidden beneath the lush covering of grass and wild flowers perhaps, and I would tumble over. I might even break my ankle, if I was unlucky. But I was gaining on him and I told myself that a warrior does not fret about such things. I wished I was wearing breeches instead of my habit. The hem of the robe whipped and caught against my legs and snagged on thistles as I passed. And yet, despite this, I was still creeping closer to Gwawrddur.

As the ground flattened out, I roared and pushed myself to even greater speed. For a few paces I was running cheek by jowl with Gwawrddur. Then, I was past him and into the gloom beneath the ash trees an eye-blink before the Welshman.

I had done it! I'd beaten Gwawrddur and now he would have to show me the secrets of the sword. Shouting out a gleeful exclamation at my victory, I leaned against the rough bark of a tree. Bending over, I drew in great lungfuls of heavy, loamy air.

Gwawrddur crashed into the undergrowth and I waited for him to regain his breath enough to congratulate me on my speed. But to my surprise, he did not halt. Instead, he rushed past me and disappeared from sight.

I panted and gasped. I was almost overcome with giddiness and thought I might faint. I had pushed myself to my limits and was unable to speak for a time. My vision blurred and sweat drenched my hair and face.

I heard Gwawrddur crashing further into the small wood. What was he doing? And then a new sound shattered the peace of the late afternoon. A sound that brought me back to full focus like a slap to the face.

From the shadows beneath the trees, in the direction that Gwawrddur had run, came the unmistakable clash of blades.

Twenty-Six

Forgotten was my exhaustion of moments before. Without
hesitation I sprang forward and ran towards the sounds of
fighting. A sudden ringing of metal on metal was followed by
silence. Another clang of blades and I reached a small clearing.
The light from the setting sun filtered through the trees, lancing
into the dust thrown up from the leaf mould by the two men
fighting there.

Gwawrddur, seemingly still fresh after the long run down
the hill, was circling a shorter, stockier man. The Welshman
held his sword high. The tip of the blade glinted as it twitched,
following his opponent's movements.

The other man was dirt-smeared and dishevelled. His shaggy
dark hair looked as though it had never been cut or combed
and his tatty kirtle was so stained with dried mud it was hard
to discern what colour it had originally been. Perhaps dark
green. In his right hand, the stranger held a long sword. Its
blade was dull in the shadows, but as I watched, he swung it in
a wild arc at Gwawrddur and it gleamed like silver as it sliced
through the shafts of mote-dancing light. Gwawrddur stepped
back quickly and apparently without effort. The newcomer's
sword sliced only the warm air.

"Put up your weapon," said Gwawrddur, his voice calm. "I do not wish to kill you."

"You will not kill me this day," replied the stranger. His voice had an unfamiliar accent, somehow similar to both the lilt of the Welshman and Drosten's burr. He jumped forward, slicing down at Gwawrddur's head. The Welshman swatted the blade away easily and stepped to the left.

"If you do not put aside your sword, you will leave me with no choice. I have seen you on the road behind us all this long afternoon and I would hear who you are and why it is you follow us. But perhaps first, you could tell us your name. Mine is Gwawrddur ap Mynyddog."

The stranger hesitated, then stepped back and lowered his blade.

"I am Cormac mac Neill."

"You are a long way from home, Cormac mac Neill," said Gwawrddur.

"What do you know of my home?" snapped Cormac.

Gwawrddur lowered his own blade and rested its tip on the ground. I noticed he did not sheathe it.

"I meant nothing by my words," he said. "I thought you must be from the island of Hibernia across the sea. Am I wrong?"

Cormac shook his head.

"No, you're not wrong. But it has been many a month since I last saw the green grass of my homeland."

"And what is it that brings you to Northumbria? I do not mean you any offence, but it looks to me like you have been sleeping in ditches."

Cormac ran his left hand through his dark thatch of hair and sniffed.

"Maybe I have," he said. "I have not had much luck of late."

"Is that why you followed us?" asked Gwawrddur. "Did you mean to wait until we slept and then slit our throats and take our silver?"

The Hibernian bridled.

"I am no thief."

"Then why did you skulk after us and hide here in this copse? Such are not the habits of an honest man?"

Cormac growled and raised his sword again.

"I am no purse snatcher," he said. "I am a good Christian man."

His words, echoing those of Beonna, made me start and I stepped from where I had been watching the exchange into the dappled light of the glade.

"So, Cormac," I said, "why were you following us, if you are not intent on robbery?"

He spun around at the sound of my voice, bringing his sword to bear. I felt strangely calm.

"I am unarmed," I said, holding out both empty hands. A bead of sweat dripped from the hair at the nape of my neck and trickled down my back. I did not allow myself to shudder.

"The monk," he whispered and made the sign of the cross. "So it is true."

"What is true?" I asked.

"That a monk is seeking fighting men to defend a minster." He paused, frowning. "Against Norsemen from the sea," he concluded.

His words shocked me. Had word travelled so widely? Then I recalled that he had followed us from Eoforwic and must have heard of our search from the people we had approached in the festival.

"Yes, that is so," I said. "Are you such a fighting man? Do you wish to offer your services?"

He raised up his sword as if I might not have noticed it.

"I am a great warrior," he said. "The men of Uí Blathmaic fear me."

"I do not know of these Uí Blathmaic," I said, stumbling over the strange words. "The men we will face are savage killers. We are few. It will not be easy and all we can offer in return is food and shelter."

"That is all I ask," he replied. His face clouded. "And a Norseman bleeds as easily as any other." He slapped the flat of his sword blade. "If my sword, Moralltach here, can cut them, I can kill any enemy."

Gwawrddur shook his head and sheathed his sword, clearly unimpressed with the Hibernian's boasting.

"Come then," he said, turning and walking back towards the hill and our camp. "Bring Moralltach and we'll see what the others make of you. And, Hunlaf," he said to me over his shoulder, "well run."

Twenty-Seven

"Cormac mac Neill at your service." Cormac bowed low.

Hereward pushed himself up from where he was tending the leg of mutton roasting over the fire. Cormac's eyes kept flicking to the sizzling meat and he licked his lips.

"Can you fight?" Hereward asked.

"I am a great swordsman," Cormac replied. "The crows and foxes of my lands are fat from feeding off the corpses of my foes."

Hereward looked him up and down, grimacing as if he had smelt something rotten.

"Gwawrddur," he said, "what say you? You crossed blades with him. Is he skilled?"

Gwawrddur sniffed.

"He is strong and does not lack speed." Cormac puffed out his chest at the praise. "But I have seen blind men more skilled with a sword. He gives away every move before he makes it and he is as clumsy as a drunk."

Cormac's face flushed.

"Why you Welsh—" he reached his hand for the hilt of his sword, but before he could unsheathe the blade, Gwawrddur had drawn his own and sprung forward. The sharp tip of his sword pressed against Cormac's throat.

The Hibernian did not move. He glowered at Gwawrddur.

"And he is reckless and easy to goad it seems," said the Welshman. He stared into Cormac's eyes. "Do not seek to raise your sword against me another time, Hibernian," he whispered. "I have killed men for less and I will not warn you again." Cormac swallowed, but after a moment he dropped his gaze and removed his hand from his sword's pommel.

Gwawrddur turned his back on him and returned to his place against the aspen.

Hereward stroked his bearded chin.

"We need men and you are clearly foolhardy enough to fight against those who are likely to kill you. I think this will be a trait that will prove useful in the days ahead. What say you all?"

Gwawrddur shrugged.

"I am going to train Killer here." He nodded in my direction. "I can train this one too, if he will listen."

Cormac's eyes widened.

"Thank you," he said, and his voice sounded like that of an enthusiastic child. I wondered about his age then. It seemed the grime and the beard hid a youthfulness that was not immediately apparent. As if embarrassed by the sound of his own youth, Cormac replaced his grin with a scowl and growled.

Drosten chuckled.

"I like the boy," he said. "Let him join us."

"If you give me your word to serve with us until after the fight," said Hereward, "I am minded to accept you into our merry band of fools. Do I have your oath that you will obey me and give your sword and even your life to protect us and the people of Werceworthe?"

Cormac grinned and was about to speak when Runolf's deep voice boomed out from the shadows beneath the aspens.

"No," he said.

We all turned to look at the Norse giant. Cormac's hand fell to his sword again.

"You disagree with me?" asked Hereward. He spoke slowly so that Runolf would understand him.

"We not take this boy," Runolf said, his heavily accented words clear to us all. He had not spoken since Cormac's arrival and on hearing his voice the Hibernian bristled.

"You have one of *them* in your midst?" he spat. "A Norse savage? Are you not planning on slaying Norsemen? You should start with this one here, it seems to me."

"Silence!" barked Hereward. "Speak no more, Cormac. Your betters are talking."

Cormac's face was thunderous, but he clamped his mouth shut.

"Runolf," said Hereward, "why would you not take the Hibernian with us?"

Runolf shook his head.

"I not trust him," he said.

"You don't trust me?" snarled Cormac. "You heathen bastard!"

"I said 'Silence'," hissed Hereward. Cormac drew in a deep breath, but spoke no more.

"Why don't you trust him?" I asked Runolf.

"He creeps in the night like a fox," he said. "A warrior would approach us and speak with his face to our faces, not skulk and hide in the forest. No, he means no good."

I pondered his words and then translated them.

Cormac erupted with rage.

"You would rather listen to a Norse heathen than to a Hibernian Christian?" he roared.

"Runolf is no longer a heathen," I said quietly, but neither Cormac nor Hereward paid me any heed. Cormac's latest outburst seemed to have sparked Hereward's own ire into searing heat. He stepped toward Cormac and slapped his hands together hard, making the Hibernian flinch.

"I would listen to a man I have seen defend the weak," Hereward said. "A man I have travelled with these last days. A man who has sworn an oath to my lord, Uhtric of Bebbanburg. Yes, I would listen to such a man over a filthy wanderer who sneaks after us like a weasel hoping to steal the eggs from a farmer's hens."

"You would turn me away?" asked Cormac, aghast at how his prospects had changed so suddenly. "But you said it yourself, you need men."

"Aye, you have the right of it. We have need of men. Men who can fight, not boys who cannot hold their tongues or swords in check. Now, begone with you."

Cormac looked as though he were about to say something else. His eyes glittered in the encroaching darkness and he looked very young in spite of his beard. He swept his furious glower over all of us and lastly his gaze lingered on the bubbling and crisping mutton.

He bit his lower lip to prevent himself from speaking further, or perhaps to stop from weeping. I could not but feel sympathy for him. He seemed so lonely. He had looked overjoyed to have been welcomed into the camp only to have his hopes dashed moments later. I wanted to say something, to call him back. But who was I to speak against Hereward and Runolf? I kept my mouth shut and watched silently as Cormac spun on his heel and strode off down the hill and into the night.

Nobody spoke until he was swallowed in the gloom.

"We will post guards tonight," whispered Hereward, still staring after the Hibernian.

Twenty-Eight

Hereward was clearly concerned that Cormac might plan some mischief against us in the night. The Northumbrian had changed, less prone to jests and often scowling as he bit his lip. The pressure of leadership is no easy thing to bear, but Hereward took up his new responsibility without complaint. He was thoughtful and fair, and never expected any of us to do what he would not attempt himself. You can ask no more of a leader of men. Now, he urged us to take watches in pairs. I would stand guard with Runolf.

I was awoken in the darkest part of the night by Hereward, who had been on sentry duty with the dour Drosten. This was probably as much to watch for Cormac as to keep an eye on the Pict, I thought. Hereward seemed to trust Gwawrddur implicitly, and so had told him to stand guard with Leofstan. I wondered about this. Why trust one man over another with so little to base an opinion? All I could think was that the prowess the Welshman had shown, coupled with his cool control in the face of adversity, had given him an aura of dependability.

"There is not long till dawn now," Hereward whispered as he shook me awake. "Rouse Runolf and keep your eyes and ears open."

Without another word, he placed a log on the embers of the fire, wrapped himself in his cloak and lay down amongst the other shadowy forms of the sleeping men. I was quickly alert. It was time for Matins, or would be very soon, and I smiled to myself in the darkness, imagining how the slumbering warriors would react if I began to sing and pray the first office of the day.

Far away in the darkness an animal screeched. Rather, I hoped it was an animal, for who knew what creatures of the night roamed the forests and hills of Northumbria? I made the sign of the cross in the gloom and crept over to Runolf's snoring bulk. Reaching out, I shook his shoulder gently. His huge hand lashed out with uncanny speed and grabbed my wrist, gripping it so tightly that it hurt. His other hand found my throat and I whimpered. I tried to pull away, but his strength was inexorable. He closed his grip and I could feel his thumb digging into my neck.

"Runolf," I gasped, barely able to make a sound. He did not respond. His hand continued to squeeze. Flames caught the log on the fire and in the sudden burst of flickering light, I saw his eyes were open, but unseeing. He yet slept, gripped by some devil-sent dream. I could not draw breath or make another sound. I slapped at his arm with my free hand, but he appeared not to notice. If I didn't waken him soon, I would pass out and then, if he did not halt his attack, I would soon be dead.

My rising panic gave me added strength and I balled my left hand into a fist and punched Runolf hard on the nose. Like a disturbed bear, he roared and surged to his feet, throwing me aside as if I had been nothing more than a child's straw doll.

He stood looking about him while I drew in a ragged breath.

"Can you two keep it quiet?" murmured Hereward, his voice already thick with sleep.

As I watched, Runolf shook his head, as if to free it of his nightmares. He noticed me, cowering at his feet and he dropped down beside me.

"I am sorry, Hunlaf," he said. "I was dreaming."

I could not speak. I rubbed my hand against my bruised neck. His eyes were wide with concern.

"It is our turn to watch," I croaked at last.

He offered me his hand. I hesitated and then, warily, I grasped it. He pulled me to my feet.

"Sorry," he whispered. "Do not wake me like that again."

"I won't," I said, wishing he had given me that advice earlier.

We moved away from the glow of the fire and sat, listening to the night.

The creature screeched again, startling me.

"Fox bitch," Runolf said. "Do not fear."

I thought of his callused hand crushing the life from me and shivered. Far out in the darkness, I fancied I saw a tiny speck of light. I imagined Cormac sleeping alone beside it.

"Dark memories are worse at night," Runolf said, his deep voice like distant murmurs of thunder.

"What memories?" I asked.

For a long while he did not speak and I thought he would not reply. The vixen called again.

"I will not speak of my memories," he said at last.

"Perhaps if you spoke of them, you would sleep lighter."

He chuckled without mirth.

"I can never sleep light again. Not after the things I have seen. What I have done."

I pushed him to speak further, but he just said, "A man's past is his alone," and would say no more.

Twenty-Nine

Despite Hereward's concerns, Cormac was not seen during the night and the dawn was welcomed with a chorus of birdsong from the trees above us. The sky was clear of clouds and it looked set to be another long, hot day of travel.

Leofstan stirred together a paste of oats and water, placing dollops of the mixture on a flat stone he had left to heat in the embers of the fire. The smell of the oatcakes filled the chill early morning air while we readied the horses. Leofstan handed out the crisp, slightly charred biscuits, and I was not the only one who burnt their tongue on them.

We were back in the saddle and riding north while the sun was still low in the east. There was nobody on the road and I looked over my shoulder as I rode, half-expecting to see a glimpse of Cormac. But I saw nobody.

When we paused to rest at midday, I asked Gwawrddur whether he would begin to teach me. He chewed a piece of cold mutton, washing it down with some water before replying.

"You ran quickly yesterday, Killer," he said. "I did not think you would be able to best me."

I glowed with pride and could not hide my grin.

"So yes, I will begin to teach you now," he said.

I looked longingly at the sword that hung from his belt, but he shook his head.

"No, no," he said. "You are not yet ready to wield a blade. You would be as likely to damage the weapon or yourself, as to learn anything useful."

Crestfallen, I sighed.

Gwawrddur ignored me and walked away from the road towards several large ash trees. Scanning the ground, he stooped and picked up a sturdy-looking branch. With deft movements, using one of his hand axes, he quickly cleaned the limb of twigs and leaves. When he was satisfied, he tossed the staff to me. I caught it in my bandaged hand. Leofstan had rewrapped it that morning in a clean strip of linen. My wounds were scabbed over now, and showed no sign of infection. Leofstan had nodded his approval and said the bandage could be removed when we reached Werceworthe.

"That stick is your sword until I say otherwise," said Gwawrddur.

I did not speak, not wishing to show my acute disappointment.

"For now, I want you to hold it, like this." He effortlessly fell into the warrior stance, both legs bent, right in front of the left, sword raised in his right hand. I emulated him as best I could. "Bend your leg. More. That's right. Now, I want you to do this." He quickly took three steps backward, shuffling and sliding his feet in the old leaves beneath the ash. Then, he immediately reversed his direction and moved three steps forward, finishing in a lunging, probing attack with his sword. He repeated this procedure three times, his movements lithe and athletic. He appeared to glide over the ground.

"Now you," he said, and I did my best to copy what he had done. He sheathed his sword and picked up another stick with which to poke and prod me whenever I did not move in accordance with his instructions. After a time, he was satisfied enough to return to his food.

"Keep doing that, over and over, whenever you have a moment to spare," he said.

By the time we came to mount up again, I was out of breath and my thighs were burning from the constant crouching position. My hand was hurting and I was sure I had broken the scabs on my fingers again. I threw the stick to the ground with a sigh of relief and clambered up onto my horse's back.

"Wait," snapped Gwawrddur. "Would you throw away your sword so easily?" He hooked his toes under the ash staff that I had tossed aside and with a quick movement he flicked it into the air. Catching it, he spun it around in an intricate pattern, before throwing it in my direction. My horse shied and twisted away, so I failed to catch it.

"Dismount and collect your sword, Killer."

The others laughed as I slid from the saddle and retrieved the wooden weapon. It took me a few moments to pull myself back up onto my steed without dropping the staff again.

"Do not lose your sword," said Gwawrddur. "From now on, you must not let it leave your sight. If you truly wish to be a warrior, your life will depend on your sword."

We rode on. As the sun passed its zenith wisps of cloud began to form in the west and the wind shifted into the north. That night we stayed in the hall of a sour-faced lord called Asser. He was surly and fed us only thin pottage. Uhtric had stayed there the day before with his warriors, and Asser grumbled about how much they had eaten and drunk. "My hospitality only goes so far," he said before stomping off to his sleeping quarters, leaving us in the hall with one sullen servant and three sombre-looking ceorls who worked his lands.

As we sipped Asser's watery stew I reflected that his hospitality didn't go very far at all. Still, we were glad of the roof over our heads when rain began to fall in the night. And as there was no need to set up sentries, we all got a decent amount of sleep.

I took advantage of the time after we had eaten to practise with my "sword". I went through the movements Gwawrddur had shown me until my arm was leaden and my legs trembled. The Welshman watched on, commenting from time to time. He offered little encouragement more than a nod every now and then. But when he finally decided I had worked hard enough and could rest, he said, "You know, Killer, I think you might make a swordsman yet."

Leofstan offered to pray with me before we slept, but I said I was too tired and collapsed onto one of the thin pallets that had been laid out for us. I placed the ash staff at my side, within easy reach. I could sense Leofstan's disapproval, but I shut my eyes and went over in my mind the moves Gwawrddur had taught me. His words of praise had filled me with warmth and I told myself that the next day I would further impress him with my hard work. As I lay there, I wondered how Cormac fared, out in the cold and wet of the night, but exhaustion brought sleep quickly and I dreamt of the weight of the ash branch in my hand and the constant burn of my muscles as I repeated lunges and sweeping cuts, and parried the blows from invisible attackers.

In the morning, the rain had eased, but a thin drizzle fell constantly and the high hills on the horizon were misted in low cloud. Perhaps, if Asser had been more generous with his board, we might have waited out the bad weather, for it was bound not to last more than a day or two, but he made it very clear that we had outstayed our welcome when he had his servants saddle our horses and bring them to the door of the hall.

We mounted up and rode through the mud of the yard and headed north once more. The day was miserable and progress slow. We were all soaked through and where we had talked and joked on previous days, nobody felt like talking as we trudged along Deira Strææt in the rain. For much of the morning, I rode at the rear of the group, behind Drosten and Gwawrddur. Frequently, I glanced back the way we had come, but I saw no sign of Cormac or anybody else. The Hibernian had probably returned to Eoforwic in search of other work. He was surely more likely to find someone to pay him in the city.

We rested in the lee of a stand of linden for a time at midday. I stretched my tight and tired muscles and practised some more. Leofstan watched me from where he sat. His intent gaze made me self-conscious and nervous, so after a while I threw down my wooden sword in disgust and sat with my back to him.

The wind picked up in the afternoon, rattling the oak and beech trees that grew tall beside the road. The rain ceased and the sun forced its way through the shredding clouds to warm the land. Our clothes and the horses' coats steamed in the sun's rays and our spirits were buoyed as we slowly dried out.

That evening, Hereward led us to the east of the road into a small wood where shiny-leafed holly grew amongst the larger beech and oak. The trees were old, gnarled and twisted, with dense canopies, and there were dry patches beneath their soaring branches. Hereward set about finding wood and lighting a fire. He sent me off to water the horses and fill the skins. Despite the rain, it had been some time since we had ridden past any streams or rivers, but on approaching this old wood, Hereward had pointed out where the lowering sun glittered on a river some way further to the west.

I sighed, resenting that I had somehow become the hostler for the group. But none of the others seemed inclined to help me and I didn't much like the idea of being away from the campsite when night fell. So I quickly unsaddled all the horses except for mine and then used a length of rope to tie their halters together so that I could lead them all. I nearly forgot to pick up my wooden practice sword, but at the last moment, I snatched it up and, holding it and the end of the lead rope in my left hand, I awkwardly pulled myself up into the saddle. I knew that Gwawrddur was watching me, but I ignored him, merely gladdened that I had not given him the opportunity to rebuke me.

The shadows were long already and while not far, to reach the river I would need to ride past the trees and down a slope of gorse. I kicked my horse forward, urging it to hurry so that I would not need to return after dark. The murmur of the men's voices was soon lost, hidden by the sighing of the trees and the clump of the horses' hooves on the leaf mould. I left the cover of the woodland and trotted out into the warm light of the setting sun. The river curled off in the distance. Trees crowded its banks, but every now and then, I caught a glimpse of the silvered reflection of the sky on the water that flowed along the valley floor. Tugging on the lead rope, I kicked my mount into a trot.

After only a few paces, a shadow to my left caught my attention. There was a tangle of elderberries running along what appeared to be a narrow furrow in the land. I followed its path with my gaze and saw that it led directly to the river. It must be a stream and was much closer than the tree-lined river. If I could get the horses down to it, it would save me some time. I hesitated, weighing up the chances that the gully would be too clogged with vegetation to be of any use to me. A warrior does not worry about such things, I thought with a smile. Swinging my horse's head to the north, I headed towards what I hoped would be a deep stream with shallow banks. The three horses trailed behind me placidly.

As we drew close, the animals snorted and tossed their manes as if they could sense the water. At first, I could see no way past the thick thatch of brambles and elderberries, so, cursing silently, I turned east again towards the river. Moments later, there was a break in the dense foliage and I could hear the trickle of flowing water. A muddy bank led down to a shadowed pool. An old willow had fallen, probably in the storms that spring. It had toppled across the stream, partially damming it and also clearing a path through the undergrowth. I offered up a prayer of thanks and dismounted to lead the horses down to the water's edge.

The water here was as wide as a beaver's pond, but I could see no gnawed trunks that would have signalled the creatures' presence. The water barely rippled. It was still and quiet here, apart from the burbling of the stream where it found its way past the damming bole of the fallen willow. At first my horse did not wish to go down into the shadows to drink. It shied away and rolled its eyes. I pulled hard on its reins and eventually, with a snort, it stepped down carefully and dipped its snout into the cool water. Its ears were back and its skin quivered. The other horses nudged and jostled each other until they too could reach the water and drink.

I looped the lead rope over a jutting root of the splintered willow. Looking about for somewhere to tether my horse's reins, I could see none so, sighing, I rammed my ash practice sword into the soft earth of the river bank. To this, I tied the leather reins. I smiled to think what Gwawrddur would say if he could see me. He would surely tell me that was no way to treat a sword. But he was back at the camp watching Hereward cook the evening meal and I was here with the horses, bringing water for everyone else. I could do with my "sword" whatever I wished.

I took the water skins from my saddle bags and knelt to fill them. I had just stoppered the first one and was plunging the second skin into the water when I heard a crack and swish of wood, as if something had snagged a twig and then it had snapped back. I listened, but all was silence again. I would have thought I had imagined it, but my horse raised its head and its ears twisted about as it too listened for danger. I stood, placing my hand on the animal's flank, as much to calm myself as the beast. There was no sound now as I strained to hear. Runolf's mare snorted, making me jolt as if slapped. Then I heard more leaves and twigs being brushed aside. There was no stealth in the sounds and I let out a sigh of relief. It must be one of the others who had followed me for some reason. I waited to see who it was. Perhaps it was Gwawrddur, come to teach me new moves to practice, or to make me run back to camp while he rode. I dropped the skins at my feet and hurriedly pulled the ash practice blade from the mud. With my left hand I gripped my horse's bridle.

The sounds of someone approaching were growing louder and I peered into the foliage that thronged the bank of the stream, but could see nobody. A finger of unease traced a line down my spine and I shivered.

"Who is there?" I called out and was angered to hear that my voice quavered. It was the voice of a timid child, not a brave warrior.

The elderberries and briars shook, and a heartbeat later, two men stepped onto the path that I had followed down to the water. I had never seen either of them before.

The first was tall and wiry, perhaps thirty years of age. His neck looked too long and his eyes jutted from his angular face. He wore a tan-coloured cloak over a dark green tunic and breeches. In his hand, he held a sword. It did not look as fine as Gwawrddur's. Its hilt and pommel were iron, its handle wooden, but it looked deadly enough and I shivered when I looked at the man's eyes. They were expressionless and blank, like the eyes of a snake.

The other man was shorter and broader. His mousy hair was cropped short and his features were blunt and brutal. In his left hand he held a wicked-looking seax. It was almost as long as a sword. Though younger and seemingly stronger, the second man appeared somehow less dangerous than the first, though I could not say why.

"Who are you?" I said, squaring my shoulders in an effort to appear brave. "What do you want?" My voice sounded small and terrified.

The thin man did not answer, he just smiled. There were gaps between his yellow teeth and his grin made me want to turn and run. But behind me there was no escape, only water.

"I told you there was but the one of them," said the shorter of the two.

"Others must be camped close by," hissed the swordsman. "Why else would he have four horses and all those water skins?" From his tone, and the way the shorter man nodded at his words, the swordsman was the leader here. He took a step closer and the horses stamped and snorted. "How many are there?" he asked, pointing his sword at me. "And where are they?"

It was my turn to give no answer, and with that small act of defiance, I began to feel the cold rage I had begun to recognise as the hidden fighter within me.

His eyes narrowed.

"No matter," he said. "Let's kill him fast and be gone from here. We can ride. And those horses will fetch us enough silver to last till midwinter."

My mouth had grown dry, but my fear had vanished, smothered by the rage that filled me. The hand that clutched the horse's bridle trembled, but not with fear now, with pent-up fury.

"If you want these horses, you will have to kill me to take them," I said. The tall man's eyes widened and for a moment, he did not move. I wondered who was more shocked at my words for I had not known I was going to speak until my mouth opened.

"Very well, monk," he said, taking a step forward and raising his sword. The shorter man did not move, but watched intently. He seemed to think he would not be needed in this one-sided fight.

"Come on then," I said, and letting go of my horse's harness, I dropped into the crouch of the warrior stance. In my right hand I lifted the ash branch as if it were a sword.

"By Christ's bones," laughed the thin man, "what have we here? A fighting monk?" He glanced back at his friend, who chuckled at what he was seeing. "It is a pity we do not have more time," the swordsman said. "I would like to know where this mad monk has come from."

"No time for that," said the stockier of the two. "If his friends are near, they might hear us and come to help him. Kill him and let's be done."

His words cut through the fog of my ire. I was a fool. Taking a deep breath, I screamed as loud as I could.

"Help me! I am under attack!"

The sound of my shout made the horses whinny and shake their heads. My mount jumped away from me and the thin swordsman snapped into action. With a growl of anger, he leapt forward.

An unusual clarity and calm descended on me. I watched as his blade flickered towards me and, as I had done countless times in the previous days, I parried. Only this time I was not defending against an imaginary foe. The wooden staff was stout and strong and it easily deflected the sword away from my face. In the next moment, as part of the same practised movement, I took a step forward and lunged.

I'd like to say that my blow was directed by skill, but the truth of it is that I was barely thinking. And yet perhaps that is what separates a true warrior from normal men. That when it matters, luck is on their side. I am sure there are those who would say that there is no such thing as luck, that my hand was directed by God, and maybe that is so, but I have ever been a proud man and I say it was my hand, not Christ's, that held that ash branch when its tip gouged into the brigand's left eye. I had continued to shout for help even as I clashed with the swordsman and now his screams of agony were added to my cries for aid. He staggered back, clutching at his face.

"Kill him! Kill him!" he raged, and his stocky friend surged forward, ready to put an end to me.

The wooden sword had not broken and I still held it before me in the defensive pose that Gwawrddur had drilled into me. He would be proud I thought and then realised the stupidity of such an idea. He might be pleased that I had managed to injure one of the two attackers, but I would be dead soon enough. Gwawrddur's pride would do me no good.

The stocky man rushed at me. His movements had none of the elegance of the swordsman and he seemed to use the seax like a cudgel, swinging it before him with furious abandon. A skilled warrior would have seen his weakness and, even armed with nothing but an ash stick, would have been able to cripple him before he reached me. But I was not a skilled warrior. I was but a young monk with dreams of another life and a stick in my hand that suddenly felt puny and insignificant when facing the burly bulk of this brigand. By reflex, I raised my wooden staff to parry his first wild swing. Splinters flew with a terrible cracking sound. The force of the blow rattled the stick and it vibrated down into my hand.

I stumbled backwards, splashing into the water. My horse, terrified now, reared up, pawing the air with its hooves. It was trying to turn in the small space of the muddy clearing, but the foliage blocked it on the one side, the seax-wielding man on the other. One of its hooves glanced from the man's shoulder and he grunted. Halting his attack on me, he leapt away, out of the reach of the animal's crazed flailing hooves, and closer to where the tethered horses stamped and strained at their bonds.

The swordsman was still cursing and screaming, but despite his face being smeared with blood, I could see that he was not mortally wounded. He would soon return to the fray and whatever slim chance of survival I had would vanish. My horse was finally able to spin about and, with a splattering of mud and a great crashing of branches, he galloped away from the stream, up the slope, past the wounded man and back into the light.

"Now you die, little monk," said the man before me with a vicious grin. He seemed to be enjoying himself as he stepped forward, hefting his heavy-bladed seax again. I could not drag my gaze from the wicked steel blade in his meaty hand. The cold water lapped about my ankles. I remembered the monks at Lindisfarnae, how they had been forced into the sea and drowned. My enemy was broad-shouldered and heavily-muscled. If he did not kill me with the seax, he would easily overpower me and force my face beneath the dark waters of the pool. The thought filled me with horror. I could not allow that to happen. I might not hold a sword in my hand, but I was not unarmed and I could still fight.

He took another step forward, still out of the range of his short arm and the cleaver-like seax. I feared that heavy blade, but I could not let that fear overcome me. With a roar of anger and terror, I sprang forward, aiming my wooden staff at his face. Looking back now, with the eyes of an old man, I can only try to remember what it was like to be so young and so foolhardy. I think I imagined myself to be blessed somehow, that I would repeat the lucky strike that had sent his comrade reeling. But even a truly blessed warrior cannot always rely on luck and must trust to his own abilities.

I sent the probing lunge at the stocky warrior and he swayed back, faster and more skilled than I had given him credit for. In the same instant, he swung his seax and hacked into the ash wood of my weapon. It splintered and snapped under the force of the blow and it was all I could do not to drop the half that remained in my hand.

Laughing at how easily he had brushed aside my attack, he raised his seax. But before he could strike, there was a tumultuous crash and a howling, wailing scream echoed around the clearing. Behind my opponent, a figure had leapt from the foliage and flung itself on the wounded swordsman. The two of them crumpled to the mud in a thrashing jumble of limbs and flashing of blades.

Thirty

Thinking back, that was the moment when I truly came to believe that I was on the path that God had chosen for me. He could have allowed me to die there. I was outnumbered and my companions were too far away to reach me, even if they had heard my screams. And when the newcomer threw himself into the fight, taking on the leader, my stocky enemy could still have remained focused on his task. I would have been dead in moments. But instead of hacking into me with his great seax, or leaping onto me and forcing my face under the water, he turned to see what was happening behind him. He made that fateful error that is many a warrior's last mistake: he underestimated his enemy.

The instant when his eyes flicked away from mine, I launched myself forward, the shattered end of the ash sword clutched tightly in my fist. My throat-wrenching scream mingled with that of the other fighting men as I plunged the sharp, splintered tip of the broken practice sword into my adversary's neck. We fell together into the mud, beside the stamping hooves of the horses. My hand was warm, and looking down, I saw that dark blood was pumping over my fingers, soaking the bandage there and colouring the water-filled hoof prints red. The man tried to push me off, but I drove the branch deeper into his throat. I did not look away from him, despite the sounds of fighting close by. He made to strike me with the seax, but I raised my weight up and pinned his arm beneath my left knee.

His eyes were dimming now, looking beyond me to whatever it is that men witness when their life leaves their mortal shell. He trembled, let out a rattling sigh and was still.

Panting, I pushed myself to my feet, wrenching the seax from the dead man's hand. Its handle was fashioned from an antler. It was warm to the touch, though not as warm as the man's blood.

The howling had ceased where the other two men were fighting and I watched warily to see who had vanquished and who it was that had come rushing to my aid. There was no doubt in my mind then or now, that without that timely intervention, I would have died there beside that stream.

Slowly, gasping for breath as if he had run a long way, one man rose. I recognised the motionless form that remained on the earth first. The pallid corpse had a curtain of blood over its face and the left eye was a ragged, ripped mess. The man who stood over the dead swordsman held a blood-drenched sword in his hand. His dark hair and his beard were an unruly tangle, but his teeth flashed bright in a grin.

"I told you my enemies feared me," Cormac said.

"My enemies too, it seems," I said. His grin widened, but I could not smile. I was only now allowing myself to believe that I would not be dead in a few heartbeats.

"Your enemies are my enemies, Hunlaf," he said. "If you'll have me."

I opened my mouth to reply, but speech seemed difficult. My mind twisted and squirmed. I was both horrified and exalted by what had occurred. And yet I could not bring forth the words to give meaning to my feelings. In an effort to hide my confusion, I staggered forward to where the thin man lay sprawled in the mud. His uninjured bulging eye stared up at the darkening sky. The gouged left socket glowered at me in silent, hideous accusation. I glanced back at the other cooling corpse.

I had done this thing.

To take a life was the ultimate sin. Had Jesu not instructed us to love our enemies; to do good to those who hate us? Could it be that I was wrong and God was sending me these tribulations as a test of my faith? I thought of the story of Job and how God had tested him. And then I remembered the tale of Abraham and his son, Isaac. God had ordered Abraham to sacrifice Isaac, only allowing Abraham to slay a ram instead after the man had tied his son to the altar, proving that he would do what the Lord commanded.

Had I failed the tests God had placed before me? Should I have offered up a prayer for the souls of my attackers, allowing them to strike me down?

I bent and picked up the brigand's sword. His fingers still gripped the hilt and I took hold of the blade to pull it from his dead grasp. Looking away from the corpse and its accusing glare, I gave a couple of tentative swings to the weapon. It was significantly heavier than my wooden staff of course, but it was well-balanced and the wooden handle seemed made for my hand.

Sounds of running feet cut through my reverie and without thinking I raised the sword menacingly. Cormac lifted his own sword, turning towards the approaching noise. Without a word, we stepped close together to stand shoulder to shoulder.

Gwawrddur came bounding down the muddy slope, sword drawn and sweat glistening on his brow.

In an instant, he took in the scene. Stepping close, he gently pushed our blades aside.

"You'll not be needing those now," he said.

Quickly, he knelt beside each man, checking for signs of life.

With practised efficiency, he searched the bodies, finding little of interest apart from a pouch of dried tinder, along with a flint and a thin rod of iron.

Moments later, Runolf, carrying his huge axe, and Drosten, armed with his knife, careened down the sloping path. They were both gasping for air after the long run from the camp in the woods. After seeing that the fight was finished, Runolf bent over, putting his hands on his knees, and gulping in great breaths. Sweat poured down his face. After a time, he straightened and wiped the back of his hand across his forehead. When he could finally speak, he asked what had happened.

I recounted what had transpired. I spoke abruptly, giving the barest of details without dwelling on the savagery of the wounds. I could not push from my mind the thoughts of the man's warm lifeblood pumping onto my hand. I kept reliving the lunge that had taken the first man's eye. My excitement at what I had done filled me with shame. What sort of man was I to revel in such violence?

Runolf looked about the clearing as if he could see the fight taking place in his mind's eye.

Gwawrddur picked up the shattered half of my practice sword. The other half jutted from the man's gore-slick throat.

"You did well," he said. "But you seem to have broken your sword."

All the while, I had gripped the sword I had picked up tightly, as if it could somehow anchor me to the spot; stop my swirling mind from floating away on the swell of my emotions.

"I have a new sword," I said, lifting the tip of the blade to show him.

He nodded and went to the swordsman's corpse. He bent and unbuckled the man's belt. With an effort he tugged it free of the dead weight and handed it to me. It had a simple leather scabbard attached.

"You'll be needing this then," he said.

I took the belt and scabbard, staring at them as if I had never before seen their like. Gwawrddur patted me on the shoulder.

"I will show you how to fasten it and how best to draw a blade from a scabbard. But later, after we've eaten."

In a daze, I staggered to where the other man was sprawled in the mud. I tugged the sheath from his belt with difficulty. Such was the trembling of my hands that it took me two attempts before I managed to slide the antler-handled seax into its leather home.

Cormac had been standing silently since the others had arrived. Now Gwawrddur turned to him.

"You may be clumsy, Hibernian," he said, "but you show a fighter's spirit. I like that."

Cormac beamed.

"You will train me then?"

Gwawrddur chuckled.

"Go and fetch Hunlaf's horse. It has run off aways."

"And then you will teach me?"

Gwawrddur shook his head.

"It seems to me you have both had enough training for one day."

Cormac looked disappointed. My whole body ached and my hands trembled. I could not imagine wanting to train or fight again. All I wished for now was to eat, drink and sleep. I wondered whether I would see the faces of the dead in my dreams.

"Go and get the horse," Gwawrddur repeated.

"You will wait here?"

"No. Follow us back to our campsite. It's in the woods to the west of here."

"I know where it is," Cormac said with a cunning grin, before turning and sprinting up the path. I wondered how close he had been to us since last we'd seen him. He must move as stealthily as a fox, I thought.

"What will we say to Hereward when we return with Cormac?" I asked.

Gwawrddur looked after the Hibernian.

"We will tell him we have another warrior to join our band." He glanced at the corpses and then looked at me. "Or perhaps that is two warriors, eh, Killer?"

Without waiting for a reply, he strode away, back up the muddy slope, leaving me to collect the water skins and the three tethered horses.

Thirty-One

After we had eaten, Gwawrddur finally agreed to train Cormac. The Hibernian was ecstatically happy. In fact, he had not stopped beaming since he walked into the camp leading my horse. By then, it was fully dark under the trees and he had been cautious and quiet at first, perhaps nervous at how Hereward and Runolf would react to him joining the group.

Hereward did not put up much resistance. What could he say, after the young man had saved my life?

"Do you give me your solemn word that you will obey my command?" Hereward asked Cormac.

"I swear."

"And do you swear to hold your tongue when you disagree with me?"

Cormac frowned, clearly torn as to what to say. In the end, with a disconsolate shake of his head, he sighed.

"I cannot do that," he said. "For what sort of man would I be to allow my leader to make a mistake without me warning him first?"

There was a glimmer in his eye, even though his face was sombre. Runolf, who was sitting on the far side of the fire, let out a bark of laughter.

"I change my mind," he said. "The boy can fight. He stay."

"I'll decide if he can come with us," said Hereward.

"Yes, yes," replied Runolf, waving his hand airily. "But he stay, no?"

Drosten laughed.

Hereward puffed out his cheeks, and blew out his breath in exasperation.

"You must swear another oath to me first, Cormac," he said.

Serious now, sensing that this was the moment that would decide his future, Cormac nodded.

"You must give your word," said Hereward, "that you will keep peace with all the others in this band." He paused. "Even with Runolf."

Cormac stared at the Norseman through the flames. He was suddenly very serious and I wondered what he was contemplating.

"You have my word," Cormac said at last, unsmiling now.

"Very well," said Hereward, clapping him on the shoulder. "You are one of our small warband."

We told riddles and tales for long into the night and slowly the tensions of the fight ebbed from me. Cormac seemed instantly to be at home in the group and talked incessantly, as if he had thirsted for company for so long that now he meant to drink deeply of the well of conversation around the flickering fire. When I had been yawning for some time and Drosten had already wrapped himself in his blanket and cloak to sleep, Cormac was still singing bawdy songs. In the end, Hereward had to intervene.

"I may yet have you swear another oath, Cormac," he said, interrupting a song about the many joys of being drunk.

"What oath?" Cormac asked, sensing a jest in Hereward's tone.

"That you will let the rest of us sleep!"

Drosten chuckled from where he lay.

"Yes," he said. "Have him swear it!"

Despite the light tone, Cormac heard the serious request for peace behind the words and fell silent. Gwawrddur took the first watch, sitting with his back to the fire and looking out into the darkness so that the flames would not burn away his night vision.

I pulled my blanket about me and tried to get comfortable. I closed my eyes, desperate now for the embrace of sleep, but fearful of what dreams it might bring.

Just before I fell into an exhausted slumber, Gwawrddur spoke.

"It is good that Cormac has joined our number."

Hereward, half awake, grunted.

"Why is that?"

"Now we are seven."

"And?"

"Any fewer, and by the dooms of the land, we are but a group of thieves."

I recalled having to copy out some of the dooms, the legal texts by which the land is governed. I had scratched the letters into the vellum under Leofstan's watchful gaze and I remembered the law about bands of warriors. A group between seven and thirty-five in number was deemed to be a warband. More than that, and it was a *here*, an army.

"I am no thief," grumbled Drosten from the gloom.

"No," replied Gwawrddur. "Not now that Cormac has bolstered our number."

Drosten hoomed in the back of his throat, but said no more.

"We are seven," said Leofstan from where he lay in the darkness. "But we are not all warriors."

He had been silent for much of the time since I had returned with my new sword from the stream. He had asked if I was well, but when he'd heard the tale of how I had killed a man, he had grown reserved and had retreated to the edge of the firelight.

"True," said Gwawrddur. "Perhaps we will need to find another to join us, if we are not to be thought of as brigands."

Nobody else spoke, and the soft sighing of the wind through the leaves above us soon pulled me into the welcome arms of sleep. Thankfully, I did not dream and when I awoke I was surprised to find that I had not been awakened for my turn at sentry duty.

"You needed the rest," said Hereward, when he saw me rising from my blanket and looking about me as the others prepared to strike camp.

"I am one of the band now," I said. "You must treat me as such."

"Or one of the thieves," he replied with a smirk.

"I am one of this band of warriors," I said, more forcefully.

He fixed me in his stare.

"You wear the habit of a monk and the sword of a warrior. You cannot be both, I fear, Hunlaf."

I had been thinking much on this and knew he was right.

"I am a warrior in the clothes of a monk," I said, feeling a weight lifted from me as I spoke the words.

Hereward held my gaze for a time, before nodding.

"Very well," he said. "Warrior it is."

I turned to see to my gear. Leofstan was watching me. I realised with a pang of guilt and shame that he had not woken me for prayers. The first thing I had thought of was that I should have stood guard along with the other men. I could sense his judgement of me, of what I had done and what I wanted to become. Or perhaps what I had already become. He could not understand what drove me. I barely understood it myself. I wanted to explain to him how I felt, but when I opened my mouth to speak, I could not find the words. I bent to roll up my blanket and then buckled my sword belt around my waist. I twisted and turned my body to get a feel for the

unusual weight of the weapon on my hip. I nodded. I liked the
solidity of it.

When I looked up, Leofstan was no longer there.

Thirty-Two

My legs ached and I was bone weary when we reached Werceworthe two days later. The long days had been tiring enough without the extra effort of sword practice, as I had opted to walk, rather than ride after Cormac's arrival. I liked the Hibernian's company, he was quick to jest and had a strange way of speaking of things that was different from anyone I had ever met before. Also, since he had come to my rescue by the stream, there was an unspoken bond between us. I felt something similar with Runolf too, I mused, as I trudged along the road, watching the rumps and swishing tails of the horses ahead of us. I had also shared a moment of combat with the Norseman. We had fought together against a common foe and I surmised that the camaraderie I felt with Cormac stemmed from the realisation that he had risked his life, and taken another man's life, for me. This thought was at the forefront of my mind when I had awoken the morning after the fight and offered my horse to Drosten.

"Are you sure?" he asked, his blue tattoos making his face seem as if he were scowling, though his tone was friendly enough.

"Yes, I would walk."

He did not need coaxing and, with a nod of thanks, he

swung up onto my horse's back. The animal snorted at the extra weight of the heavily-muscled Pict and Drosten patted its neck and offered me a smile that I am sure was meant to show his gratitude, but appeared like a monstrous leer from his tattooed face.

It was true that I was glad to walk alongside Cormac, to hear more of his tale, though I soon found out that whilst he talked a lot, it was difficult to glean much of the story of his past and how he had come to be in Northumbria seeking someone willing to pay him for his sword. But above this, I knew the real reason I had decided to walk rather than ride. I could not bear the thought of Cormac speaking to Gwawrddur all day without me. Whatever techniques and tricks the older man might impart, I would hear them too.

When we halted at midday and after the camps were set up at night, Cormac and I trained. Gwawrddur made us both run through routines of movements, growling at us to attend to our footwork.

"A swordsman is only as good as his speed and balance," he said.

It was clear that despite great enthusiasm, Cormac was as unskilled with a blade as I was. I had the advantage of having performed some of the movements over the last few days, and so I moved through them fluidly and more naturally than the Hibernian. But I was only used to practising with a stick, and the weight of my newly acquired blade soon had me panting and sweating from the exertion. My fingers throbbed and my shoulders burnt with the effort. Cormac made up for his lack of skill with his overwhelming physical presence. He swung his sword hard and fast, leaping forward and backward, rather than the quick shuffle that Gwawrddur advocated, causing the Welshman to shout out.

"Speed and skill, not strength, will win a fight."

Cormac would bite his lip then, forcing himself to do what

he was told, but soon enough, he would be swinging and thrashing with his blade again. Gwawrddur shook his head.

"You are like an angry child. If you wish to cut oats or barley, I will buy you a scythe. You will not be needing that weapon."

Cormac grumbled, but nodded, acknowledging the swordsman's words. Once more, he began to follow the instructions more closely, but after only a short time, his sword was flailing about wildly.

The evening before we reached Werceworthe, Gwawrddur rose from where he had been watching us train and clapped his hands together. The sound was loud and caused us both to halt. I was glad of the respite, as my arm and shoulder were on fire and my thighs ached from the constant crouching.

"Sheathe your blades," Gwawrddur said. "Now, take these." He threw each of us a staff the length of a sword. He must have found the wood and cleaned the branches of twigs and offshoots while we had been practising. "Unbuckle your belts," he went on. After a moment's hesitation, I did what he asked. I noticed Cormac, frowning, seemed reluctant to remove his sword from his waist. "You are either my pupil, or you are not, Cormac," Gwawrddur said, shaking his head. "If you will not obey me, then we are done." He turned to me. "It seems we are back to just you and me," he said.

"Wait," said Cormac, quickly tugging at his belt's buckle.

Gwawrddur waited for him to discard his sword and belt before continuing.

"Now the two of you will pit yourselves against each other."

Cormac grinned at me, but I did not return his smile. I could feel the eyes of everyone on me.

"And listen, both of you," Gwawrddur said, his tone hard and stern. "I do not want any lasting injuries. This is not about maiming or crippling your opponent, it is about getting first touch. And there are to be no hits to the head, face or neck. The first to three touches will win. If I call halt, you will cease immediately. If I deem either of you to have breached my rules by hitting too hard or by aiming above the neck, I will award the other combatant a hit. Is all that understood?"

We both nodded. I noted that Cormac looked less pleased now, clearly concerned that he might annoy Gwawrddur and forfeit a point.

"Before you commence, I would tell you that I believe Cormac to be the stronger of the two of you. Do you agree?"

Cormac's smile returned.

"I will not argue with you on that score," he said, swishing his staff before him flamboyantly.

I appraised him. The Hibernian's shoulders were broader than mine, his neck thick and his hands wide and strong. I could not deny what Gwawrddur had said. I said nothing.

Seemingly satisfied, Gwawrddur said, "Now, prepare to fight."

The Welshman's words had sparked a deep resentment in me. I may not be as strong as Cormac, but I was fast, and I had proven myself. I would show them both. I dropped into the warrior stance, the aches and pains of moments before forgotten now.

"I will try my best not to bruise you too much, monk," Cormac said, and in spite of the friendship I had felt towards him since the fight at the stream, in that moment, I hated him.

I did not speak, but fixed my gaze on his eyes, allowing my vision to take in his whole body as Gwawrddur had taught us, watching for movements in his feet and the direction he turned his chest. That was how you could see where a warrior would strike.

"Fight!" said Gwawrddur, and the next instant, as I had expected, Cormac sprang forward, swinging his practice sword wildly for my midriff.

Without thinking of my response, I took three quick steps backwards, allowing his blow to whistle harmlessly past. He was off balance for a heartbeat, but without the weight of iron and steel in his hand he would recover in an instant. But I was also unencumbered by the weight of a sword. The staff felt as light as air in my hand after the gruelling drills we had been running through. The moment his practice blade swiped past me, I lunged, landing a touch to Cormac's ribs. I did not put my full weight behind the strike, but it was harder than I had anticipated and Cormac grunted. I sensed he would retaliate in anger, so I skipped back again as he bellowed in fury, aiming a cut at my head.

I raised my staff, parried the blow, then sent a slicing riposte into his shoulder.

"Two strikes to Hunlaf," said Gwawrddur.

We pulled apart and Cormac rubbed at his chest where my first blow had landed.

"Bastard," he spat. Gone was the smile and the glimmer of humour in his eyes. He was furious. I felt the familiar serenity of combat wash over me. There was nothing now in my world apart from Cormac and his weapon.

"Be glad the fight is not over, young Cormac," Gwawrddur said. "Your last strike was directed at Hunlaf's head, was it not?"

Cormac did not reply, but with a growl, he jumped forward once more.

It was all over in a heartbeat. I barely knew what had occurred. The vibrations of collision thrummed in my right hand and then Cormac grunted and pulled up short. He bent over and retched. Drosten and Runolf's laughter rang out in the sudden quiet of the dusk. Hereward shook his head and tended to the food he was cooking over the campfire.

As I watched Cormac slowly straightening up, rubbing at his groin, my mind caught up with what had transpired. Cormac had rushed me, once again signalling his movements and swinging his weapon with great force. With the speed borne of days of practice, I had parried his attack with ease and sent my counterattack slamming between his legs.

"The fight is Hunlaf's," said Gwawrddur, striding forward and snatching Cormac's stick from him. He then held out his hand to me. I handed him my staff. Then, to my surprise, he picked up both of our sword belts. "I will look after these for the time being," he said.

I went over to Cormac and offered him my hand. He stared at it, his face dark and clouded with anger and pain. After a time, his expression lightened and a sheepish smile lit his face.

"I am sorry," I said.

He grasped my forearm in the warrior grip.

"No need to be sorry," he said. "You won. That is all." He turned to Gwawrddur. "Very well. I understand."

"Do you?" asked the Welshman. "What have you learnt here today?"

Cormac massaged his shoulder.

"Apart from the fact that Hunlaf is a better swordsman?"

"Yes," said Gwawrddur, "for that is not necessarily the case. He has natural skill, it is true." I looked away from Cormac, so that he could not see the pleasure on my face at Gwawrddur's praise. "But," Gwawrddur went on, "you are stronger and have speed and courage."

"And yet I lost."

"And yet you lost," Gwawrddur agreed. "So what have you learnt?"

"That I should listen to what you say," Cormac replied.

"Yes, but more than that?"

Cormac, seemingly fully recovered now, scratched at his beard.

"That it is skill and not strength that wins a fight."

"Even more than skill. It is preparation and sticking to a plan that will conquer a foe," replied Gwawrddur. "Particularly one who allows himself to be governed by his anger and emotions.

The only thing separating you from Hunlaf, was that he focused on what I had taught him. He did not succumb to fear or fury, but awaited your attacks and countered them."

Cormac nodded.

"Good," said Gwawrddur, "if you have learnt this much, this evening has not been wasted."

"Listen to the man," said Hereward from the fire. "The only time a warrior might cast aside caution and preparation is to save a shield-brother. Even then, he must not neglect his duty to the warband. For what good is it to save one brother and to have the whole shieldwall crumble?" He spat into the flames. "Tomorrow we will reach Werceworthe and our planning will begin in earnest. We are few, so it will not be strength and sword-skill that will win against the Norse when they come. No," he tapped his head, "it will be what traps we have laid for them and the defences we have built. Only with discipline and forethought can we hope to prevail."

I thought on the fight with Cormac and Hereward's sombre words as we finally trudged into Werceworthe where it nestled in the crook of the river Cocueda. Everything was familiar to me and my first feelings were of relief. The Norse had not come here. I looked to the sky, where dark clouds swarmed in the north. The weather had remained unsettled for much of the journey from Eoforwic. The closer we got to Werceworthe, the darker and more brooding grew the clouds, and a cold wind blustered into our faces from the north. It was still midsummer, but there was an almost wintry chill in that wind.

"Good sailing wind," Runolf had said ominously in Englisc that morning. Nobody had replied, but the meaning was clear and we had pressed on with renewed haste.

The swirling storm clouds on the horizon seemed to mirror my mood as we passed the buildings of the lay people of Werceworthe. The houses and trees were the same as when I had left only days before. The church still rose above the huts of the villagers who tended the land, the sounds of work and stink from Aethelwig's tannery, the clang of hammer on hot iron, the scent of the smoke from Garulf's forge and the distant lilt of singing that came from the minster in the distance were all things that made me think of safety and home. Nothing had changed here and I was soothed by the sense of homecoming. And yet, as we passed the houses of the ceorls and made our way towards the vallum ditch and the minster buildings, I could not shake the feeling that I was not the same. Men and women peered from their homes, but they did not venture out to greet us.

"This is not the welcome I was expecting," said Drosten.

"They are frightened of you," Leofstan replied. "Armed men do not often bring peace with them."

I wondered if I too now scared them. Did I frighten Leofstan? He had barely spoken to me in the last few days. I saw the tanner's wife, Wulfwaru, tiny Aethelwulf on her hip, staring at me and I smiled, glad to see her comely face. She had always been kind to me, but now her face was grim and pale. Was that fear I saw in her expression? Her eyes flicked down and I understood what she was seeing. The sword was again belted at my hip and she must have seen the truth of what I had said to Hereward in my demeanour and the weapon at my side. I was no longer the monk she had known. I was now a warrior merely clothed in the habit of a monk, nothing more.

I wondered what Aelfwyn would have seen if she were yet alive to witness this change in me? She had known me as a boy and as a shy monk. Would she have recognised this harder, colder man who now wore the monk's clothes, but carried a sword and had taken lives with his own hands? The vision of her as I had last seen her, terrified with panic and fearful for her own life and that of her husband, flitted into my mind like an unwelcome bat in a hall. For a heartbeat, I saw anew her husband's corpse and could smell the smoke from the fires that had consumed her and much of Lindisfarnae. With a grimace, I pushed the dark memories away. Clutching the pommel of my sword as if for support, I pressed onward. On the day the Norsemen came to the holy island, the innocent monk had ceased to be, as dead as if he too had been thrown into the inferno of the burning barn alongside Aelfwyn.

When we reached the minster buildings, Brother Seoca, whom I had known since our time together at Magilros, came out to greet us. He led us all to the dormitory hall where Uhtric and his men had slept on our previous visit.

"Make yourselves comfortable," he said. "Food and drink will be brought to you soon."

"That is more like it," said Cormac, who always seemed to be hungry.

Leofstan followed Seoca out of the hall, but Seoca hesitated at the door, turning to me.

"Brother Hunlaf," he said. "Please take your belongings to your cell and then join us for Vespers in the chapel." I placed a hand on the pommel of my sword but made no move to follow him. He looked down at the weapon, his eyes widening in shock. His mouth fell open, but he made no sound.

"Hunlaf will not be joining us at Vespers," Leofstan said, and his voice sounded hollow and tinged with great sadness.

"But... but..." stammered Brother Seoca.

Leofstan met my gaze and gave me a small nod of encouragement.

"Isn't that right, Hunlaf?"

I reached up and ran a hand over my head. My scalp was no longer shaved bare in a tonsure. Where the bald circle of skin had been, now the bristles of new hair grew.

"Leofstan speaks the truth of it," I said. "Thank you, Brother Seoca."

Seoca stared aghast. I returned his gaze, unmoving. Leofstan touched him gently on the arm. Seoca turned, shaking his head and muttering as he left the hall.

We threw our bags and packs in one corner and pulled benches from where they were propped against the wall. Shortly afterwards, Osfrith entered, carrying an earthenware pitcher and a stack of wooden cups on a tray.

"What have we here?" asked Cormac.

"Ale," Osfrith said in a timid voice. He could not stop looking at me, as though my physical form had changed beyond all recognition. I offered him a thin smile and he hurried away.

We drank ale and the others talked quietly about what we had witnessed when we had arrived. They spoke of the distribution of the houses and work huts of the lay folk, how the river encircled a good part of the minster, the steepness of the cliffs that fell down to the water in the west, the position of the ferry crossing and where the nearest ford was. Gwawrddur asked about the river. How close was its mouth to the sea? What of the island they had mentioned, could it be seen from here?

Hereward answered most of their questions, but as the one who had lived here for two years, it was up to me to give them the details they needed. I answered their questions as best I could, but I could not concentrate and more than once Hereward had to angrily bang his hand on the board before him to get my attention.

"Wake up, Hunlaf," he said.

"He is away with the fairy folk," said Cormac, and absently I crossed myself to ward off the possible curse of the evil elves.

I took a sip of my ale.

"Sorry," I said. "I am tired."

Hereward accepted my excuse, but I knew it was a lie. It was not my fatigue that plucked at my concentration like a thread being snagged from the hem of a cloak, pulling and unravelling my thoughts. No, I had that feeling of excitement and dread that presages a thunderstorm. Or battle. I could not focus because I was certain that something portentous was about to happen.

I did not need to wait long to find out what it was.

Thirty-Three

"You are still certain that this is what God has called you to do?" Abbot Beonna asked me.

He had sent for me before the evening meal and I had walked the short distance to his quarters with a feeling of dread. I recalled feeling the same way when my older brother, Beornnoth, had stolen a jar of Father's favourite mead and convinced me to drink it with him. Not only had we both become puking drunk, but in our inebriated state, we had smashed the jug too. Father had summoned us before him shortly after we had returned from the top fields, where we had spent the afternoon drinking and playing childish games until we had grown so drunk we had collapsed in the waving barley. We had stopped vomiting by the time we stood before Father, but my head pounded and I could barely walk in a straight line.

I had been ten summers old, already full of defiance and anger, but I had been no match for my father, who had put me over his knee and spanked me with a wooden butter paddle until I could not sit down. Beornnoth had fared no better. Father had not listened to my protestations that it was Beornnoth who had stolen the jug and goaded me into joining in with the drinking, and we had both received the same punishment.

I had cried with frustration and pain as Aelfwyn had

consoled me later. She'd listened as I had raged against the injustice, nodding because she had known the truth, saying little as no words would alter my father's mind or take away the punishment I had received.

I was no child of ten now, but I felt the same overpowering urge to weep and I half expected the abbot to tell me to bend over so that he could exact a beating on me for being a wayward son.

He did no such thing. Instead he looked at me from his desk, his eyes rheumy and sad. Leofstan was seated in the same chair he had occupied the last time I had been there.

"Hunlaf," he said, his voice gentle. "You must answer the abbot."

Startled out of my thoughts, I nodded.

"Yes, father," I said, and it was the truth. "The vision was clear to me and since then the good Lord has saved me from what should have been certain death. I am sure He means for me to help to protect the minster from the heathens."

"And the Norseman?" Beonna said. "Leofstan tells me he is now baptised into the faith."

"Yes, father. The king insisted it must be so if he were to remain in his kingdom. He was baptised and then oath-sworn to Uhtric."

"Do you believe we can trust him?"

I pondered this for a moment only.

"Yes, I do. He is a man of his word. His ways are foreign and strange to us perhaps, but I believe he is a good man."

"And are you a good man?" asked Beonna, frowning at me in the gathering gloom.

His words took me aback and I did not know how to respond. I looked to Leofstan, but he did not return my gaze.

"I am a sinner, like all men," I said at last. My mouth was dry and I swallowed. "But I try to be good. To live by the teachings of the Scriptures."

"And is it the Scriptures that teach the killing of your fellow man?"

I bridled at that, feeling that same defiance and sense of injustice that had so angered me when my father had beaten me. I bit back the words that threatened to burst forth.

"No," I said, keeping my voice steady with difficulty. "I know that to kill is a sin. But is not the defender of the weak forgiven by God?"

For a long while, Beonna did not speak. He reached for the flask I recognised from my last visit and, like then, poured out three cups of mead. He handed one to Leofstan, who took it without comment, the other he passed to me. He drank deeply of the third cup.

"The Almighty can forgive anything, if a man comes to him truly repentant and with an open heart," he said.

I did not speak, but his words gave me some comfort. The thought of eternal damnation had been gnawing at me ever since the horrors of Lindisfarnae.

"But a man who seeks war and killing," he went on, "is surely not penitent." He stared at me. The evening was drawing in and only a dim light shone from the small window in the room. His eyes were shadowed; hidden from me beneath his heavy brows.

"I have thought and prayed much on this and waited for your return before I made my decision," Beonna continued. "Leofstan has told me of the events that have transpired, but I wanted to be certain of your mind before I pass judgement."

His words were ominous. Again I felt like the child about to face punishment and, just as when I had stood before my father, I was certain I had done nothing wrong. I bit my lip.

"Do you choose the sword over peace, Hunlaf? Will you allow war to govern your life, rather than God's love?"

"God has placed a sword in my hand and given me the skill and strength to wield it to protect his own." I sat up straight and puffed out my chest. Pride is a sin too, but I cannot deny that I felt proud of the battle-skill I had unearthed from within me. "I cannot turn my back on that."

"The Lord places many things within our reach," Beonna said, shaking his head. "We decide which we pick up. The choice is ours and ours alone."

"I can feel your disappointment in me," I said, tears stinging my eyes. I blinked and took a deep breath. I would not cry.

"No, no, Hunlaf," Beonna said. He leaned forward and patted my knee. "We are not disappointed. We are scared of what will become of you. You were sent to us as a boy by your father, and we will suffer his wrath if you leave us, but you are a boy no longer. And each man must make his own choices."

I had not thought that far ahead, or how my father would react to the tidings of his second son abandoning the post he had secured for me. He would surely cease to pay whatever silver he placed within the coffers of the church for my upkeep when he learnt of my change of heart.

"Leave you?" I said, a new fear gripping me. "I do not wish to leave. I have brought the band of warriors to defend the minster, and those I love." My voice cracked. "And I will stay to aid them."

"And you are welcome here, my son," Beonna said softly. "Know that you will always be welcome." He hesitated. "But as you no longer abide by the *Regula Sancti*, you cannot remain part of this brethren."

I opened my mouth to protest, but the words did not come. Hereward had said the same, and the truth was that I had already made my decision. I had not thought of my father's reaction to the news, but that would not change my mind. The abbot and Leofstan could clearly see as much and were merely formalising it. I looked down at the cup in my hands and nodded. I emptied the contents and welcomed the burning sweetness of the strong mead. A warrior's drink, I thought with grim irony.

"There is no shame in this, Hunlaf," said Leofstan.

I nodded again. If Leofstan spoke truly, why did I feel so shameful?

"Perhaps one day you will return to us," said Beonna, "but for now, it seems the Lord has other plans for you. Now, let us pray together for the days that are to come."

At the time, filled with the passions of youth, I could not imagine ever returning to the life of a monk. Something had awakened within me when I took the life of that raider on Lindisfarnae, and I had found my true calling when I picked up the sword from the brigand's dead hand on the muddy stream bank. I was a warrior now and would not look back at who I had been. But the abbot was a wise man. Beonna is long since gone now to sit by the throne of our Heavenly Father, but I often think of him and pray for his eternal soul. Not that the prayers of a sinner like me are needed for such a holy man. For in the end, his words proved true. Fighting and killing are the pursuits of young men and, as the years passed, with increasingly fewer of my friends surviving and my bones aching whenever there was rain in the air, the prospect of quiet contemplation and prayer appealed. Eventually, I made my way back to the minster at Werceworthe, and found the abbot's promise had been passed on to his successor, Criba. He did not like me, or what I stood for. I am sure he would rather I had died in some distant land, but somehow I had managed to outlive all of my warrior brothers and whilst I was not welcomed like the prodigal son with open arms, I was allowed to take up my place within the minster, and for that I am thankful.

But back then, in the abbot's room, I could only see as far as defending the minster against the Norsemen. If I lived beyond that, time would tell where God and my wyrd would lead me. We bowed our heads and Beonna led us in prayer. With each word I felt my old life drifting away, like dark dye leaching from cloth in hot water. The abbot's words and his and Leofstan's love comforted me, and yet, at the same time, I knew that when I left that room, I would be a monk no more. I would discard the habit and the tonsure, wear a sword and ride rather than walk. Men and women would look at me differently, expecting things of me that I had never truly contemplated before.

The future was unseen and I could not imagine the great deeds I would witness in later years. As I knelt there in the abbot's darkening room, all I knew for certain was that when the Norsemen came again to our shores, I would not cower in the church with the holy men, or flee before them with the women and children and the ceorls who toiled in the fields. No, I would face them alongside my new brothers. I might die on the cold iron of the Norse axes and swords, but I would fight to protect the lives of those unable to fight for themselves. I would not run from battle, but towards it, and I would stand as a warrior, blade in hand and willing to give my blood and my life in the defence of my friends.

There was a time for prayer and forgiveness, and there was a time for swords.

Thirty-Four

When I returned to the dormitory, the boards had been laid out for the evening meal and the smell of cooking filled the air as I passed the kitchen. The conversation with the abbot had left me in a daze. My mind was clouded, as if I had drunk much more than the single cup of mead.

My discomfort must have been plain to see, for as I walked, stiff-legged, to find my place on the benches, Hereward caught my arm. I looked down at him, a blank expression on my face.

"Are you ill, Hunlaf?" he asked.

I shook my head but said nothing. Frowning, he released me and I stumbled on.

The brethren traipsed in after Vespers and the food was served. I noticed Osfrith staring at me, and when I swept my gaze about the gathering, all the faces that looked back at me seemed cold and unforgiving, as if I had been judged and found wanting.

The fare was simple enough; a pottage and a thick slice of fresh bread each. But this was followed by a treat as tasty as any morsel on a lord's table. Freothogar, a man from the village, had baked some of his fabulous honey cakes. Everyone in Werceworthe agreed that Freothogar's cakes were better than any other, but when asked what made them so delicious, he was always tight-lipped and would merely smile and tap his nose.

I did not think I had an appetite, but the thought of one of Freothogar's honey cakes changed that, and when a steaming bowl of stew was placed before me, I ate ravenously, mopping the bowl clean with the bread.

The older men seemed to understand that I needed time to myself and none of them tried to engage me in conversation, but Cormac slid onto the bench beside me, speaking incessantly and asking all manner of questions about the brethren, the minster and its environs.

"Speak to Leofstan," I growled, "if you wish to hear about the minster and the monks."

"But I would rather hear it from you, Killer," he replied, using the name that Gwawrddur had given me. When the older man called me that, it did not rankle and I took it in the spirit it was meant. But the name on Cormac's lips saw me flying into a rage. I hammered my fist down on the board and the cups and plates rattled.

Drosten cursed as his cup of ale tumbled over.

"That is not my name, you Hibernian fool," I snarled, my voice ringing out loudly above the murmured hubbub of the hall.

The room fell silent.

"I meant no ill," Cormac said.

"Come now, Cormac," said Gwawrddur, his tone soft in the sudden stillness. "You have keen eyes. Can you not see that Hunlaf does not wish to converse with you this night? Leave him be. He has no time for your prating tonight."

I nodded my thanks to the Welshman and mumbled an apology to Cormac before pushing myself up and stalking to the corner where lay all of our belongings.

Everybody watched me and I wanted to scream at them to let me be, but soon enough the room was abuzz with the drone of the warriors' conversations, while the monks ate in their customary silence.

Osfrith used his hands to sign at me, asking if I was well.

I made the sign for "yes" back at him and offered him a thin smile. I would have to find time to talk to him. We had been friends ever since coming here, and he looked up to me like an older brother. The change to my circumstances would surely hit him hard.

But for now I ignored him and the rest of the men in the hall and went about what I had been thinking of doing for the last few days but only now, after speaking to the abbot, dared to do.

Thirty-Five

"What is that up there?" asked Hereward. I looked in the direction of his pointing finger, peering through the mist of drizzle at the mouldering buildings that stood on the high grounds that overlooked the monastery.

"That is Werce's Hall," I said.

"Werce? The lord of this place? I thought it was just monks and ceorls."

"He was the lord once, I am told, but it has been close to a hundred years since this land was gifted to the brethren of Lindisfarnae by King Ceolwulf."

"Does nobody live there now?" Hereward asked.

I shook my head. I had been up there before with Osfrith. Neither the large building, nor the smaller huts near it, were in use. The thatch had fallen in and rotted through in places and one of the walls had partially collapsed, but it seemed to me as though it had been used by either the villagers or the monastery until quite recently. It had certainly not been abandoned for a century, for if it had been, there would be nothing to see but rotting timbers in the grass.

"It has been empty for as long as I have been here," I said, eager to give Hereward an answer. Gone was my sullen silence of the night before. I had awoken with fresh purpose. I had chosen this life and, if I was to prosper in it, I would need to make myself useful.

Hereward exchanged a glance with Gwawrddur. The Welsh-man said nothing, but nodded slowly, as if in response to some unspoken question. I marvelled at how the two warriors seemed to understand one another with barely a word uttered. It was not the first time I had noted this since we had set out that morning to survey the land.

"We shall have to go up there to take a closer look," said Hereward.

I looked up at the grey sky. The light rain moistened my cheeks and I wished I had a cloak to keep me dry.

"It will be slippery on that slope," I said.

Hereward smiled.

"Good," he said, and began walking across the fields towards the high hill that rose to the south of the promontory that was made by the loop of the Cocueda.

We skirted the green barley that dropped under the weight of the rain. The nettles and weeds that grew along the verge were wet and soaked our clothes as we passed. It had started raining in the night and, though it was not cold, I was glad of the extra protection from the mud and the moisture on the long grass that my new leg wraps provided. I had cut the bottom half of my habit using the sharp seax I had taken from the dead brigand by the river. What had been my long robe was now a short kirtle, the tattered, un-stitched hem of which hung to my thighs. The remainder of the woollen cloth I had cut into strips. In the morning I had bound them about my lower legs. I wore old breeches that I had brought with me to the minster when I had first come from Magilros.

Hereward had raised an eyebrow when he'd seen my new attire, but he'd said nothing.

Cormac had grinned and said, "You look every part the warrior now, Hunlaf." I had returned his smile. I did not wish to argue with him or any of the others that morning. But despite the change to my clothes and the heft of the sword at my hip, I did not feel like a man of war. As we trudged through the rain along the southern and eastern edges of the land upon which the minster nestled, I felt strangely out of place. I knew the surroundings well, the sandbars in the river, the shingle beach where the ferry landed, the alders that skirted the waters of the river and the fields of barley that grew in the east between the river and the hill of Werce's Hall. I answered Hereward's questions quickly and as fully as possible, but as I walked beside these men of action, these killers, I could not shake the feeling that I was an impostor amongst them. A cuckoo in a nest of falcons.

Drosten pointed out likely places where it might be possible to ambush the Norsemen. Gwawrddur said that it was clear they would need to sacrifice some of the buildings, if they were to stand any chance against superior numbers. Hereward listened to their suggestions, his eyes ever roving over the land in search of weak spots or places that could be more easily defended. I did not look at the land with the eyes of a warrior. I had much to learn if I wished to be of real use to these men. Cormac, I noticed, was uncharacteristically quiet. Perhaps I was not the only one feeling out of my depth and adrift.

Grass grew thick and lush on the hill that loomed over the settlement and minster of Werceworthe. As I had warned, the rain made the going difficult. The ground was slick and we had to use our hands to steady ourselves as we ascended. When we reached the summit we looked down at the houses of the lay people and in the distance, at the far northern tip of the jutting piece of land, the church and minster buildings by the river's edge. The rain stopped as we stared out over Werceworthe. In the north, far off on the horizon above the distant hills, the clouds parted and a ray of sunshine lit the land below. Even up here, there was scarcely a breeze. It was yet high summer and the sun was hot. The cooling effect of the rain was quickly forgotten and it soon felt uncomfortably warm and clammy.

Hereward led us over to the western side of the hill and we looked down the steep bank at the river below. This side was much steeper than on the east, and the slope was heavily wooded with alders and sallows.

"They won't be wanting to come that way," said Gwawrddur. I wondered at his words, but did not wish to appear foolish, so kept silent. Why would the Norsemen seek to climb this hill at all, when the settlement was below us?

Seemingly satisfied with what he saw, Hereward turned and went to the hall. It was a large building and must have been imposing before it fell into disrepair. There were two smaller outbuildings, but both of those looked to be in an even worse state than the hall. We walked around the outside of the building before eventually stepping inside through the doorway. The door had fallen from its leather hinges and lay rotting on the floor inside. The place was redolent of mildew and damp. Pigeons, disturbed by our arrival, fluttered and cooed in the rafters. Rotted thatch, broken timber, bird shit and mouse droppings littered the floor.

Hereward slid his seax from its sheath at his belt and went to the thick pillars that supported the beams of the roof. He jammed the tip of the knife into the wood in several places, prying and twisting the blade and examining the damage. Turning back to us he nodded, a grim smile on his face.

"The timber is sound enough," he said. "For the first time I am beginning to think we might actually do this thing."

We left the stinking shaded interior of the hall and stepped once more out into the steaming warmth of the sunshine. Hereward and Gwawrddur were both pleased with what they had seen. Drosten, his tattooed face making him appear to be frowning, surveyed the land from the hall's vantage point. As if he too understood what Hereward planned, he nodded silently to himself. I glanced at Cormac. The Hibernian raised an eyebrow sardonically, inviting me to ask the question that I thought was probably also on his mind. Again, fearing appearing foolish, I clamped my mouth shut and said nothing. Instead, I led Hereward and the others to the south of the hill. There it dropped away in a shallow incline. A huge solitary oak stood there, like a sentinel, and we could clearly make out a deep ditch that led from east to west across the outcropping of land that was largely encircled by the river's meandering loop.

The ditch was too straight to be natural. Wide and as deep as a man is tall in places, it seemed that the only reasonable explanation for it was defence, but its banks were eroded and overgrown; clogged with weeds and brambles.

"It seems that men long before us defended this place," said Hereward.

"Nobody knows who dug it," I said. "It was here when the monks came, and they say even before Werce's Hall."

Hereward rubbed his bearded chin, surveyed the land all about, before nodding in approval at what he saw.

"This is a good place," he said. "I imagine men have lived here for generations. Who knows, perhaps they even made this hill."

I gazed about the expanse of the raised mound where we stood. I took in the shallow slope to the east, and the steep wooded fall down to the river in the west.

"You think that is possible?"

"Anything is possible, Hunlaf," said Hereward, with a smile. "Even a monk becoming a warrior."

My face grew hot. Hereward laughed at my expression and slapped me hard on the shoulder.

"Relax, young Hunlaf," he said. "Your secret is safe with me."

"My secret?"

He looked at me and shook his head.

"Pay me no heed," he said. "I am merely jesting with you."

His words added to my unease. From the distance came the echoing clang of the church bell. I realised with a start that it must be Sunday, for that was the only day the abbot allowed the piece of metal that had been fashioned by Garulf, the smith, to be hit to call the faithful to mass. Without thinking, I turned towards the north and began walking briskly towards the church. Hereward laughed.

"Not much of a secret," he said.

I paused, frowning at his meaning.

"You can take the monk out of the monastery," said Cormac, "but you cannot take the monastery out of the monk as easily." He chuckled at his own wit and the sound of his laughter chafed against my nerves.

"That is the sound of the call to mass, Cormac. I may no longer be one of the brethren here, but I am yet a Christian." I looked about the men, unable to hide my displeasure. "Are we not all good Christians?" I asked.

Hereward held up his hands in a placatory gesture.

"Well," he said, smiling, "I am not too sure about him yet," he nodded in Runolf's direction, "but I take your meaning. Come, boys. Let us to mass. If we are to make this work, we will need God on our side." Runolf frowned, an expression of consternation on his craggy features.

"What say you?" he said. "And what is that noise? An attack?"

For a heartbeat nobody made a sound and then, as one, we all laughed. Runolf, confused, asked, "What? What is the sound?"

When we had stopped laughing, I explained to him in Norse that the metal clang was the sound of us being called to worship. He frowned again, still unsure why we had laughed. I chose not to explain further and felt a thin prickle of shame at my behaviour. I knew it was craven of me, but I could not deny that it had felt good for the others' ridicule to pass from me to the huge Norseman.

We arrived at the church when the mass had already commenced. Abbot Beonna had welcomed the congregants and was now reading the first lesson. We shuffled in at the rear of the building and the abbot fell silent for a moment at the disturbance. The curious faces of the villagers and the brethren turned towards us and I knew not how to respond to the expressions I saw there. Sweat beaded my brow and I rubbed uncomfortably at my itching scalp, where the bristles of my disappearing tonsure grew. I looked down at the ground, closed my eyes and focused on the words of the service. Once again the sensations and sounds were so familiar to me that it was easy to imagine that nothing had changed. But I was not standing with the brethren at the front of the coolly shadowed building, I was huddled by the door surrounded by hard men who, whilst bowing their heads and muttering the necessary responses, were clearly not well-versed in the sacred rites of the mass.

The abbot droned on and, automatically, my mouth uttered the correct words in reply. When the brethren chanted the epistle, I sang with them. By the time the moment came to partake of the Eucharist, my sweat had cooled and I shivered. Was I yet welcome here in the house of God? Despite the words I had said to the abbot and Leofstan, here, standing in the presence of the Lord in His house, I questioned whether He would truly forgive me the sin of murder.

"What must I do?" rumbled Runolf beside me.

I looked up at him, suddenly aware that his discomfort must have been greater than mine.

"Follow me," I whispered. "It is but a mouthful of wine and a piece of bread."

He clearly had no understanding of the significance of the symbols and I vowed to myself that I must spend time explaining the rituals and the true faith to him. He was baptised and tied to the king of this land, so it was only right that he should understand the religion he now ascribed to.

Runolf walked hesitantly behind me up to the altar. On my instruction he knelt beside me and without comment he drank wine from the ornate silver cup the abbot offered. He watched me closely, as I took the bread on my tongue from the abbot's hand. I chewed and swallowed, watching as Runolf did the same. How easily men adapt. Heathen becomes Christian; monk becomes killer.

At the end of the mass, when Beonna dismissed the faithful, the brethren and lay people filed out into the welcoming sunshine of the afternoon. Hereward stepped before the abbot as he prepared to leave the church. Signalling for the others to go on ahead, Beonna moved back into the gloom of the building and nodded for Hereward to speak.

"We have walked the perimeter of your lands," Hereward said.

"And what did you find?"

"The good tidings are that, with God's grace, and with enough time to prepare, we might be able to protect your people."

"These are good tidings indeed. Praise be to God that in His wisdom he has brought you here to this place."

"And praise be to my Lord Uhtric," Hereward said, "for it is he who has granted us permission to come to your aid."

The abbot waved his hand dismissively.

"Of course," he said. "God is good and so is Lord Uhtric."

"There is much work to be done if we are to have a hope of vanquishing the Norsemen when they attack."

"If they attack," the abbot corrected.

"When they attack," Runolf said. His voice was firm. He may not have understood every word we said, but he understood this much, that was clear.

The abbot ignored him, but Hereward nodded.

"When the Norsemen attack," he said, "there will be many of them and there are few of us."

"What is it that you are asking for?" asked the abbot, astutely recognising the request couched in Hereward's words.

"We need people to help prepare the defences," Hereward answered. "To make spears, to dig ditches, and to repair the buildings on the hill."

"Werce's Hall?" asked Beonna.

"Yes. The hall must be repaired so that once more it can house people."

The abbot scratched at his scrawny throat, pondering Hereward's words. At last he nodded.

"I will order some of the brothers to aid you with the construction work at the hall. It is good that you do not stay here at the minster. Your presence is a distraction to the less devout of my charges."

He did not look at me as he said the words, but they stabbed all the same.

"No, no," said Hereward. "You misunderstand me. The hall must be readied so that every man, woman and child in the minster and village can be housed there."

The abbot's mouth fell open, aghast at what was being suggested.

"But... but..." he stammered. "Such a thing is madness. What of the church? The scriptorium? The cells? My room? You would have us abandon them all?"

Hereward's expression was stern, unflinching.

"It is the only way we can save the minster. When the Norse come, we must be prepared for everybody to go to the hall on the hill. We will defend that place and that place alone."

"But what of all the other buildings?" Beonna waved his hand to take in the fine cross on the altar. "What about the gold cross. The reliquaries? The finger of Saint Edwin?" His eyes widened as he thought of all the treasures in the minster. "What would become of the books in the scriptorium? We have one of the finest examples outside of Roma of *Exposito psalmorum* by Cassiodorus!"

"All that is left here," said Hereward, his tone brooking no argument, "will be taken by the raiders. We cannot make you and the brethren, or anyone do what we say, but know this, if you do not come to the hall when the Norsemen arrive, you will be killed or enslaved. We will not be able to save you."

For a time the abbot was speechless. His face had drained of colour and he looked as if he had aged a decade in a heartbeat. Absently, he wrung his trembling hands. He looked as though he would welcome a cup of his strong mead, but that would have to wait. I felt sorry for him. It was no easy thing for a man of peace and learning to imagine the destruction the Norse would wreak on the minster. But I had been there. I had heard the screams, felt the heat of the flames, smelt the smoke and charred flesh on the breeze.

"It is the only way," I said.

"How can you be so sure they will attack the hall?" he asked, trying to find fault with Hereward's plan.

"I hope they do not," said Hereward. "I hope they look upon the defences, and the position of the hall, and sail on in search of weaker prey. But make no mistake, Beonna, these men come for slaves and for riches. They do not seek land to till or buildings to settle, they come in hunt of able men and young women, silver and gold. And all of those things will be in Werce's Hall or buried somewhere near. The Norse will attack us on that hill, or they will leave empty handed."

Thirty-Six

We left Beonna by the altar in the dark interior of the church. I looked back and felt a terrible pity for the man. He had come here as the leader of a house of holy men, to lead them in prayer and the study of the Scriptures. The minster was far from the borders of Northumbria. There was no reason to expect war might descend upon his small peaceful domain. And yet, the more that Hereward had spoken, the more Beonna's shoulders had slumped. Hereward's words were hard and unyielding, like stones. And that such a man as this, a hearth-warrior of the lord of Bebbanburg, would speak thus, gave the meaning all the more weight.

He had tried to believe this would not happen, that it was some distant event that might never come to pass. So it is with all men, even those as wise and caring as the abbot. It is one thing to hear of something that has occurred elsewhere and to weep for those lost, and rage at the injustice of it. Good men, like the abbot, feel great compassion for others and will pray for the souls of those less fortunate than themselves. But when confronted with the possibility that their lives might be thrown into disarray by some unseen threat, it is hard for any man to truly believe it. It is this same trait that makes young men believe they will never die.

But the abbot was no fool and he was no young man. Listening to Hereward's instructions and predictions his face had crumpled and he had made the sign of the cross several times.

"I trust that the Lord will protect us all," he muttered at last. Hereward nodded.

"Well, the good Lord sent us and we will do our best," he said. "But if you do not follow my orders, I fear that God might believe you have decided not to take the help He has bidden unto you."

With that, Hereward had stalked out of the stone church. He did not wait for a reply from the abbot. As I glanced back at the old man's drawn, pallid face, I deemed it for the best. Beonna needed time to come to terms with what Hereward had told him. He would pray, asking for guidance, I was sure, but in the end, he would realise that the warrior spoke the truth. Yet such decisions could not be hurried, and so we left him alone to his prayers and worries.

"I am starving," Hereward said once outside in the warm humid afternoon sunshine. "Let us see what food we can find." We had been given the same as the monks to break our fast, a watery gruel and a slice of stale bread, and it was clearly less than the warrior was accustomed to.

The monks were eating in silence when we returned to the hall. There was food laid out for us, and we sat and talked about what we had seen and the plans that would be needed. The men's voices were loud and jarring in the quiet of the refectory and I wondered how long it would take me to speak freely as I ate, like them. Hereward spoke with seemingly no care for who overheard and I wondered if this was part of his plan. I glanced about and saw that the monks were clearly listening. Hereward was a wily one. Easier perhaps for Beonna to be persuaded of what he needed to do from his own brother monks. And even if he were already convinced of what must be done, in this way, his brethren would be less shocked when he informed them.

After a time, the monks rose from the benches and left to perform their chores and to attend Sext. We were left alone. The food, a wholesome pottage flavoured with small flakes of pike caught in the Cocueda, whilst more plentiful than the morning meal, was still not to Hereward's liking and all of the bread had already gone. I was full enough after my serving, as was Gwawrddur, but Drosten, Hereward and Runolf all ate two helpings. Cormac, as hungry as ever, ate three whole bowls of the stuff.

"By Christ's bones," said Hereward, "where do you put all that food?"

Cormac grinned.

"I grew up with four brothers and three sisters," he said, chewing the last mouthful. "I learnt to eat quickly and not to waste anything. If I didn't eat it, someone else would."

"I have four brothers also," said Drosten. "Are yours all back in Hibernia?"

Cormac's face darkened and he stared into his bowl.

"Yes," he mumbled, his voice catching, "they are all in Hibernia."

Cormac's shift of humour had soured the mood between us and an awkward silence fell.

"What we need is a good drink," said Hereward, casting about for something stronger than the weak ale we had been served. Noticing a movement at the far end of the hall as someone stepped in from the bright sunshine outside, Hereward smiled. "Perfect," he said, beckoning the figure over. The newcomer was silhouetted in the light from the doorway, but the sway of the hips and the narrow waist gave away that it was a young woman. "Fetch us some mead, girl," Hereward said and aimed a playful slap at the woman's rear.

As quick as thought, the woman stepped out of his reach and hit his hand away. The report of her palm against his skin echoed in the room.

"I am no maidservant or slave for you to grope," she snapped. On hearing her voice, I looked up at her face and finally recognised her. Wulfwaru, the tanner's wife.

"Forgive me, goodwife," Hereward said, rising to his feet. I saw his gaze drop to the keys that dangled from her belt and then up to the wimple that covered her head. "This ale must be stronger than I thought." He was flustered and his cheeks burnt red.

She glowered at him.

"I came to offer my services to you," she said.

Cormac, his previous sombre mood seemingly forgotten, whistled. Drosten laughed. A stern look from Wulfwaru silenced them both. Gwawrddur narrowed his eyes and said nothing.

"And what services would those be," asked Hereward, maintaining a serious mien.

"We all know why you are here," she said. She cast her gaze over us. She offered Runolf a small nod of recognition, presumably for what he had done for her by saving Aethelwulf. "But we are not fools," she went on. "We can count and you are but six men. You need help."

"You are right," replied Hereward. "We will be asking for people to help dig and build defences. Everyone will be needed, if we are to survive what is coming."

"We will all do our share of what is required," she said. "The people of the minster are hardworking and strong. But it is not the sweat of my labour I offer you."

"What is it then that you are offering?" Hereward's brow furrowed.

"I would fight alongside you," she said, her voice firm and hard. "Where you are six, I will make you seven."

For a moment there was silence in the hall. Then Gwawrddur spoke for the first time.

"Well, Drosten, you should be pleased," he said, the ghost of a smile on his lips.

"What are you speaking of Welshman?" asked Drosten, confused.

Gwawrddur's smile broadened.

"With the addition of the woman," he said, "we are once more no longer a band of thieves."

Thirty-Seven

Runolf heaved on the oars of the small boat, pulling us quickly and effortlessly towards the mouth of the Cocueda on the outgoing tide. For a time Drosten had sat on the thwart and manned the oars, but the skiff had meandered left and right and we had made slow progress. We had barely reached the next looping turn in the river to the east of Werceworthe when the Pict had sent the craft into a dense stand of rushes. With a growl, Runolf had pulled him away, almost tipping the boat over in the process, and positioned himself at the oars. He was clearly a much more experienced oarsman, and he soon had us speeding along the river towards the sea. His skill, coupled with his prodigious strength, would quickly take us out of the river and into the open waters of the North Sea. I had travelled in this boat several times before, and I had even manned the oars, but we had never made such rapid progress as when Runolf powered us along, his shoulders and arms bulging with each pull.

As one of the youngest members of the brethren of Werceworthe, it had often fallen to me to help take provisions to Cocwaedesae. Even though this was an unscheduled trip to the island, we had decided to bring some things for Anstan, the old monk who lived there. We could not carry much though, just a small barrel of mead with the abbot's greetings, a sack of flour and a linen-wrapped hunk of ham. Usually there would only be two of us in the boat, leaving much more room for supplies, but today, as the sun lanced through the trees that lined the Cocueda's edge, the small boat was already low in the water with its four occupants. Hereward was sitting at the stern, looking ahead, past Runolf. He had not spoken for some time, but I knew we were not done with the subject that had resurfaced as we loaded the boat back on the shingle beach at Werceworthe.

Hereward's eyes darted and he was suddenly alert, peering to the left at the shadows of rushes and trees as we passed. Curious and on edge, I followed his gaze. Had he seen some hidden danger? His obvious unease was making us all nervous. A flicker of iridescent green and blue flashed against the shadows. With a sigh I realised that what had caught his attention was the darting of a dragonfly, low over the water. I trailed my fingers into the cool waters of the river and then splashed a few drops on my face. The sun was not yet at its zenith but the day was already hot. The drizzling rain of yesterday was now a distant memory and the sky was a pale egg-shell blue. The trees that towered over the river rustled and sighed with the light northerly breeze, but here in the wind-shadow all was still, the only sound the gentle splash of the oar blades cutting through the water and the soft creak of wood on wood.

"A woman!" Hereward blurted out suddenly.

Runolf snorted and shook his head. We had all heard Hereward voice his disapproval many times. I wondered when he would accept what had happened and move on. Ever since Wulfwaru had come to us the day before, Hereward had continued to circle back to his outrage at her proposal to help in the upcoming fighting. I did not know what else to say that had not already been said. It was unusual for a woman to offer to stand with the men in combat, that much was true, but after our initial doubts had been put to rest by Wulfwaru's determination and obviously useful skills, we had all voiced our opinion that her aid would be welcome. This had seemed to incense Hereward, as if somehow our acceptance of the woman's help made us traitors, that he could no longer trust us.

"But you are... you are..." Hereward had stammered the day before, looking up at Wulfwaru, who stood with her fists clenched and pressed against her hips in a clear expression of defiance.

"I am what?" she asked.

"A woman!" replied Hereward.

"My husband is pleased of that," she said. We all laughed, except Hereward, who gave us a dark look. He stood up then, his face flushed with rage, but clearly unsure how to proceed. Wulfwaru met his gaze and did not flinch.

"We need weapons, not spindles and cooking bowls," he blustered, but his anger seemed to quickly lose strength, like a summer storm that blows over and is soon gone, leaving behind it just wet ground and the memory of squalling rain and wind.

"I can offer you more than weaving and baking bread," said Wulfwaru.

"What can you offer us, woman?" asked Hereward, his tone dripping with disdain.

Wulfwaru, her comely face stern and severe, turned and walked towards the door.

"Come outside and I will show you," she said. Not waiting for a response, she left the building.

"This is madness," grumbled Hereward, as we all stood up at the same time with a clatter of benches being slid back.

"We lose nothing by seeing what she has to show us," said Gwawrddur, already walking towards the exit. The rest of us followed and Hereward, after a moment's hesitation, cursed and joined us.

Outside in the warm sunshine, Wulfwaru was standing, waiting for us patiently. In her left hand she now held a hunting bow of yew. In her right was a long arrow, its white goose-feathered fletching gleaming in the bright sunshine.

"What are you going to do with that, girl?" sneered Hereward.

Wulfwaru sighed, but seemed otherwise immune to the warrior's taunts.

"My father too believed that girls were of no use," she said. "But he had no sons and so he had to make do and teach me the things he would have taught boys, had he been blessed with them."

"And he taught you to use a bow, I suppose," said Hereward, apparently tired with this conversation.

"He did." She nodded towards three small objects in the distance. Each was a figure made of tightly-wrapped straw, not much larger than a child's toy, perhaps the length of a man's arm. They were propped against the trunks of three alders that rose up tall by the river. "You see those dolls?" she asked. We all nodded. They were some fifty paces distant. "Imagine they are three Norse raiders," she said.

"Aren't they a little short for Norsemen?" said Cormac with a chuckle.

Without answering, and moving with a fluid strength that spoke of years of practice, Wulfwaru nocked the arrow, drew and loosed. It flew straight and unerring, skewering the straw doll's head and pinning it against the tree. Her prowess with the bow could not be disputed, but before the first arrow had hit its target, she had pulled a second arrow from the ground by her feet. This, too, she sent flying, this time towards the second of the straw men. And instantly after loosing the second arrow, she reached for a third, sending that after the others. The third arrow penetrated the third straw man in the centre of its head. None of us had moved or uttered a sound. The three arrows had all been loosed with exacting skill and deadly force in as many heartbeats.

Cormac let out a low whistle.

"You don't have any sisters, do you?" he asked, grinning at Wulfwaru.

She allowed herself a small smile in return.

"Alas, I was my father's only child," she said.

"But what of your husband?" asked Hereward, his tone gruff.

"He will do his duty along with everyone else. He is a brave man and will stand and fight." She hesitated. "But his father did not make him practise with the bow every day."

Hereward glanced at the arrows. The white feathers were bright in the shadows under the alders.

"You have a babe," he said, turning back to Wulfwaru. "What of your son?"

Wulfwaru met Hereward's gaze.

"I have known the helplessness of my son being taken from me. I will not allow that to happen again."

"But your place is with him, not with us."

"I will worry about Aethelwulf, Hereward," she said. "He is not your concern. He is mine and my husband's. And when the raiders come, as you say they will, I will serve him best if I put my bow to good use in defence of our home."

Hereward scowled at her, perhaps thinking of other arguments to use against her reasoning. But before he spoke again, Gwawrddur stepped forward and said what we were all surely thinking.

"Well," he said, "anyone who can shoot a bow like that can stand by me in battle."

As we progressed along the Cocueda, the oars groaning quietly in their tholes, Hereward's disapproval was still plain to see. He seemed to consider it a betrayal of sorts that we had all agreed that Wulfwaru would be a welcome addition to the defenders of Werceworthe. I wondered at the depth of his anger about this issue, but no matter how much we pressed him on it, he would say no more apart from that it was not a woman's place to put herself at risk in a fight. Still, whatever his misgivings, he had in the end grudgingly agreed that Wulfwaru would be useful, at least in the preparations for the defence of the minster.

He had left Gwawrddur and Cormac behind with instructions to begin training the villagers and, with Wulfwaru's help, to start organising the defences. True to his word, the abbot had sent a group of monks up to Werce's Hall that morning to assess what materials they would need to repair it. Hereward had allowed himself a thin smile when he saw another group of monks enter the church with chests, clearly with the objective of packaging up the treasures there.

"The only way any of this will work is if we have warning of the Norsemen's approach," said Hereward that morning when he had asked the abbot for use of the boat.

I was not sure exactly what Hereward had in mind, but we were heading to Cocwaedesae, the island that was visible from the mouth of the Cocueda. The island was small, with only a single hut upon it, where old Anstan spent his days in quiet reflection of God, at peace with nature. When I said as much to Hereward, he merely nodded and said, "Let us see what we see."

Now, as the waters of the river opened up into a natural harbour surrounded by sandbanks to the north and rocky outcrops to the south, the island of Cocwaedesae hove into view, squat and low on the slate-grey expanse of the Whale Road. I always loved this part of the journey. The land about the estuary was seething with birds. Redshanks and oystercatchers strutted through the shallows, dipping their long beaks into the mud. A huge flock of dunlin twittered and fluttered at the water's edge, rising into the air as each wave broke and then settling again as the water hissed back away from the sand. In the sky, gulls wheeled and shrieked. Out over the dark waters flew a group of gannets, and every now and then, they speared down into the water, diving deep in search of prey. On a twisted stump of a washed-up tree, two cormorants sat, wings open to the wind and sun, drying their feathers after fishing.

"It is a pity that Wulfwaru is not here," said Drosten with a wink at me. "She could shoot us a couple of birds for our supper."

Hereward spat over the side of the boat.

"Do you need a rest, Runolf?" he asked. "There is still a way to go for the island."

Runolf did not turn to me for a translation and I had learnt that meant he had understood. His command of Englisc was improving by the day. The Norseman looked over his shoulder and laughed.

"That is not far," he said. "I not need a rest."

He pulled hard on the oars with renewed vigour and the small craft sped forward. I had been peering at the cormorants, wondering why it was that they needed to dry their feathers while the other birds did not, and Runolf's heave on the oars caught me unawares. I lost my balance and had to clutch the top strake of the boat to avoid tumbling into the deep water.

I glowered at Runolf, but the Norseman just laughed.

The sound of his laughter reminded me of Skorri's cruel cackle and I shivered. I scanned the horizon, suddenly convinced that I would see the sails of the Norse raiders' ships there, sliding out of the north, coming for more easy conquests from the holy men of Northumbria. But there were no ships. I let out a long breath in an effort to calm my nerves.

It was harder going once we were out on the sea and the boat was caught by the waves. We slid up and then crashed down with a splash of spray. I could taste salt on my lips and we were soon all drenched. Despite the sun, a chill wind blew from the north and by the time we reached the pale sands of Cocwaedesae I was cold and shivering.

Runolf was true to his word and had brought us to the island more quickly than I would have thought possible. As the keel grated against the sand, he leapt over the side of the boat, splashing into the knee-deep water and, seemingly without effort, he dragged the vessel with us and the provisions inside, up the beach and out of reach of the waves.

"Out and help," he said. We clambered out of the boat and lent our weight to pulling it above the high tide line that was marked with a jumble of flotsam; driftwood and seaweed.

Runolf looked about him, staring out to sea. I wondered if he too imagined the ships of his countrymen ploughing through the waves, sliding as inexorably towards us as death. After a moment, he nodded.

"Yes," he said. "This is the island Skorri will sail to." He gazed towards the river mouth and its teeming birds. "Easy sailing," he said, scratching his beard.

Hereward and Drosten had already taken the provisions from the boat and were striding up the grassy slope towards the small timber hut on the highest part of the island.

"Come on," called Hereward.

Runolf made to follow, but I pulled him back.

"Do you think they are coming?"

He nodded, his expression grim.

"Good sailing weather," he said. "They will come."

"Now?" I asked and I cursed myself for sounding so timid.

He pondered my question and then shrugged.

"Who can say?" He stared out to the north. "Perhaps they will wait till after the harvest."

"Truly?" I said, my eagerness shaming me. But what was there to be ashamed of? Harvest was weeks away. That would give us time to repair the hall and prepare the defences. And yet I knew the true reason for hoping the Norsemen would not come sooner. Harvest was far enough in the future to seem like a dream; unreal.

"Perhaps," he said. He looked up at the cloudless expanse of the sky and again dropped his gaze to the northern horizon where the pale blue met the dark grey of the sea. "Yes," he said. "Perhaps."

He walked off after the others and, frustrated at his non-committal words, I followed him.

The island was small and we were soon at the tiny shack where Anstan lived. The door was closed and there was no sign of the old hermit. Hereward looked at me inquiringly. I shrugged and, stepping forward, I rapped my knuckles on the door. It rattled in its frame. When the winds blew in from the sea, the whole building must shake and the weathered timbers of the walls wouldn't keep the cold out.

I raised my fist again, but before I could knock, a voice called from inside.

"If you have rowed all the way over here, you surely have strength enough to open a door."

I tugged at the leather handle and the door creaked open, dragging in the dust so that I had to lift it as it opened or it would become snagged on the ground.

"Come in, come in, young Hunlaf," came the raspy voice of Anstan. I stepped into the gloom and the others crowded in behind me. I blinked against the darkness inside after the bright sun. Anstan was old, with skin as dark and wrinkled as oak gall tanned leather. His limbs were spindly but strong, and usually when I had come to the island on such a day as this, he would be found waiting for us at the beach. He liked his solitude, demanded it, in fact, but he always seemed pleased of company when it came to his island retreat, and he was especially fond of the mead we brought him. I was surprised to find him lying in his low pallet. His eyes gleamed from his sallow face.

"When I first heard you outside," he said, his voice reedy, "I thought you were the Norsemen, come to send me on my way to meet our Heavenly Father."

"You know of the Norsemen?" I asked.

"Yes, yes," he replied, "I am old, not stupid." He laughed, a dry sound that reminded me of the rattling door. After a moment the laugh turned into a cough. He hacked, struggling with the effort, before reaching his bony fingers for a stained cloth. He lifted it to his mouth and spat into it. "Besides," he wheezed, "Beonna sent someone to tell me the tidings. You had gone to Eoforwic, and now you seem to have brought some friends back." He stared at the others, and then at the sword scabbarded by my side. He stared at me for a long moment. "It seems you have brought back one more warrior than expected. No longer a man of peace, eh?" I blushed, awaiting a rebuke. But none came and I shrugged in response, unsure how to put into words the change that had taken place within me. He let out a ragged sigh. "I miss being young," he said.

"And this must be the Norseman," he said, looking up at Runolf. "The one who saved Aethelwig and Wulfwaru's child."

"Yes, Anstan," I said. "This is Runolf Ragnarsson. He has been baptised," I added.

Anstan nodded, but said nothing. I wondered if he had heard what I said. I was shocked at the change in the old man. He had always seemed ancient to me, but he was ever vital and full of energy.

As if he could hear my thoughts, he said, "Do not look so glum, Hunlaf. I am old and I am unwell. When you reach seventy-six years old, I wonder whether you will look as good, hmmm?"

I did not know what to say and so said nothing.

Anstan turned his attention to Hereward.

"You look like one used to being obeyed," he said. "What is it you have come to speak to me about?"

"First, I bring you some provender," Hereward said. "Some ham, some—"

"Is that mead I spy?" interrupted Anstan.

Hereward smiled.

"Indeed it is," he said. "Where are your cups?"

"Hunlaf knows," Anstan replied. I hurried to fetch some small cups from the shelf at the back of the hut. Anstan might be old and ill, but he was tidy still, and everything was in its place.

I held out the wooden cups and Hereward poured a small amount into each one. He filled Anstan's to the brim and handed it to him.

"To good health and long life," croaked Anstan before draining his cup. He smacked his lips and chuckled. "I seem to have lost one now, but I have managed the other, with the Lord's help, of course." He held out his cup for a refill. Smiling, Hereward obliged him. Anstan sipped at the mead and closed his eyes. "This is fine mead and the abbot is a good man," he said. "I take back everything I have ever said to the contrary."

Hereward snorted and raised his cup.

"To fine mead and good men," he said.

Anstan drank some more.

"Now, tell me why you have come here and disturbed my prayers?"

Hereward drank the remainder of his mead and handed me the empty cup.

"It had been my intention to build a beacon here, on the island. I was hoping that we could have someone watching from the mouth of the Cocueda with another beacon. When the Norse ships can be seen from here, the beacons would be lit, and in that way, we would be forewarned in Werceworthe."

The old man nodded slowly.

"You have a plan for the defence of the minster?" he asked.

"Yes, but it relies on having some warning of when the raiders are coming."

Anstan's eyes glittered with the intense energy I recognised from previous visits.

"You will retreat to Werce's Hall?" he asked. "Force them to attack you there?"

"Yes," said Hereward, as surprised as I was at the old man's words.

"It is a good enough plan," continued Anstan. He propped himself up in his bed. He seemed somehow younger than moments before, whether from the mead or the talk of battle preparations, I could not tell. "It is what I would do." He closed his eyes and I wondered if he was going to drift off to sleep, but he must have only been picturing the layout of Werceworthe. "You will make the land to the north a killing ground? Force the Norsemen to move between the buildings where you can ambush them?"

"That is my plan," said Hereward.

"You must be careful of the east, that will be the weakest approach, I think."

"Thank you, Anstan," Hereward said. "You have a good mind for strategy."

"Once, perhaps," he said, "in another lifetime. But you said it *had* been your intention to build a beacon here. What has changed your mind?"

"Well, I have now seen the lie of the land." He hesitated, and then went on, "And when I saw that you were sick, I decided that it would be best to take you back to the minster, where you can be cared for. And now that we have spoken," he smiled, "I think also you could help me with the preparations."

"And what of the beacon? How will you know when the Norsemen are coming?"

Hereward shook his head.

"I am not sure yet. I will have to think of a different plan."

"What other plan is there?" asked Anstan, his tone acerbic and urgent. "Will you set another here to light the bonfire?"

Again, Hereward shook his head.

"Now that I have seen this island, I fear that any who lights a beacon would invite the wrath of the Norse. There is nowhere to hide. Anyone here will surely die."

Anstan sighed and then began coughing again. As the coughs abated, he held out his cup and I refilled it with mead.

"That seems most likely," he said after he'd had another sip. "Well then, it is settled. You will send over timber and build the beacon here, near my home, and I will stay and light it when the time comes."

"But Anstan," I said, "you will die."

"I am dying anyway," he said with a sad smile. "I would rather be of use to you all before I go to meet the Lord in heaven."

The old man's casual bravery shamed me, contrasting so starkly with my own fear of the future. There was a firmness to his words, a determination. It felt to me as if this conversation had already been played out. It was as if we were all pieces in a game of tafl, and the Lord had placed us in our positions on the board already. Surely, this was all part of His plan.

"What if I forbid it?" said Hereward. His voice was tight and filled with emotion. "What if I tell you that you must return with us?"

Anstan chuckled to himself.

"Then I will tell you to let an old man be." He reached out and patted Hereward's leg. "You may be in command of your warriors," he said, "but you do not command me."

Hereward looked away. He blinked several times. After a long while, he sighed and turned back to Anstan.

"If I allow this thing, old man," he said, a hard edge to his tone now, "what is to say that you will not die before the Northmen come?"

For a heartbeat nobody made a sound. I could scarcely believe that Hereward had voiced such a concern. How could he be so uncaring?

But Anstan threw his head back and laughed long and loud. After a time, his cackling turned into his barking cough and I leaned forward to pat his back. When he had regained his breath, he hawked and spat into his rag.

"Well, I cannot promise that the Lord will not take me before, for no man can see what will pass. But I do not believe that is His will. Do you?" He looked at me then. He must have felt it too, I thought, the sliding into place of the different pieces in this deadly game. "I think it is God's will that I remain here," he said with conviction. "I have prayed long and hard on this these past weeks and I am a stubborn old goat."

Hereward laughed at that.

"I barely know you, but I already know that you do not lie when you say you are stubborn," he said.

"I was a warrior once too, you know?" Anstan went on. "I know what it is to rely on others. And I will not let you down." He gripped Hereward's arm in the warrior grip, his spidery fingers clasped around the tautly muscled forearm, and stared up at him with unblinking eyes. "I will live long enough to light the beacon. When the time comes, you can rely on me."

We were quiet and subdued as Runolf rowed us back towards the Cocueda. I stared out over the waves at the diving sea birds. Drosten was silent and Runolf was stony faced as he heaved on the oars and the boat sped over the water. As we drew closer to land, the waves became larger and cold surf sprayed up over the prow. I glanced back at Hereward in the stern. He was twisted around, looking back at the island and the small hut. When he looked away from our wake, I saw that his eyes were red and his cheeks wet.

Thirty-Eight

The sun was in the west when we reached Werceworthe. We had spoken little on the return journey. Hereward had brooded silently at the rear of the boat while Runolf rowed. Drosten seemed content to watch the land slide by as we travelled up the Cocueda. It was slower in this direction as we were heading against the flow of the river. When the keel of the boat grated against the small shingle beach, Runolf's forehead was beaded with sweat. He climbed out to drag the boat from the water and I hurried to help him. The back and chest of his kirtle was dark and wet from his exertion.

"You are mortal then?" I said, nodding at his sweat-drenched clothing. He looked confused, and so I added, "You sweat, like anyone else. I thought you never tired."

Giving the boat one last tug, taking it fully out of the water, Runolf gave me a strange look.

"We are all mortal," he said. His tone was sad.

"You think we are wrong to leave Anstan there?" I asked.

He shook his head.

"There is no better thing for a man than to decide the manner of his death."

Hereward spat into the river and, clearly not wishing to be part of this conversation, pushed past us and headed towards the minster buildings. Drosten followed behind him.

I had not stopped thinking about Anstan since we had left him snoozing in his bed. "I will keep watch outside once the beacon is built," he said. "But there is no point in me losing sleep until then. Even if I saw the Norse, I could do nothing to alert you."

I marvelled at his courage.

"Anstan is a truly brave man," I said. I had always thought of him as a nuisance, a talkative old man whose stubborn desire to remain on the island had given me extra work to do. I saw now that I knew nothing of the man, or the life he had led before joining the brethren.

"He is that," said Runolf.

"I do not know where he finds his strength."

"Is that not from your Christ god? I thought this is why you prayed to Him."

For Runolf to remind me of my faith filled me with shame.

"Yes, you speak true. You are learning much of our ways," I paused. "*Your* new ways," I corrected myself. "Surely, as you say, Anstan must find courage from his faith, but I do not know how he can be so resolute in the face of certain death."

The thought of his frail form, alone on the windswept island saddened me. To decide the manner of your passing might be a good thing, but did any man truly wish to die alone, with no friend or kin beside him in the end?

I became aware that Runolf was staring at me, his head cocked to one side, as if unsure of what he saw.

"What is it?" I asked.

"You say you do not know how the old man can face death."

"Yes, but what of it?"

"Is that not what you are doing here? What we are all doing?"

Despite the warmth of the afternoon, a chill ran through me.

"You think we cannot prevail?" I asked, my voice small. Was that what they all thought? Did they all believe we would die here?

Runolf looked at the river for a time. A fish jumped with a silver gleam and a splash. The ripples faded quickly, leaving no trace of it.

"Christ knows," he said at last, using one of the terms Cormac was fond of. I might have smiled at the sound of it, if I had not been gripped with a cold anxiety. He turned and walked after the others. "Anything is possible."

I watched after him, unsure whether I wanted to laugh or cry.

When I caught up with him, I saw he was heading away from the minster and the refectory. My heart sank. We had not eaten since shortly after dawn and my stomach was empty and grumbling. It looked as though I would not be getting fed any time soon. In the distance, Hereward and Drosten were striding towards a large gathering of villagers. I trotted to catch up with Runolf and fell into step with him.

Some of the people turned to welcome us as we arrived. I knew them all, of course, and nodded greetings. I could not be sure, but it seemed to me as though they were looking upon me with less suspicion than the day before. Perhaps in time they would come to accept this new me with a sword on my belt. *Not if we were all dead*, whispered a small voice within me. I ignored it with difficulty and surveyed the activity.

There were three distinct clumps of villagers in the open yard outside Aethelwig's hut. As I watched, yet more came from the south, carrying a bundle of long branches of what looked like ash wood.

A small smoky fire burnt and several people were placing long staves into the flames, twisting the wood constantly, then pulling it out to inspect the tip. The smell of woodsmoke filled the hot air.

I spotted Gwawrddur walking between the different groups, offering advice and encouragement.

One of them was using knives and axes to clean the twigs and leaves from the branches, leaving straight shafts, longer than a man is tall. The next group was involved in cutting a point into one end of each haft. These sharpened staves were then handed to the final group, who plunged the sharp ends into the fire.

"I see you have put the people to work," said Hereward. He sounded pleased with what he saw. Gone was the sombre mood that had fallen over him since the meeting with Anstan. I thought about the sudden change and realised that this was the mark of a leader. It was his duty to these people to give them hope, not to burden them with his fears and woes.

Cormac waved from where he was kneeling. He was with the group that was sharpening the wood. He held a wicked-looking knife in his hand. I noticed Wulfwaru beside him, her head bent over in concentration. Aethelwig walked over from the fire and offered her a cup of water he had filled from a bucket. She smiled her thanks and drank, before handing the cup to Cormac to finish.

One of the older women shouted at some screaming boys, telling them to quieten down. The children were throwing the discarded twigs and branches at each other in a mock battle. They jeered and shouted even louder at the woman before sprinting off through the trees that led down to the river. There was a relaxed, convivial atmosphere about the place. These were simple folk with a purpose. The seasons did not cow them as they toiled to till and sow and harvest, and they were not daunted by the prospect of men coming to steal what they owned. I remembered the sleek, beast-headed prows of the Norse longships, the leering raiders, with their swords and axes and savagery. It was good that the villagers smiled and laughed as they worked. They would have time enough for fear.

"Work has started on the hall and its buildings," said Gwawrddur, "but I have left that to Brother Eoten to organise. He seems to know what he is about and has willing hands to help him." He cast a glance about him at the gathered people all working on a common goal. "I thought it would be a good idea to start working on something the people could hold and understand quickly and easily."

Hereward smiled at what he saw.

"You have done well," he said. "Everyone should be armed with a spear at least. And we will need more sharpened stakes for what we have in mind."

"Tomorrow, I will begin to train them in their use."

Hereward walked over to the pile of completed spears. Each had a blackened, sharpened tip, but other than that, it was just a branch that had been cleaned of leaves and offshoots. Runolf, frowning, took the spear from the Northumbrian. It looked flimsy in his huge hands. He made a couple of thrusts with it, before inspecting the fire-hardened point.

"This is no spear," he said in Norse. "It is a twig."

Hereward looked at me questioningly. I interpreted the Norseman's words.

"We do not have enough iron or time to fashion blades for them," said Gwawrddur. I translated and he continued. "But a thicket of these will hold an attacking force at bay."

Runolf looked sceptical. He thumbed the blackened tip, shaking his head.

"If a spit can pierce a hog," said Cormac, "one of these can skewer a heathen Norseman."

Runolf waited for me to translate the words, then he scoffed.

"A twig would not kill me," he said, his rumbling voice tinged with disdain.

I was aware that the activity around us had ceased. Silence fell as the men and women observed the interplay between Runolf and Cormac. Sensing the morale-damaging shift in mood, Hereward stepped forward and clapped Runolf on the shoulder. He took the spear from him, gave it a nod of approval and tossed it back onto the heap of them that the villagers had prepared.

"Luckily for us," he said loudly, "these spears only need to kill heathen Norsemen, and you, my huge friend, are a good Christian man."

Thirty-Nine

It was late when I entered the refectory, but I was certain that Hereward and Gwawrddur would still be awake. Despite the long days and the backbreaking labour, the two of them never seemed able to find sleep easily. Tonight was no different. I took off the woollen cloak I wore and shook out the worst of the rain at the entrance before making my way inside. The room was wrapped in shadows, the only light coming from the flickering flame of a rush lamp. I could see the mound of blankets where one of the others slept. I recognised Runolf's loud snores and grimaced. As tired as I was, the sawing noise was bound to keep me awake, as it had so many nights before.

Hereward looked up from where he sat on a bench. The lamp was between him and the Welshman, their features bright in the darkness, their eyes lambent.

"Still raining then?" Hereward said.

I nodded and moved to the bench beside him, lowering myself with a groan, down onto the wood and stretching my legs out before me. My lower back and arms ached from digging the deep ditch to the east of Werce's Hall. We had been digging for days. Another task to add to the many other gruelling jobs we had performed in the previous weeks.

As well as the ditch to the east, which we hoped would deter the Norse from that approach, we had constructed fences to help us channel the attackers and also dug deep pits in which to entrap them. It seemed as if the work would never be finished.

"You think Drosten will stay awake tonight?" asked Gwawrddur, pouring me a small measure of mead and pushing the cup across the board towards me. I shrugged.

"Well, he was alert and open-eyed when I left him."

"The Pict will not sleep again on duty," said Hereward with finality.

A week ago, Hereward had gone up the hill in the darkest part of the night. He had been unable to sleep. Drosten, it transpired, did not have the same problem. We knew that it was unlikely the Norse would come at night. When we had asked Runolf whether they might attack in darkness he had shrugged and infuriatingly said, "Anything is possible". He had gone on to say that it was very unlikely, that it was too dangerous to sail without light, especially in waters they did not know well, but his first comment had sowed the seeds of doubt and so it was that Hereward had ordered one of us to be on watch in the hall on the hill at all times. When he had found Drosten sleeping, he had been furious, vowing that if he found him in dereliction of his duties again, he would send the Pict away.

"I would rather have fewer blades wielded by men I can trust," he'd said, "than by an untrustworthy Pictish cur."

Drosten had bridled at that, squaring his shoulders and jutting his chin out belligerently. He took two steps towards Hereward, the sinews of his neck and jaw bulging with his pent-up fury. Hereward did not move. "Think very carefully what you do now, Pict," he said, his voice barely more than a whisper but carrying with it the threat of a whetstone dragged along a finely honed blade.

Drosten clenched his fists and I thought he might seek to strike Hereward. But with a great effort the tattooed warrior swallowed back his anger, bowed his head and stalked away.

We had not seen him again until that evening when he'd walked into the refectory and approached Hereward.

"I am sorry," he said, and his emotion made his Pictish accent thicker than normal. "It will not happen again. You can trust me."

Hereward had held his gaze for a long time before finally nodding and handing him a mug of ale.

"Your punishment," said Hereward, "is to collect the brambles to fill the east ditch."

Drosten had let out a long breath, but nodded. We all hated the task of cutting brambles and carrying them to be piled in the trenches we were digging. We had placed sharpened stakes in the earth at the bottom of the ditch, but Gwawrddur had pointed out that the Norsemen would come on foot. Horses would be impeded by the stakes, but men would be able to climb past them easily enough. Wulfwaru had come up with the idea of filling the depression with briars, which would slow a man and cause him great suffering if he were to force his way through. It was bloody, agonising work to hack down clumps of the thorn-laden plants and we all had scratches to remind us of the odious task.

Over the next days Drosten did not once complain about his punishment, but by the time he had brought enough brambles to satisfy Hereward, his hands, arms and face were a welter of thin scratches, their red lines adding a bloody counterpoint to his woad tattoos.

No more had been said of the incident and Hereward seemed content with Drosten's apology.

I sipped the strong mead that Gwawrddur had given me, enjoying the warming sensation as it trickled down my throat. None of us drank to excess. Hereward had forbidden it. But

I thought that a few swallows of mead might help to dull my senses enough that I could sleep through the incessant snoring from Runolf's corner of the room.

"It would matter little whether he is awake or asleep, the weather as it is," I said. "If Anstan is even able to light his beacon in this weather, something that I doubt, how we would manage to see it through this driving rain is beyond me."

"Have faith, young Hunlaf," said Gwawrddur, with a thin smile. "Of all of us, that should be easiest for you."

Anstan too had told me to have faith when we were building the beacon on Cocwaedesae. My doubts as to his ability to carry out the task of lighting the fire must have been plainly written on my face as I looked at the frail hermit. It had taken us three days to chop and transport enough timber to the island. Hereward had given me the task of overseeing the construction of the beacon and whilst the toil had been exhausting, I had enjoyed the time spent with Runolf cutting down trees in the forest, splitting the logs and then piling as many as possible onto a raft that we could float behind the small skiff and rowing them out to Anstan's island retreat.

The laconic Norseman had relaxed noticeably away from the eyes of the villagers and he seemed to revel in the simple task of swinging his huge axe into the trunks of the trees. It was plain to me that he was as skilled a woodsman as he was a warrior, aiming his axe deftly and showing me how best to split the wood. He explained all manner of details about the timber he hewed, how wooden wedges were best for making straight planks and how the planks could be bent to any shape needed by steaming them in fire pits. His face lit up as he talked about working the wood. I wondered about his past life, but when I asked him of it, he grew sombre and withdrawn and I was sad to have dispelled the easy atmosphere between us.

Later we sat on the beach looking out to the darkening sky and listening to the constant growl and hiss of the waves washing up and down the sand. A melancholy had come upon Runolf and I did not wish to press him further about the life he had left behind. So, although I wished to learn more about his past, I told him of mine. I spoke of my father and my almost-forgotten mother, of how my older brother had always seemed to please my father, where I had only disappointed.

"Beornnoth lives in Berewic now," I said, watching a puffin streak low across the water, its wings beating furiously as it headed north towards the Farne Islands no doubt. And beyond them Lindisfarnae and then, at the mouth of the Tuede, Berewic, where my brother lived. "He serves Lord Cerdic there as a warrior and he has done well for himself, by all accounts." I picked up a pebble and flung it out into the surf. "But Father could only afford the heregeat for one of us, or so he said, and so I was sent to Magilros to become a monk."

"'Heregeat'?" enquired Runolf. "What is this?"

"A warrior's gear. Sword, byrnie, horse and saddle."

I sat in silence for a time and wondered at the twists and turns of fate. It was all God's plan, I supposed. Despite being envious of my brother, I had been happy at Werceworthe. I looked sidelong at Runolf and thought how our lives had become as inextricably linked as wool woven into a cloak. What did I truly know of this massive man I asked myself. He had come into my life on a wave of blood and violence. Had my actions on that day signalled the end of my happiness as a member of the brethren? I had lusted for vengeance and blood. I had killed. My sins were plain for all to see.

Or was it when Oslac had shown us *The Treasure of Life* that my fate had been sealed? For from that moment I had been consumed with the desire to know more of the secrets that lay within the heretical text. Where there was one such marvellous book hidden deep within a scriptorium, there must be more. But even if the book had survived, if the Norse had not come, would I have been content to return to Werceworthe, to resume my duties and live a simple life of contemplation and learning under Leofstan and the abbot? Would the study of books have proven sufficient for me?

Perhaps.

I would never know. For suddenly, on that terrible day of slaughter and horror, everything had changed forever.

"All fathers have a favourite child," said Runolf, taking a swig from the costrel of ale we had brought from Werceworthe. "Good fathers try to hide it from their sons. They ensure they do not favour one over the other, but they cannot conceal the truth from their heart." I glanced at him, wondering at his words, but he was staring out at the Whale Road, lost in his own thoughts. I wanted to ask him if he had children, but I remembered his reaction when questioned that afternoon and I surmised it would not be wise to broach the subject with him.

The following day we had completed the beacon. Runolf had directed me, telling me where to lay the planks and logs, building up a great mound of wood, with enough gaps in between the pieces to allow air to flow and feed the flames. When we had finished we took a final drink with Anstan and I handed him an earthenware jar that was sealed with wax.

"This is fish oil," I said. "It will help feed the fire, if it is wet."

"Yes, yes, young Hunlaf," the old man said. He hawked and spat a gobbet of bloody phlegm into the grass. "I am no child that you need to teach me how best to strike a light. I will manage to set this bonfire aflame when the time comes, never you fear."

In spite of his frailty, and the sickness that had a hold of him, I believed his words. Over the course of the days in which we had constructed the beacon, Anstan had seemed to grow stronger with each passing moment. I had commented as much to Runolf the day before.

"A man needs to know what his purpose is," he said. "A man with no purpose, is merely awaiting death."

I did not care to mention that Anstan too was surely awaiting death, but rather than one caused by the illness that consumed him, a bloody and violent end at the hands of Runolf's countrymen.

I looked over now at Runolf's sleeping form and again wondered at the friendship between us. As the days had passed, the bond between us had grown stronger. And not only between me and the Norseman, but with all of the warriors in this strange band to which I now belonged. At times I still felt an unusual disquiet to be surrounded by the brethren of the minster and yet to no longer be one of them, but I had left one brotherhood for another. I had worked hard alongside these men, and Gwawrddur had continued to train me and Cormac. We had both improved, building up our strength and our skill. I still often felt like an impostor amongst these strong men of war, but every now and then, in an unguarded moment, I would forget that I had once been a monk. I could best Cormac more often than not with a blade now. The sword felt natural at my side now, and my hand often dropped without thinking to the hilt to prevent the scabbard from snagging on things as I moved about. How rapidly what had once seemed strange had become familiar.

"How does the roof fare?" Hereward asked, his voice bringing me back from my thoughts. The day before, the tall monk, Eoten, had finished laying fresh thatch on the timber frame, parts of which had been replaced with freshly hewn beams. The constant rain since had been a test of his skill.

"The hall is dry," I said. "Eoten has done a good job."

"Good," he said. "Tomorrow we will bring the treasure up to Werce's Hall. After that, we will all sleep there too."

"It will please the abbot to have us out of the minster," Gwawrddur said.

"It will," I replied. "You think the Norse will come soon?"

Runolf's snoring was suddenly interrupted with a choking

cough. We all turned to look at the sleeping giant. A moment later, his constant snoring resumed. Hereward frowned.

"Runolf says they will come in the next fortnight. Do not ask me how he knows, something to do with the winds and the weather, but he seems sure of it, and I see no reason not to believe him." He drank sparingly of his mead. "Yes," he continued, his voice grim, "I think they will come soon."

"Are we ready?" I said. This was the question that preyed on everyone's minds.

"No plan survives the first meeting with the enemy," Gwawrddur said, "but we are as ready as we can be. The hall is prepared. We will take the gold and silver up there tomorrow. We have already carried the bell up there." Garulf's iron bell had been installed outside Werce's Hall, and it was no longer used to call the faithful to mass on Sundays. The inhabitants of Werceworthe had all been drilled in what to do when the bell rang out the next time. The monks, most of the women, children and the elderly, would come rushing from their homes to the protection of the hall. Others had more dangerous tasks assigned to them. We had all run through the plans many times over. There were so many things that could go wrong, and all we could do was trust in our preparations, God, and the men and women around us.

"How many archers has Wulfwaru trained in the end?" asked Hereward.

Over the weeks he had come to grudgingly respect her. She was hard working, with a keen mind, and I had noticed recently how he had turned to her on more than one occasion to seek her advice. We had all seen her skill with a bow, but she had also taken it upon herself to make more of the weapons and train other women in their use.

"I believe there are five now who are passable shots," Gwawrddur said. "None of them are anywhere near a match for Wulfwaru, but if the Norse stand still for long enough, they might be able to injure a few of them." He smiled and Hereward chuckled, but I sensed no mirth in his laughter. Gone was the man so quick to jest whom I had met all those weeks before on the windswept island of Lindisfarnae. "But it matters little," Gwawrddur went on, "as their arrows will be spent soon enough, I think."

Whenever Wulfwaru had a moment spare, which was not often, what with tending for her child and her husband, and helping with the defences, she could be found making simple, but effective arrows. She had a small collection of iron-headed hunting arrows, and Garulf had made her several more. Wulfwaru had convinced a couple of the other women to help her make the arrows, cutting the feathers, gluing them to the wooden shaft using birch tar and then binding with sinew.

"When the last of the ditches is finished, perhaps we can help her to make more arrows," Hereward said. "If nothing else, it will keep us occupied as we wait." Cormac and I had already made a few arrows under Wulfwaru's expert supervision. I had enjoyed the painstaking concentrated effort, inserting the tang into the wood and then slowly winding the sinew twine tight at the connection of the shaft to the head. I missed the exacting work of putting quill to paper and Hereward's words pleased me. It would be good to have something to do with my hands in the days ahead. Days that would all too soon bring chaos and death. I pushed my dark thoughts aside and stood, stifling a yawn.

"I will try to sleep, I think," I said.

As if in answer, Runolf let out a rumbling fart to rival the noise of his stertorous snores. Hereward chuckled.

"By God," he said, "perhaps his wind will blow out the candle to help you find rest."

"I am scared that his noxious stench might kill me long before the raiders have a chance."

They laughed at my dark humour. Leofstan would have been appalled by my words, but I had learnt that this kind of jest was appreciated by men who chose to live and die by the blade.

I was casting about in the shadows for where my blanket lay, when a crash came from outside. This was followed by the screaming yells of a distraught woman, the bellowing roar of a man's deep anger and, above it all, the piercing, howling wail of an infant.

The sounds, cutting through the night-time stillness like a seax blade through warm tallow, shocked me into immobility. Had the raiders come unannounced and unnoticed? Had Anstan lit his beacon only to have it unseen in the sheeting rain? Or had it been seen by the monks who waited on the coast and then they had struggled to light their own bonfire? Had I missed the sign of the light in the darkness to the east? Was Drosten asleep again at his post?

All these thoughts swarmed in my head like crows, battering my senses with their confusing wings. I was yet standing there, unmoving and seemingly frozen to the spot, when Runolf leapt up from where he had been sleeping. His great axe was already in his hand and he shook his head as if to free it of sleep as a hound shakes off water. The sounds from outside were growing louder, closer perhaps, and I glanced from the massive Norseman to the door, as a blast of the wet cool air of the night blew inside.

Hereward and Gwawrddur, with none of my confusion or temerity, had moved without hesitation and rushed out into the darkness. Runolf cocked his head, listening to the night. There were voices there, behind the hiss of the rain. Angry voices, scared voices. And still that baby wailed.

"Come, boy," roared Runolf, bounding towards the door. And then, as if he knew exactly what I was thinking, he turned and said, "No time to worry now," and ran out into the gloom of the rain-slick night.

I took a deep breath, pulled my sword from its scabbard and, feeling some comfort from its heft, hurried after him.

Forty

I sprinted after Runolf, splashing through puddles and sliding through the mire of the path. There was light ahead, not within the minster, but amongst the buildings of the lay people. I stumbled as I jumped over the shallow ditch of the vallum that surrounded the monastery. I could just make out the shapes of Gwawrddur, Hereward and Runolf before me and it was all I could do to keep up and avoid slipping in the mud.

How had the Norsemen reached the village without coming to the minster first? Had they passed unseen and landed on the western edge of the settlement? Had all our plans been for nought? And why was Drosten not hammering on the metal that hung outside Werce's Hall?

I skidded and slid into the clearing before Aethelwig's house. There were people there and the baby was still crying, its voice pitiful and full of rage and fear. At first, I could not make out the details of what I saw. Hereward, Gwawrddur and Runolf had their backs to me and there were a few others standing in the mud as the rain fell relentlessly from the dark sky. There were not as many attackers as I would have expected.

I spun about quickly, suddenly convinced that there was a horde of warriors creeping up behind us, but the night was empty, dark and still except for the constant murmur of the rain that was easing now.

Returning my gaze to the huts and the gathered people, I tried to make sense of what I saw there. The illumination was spilling from the open door of Aethelwig's hut. Figures were circling each other on the open ground before the building. The dim light from a rush flame or lantern caught the wet, deadly blade of a sword. At the same moment the light limned the features of the bladesman and I recognised him; Hereward's voice, loud and hard, cut through the noise.

"Cormac!" he snapped. "Put up your sword."

The Hibernian ignored him, holding his blade aloft and stepping slowly around so that his adversary would be lit by the light from the open doorway. He was stronger now than when we had found him, weeks of good food and hard work had broadened his shoulders and added bulk to his arms and legs. But his step was lighter, his movements more thoughtful and controlled. Gwawrddur was a good teacher and even though I was able to best Cormac frequently now, he was a formidable opponent, especially if the one who faced him was not trained in the use of a blade.

Light spilled onto his enemy's features and I knew there would be no good outcome to this fight. It was Aethelwig who stood before him. The tanner was a burly, round-faced man, as strong as an ox, but slow. He was not a fighter. Not a killer of men. But his face was twisted with ire and in his hand he held a long knife.

"Cormac!" shouted Hereward again. "Do not forget your oath."

Cormac hesitated, but did not lower his weapon or remove his gaze from Aethelwig.

"The man is mad," Cormac said. "I have done nothing wrong."

"Then why do you come to my house in the dead of night,

creeping like a thief?" shouted Aethelwig, his voice trembling with rage.

"I did not wish to wake Aethelwulf," Cormac said.

The baby was still crying loudly. I noticed that it was not Wulfwaru who held his swaddled form, but Mildrith, her friend, who had two children of her own.

"Well, Aethelwulf is awake now," bellowed Aethelwig, "and so am I, and I will gut you like the Hibernian pig you are."

I saw Cormac's shoulders bunch and I knew he was going to lunge. This was his weakness and the manner in which I could often beat him. It was possible to goad him to make the first move, from which a skilled swordsman could parry and counterattack. I was fast and found that a well-timed insult would provoke a response from which I could win a practice bout. Aethelwig, though, was not a skilled warrior and I could already picture how Cormac would bury his long blade in the tanner's body.

Hereward and Gwawrddur both sensed what would occur at the same moment and, as one, they shouted out, "No!"

Perhaps their voices would have halted him, but in the same instant Wulfwaru slid between the two fighting men. Her back was to her husband and in her hands she held a fully drawn bow. The iron tip of the arrow looked dull and dark in the night, but her aim was unwavering. The arrow was pointed at Cormac's chest.

"Nobody will gut anybody here tonight," she said, her voice tight with anger.

"You would defend him over me?" said Aethelwig. "He is your lover, I knew it! I demand a husband's justice."

She did not turn to face him. Her arms did not tremble as she held the arrow aimed at Cormac.

"Husband," she said, her tone softer now, "you must trust me when I tell you there is nothing between Cormac and me."

"And yet you defend him!"

"My arrow is aimed at his heart, not yours," she replied. And then, in a soothing, sad tone, "And my heart is yours and not his."

"But... Why... Why did he come here in the depth of the night?"

"I cannot speak for another," she said. "Cormac, explain yourself. My arm is growing weary."

Cormac seemed to finally grasp the situation he was in. Slowly, he lowered his sword, then sheathed it. For the first time he looked about him at the people who had gathered there, pulled from their beds into the wet night by the sound of his confrontation with the tanner. Wulfwaru still held her bow high, the string pulled taut. Cormac swallowed.

"I meant no harm," he said. "I could not sleep."

"And you thought to visit my wife, that she could help you find rest," said Aethelwig, spitting each word furiously. "Is that it?"

"Hush, husband," said Wulfwaru softly. Carefully, she unbent the bow, lowering the arrow until it pointed at the mud. "Why did you come here?" she snapped at Cormac. "What could you want here? It is dark and we were sleeping." Wulfwaru seemed even more enraged than her husband, but also more deadly: Aethelwig had shouted and yelled and swung his knife about in anger, but we could all see that the Hibernian would have defeated him if it had come to blows. Wulfwaru was quieter and more controlled and it was clear that she would not hesitate to slay Cormac, if he attacked.

"I..." Cormac's voice trailed off, and he looked again about him. He bit his lip. "I thought I could perhaps help you to make some arrows..."

Her eyes widened.

"In the dead of night? Are you mad?"

Cormac did not seem to know how to respond. He opened his mouth, but no words came.

"Enough of this," said Hereward, stepping forward. "Now is not the time for more talk. Cormac, apologise to Aethelwig and Wulfwaru."

Cormac glared at Hereward. The Hibernian's hair was soaked and plastered to his face, giving him a wild look.

"Apologise," Hereward repeated, "and return to the refectory. We will speak of this in the morning."

After a moment of hesitation, Cormac mumbled, "I am sorry." And then, without waiting for a response, he turned and was lost in the night. The excitement over, and rain once again beginning to fall heavily, the other villagers dispersed, hurrying back to the warmth and shelter of their homes.

"I do not want that Hibernian anywhere near my wife," growled Aethelwig. "It is bad enough that she spends all her days practising with that thing," he nodded towards the bow in her hands, "and neglecting her duties. Now I have to worry about you warriors turning her head."

Wulfwaru pushed the bow and arrow into her husband's hands. He already held the big knife, so took them awkwardly. With a nod of thanks, she retrieved her son from Mildrith. Cuddling him to her breast, she patted the baby's back and he began to quieten.

"The only thing you have to worry about is whether we will survive when the Norsemen come." She shook her head. "If you cannot see that, then you are a fool, Aethelwig." She strode back into their hut and slammed the door behind her, leaving us all in the dark.

For a time, the only sound was the rain. And then came the voice of Aethelwig in the gloom.

"By Christ's blood," he said, "if I live to see a hundred summers, I will never understand womenfolk."

★ ★ ★

"I knew she would be trouble," shouted Hereward, as he came through the door and slung his wet cloak across the room.

We had not spoken much as we awaited his return. He had said he would go up to Werce's Hall and let Drosten know what the commotion was about. I hoped that the Pict was alert, for God alone knew what Hereward would do to him if he found him asleep.

Gwawrddur had poured us each a cup of mead and we had sat in the light of the flickering flame of the single rushlight, each pondering what had happened. I could make little sense of it, but I liked Cormac and hoped that some of Hereward's ire would have washed away in the rain as he walked in the night.

I was disappointed. If anything, his anger seemed to have grown more intense. He took the cup Gwawrddur offered him, drained it and slammed it onto the board with a crash.

Cormac started as if slapped.

"It was not of her doing," he said. "I am a fool."

Hereward barked out a humourless laugh.

"There is no doubt of that!" he said. "One sniff of a cunny and you have lost what little sense you ever had."

I blushed at Hereward's words.

Cormac bristled.

"It is not like that," he said.

"No? Then tell me how it is, Cormac mac Neill." Hereward's tone was scathing. "What were you thinking of? Did you think she would welcome you into her home while her husband slept?"

"I just thought—"

"What did you think?" Hereward interrupted him. "You thought nothing apart from wetting your cock!"

"Do not speak thus," Cormac shouted, springing up from the bench to stand, fists clenched before Hereward.

Hereward stared at him impassively.

"Why?" he asked. "Is it not true that you desire her? That much I can understand. She is a comely enough wench. By God's bones, that is why I should never have allowed her to stand with us. But what did you think would happen?"

"The other day," Cormac said, his voice not much more than a whisper, "she told me she could not sleep at night. That she lay there awake and worrying of what might come."

"So Aethelwig was right! You thought you would go to her, is that it? To put her at ease."

"No!" He looked down at his feet. "Yes... I don't know. I thought perhaps..." He hesitated as if he knew how his words sounded. "I thought we could make arrows together. It would calm both our nerves to be doing something useful."

"Good God," spat Hereward, "it is a pity that Aethelwig did not kill you."

"What does Cormac say?" asked Runolf.

"He says he went to Wulfwaru's home to make arrows with her."

Runolf guffawed.

"To make arrows! I have never heard it called that before."

Cormac spun around, his face dark with anger.

"You shut your mouth, you Norse bastard!" he raged.

Hereward shook his head in disbelief.

"Aethelwig will not need to worry any longer, if you choose to fight Runolf," he said. "You have gained some skill with the sword, thanks to Gwawrddur here, but the Norseman would snap you in two."

Cormac glowered at Runolf, who had not stopped chuckling. I wondered if Cormac would attack him, but then, he let out a shaky breath, turned and went to the furthest corner of the room. There he shook out his blankets and threw himself down on the ground with his back to us. I took a step after him, but Gwawrddur caught my shoulder and shook his head.

"Leave him be," he said. "There is no point talking to him now. It would be like trying to bathe a wild cat."

Forty-One

The rain blew over in the night and the next few days were dry, but overcast. Dark, gravid clouds loomed in the north and west, a constant threat of more rain to come. The final ditches had been completed and the defences were ready. But we were anxious and on edge. After the night-time madness that had gripped Cormac, the atmosphere in the settlement was strained and it was with a sense of relief from Beonna that we moved our scant belongings up to Werce's Hall, where we would reside from then on.

In the years since that late summer at Werceworthe, I have learnt that it is the waiting for battle that is the hardest to endure. Your mind picks over the possibilities of what might occur and whilst the grim reality of combat is never pleasant, the constant brooding terror of anticipation is worse. When battle is joined, the world is filled with the screams of the injured and dying, the clash of blades, the savage roars of rage and the searing pain of wounds. Fear is banished, pushed aside in that moment, as all you can do is look to victory and survival. It is the time before and after a fight when the claws of fear gouge at your self-worth and certainty. In the long days before a confrontation, you question your ability, the decisions you have taken to reach that point and whether you have done all in your power to grant you victory.

In the aftermath of battle, the wounds of your soul ache more than those of your body. If friends have died, could you have saved them? If the battle was lost, was it your fault? Did the men you slew deserve death? I have known many warriors in my time and there are those who will tell you they care nothing for these concerns that seem to plague me. Maybe they speak the truth, and they walk away from the carnage of battle without a care, but it is my belief that all men, no matter how hard and callous they appear in the face of killing, feel more than just the physical blows they receive from their enemies. A warrior's scars are many, and not all of them leave their mark on the flesh.

We maintained a constant vigil from our new accommodation, with one of us looking east at all times for a sign of the Norsemen's arrival. At night we peered into the darkness for the glint of a far-off fire, and during the dull, hazy days, we scanned the horizon for the great billowing of smoke that would pour from the beacons we had constructed. We might well be able to see the smoke from Anstan's fire on Cocwaedesae, but if not, we were sure we would see the flames or smoke from the beacon we had placed on the coast. It was constantly manned by one of the younger monks or men from the village and they had been given instructions to light the fire when they saw Anstan's beacon afire, or the Norse approaching, and then to flee for safety. The young men of Werceworthe knew the land, and it was unlikely that the raiders would wish to tarry long enough to search for the one to light the fire on the beach. The longer the Norse remained on Northumbrian land, the more chance they would have of being pinned down by King Æthelred's forces. They would wish to attack, steal what they could load aboard their ships, and head back out to sea, where there was no chance that they would be caught.

Runolf looked at the clouds on the horizon and scratched at his thatch of a beard. A great murmuration of starlings swarmed through the sky, diving and wheeling about as if of one mind, unaffected by the strengthening wind that had picked up that afternoon. The lowering sun gleamed from beneath the banks of clouds.

I wiped sweat from my forehead as I joined the huge Norseman to stare into the distance. I had been training with Cormac under the watchful eye of Gwawrddur and, even though I was winded and sweating from the exertion, I would have happily continued. It kept my mind from dwelling on the future. But Hereward had attracted the Welshman's attention with a whistle. Gwawrddur had understood the signal, nodded and told Cormac to go and check that all the defences were intact before it got dark.

"I would rather continue practising with Moralltach," he said, swishing his blade in a flourish.

"I did not ask your opinion on the matter, boy," said Gwawrddur. "Do what I say."

"But—"

"I want to hear no further dissent from you," Gwawrddur's voice was flat and unyielding. "You gave us your oath that you would obey, so obey. Go now."

Cormac looked as though he might argue, but ever since the incident outside Aethelwig's house, his often ebullient character had become more subdued. Hereward was still furious with him and Cormac knew that he was on unsteady footing with our leader and so, after the briefest of hesitations, he angrily slid his sword into its scabbard and headed off down the shallow southern incline.

As I reached Runolf's side, I saw what had prompted Hereward to send Cormac away. Wulfwaru was trudging up the steep slope towards the hall. We all turned to watch her as she approached. Her face was stern. She carried her bow in her left hand and a bag of arrows hung from her belt.

"I am sorry for what happened in the night," she said to Hereward, ignoring the rest of us.

"It was not of your doing," Hereward said, his tone gruff. "I will keep Cormac at a distance from now on."

Her features softened, as if with sadness, but she nodded.

"It is for the best," she said. "My husband is a good man."

"I do not doubt it," said Hereward. "Cormac is a fool."

She smiled.

"Most probably. But he is young and a good man too, I think."

An awkward silence fell over us then. Eventually, Hereward cleared his throat.

"There was something else?"

"Yes," she replied, shaking her head at her own forgetfulness. "Everything is ready. My archers are prepared and if things go as we have planned, we will give the raiders a welcome they will not forget in a hurry."

Hereward nodded.

"You have done well." He gave the praise grudgingly and she smiled at his reticence.

"Thank you," she said. "Let us hope all of our plans are enough."

"They will have to be," said Hereward. "If we are resolute and keep to what we have decided, I believe we will succeed in sending the Norsemen away. It will not be easy, but God is on our side."

Wulfwaru nodded and I wondered if she was convinced by the words. I was not, and I asked myself whether my doubts were sent by the Devil.

"I was also going to ask whether you men would wish to help with the harvest tomorrow. It looks as though the rain will stay away and if we do not bring in that barley, there will be no reason to save the people from the raiders. We will starve over the winter without food."

"It will do us good to keep busy in the fields," Hereward said. "And we should show the people that we are good for more than fighting and digging ditches too." He glanced over to where I was standing beside Runolf. "What say you, Runolf? You think we have time to help with the harvest?"

Runolf shrugged his massive shoulders.

"Anything is possible," he said. Drosten groaned. This was how the Norseman answered most questions. Runolf offered the Pict a twisted smile. "But I think my people will also be needing to bring in their harvest. If they have not come already, they will come after. And if we keep our weapons to hand, and a man to watch from here, we will have warning when they come." He peered out at the horizon and the distant hills to the north. He stuck his forefinger in his mouth and then held the wet digit up in the air. After a moment, he nodded. "But they will be coming soon. I am sure of it."

I had not needed to interpret his words. His Englisc was much improved and apart from his thick accent and some missing words, it was easy to understand Runolf now.

Wulfwaru clearly had no trouble comprehending him.

"What will it be like?" she asked, her voice fragile and timid.

Runolf glanced down at her.

"What?" he asked.

"When they come?"

The wind rustled the alders that lined the river's edge and I shuddered. Sometimes, when I closed my eyes at night, I could see the terrified faces of the men and women of Lindisfarnae on that fell morning when the heathens had landed in the harbour. I could hear the screams of the violated, and smell the acrid stink of spilt bowels. I recalled the vivid crimson and heat of the Norseman's blood as it had gushed over my hand. I shook my head to clear it of such visions.

Wulfwaru was waiting for an answer, but I sensed that none of us was inclined to tell her truly what to expect. At last, Runolf sighed and turned his attention to the young woman.

"They will come seeking death," he said. "There is nothing more to know. We must stand and fight, and with Óðinn's favour, we will live and they will die."

Nobody spoke, but the finality of Runolf's words landed like axe blows, each cutting deeply into Wulfwaru's resolve. Nobody said anything about his use of the name of the father of the old gods his people worshipped. Wulfwaru's face grew pale. She bit her upper lip. I wanted to say something, anything to take away the sting of Runolf's pronouncement, but my mind was thronged with darkness and I could think of nothing good.

"They will leap from their ships like devils," said a new voice with a familiar Hibernian lilt. We all turned to see that Cormac had returned.

"I told you to check the defences," growled Gwawrddur.

Cormac ignored him. He stared at Wulfwaru, as he stepped forward.

"They will scream in their heathen tongue as they burn your homes. Your father and brothers will rush out to defend your land, but they will be hacked down, turning the stream red with their blood." He walked toward Wulfwaru, his eyes brimming with tears.

Gwawrddur reached a hand out to stop him, but Cormac shrugged it off.

"One of the bastards," he went on, "a huge man with a great helm that covers his face, and only leaves his great red beard showing, will watch as your mother is raped and then, when you try to stop them taking your infant sister, the brute will rip her from your grasp and then..." His voice cracked and he let out a shuddering sob. "And then..."

"Cormac," said Runolf, his voice gentle, as if talking to a child.

Cormac's face twisted into a sudden fury.

"Do not speak to me, you red-bearded savage!" he screamed. Tears streaked his cheeks. His hand dropped to the hilt of his sword.

"Cormac!" bellowed Hereward. "Enough!"

Cormac's hand tightened on the grip of his sword, but he did not draw it from the scabbard. He flicked his gaze from Wulfwaru's delicate face to Runolf's craggy features and fire-red beard. Nobody moved but I could sense Gwawrddur readying himself for action. I held my breath. If Cormac pulled his blade and attacked Runolf, I would have no time to think, I would need to act. I was just coming to the conclusion that I would defend the Norseman should it come to that, when Cormac let out a ragged breath. Swiping the tears from his cheeks, he turned on his heel and ran from the hill.

I started to head after him. He was my friend and it saddened me to see him thus.

Gwawrddur pulled me back.

"Let him go," he said. He looked after the young man and sighed. "Sometimes a man needs to be alone with his ghosts."

Forty-Two

In the days that followed we worked as hard as any of the ceorls in the fields. We grumbled at having to labour in the fields, harvesting flax and carrying the sheaves to the steeping pools; hoeing and weeding, scything the hay, reaping the barley. Our backs ached from stooping, and by the end of each day, as dusk was swallowed by darkness noticeably faster than at the height of summer when the days had seemed almost endless, we staggered back up to Werce's Hall. We ate and we slept, but we had little time to fret over what would come, for there is always work to do during the sunny days when preparing for harvest and the dark winter that follows.

The worst moments were when all the others slept. I often found myself startled from slumber by some sound that I could not make out on waking. I would lie there, listening to the sounds of the night. Runolf's snoring, the pop and crackle of an ember on the hearth, the creak and groan of the timbers as the building settled and cooled. At such times, I would try to think of anything to avoid facing what we were all certain would come. I prayed for forgiveness for my sins and asked God to grant us victory when the Norse came. Sometimes, I would manage to focus on my prayers for long enough that sleep would come again, but more often, I would decide that

I would not find more rest that night. At such times, I would rise and go outside, to stand watch with whichever one of our number was on duty.

On the first night this happened, I found Cormac leaning against the wall of the hall, his face a shadow in the dim moonlight that filtered through the clouds. It had drizzled for a short while during the afternoon, and the villagers had looked to the heavens with furrowed brows. If it should rain heavily, much of the barley would go to ruin. It would rot if they were not able to bring it in dry. One wizened man, who looked old enough to be Beonna's grandfather, had gazed up at the clouds and the smirr of rain and pronounced that it would be dry on the morrow.

"There will be time enough for the harvest before the rains fall in earnest," he said, nodding and smiling a toothless grin. Some of the other villagers seemed happy, and nodded, as if the greybeard had the power of prophecy. It had looked to me as if it was set to rain for days. The clouds had brooded over us for a long time and they were heavy and dark.

But as I stepped out of the hall into the darkness, the air was dry. The clouds yet covered the moon, that lit up the sky with its pallid white light, but there were breaks in the clouds from which the chill light of stars shone. Perhaps the old man had been right after all.

There was no fire out here. One might be welcomed by the sentry on duty, but the light from the flames would impede a man's ability to see in the dark. We could not afford to miss the beacons when they were lit and so there was no fire. I shivered, noting the coolness and how my breath steamed about my face. Winter was a whisper in that chill air.

Cormac did not turn as he heard my approach, but despite the darkness, I knew him from the angle of his head and the line of his neck. I stood close to him and leaned against the timber frame of the hall. I could smell the sap of the wood and the earthy scent of the daub that had been applied recently to the wattled walls between the timbers. If the hall was to remain intact and dry through the winter, it would need at least one more coating of the manure, mud and straw mixture. The previous layers had begun to crack as they dried out.

For a time we stood in silence. It had been two days since his outburst and none of us had spoken to him about it. I realised I knew nothing of his past life, of the time before he had joined our band, but the things he had said had allowed me to see a glimpse of the terrible anguish that beset him. He hid his pain well behind a screen of humour and bravado. And yet, it seemed to me, that the wall he protected himself behind was, just like the daub on the hall, cracking and threatening to flake and peel away. I longed to tell him that he could confide in me. We were close and had spent much time together in those long, hot summer days, but in the way of men, I knew not how to say these things to him.

"She reminds me of my sister," Cormac said into the silent darkness.

"Who?" I asked, but I knew the answer.

"Wulfwaru," he replied, in a voice not much more than a whisper. True to his word, Hereward had kept Cormac away from her since the confrontation with Aethelwig. The day before, when the rain began to fall, we had headed for shelter under a stand of willows by the river. Aethelwig and Wulfwaru were there, and Cormac had halted in his tracks and run off towards the church where a few others had gone to stand out of the rain. Before he had gone, I'd seen the sadness that had washed over him. I wished I'd gone with him, but instead I had watched him go and wondered at his infatuation with Wulfwaru.

"You should have told us," I said.

"What? That she reminds me of my older sister, Darerca, who was defiled and murdered?" He sniffed quietly in the gloom. "What would be the point? They had all made up their mind about what it was I wanted from her. They think me as bad as the Norsemen."

"They think you a man. Nothing more."

Silence grew between us again and I thought of all the horrors that had brought us to this place.

"He is a good man," I said, after a time.

"Who?" he asked. Apparently it was his turn to act as though he did not know the answer to his question.

"Runolf," I replied.

"He is Norse," he said.

"He is a man. No more than you." I hesitated, but I had to speak now. Cormac had opened the door to this conversation and I had to step through it. "He did not do those things to your family."

"I know it," he said. "But he would have, wouldn't he? If he had been there."

"I cannot say. But in the time I have known him, I have seen him save children's lives and only take those of men wishing to cause me and others harm."

Cormac sighed. The moonlight caught the cloud of breath that drifted for a moment about his face like cobwebs, or the ghosts of memories.

"You have oft spoke of this," he said, "and yet when I look at him, I see that heathen bastard..." His voice trailed off. He let out a shuddering breath. "Everything I had was taken from me when that serpent-prowed ship landed on the banks of Loch Cuan. Vengeance is all I have now."

I didn't know how to respond to that, and so I said nothing. We each had our reason for being here. Vengeance was as good as any.

After that night-time talk, Cormac's mood seemed to lighten somewhat. He had never spoken of these things before and it seemed that the act of describing what had happened to his kin had perhaps begun to allow their shades to depart, leaving him less burdened by their suffering.

He made more of an effort to talk to Runolf without his usual rudeness and a few nights later he sat with us in Werce's Hall. The harvest was over and we had celebrated with a roasted pig. It had been cooked over a great fire and the succulent meat had been shared by everyone, lay people, monks and warriors. The atmosphere had been buoyant and more than one person said they thought that all the work we had done on those hot summer days preparing defences had been a waste of time.

Beonna had come over to where Hereward lounged in the shade of a willow.

"Thank you all for your help with the harvest," he said. "It seems that the Lord smiles upon us. The rains have held off and so have the Norse." He smiled and looked about at the happy faces around us. "I pray to Jesu that the defences you have all toiled so hard over are never needed. Perhaps soon we can return to the life we used to live."

Hereward chewed the meat in his mouth and washed it down with some ale from a large wooden cup.

"I too pray the Norse do not come," he said. "But the seas are yet mellow enough for travel. I will not trust that you are safe until the storms come that will see the raiders holed up in their northern lands until the thaws of spring."

Beonna was not happy with that answer and had trudged away, muttering and shaking his head.

"So," said Leofstan, who had been standing close to the abbot, "you still think they will come?" I had scarcely spoken to him these last few weeks. Whenever we crossed paths, we would exchange greetings and pleasantries, but truth be told, I was nervous in his presence. Whenever he looked at me, I felt that I was being judged and found wanting. I much preferred to ignore my feelings of guilt and uncertainty when it came to my motives. We were all sinners, but Leofstan had a way of making me see what I must look like in his eyes: a lapsed monk who had turned his back on Christ and instead chose murder and violence as his creed.

"Runolf says they will," I replied.

"And you believe him?"

"I have no reason to doubt his word."

"I hope he is wrong," he said, but I could tell from the slump of his shoulders that he too believed the Norseman. Leofstan had witnessed the frenzied attack on Lindisfarnae and knew, deep down, that the heathens, having feasted on the flesh of Northumbria, would have a taste for it now and would return soon enough for more plunder. Leofstan turned to walk away, then halted.

"Hunlaf," he said, fixing me with his sad stare. "When the fighting starts, you must forget who you were." He looked away from me up at Werce's Hall, but not before I saw there were tears in his eyes. "The bright boy who wants to understand everything under God's heaven will not survive a battle."

"I know not if that boy still lives," I said.

"I think he does," he said, turning back to face me. His eyes were full of sorrow. "But when the Norse come and the bloodletting begins, you must push that boy deep inside yourself. That Hunlaf would be slain in an instant. Battle is not a time for pondering and thinking. When the time comes, you cannot hesitate."

His words shocked me.

"You are not disappointed in me then?" I asked.

Leofstan sighed and shook his head.

"What I think is unimportant. What God sees within your heart is all. He can forgive any trespass."

Leofstan's words lifted my spirits. I had craved his approval, and whilst I knew he would never give me that, it was good to know he understood the difficult decision I must take to defend the minster.

That night we were all sated, full of roasted meat, good fresh bread and a thick pottage of peas, beans and onion that the women of Werceworthe had made. It was full dark by the time we reached Werce's Hall, but although we were tired from days of working hard in the fields, the atmosphere of celebration hung in the air as much as the scent of the roasting pig. We had all drunk more than Hereward usually allowed, sneaking in an extra cup or two of the good ale that the monks had brought out for the festivities.

Hereward had taken over from Drosten, who had been on watch that afternoon, and now the Pict sat in the hall beside the newly lit hearth fire and ate the food we had brought him. The talk always seemed to flow more easily when Hereward was not in the hall and so it was that night. When being led by Uhtric, he had been a man prone to jest and gripe. That had changed after he had found himself in command, and none of us could truly be at our ease in his presence. He was only just outside the door and might very well be able to listen to our conversations, but even the fact that we could not see him made the men relax and speak more freely.

Cormac lay back and belched.

"So, Drosten," he said with a smile, "you all know why I am here. What of you? What makes you happy to risk your life for the men and women of this place? Why are you not at home?"

Gwawrddur shot me a wary glance, clearly concerned that Cormac was going to rake over the coals of his own past, kindling the fire of his distress once more. I shrugged. Cormac seemed much more at ease now that he had spoken to me and I could not deny that I was as interested as anyone to know what brought the tattooed Pict to Northumbria and made him willing to stand here with us against the Norse. As far as I knew, Drosten had never spoken of his past and none of us knew more about him than that he had fought with his fists for money at Eoforwic and that he had been robbed there.

Drosten took a bite of the meat, savouring it and chewing slowly. The tattooed lines on his face writhed like serpents as his jaw worked. We knew he was not a man prone to speak quickly and so we waited patiently for him to finish. He took a long draught of ale and stared into the flames of the fire. Just when I was sure he would not reply to Cormac's question, Drosten spoke.

"I am a warrior," he said, keeping his gaze fixed on the dancing flames. "What better place to be than where there is fighting?"

"But why here?" asked Cormac. "Northumbria is not a friend of the Picts. You would be better served standing with your people against Æthelred, rather than here, defending his folk."

A chapman had passed through the previous week with tales of battle in the north. Æthelred's forces had clashed with those of Causantín. The peddler was not clear which of the two sides had won, but he had eyed Drosten fearfully and declined to spend the night at Werceworthe, instead hurrying southward. Drosten had listened to the news of war without expression.

"I have no home," Drosten said, his voice as grim and hard as the mountains of his birth. He took another gulp of ale. "Not now."

"Why?" prompted Cormac. "What happened?"

Drosten drew in a deep breath and I saw his knuckles whiten on the wooden cup he clutched in his huge fist. The hall was silent. Much as I wanted to hear the answer, I was concerned that the Pict might launch himself at Cormac. It seemed that all of us held our breaths. It always surprised me that Cormac could be so dismissive of others' feelings when his own were so raw.

After what seemed a long time, Drosten sighed and set his cup aside.

"I was accused of a crime," he said.

"What crime?" Cormac asked.

Drosten shook his head and smiled ruefully.

"They said I stole something of great value." He shook his head and watched the flames flick and dance. "But I am no thief."

"If you are innocent, you should return."

Drosten snorted in derision.

"It is not so simple, boy," he said. "Nothing ever is." He picked up a stick and prodded at the fire. "No, I can never return." His tone was distant and filled with sorrow and memories of things that were lost. "But I am no thief. I'm still the man I always was, and it is right that a warrior stands in defence of the weak and helpless."

"Like the people of Werceworthe," said Cormac.

Drosten offered him a thin smile. The lines on his face and the shadows from the flames gave his features a sombre, almost monstrous aspect.

"Yes, like the people of Werceworthe," he said before falling silent again. He refilled his cup and drank. "You asked me why I would stand with you against Norsemen who seek to kill and enslave the monks and people here." He fixed Cormac in his gaze, but it seemed to me that he was speaking as much for himself as for the young Hibernian. "I do it because it is right. And while I do what is right, I know I am not the man they tried to make me become with their lies and deceit."

Cormac opened his mouth to ask another question, but Gwawrddur, sensing that it would be best to leave the Pict to his memories, cut the Hibernian off, speaking over him.

"What of you, Hunlaf?" he said. "What truly made a monk decide to throw away all that learning and prayer? To put down the quill and pick up the sword?"

They all turned towards me and I blushed under their scrutiny. How could I explain to them what I barely understood myself? Unsure how to answer the question, I reached for a log, one of the oak offcuts from when the hall had been repaired, and tossed it onto the fire. Sparks showered up and Drosten cursed, stamping out a smouldering ember that had landed on the fresh rushes that covered the floor.

"Sorry," I mumbled. Drosten just shook his head and took a sip from his cup. None of them uttered a word and I looked at each of them in turn. What could I say that would satisfy these men of action, warriors and killers all? And then, with a start, I understood that I was one of them by my own actions, just as much, if not more so, than I had ever been a man of God. I had fought and slain my enemies and I had felt that rush of ecstatic power that came from fighting for survival and winning. No words can truly capture that feeling, and any man who has not felt it, cannot understand how it feels. Or its allure.

"My father wanted me to become a monk," I said. "My brother, Beornnoth, became the warrior. I was happy enough, I suppose. I learnt quickly and I have a good hand when it comes to penmanship. I followed the order of the brethren, praying, fasting, working, studying, scribing and I think I would have carried on that way until I grew old like Leofstan, I suppose." I scratched my head and was surprised at how long the hair on my crown had grown. There was almost no sign that once I had worn the tonsure. "If I had not been on Lindisfarnae when the Norsemen attacked." I scanned their faces in the firelight. They were rapt, eyes glimmering, intent on my words. I had chosen to make this the tale of how I became a warrior, but even then I could feel the pull of knowledge, the desire to read and to write and learn about the world and its mysteries. I wondered if this was how a scop feels, to have the attention of everyone in a hall on him and to mould his story according to his audience. A tremor of excitement scratched the back of my neck. I had never enjoyed being the centre of attention before. How many other things had changed in me?

"When they landed, it was as Cormac said. They were like devils. People were screaming," I hesitated, seeing again in my mind the terrified faces, Tidraed's expression as he had been defiled, the blood of slaughtered innocents staining the surf. "Men and women were dying. They were being hacked down and they were defenceless. We were not warriors. We had no weapons." I could feel the memory of the sensations of that day, the growing anger at what was happening around me. "And it was then that something snapped within me. I did not know it at the time, but I think now, looking back, that it was in that moment that I ceased to be a monk."

"What happened?" asked Cormac, his eyes wide.

"People were fleeing away from the raiders, running as fast as they could." I reached for the ale and poured myself another cup, even though my head was already fuzzy with drink. My hand was shaking. I took a swallow. "But I did not run with them. I was filled with an ire such as I had never felt before. I had to do something to defy these heathens who had come with the dawn tide. I knew not what I could do, but instead of running away, I ran towards them." I thought of Aelfwyn and how I had desperately wanted to save her. But I did not mention her. "My fury was greater than my fear and as I ran, I grew more and more angry. I snatched up a seax, much like this one." I placed my hand on the weapon that now hung sheathed at my side, wondering what had happened to the weapon I had used that day, for my first kill. I swallowed at the lump in my throat. "I picked up a seax from the corpse of one of them and I threw myself at another man. I'll never forget him till the day I die." For a heartbeat I could not breathe, could not speak as I recalled his eyes, the scent of his breath, the strength ebbing from his body as I drove the blade into his flesh. "I took his life and it was easy. His blood covered me and I ran on... Looking back, so help me God, but I think I enjoyed it." I shuddered, suddenly feeling exposed. I had said too much, shown too much of myself. This was a truth I had scarcely allowed myself to admit, let alone speak out loud. "What sort of sinner does that make me?" I asked, not expecting an answer.

"I would say it makes you one of us," said Gwawrddur. "We are all sinners, are we not, Killer?" I was uncomfortable by the use of the name he had given me. Is that who I was now?

"All men are born of sin, it is true," I said, feeling sad. "But what kind of man revels in killing?"

"You are not a bad man," the Welshman replied. "You are a natural warrior, and too often the world needs men who run towards danger, rather than away from it." He reached over and gripped my shoulder. "But it is who you choose to fight that decides what manner of man you are and how you are remembered."

I took another mouthful of ale. I was not so sure. I was a killer and did not God command us not to kill?

Gwawrddur watched me through narrowed eyes for a time, and then, as if deciding that I had had enough, he turned to Runolf.

"It was there you met our Norse friend, was it not?" he asked.

I nodded. They all knew this story, but I was glad to move away from my own part in it.

"He was one of the raiders," I said. Hearing how the words sounded, I quickly added, "but he stood against some of his countrymen. He saved the lives of two children."

"And your own?"

"Yes. I too owe him my life."

"What is your tale then, Runolf?" asked Gwawrddur. "Why are you here?"

Runolf scowled. The firelight made his beard glow like iron hot from the forge.

"I have no choice," he growled. "I swore my eiðr, my oath, to your king. And I am a man of my word."

Cormac spoke up then and I groaned to hear the edge of accusation in his tone.

"You speak of being a man of your word," he said, "and yet you turned on your own. Where is the honour in that?"

"Easy now, Cormac," said Gwawrddur.

Runolf held up a huge hand, waving away Gwawrddur's concern. He fixed Cormac in his pale stare.

"I did not break my oath," he said. "And I do not make war on children. I defended them against bad men. Those men had stood beside me in raids before. They knew better than to cross me."

"You have children of your own?" asked Gwawrddur.

Runolf went very quiet. His shoulders sagged and his gaze dropped to the fire. Where moments before he had seemed a giant, a man to fear, now he appeared diminished. He drained his cup of ale.

"Once," he said, his voice a rasping growl. "No more." He scratched at his beard and then combed his thick fingers through his hair. As with the hair on my head, there was little reminder of the tonsure I had shaved. He squared his shoulders and with an effort of will appeared to regain his strength. "I will not stand by while the defenceless are slain."

For a time nobody spoke. The log I had placed on the fire shifted as it burnt, sending fresh sparks into the smoky air.

"There is one thing I do not understand," said Drosten, breaking the silence with his thick Pictish brogue.

Runolf looked at him and raised an enquiring eyebrow.

"Why did your people leave you behind on Lindisfarnae?"

Runolf shrugged his massive shoulders.

"Who can say? Mayhap they thought me dead."

"Or they wanted you dead," said Drosten, rubbing his chin.

Runolf flashed him a dark look.

"Perhaps soon we can ask them." He glowered over the rim of his cup as he emptied it. There was death in that gaze. If the

Norse returned, there would be little in the way of talking and asking of questions, I thought.

"What of you, Gwawrddur?" asked Runolf, pushing his memories and anger aside. "You have asked many questions this evening. But you have spoken nothing of yourself. Why are you here?"

The slender Welshman smiled and raised his cup to the Norseman.

"You speak truly," he said. "I have been content to listen to you all. A wise man once told me that a man learns much more from listening than from speaking. And so I listen and I learn."

"And you teach," said Cormac.

"Yes, I teach, as others have taught me. Or at least as well as I am able."

"Both Hunlaf and I are thankful for your teaching. You are a formidable swordsman, and we are blessed that you would devote your time to us."

Gwawrddur smiled at the compliments.

"I have done my best to equip you with the skills needed to survive when the sword-song begins. I feel the rest is up to you both. I have helped to forge you, now it is for you to temper yourselves in the fires of battle."

He sipped at his ale.

"I had not imparted sword-skill to others before. I have always been reticent to do so, but I cannot deny that I have enjoyed seeing you both improve until you each bear yourselves like men, not boys. Like warriors." Cormac and I grinned at the rare praise from our teacher. "And yet, that is not the answer to your question of why I have come here, to this place, where few will stand against many."

"What is your answer then?" I asked.

Gwawrddur pondered a moment before replying.

"I have fought the best swordsmen from every corner of these islands. I have tested my blade and my skills against the greatest warriors I could find. Some have been in contests of skill, where the winner took silver or gold, others have stood against me with naked steel, where defeat brought death." He looked into the flames and I wondered what memories he saw there; how many dead enemies. "I have defeated all who have stood before me," he said, taking another sip of ale. "Every warrior wishes to test himself against others. There are no adversaries who can best me in these islands, perhaps one of these raiders from other lands can challenge me."

I thought about his words. There was a hollow sadness in them. Some men are born thus, never content with their lot, always striving for more. For many, they lust over power and gold. Gwawrddur sought the constant betterment of his own skills. With each opponent he defeated, rather than feel that his skills were validated, he thought that he had yet to find a worthy enemy.

"But when," I said, and then corrected myself, "*if* you find the man who can beat you in combat, you will be slain."

"That would seem to be the most likely outcome," he said, with a grim thin smile. "Then we must hope that I do not meet my match too soon."

I shook my head, unable to understand the man's desire to face ever-increasing odds against him. What made him seek danger in this way? But was I not in my own way doing the same? I did not voice it in such stark terms as Gwawrddur, but I too had decided to throw myself towards danger where most would flee. Perhaps we were all moonstruck in our way. Maybe the Devil had his claws in all of us, damning us to be killers. Condemning us to violent deaths.

I was trying to weave my feelings into the cloth of words, when a loud clanging rent the quiet night. I started at the sound and for the briefest of moments, none of us moved. And then, as one, we surged up from where we lounged about the fire and rushed out into the darkness.

Hereward was hammering the rusting piece of metal that hung from the rope outside the hall. The ringing cacophony filled the night. In the settlement and minster buildings below us, I could see small sparks of light as men and women rushed out of their homes and monks tumbled from their cells. I fancied I could hear shouts and calls in the distance, but the jarring crash of the iron bell drowned out all other sound.

Hereward continued to pound the lump of iron and I looked to the east. The night was dark and at first I saw nothing of note. And then my eyes became accustomed to the gloom and I saw it, a flickering of distant flames. As I watched, another light flared in the darkness. Not one but at least two of the beacons had been lit.

Hereward finally stopped hitting the bell. My ears rang and jarred as if the sound echoed within my skull.

"Sounds carry far in the quiet of the night and your talk has made for interesting listening this night." Hereward scanned our faces. The ruddy light from the hearth spilled out of the open door of the hall, illuminating his features. His teeth flashed in a grin. "You each have your own reasons for being here. But all that matters now is that the time has come for us to stand together. The few against the many. We have readied ourselves for this moment, and I can think of no men I would rather have at my side when the storm of steel begins. If we stick to what we have planned these last weeks and you do what is asked of you without hesitation, I say we will prevail. We will be outnumbered, but we have something important in our favour."

"What?" asked Cormac.

"This is a minster," Hereward said. "A holy place." Cormac looked blank. Hereward laughed, too loudly. "We have God on our side!" he bellowed.

I met Runolf's gaze. Both of us had been on the holy island where the bishop of Northumbria resided. God had not protected them from the fury of the Norsemen. I clenched my jaw, forcing aside the voice of doubt that threatened to smother my resolve. God might have allowed many to die that accursed day, but He had also brought us all here together. It was the Lord who had called me to stand with these warriors and, with His grace, we would be victorious.

Forty-Three

For a time we stood, staring out over the dark land, each lost in our thoughts of what was to come. We had been preparing for this for weeks, but it was only then, with the flash of flames in the distance, that I truly believed the Norsemen were coming and suddenly our plan and the skill and strength I had built up under Gwawrddur's tutelage seemed inconsequential. What could the few of us and a couple of dozen ceorls hope to do against the battle-hardened raiders who swept from the Whale Road aboard their serpent-headed wave-steeds?

I peered into the east, at the tiny flecks of light and thought of Anstan on his rocky island. Had the men gone to his hut and slain him for his temerity in lighting the beacon? Had he found the kind of death he craved or had they merely slid by on their long ships, leaving him to succumb to the rattling cough and sickness that consumed his feeble body? If they had not gone to the island, they would already be in the mouth of the Cocueda. I could picture the banks of oars rising and falling like great wings, propelling the ships and their savage crews ever nearer to Werceworthe.

"Come on," snapped Hereward. "We have looked long enough. Would you be standing here when the Norsemen arrive? Go and help the people up here to the hall."

Nobody moved. It was as if all we had prepared so carefully in the warm days of summer had been forgotten in the darkness of that night with the breath of approaching winter in the cold air.

"You know what to do," growled Gwawrddur. "Go!"

Like oxen goaded with a hazel switch, we all jolted into motion and hurried to fulfil the roles that had been assigned to us.

The first task was to get all of those who would not fight up to Werce's Hall. And so, for what seemed an endless amount of time, we carried children and belongings up the hill. The monks and greybeards helped, as did the women. All the while, as babies cried and women shouted at their offspring, I imagined the Norsemen heaving on their long oars with the strength and ease I had witnessed from Runolf. Their sleek ships would slide quickly up the river and I kept on glancing down to the water, expecting to see a horde of armed men, all savage, leering grins and the dull-glint of deadly iron.

But no attack came and soon enough all the people who did not have a role to play in the plans we had devised were in the hall. It was packed and already some of the monks had decided to sit outside in the scant shelter of the ruined store huts, rather than being uncomfortably squashed inside the hall with the crush of villagers. I nodded, grim-faced, at the anxious monks and tried to emulate Hereward with words of comfort and a cheerfulness I did not believe.

I did not see Osfrith amongst them and recalled with a sinking feeling in my gut that he had been manning the beacon at the river's mouth. Had he been found by the Norse? Was he even now being abused, tortured and murdered while the raiders laughed at his plight and ignored his pitiful screams?

I shivered at the thought and pulled the cloak I wore more tightly about my shoulders. I had been sweating moments before as I helped the lay people and monks to climb up to the hall, and now I felt the chill of the night against my skin.

Hereward called me over. Drosten and Runolf were with him.

"Look," he said, pointing into the east. I followed his gaze, but could see nothing. I did not understand. And then I saw it.

"The beacons have gone out?"

"Or they have been extinguished. Whatever has occurred, you must all take your places. They might attack at any moment. Go!"

I hurried down the slope, slipping more than once on the wet grass. Leaving Runolf and Drosten with a whispered, "God be with you," I ran on to where I would wait for the coming of the Norsemen.

My sweat cooled on my brow and I shivered as the night drew its cold dark arms about me. I was close to the water's edge, in a stand of alders and with a clear view down to the river. I propped my spear against one of the trees and watched as a thin mist began to form over the slow-flowing waters of the Cocueda.

Silently, I recited the paternoster, all the while thinking of what might have happened to Anstan and Osfrith. I stood and stretched my arms and legs, bending and twisting my body. The plan relied on the element of surprise and my speed. I could feel the cold of the night seeping into my bones. If I was not careful, I would only be able to hobble stiffly from this place rather than sprint. I had been so proud of myself when Gwawrddur and Hereward had named me for this crucial role. I knew Cormac had been disappointed that it was not given to him, but Gwawrddur had confided in me.

"You are not only the faster runner," he said, "but you can hold your head when all about you has turned to chaos. Yours is the most important position in the plan of the first defence. You must hold your nerve and then you must act, and act fast.

And," he gripped my shoulder and gave it a squeeze, "run like the wind, as if the Devil himself is chasing you."

"Not just one devil," I said, grinning at my own wit. "A whole horde of them."

That had been weeks ago. The days were warm then and the prospect of actually being here, hunkered down in the lee of an alder and watching for sign of the arrival of the Norse had seemed very distant. Now that the moment was upon me, I would have gladly traded places with Cormac. He would not have been as terrified. His bowels would not have turned to water and his hands would not have shaken like the leaves of the trees above in the stiffening breeze.

But Gwawrddur was of course right. Cormac was not best suited for this role. He was possibly fast enough, but at the sight of the Norse, he might well forget himself and throw the whole plan into disarray, such was his anger. I hoped he would be able to hold his fury in check when the time came. Gwawrddur had warned us both that we should master our ire.

"Your anger must be under your command," he had told us. "For if you cannot control it, you will become the slave of your rage, and it makes a poor master."

I tried to recall the surging anger that had coursed through me on Lindisfarnae, but all I felt was creeping fear. The Norsemen, sharp steel in their hands and murder in their heathen hearts, would come upon my hiding place and sheathe their swords in my flesh, I was sure of it. I began to tremble. I loathed my own weakness, but the more I tried to convince myself that our plan would work, the more I shook. I gripped the haft of the spear and renewed my prayers. If I was to die soon, I did not want the Lord to think I had forsaken Him. I vowed that if I survived the night, I must seek out Beonna that he could hear my confession. I must not face the end without being shriven.

The screeching call of a night bird in the distance startled me. I stopped breathing, fearful that the smoke of my breath might show my position to alert eyes in the darkness. Peering from behind the bole of the alder, I stared down at the wide, black waters of the Cocueda. The water was wreathed in wraiths of mist. The night was as silent as a barrow mound. I strained to hear any sound.

A rising breeze caused the leaves high above to murmur a secret susurration. A quiet stealthy splash. Was that the fall of an oar blade into the water or a nocturnal fish in search of some insect flitting on the river's surface? I leaned forward, listening for any other sign; a whispered command, the scrape of a ship's keel against sand, the creak of an oar against a thole.

I heard nothing save for the pounding of my heart. I let out my breath very slowly.

The screech of the bird echoed out again, loud and piercing like the scream of a dying man. I jumped and almost dropped the spear that was clutched in my hands like a talisman, as if the ash wood topped with a sharp leaf of iron could somehow save me from the horrors that lurked out there in the dark. I forced myself to breathe slowly. It was just one of the pale-faced owls that frequented the land and roosted in the church roof, I told myself. Or was it perhaps a man, imitating the call of an owl, signalling to his comrades that the coast was clear?

I lifted the spear in my trembling grip and readied myself.

A twig snapped loud and clear in the gloom. A rustling footfall, sighing through the leaf litter. No matter how hard I tried now, my breath came fast and it was all I could do not to give away my position with my panting gasps. The Norsemen were coming. Here, now, in the darkness. And I would be the first to stand before them. My blood rushed in my ears.

Think, I told myself with an effort. Think and remain calm. This is the plan. It is right that you have heard their approach. Your sword-brothers are where they should be. You are not alone. You will lead the raiders to their doom and you will live to see the dawn. This was why Gwawrddur had chosen me over Cormac and I would not let him down.

Another scraping step. Closer now, almost upon me. It was coming from the east and someway behind me, back towards the settlement. I could not let the attackers get behind my position. If they cut me off, I would be killed and all the planning and preparation would be for naught. Slowly, stealthily, I left the dark shadow beneath the alder and set off after the raiders who were passing close by through the woods.

I carried the spear in my right hand, using my left to reach out before me to avoid stumbling into low branches. I took a few steps and then halted, listening. The sounds of movement stopped and the night was silent again. Had they heard me? I breathed through my mouth and listened.

There! A footfall, then another. A sudden gust of wind shook the trees and I was sure I heard my quarry take several fast steps, perhaps hoping to mask the sound of their passage with the rustle of the boughs. I moved quickly, certain now of the position and direction of my quarry.

Far off in the distance, the owl called again.

The footsteps were coming closer, more quickly now, seemingly with no effort to hide their crunch in the undergrowth. I spun around, looking behind me, suddenly certain that the Norse had somehow encircled me and were about to plunge their blades into my back. There was nobody there.

The sounds of approach grew louder. I frowned. I could only make out one or perhaps two people. Where were the rest of them? I offered up a prayer that they had not separated to come at Werceworthe from different directions. I had positioned myself in the path of the oncoming Norse and there was no time now to change the plan. A twig snapped very close, its report as loud as a slap in the almost absolute darkness beneath the trees.

Taking a deep breath, I raised the spear above my head, preparing to throw it as hard as I was able, and stepped out from behind the broad trunk of a tree.

Forty-Four

My muscles thrummed, as taut as a bowstring at full draw. I pulled my arm back, ready to let fly the spear. All of my pent-up fear from the long night-time solitary vigil would be unleashed in that throw and I knew, if the iron spear point struck its mark, it would pierce the links of any byrnie. If the man it hit was not wearing an iron-knit shirt, it would plunge easily into flesh, severing arteries and smashing bone.

If my throw was true.

I drew in a breath of the damp, loam-redolent air of the wood, scanning the gloom for my target. There! A shadowy shape of a man. There was only one of them! My heart thundered against my ribs. No time to ponder this mystery now. I knew what I was about.

I began to snap my arm forward. I was sure of my strength and my aim. The spear would fly true and its blade would find its target.

"Hold, Hunlaf," hissed a voice.

What? Who was this enemy that knew my name?

Without conscious thought, perhaps by the power of the Lord Himself, I did not release the spear. And thus, I was prevented from murdering one of my oldest friends.

"Osfrith?" I whispered.

Horror washed through me as I realised how close I had come to killing him, spitting him on the point of my spear like a boar cornered in a thicket. With trembling hands, I lowered my weapon, but I did not lower my guard. Scanning the darkness behind him, I fancied I could see enemies lurking there in the gloom.

"Where are the Norsemen?" I asked, my voice sibilant and harsh in the still of the night.

"I know not," he replied, stepping closer. His breath was ragged and I detected the sheen of sweat on his brow, his hair wet and slick against his forehead and the nape of his neck. "You saw the beacon then?"

"We did," I said. "We have been ready for the attack all night. I thought you were a Norseman." I blew out a breath. It steamed briefly around us. "I almost killed you."

I sensed as much as saw him make the sign of the cross.

"Well, thank the Lord you did not." I could hear the smile in his voice. There was always a levity between us when we were alone. We were both devout enough, but we were young and enjoyed escaping from our chores and prayers when we were able. Together we had roamed all over the area surrounding the minster. But we had never been out in the dead of night before. The owl shrieked again and Osfrith tensed.

"Only a bird, I think," I said.

"You think?"

"Well, I thought you were a Norseman, so anything is possible." I smiled in the darkness despite myself, at my use of Runolf's favourite phrase. "I am glad I did not kill you too," I added.

Osfrith snorted.

"What happened?" I asked.

For a few heartbeats he was silent and I could imagine him reliving the horrors he had witnessed. The visions of

Lindisfarnae threatened to loom up in my own mind's eye and I pushed them back with an effort.

"The Norse came at dusk," Osfrith said. "They were just as you said they would be. In three massive ships, with the beast prows and those huge square sails. Sleek and fast are those ships." His voice was filled with awe. He loved the sea and boats and we had often enjoyed rowing out to the island of Cocwaedesae together, he entranced by the waves and me with the birds.

"Enough about their ships," I snapped, my anxiety lending a sharp edge to my words. "What happened?"

For a moment, he did not reply and I imagined him pouting at my tone. We would often fight and disagree on our adventures around Werceworthe. We bickered and sometimes even came to blows, but we would always shrug off our differences in time. Osfrith must have decided there was no time for us to play that game, as, after only a brief hesitation, he answered me.

"Anstan lit the beacon. They must have seen it, for they hove around and landed on Cocwaedesae," he said. "I watched them from the beach. I was terrified. I knew I should light my beacon, but if I did, I was sure they would come for me and so I held back and did nothing for a time." His voice cracked and I placed my hand on his shoulder.

I said nothing, waiting for him to finish his tale.

"They slew Anstan. They hacked at him... I think I could hear his screams." He sobbed then, as the images flooded his mind again. I doubted that he could have heard anything over the waves. Perhaps he had heard gulls. But I said nothing. "And then they threw him onto the beacon." Could he truly have seen such details from the beach by the mouth of the river?

I have learnt over the years that after battles or moments of strife, men often believe they have seen things which do not stand up to scrutiny in the calm light of a peaceful day. But it is a fruitless task to debate such things. I doubted that Osfrith could truly have seen what he claimed to have witnessed, but even then, young and impetuous as I was, I knew better than to question him further.

"What did you do then?" I asked, keeping my voice soft.

"I lit the beacon."

"You did well. We saw it. And you did well to hurry back here without being captured."

"I did not come hither directly."

"Did you have to head away from the river to be safe?"

"No," he replied, "when I set off for Werceworthe, I came by the most direct path I could. If I had not got lost in the dark and missed the place, I would not have reached you. I would have turned off sooner and crossed the fields and headed directly for the hall on the hill."

I nodded. He must have been following the river and in the dark not have realised he had reached the loop in its course which should have seen him turn left and away from the water.

"Is that what you meant when you said you did not come here directly?"

"No," he replied. "I mean I stayed beside the beacon for a time. The flames raged high into the darkening sky and I am sure they saw the fire and me, lit as I was by the flames. And yet, I stood there and stared out at the island with their ships pulled up on the sands of the beach."

"But you came at last," I said.

"The fire was burning down and it was dark. There was not enough of a moon to show me anything."

"Anything of what?" I asked, confused.

"Before it became too dark to see, I watched them. I had thought they would put to sea and come to me. I was filled with a righteous anger at what they had done to Anstan and I think I might have remained there, if they had come."

I could scarcely believe what I was hearing.

"But they did not come," I said.

"No," he replied, his voice sounding small and lost. "They remained on the island and I fled as the beacon turned to embers."

"What do you think they will do?" I asked.

"I know not," Osfrith replied. "But I have thought much on this as I walked the dark paths of the night."

"And what did you come to think on the matter?"

"That we must remain vigilant," he whispered in the gloom. I noticed that I could make out his features now. The wolf-light of dawn was tinging the sky. "The Norsemen have come with one purpose and they will not tarry long on Cocwaedesae."

I nodded, but said nothing.

"The beacons have done their task and forewarned us," he said. "This has given the northern raiders pause, but the fires have done something else."

"What?" I asked.

"They have told the heathens that we know of their coming."

Forty-Five

I have oftentimes had to endure long waits. Once, Al-Hakam Ibn Hisham Ibn Abd-ar-Rahman, the blood-thirsty Emir of Cordova, made me linger in his palace for three whole days before he would deign to honour me with an audience. But I have never known a more interminable day than the one of exhausted tension that followed that long night.

As the dawn lightened the sky to a dull, cold iron grey, I sent Osfrith on to the hall to inform Hereward of what had occurred at Cocwaedesae. I dared not leave my post and so I remained there, stiff, cold and hungry and above all else, tired. The previous day we had toiled hard in the fields and afterwards eaten our fill and drunk more ale than was good for us, and then, just as we had longed for sleep, we had seen the flare of the beacons and set about putting our plans into motion and moving to our positions. I had not slept, but after so long expecting action and battle, despite the prospect of the Norsemen looming out of the morning mists, with their savage smiles and sharp blades, I found my eyelids drooping. I shook my head and forced myself onto my feet.

The woodland awoke around me and the familiar chirrups of siskins and finches, and the distant thrum of a woodpecker, made me even more drowsy. I leaned against the trunk of a willow and closed my eyes. I must have only dozed like that for a short while, for the day was still young when I was startled awake by the sounds of someone coming from the settlement. My face reddened with shame. What if the Norse had attacked while I slept? I would be dead and they would even now be stalking into Werceworthe unannounced.

Turning, I saw Cormac walking towards me in the early morning shadows. He carried a basket, which he placed on the ground beside the willow.

"Christ's teeth," he said, "you look done in." He gestured at the basket. "There is some food and drink in there."

I took the hard bread and piece of smoked cheese from the basket and ate.

"I am so tired," I said, through a mouthful of bread and cheese. "I think I could sleep standing up."

"I think you were doing just that when I arrived."

I gave him a sidelong glance, but saw no malice in his comment. I offered him a rueful smile. He winked and said, "Lie down and rest a while. I will watch for the Norse."

Nodding my thanks, I sat and propped my back against the willow. Pulling out the leather flask from the basket, I unstoppered it. I sniffed the contents. There was a faint memory of the odour of mead, but the vessel was filled with refreshing water. I drank deeply, only then realising how thirsty I had been.

"Hereward thinks it is unlikely they will attack during the day," Cormac said.

I was unsure how I felt about that. My neck and shoulders ached from tension and I did not relish the thought of another long day and perhaps night waiting for something to happen.

"When does he think they will strike?" I asked, stifling a yawn.

Cormac shrugged.

"Hereward talked to Gwawrddur and Runolf about it for a long while. Beonna thought that perhaps the beacons and the threat of a ready defence might have scared them off. Runolf laughed at him."

In my memory I saw the savage men who had descended upon the holy island, picking it clean of treasure and slaughtering all those that did not serve their purpose. I could not imagine them retreating at the possibility of a fight.

"Runolf is certain they will attack," Cormac went on. "But he said they are not foolish and will not wish to wait too long. They are not afraid to fight, he said, but they do want to live to return to their homes. The longer they wait, the more chance that the king will send warriors to fight them. He thinks they will wait until nightfall. But no longer."

I tried to picture sprinting through the darkness, leading the Norse after me without tripping or slipping on some unseen obstacle. My stomach twisted. I did not want the Norse to come at all, but I certainly did not want them to strike at night when I could not see where I placed my feet and every sound in the looming shadows of the woods filled me with fear.

I closed my eyes and listened to the birds chitter and chirp in the boughs all around me. It was hard to imagine the terror that had gripped me in the night, or the threat of the Norse, who were sure to attack all too soon.

I thought again of the plan we had put in place. The ditches, pits and fences to corral the Norsemen. I could barely believe that I had talked passionately in favour of me being the one to lure the attackers to the killing ground we had created in the village. Hereward had been against it, saying it was too risky and too prone to something going wrong. Cormac of course had agreed with me, saying it was a good plan, and when asked for his opinion as to whether it would work, Runolf had shrugged and said, "Anything is possible." Drosten had frowned and said the plan had its merits, but he was noncommittal. Wulfwaru was an unexpected champion of the idea. She said it gave us the best chance of allowing our archers to have some unmoving targets.

"Whatever helps us to kill more of the bastards," she'd said, making me blush at her language.

But it was Gwawrddur who swayed Hereward's mind.

"The boy is fast and brave," he'd said. "It might just work. If it doesn't, we will be no worse off, unless he gets himself killed, of course."

He'd winked and I had returned his smile, pleased with his praise and belief in me. But now, faced with the reality of being alone in the woods with the Norse baying at my heels, I wished I had not managed to persuade him that this was a good idea. There would be danger ahead for all of us, but this was madness. I offered up a silent prayer that Abbot Beonna was right and the Norse had fled after seeing the beacons.

I sighed, knowing that was a vain hope.

I awoke to Cormac kicking my foot.

Rubbing my eyes, I sat up, confused momentarily by my surroundings. The sun was high in the sky, but its light was muted and watery as it fought to shine through the thick clouds that blanketed the sky above us.

"How long have I slept?" I asked, ashamed that I had succumbed to sleep so readily.

"Long enough," Cormac said with a grin. "Gwawrddur will be furious with me, I am sure. But better that you are awake when the Norse come, eh?"

I pushed myself to my feet and thanked him.

"Not long now," he said, slapping me on the shoulder before trotting off back towards the settlement.

I waved and nodded, fixing a smile that felt like a lie on my face. With Cormac's parting words still swirling in my mind, I set about resuming my vigil and remaining alert and ready for what I was sure would come.

I walked down to the river's edge and splashed some of the cold water on my face. I stretched and performed some exercises with my spear and seax. I had left my sword back with the others. I had wanted to wear it scabbarded at my belt, but Gwawrddur had convinced me that it would only slow me down.

"If you need to turn and fight with a blade," he said, his expression dour and stern, "you will be lost. You must be as fast as the wind through the trees. Faster than any Norseman wearing an iron-knit shirt or carrying a sword." His words had seemed to sit in the pit of my stomach like two boulders. The weight of them would surely hold me back, slowing me more than any sword. But I had left the blade behind. The Welshman was right, I knew. I would be faster without the scabbarded sword slapping at my legs and threatening to trip me. But I had grown used to its solidity, the heft of it resting on my hip and thigh, and now, preparing to face three ships' crews of marauding Norsemen without even the comfort of my sword, I felt naked.

After a few lunges with the spear, I twisted my waist and stretched my legs. I felt more awake now and returned to my position beside the thick trunk of the old willow. A light drizzle began to fall and the woodland hushed as birds returned to their roosts. I pulled my damp cloak about me and hunkered in the thin shelter of the tree.

The day wore on, the slowly drenching drizzle soaking through my clothes and making me shiver. There was no movement from the river and I began to wonder if perhaps the Norse had in fact decided to leave in search of easier prey. I knew such thoughts were folly, and my spirits swung and flapped about from hope to abject misery like a flag caught in a strong breeze. One moment I was hopeful that the Norse would avoid Werceworthe altogether, leaving us in peace, the next, I was languishing in the deepest abyss of doom, certain that not only would they come, but all of our carefully laid plans would serve us for nothing and we would be slaughtered like so many cattle when the long nights of wintertime draw in.

I watched as the rain dripped from the leaves above me and puddled in ruts and depressions on the path. I had visions of our blood swilling down the muddy lanes of Werceworthe, turning the earth into a gory quagmire.

Wulfwaru came to me when I had fallen into the deepest despondency. I still had my wits about me enough to turn at her approach, but the expression on my face must have told her all she needed to know.

"You have been alone here all day?" she asked.

"Cormac brought me some food just after dawn."

She looked up at the slate grey sky through the canopy of the trees.

"It is almost dusk now," she said. "The waiting has been bad for us all, but for you, here alone, it must have been terrible."

"It is not that bad," I lied. No man likes to admit weakness before a woman, particularly not a pretty one, and especially not a pretty one with the tough spirit of a fighter, like Wulfwaru.

She nodded, pretending to believe me.

"I have brought you some food," she said, handing me a linen-wrapped bundle. My stomach groaned with hunger as I uncovered the piece of bread, an apple and a slice of meat from the roast pig inside the parcel. "The bread is stale," she said. "Sorry. We have not baked today. We should have though, I feel. Runolf said they would not come till nightfall, but Hereward would not allow us to take the risk of going down to the ovens."

I chewed the food, feeling my mood lift.

"Thank you for this," I said, careful not to spit crumbs as I talked.

For a time she was silent, watching the river and listening to the murmur of the light rain through the trees, while I ate.

"You are a good man, Hunlaf," she said, interrupting the quiet. I almost choked, but managed to swallow the food that was in my mouth.

"I do not feel good," I said, frowning and choosing not to utter the thought that I also felt more like a boy than a man.

"It is a good thing you have done," she went on, "bringing these men here to protect us. You have given up much. Risked your life even. For us."

"So have you," I muttered. My cheeks burnt. I was uncomfortable with the woman's praise. It seemed unwarranted and I felt unworthy.

"Cormac didn't mean to cause you upset," I said, wishing to change the subject. "The other night. It was foolish, but you remind him of his older sister."

She smiled sadly.

"That is not foolish," she said. "Coming to my home in the dead of night was folly though, of that there can be no doubt." The rain began to fall more heavily, whispering through the woods all about us, rippling the river's surface. "Aethelwig could have killed him."

I nodded, thinking it much more likely that Cormac would have killed the tanner, if she had not intervened.

"Cormac is sorry for what he did," I said.

"He is a good man too, I think," she said, "though he masks it better than you."

I blushed again.

"Perhaps when this is all over, you can tell him as much."

"Perhaps," she said.

Something drew her attention and she stared open-mouthed over my shoulder. Her eyes widened. I spun about, knowing what I would see before I did.

Through the grey boles of the trees, sliding silently through the dark, rain-rippled waters of the Cocueda, came the three high-prowed ships of the Norsemen. Their sails were furled and the rows of long oars rose and fell, dipping silently into the water, just as I had imagined them. As silent as death came the Norse raiders. There were so many of them. Dozens of hardened men, with plaited beards, pagan amulets about their necks and warrior rings on their muscled arms. At the prow of the foremost ship stood the massive man I had seen take Tidraed's life on Lindisfarnae. The same blood-red cloak hung lank about his broad shoulders.

Skorri.

The jarl raised his hand, indicating for his helmsman to turn the ship and, a heartbeat later, the sleek vessel began to swing into the sandy shore. My mouth dropped open, amazed that this first part of the plan had worked. We had spent a long afternoon clearing the beach of debris and jetsam, hoping to make it an enticing landing point for the Norse when they came. As the ship swung toward the land, the tall jarl scanned the forested banks. His grey gaze roved for signs of an ambush perhaps. Or more likely, given the wolfish look of the man and the ranks of raiders behind him, he was looking for prey.

Watching him from the shadows beneath the trees, I knew what it was like for the vole to stare at the owl, or for the hare to look into the eyes of the oncoming wolf. I could not move. I had a terrible urge to piss and I worried fleetingly that my bladder would loosen.

The Norse leader turned and called out quietly to his men. I could not make out the words, but they laughed, a hard, jangling sound in the still of the late afternoon. With that sound, the spell was broken and I turned to Wulfwaru. I pushed her away, so hard that she stumbled and almost fell.

"Run!" I hissed. "Now, quickly, before they land!"

She didn't move. Her eyes flicked from me to the ships and their cargo of murderous heathens.

"Run now or Aethelwulf will lose his mother, and all our

planning will be for nothing." I took hold of her shoulders and shook her. "Go, now!"

At last, she turned and without a word, she sped off towards the settlement of Werceworthe.

Suddenly calm now, I turned to watch as the first of the ships landed on the beach. I could see every detail as the hull crunched into the shingle. The grain of the oak strakes, the pine resin oozing from the caulking between the planks, the iron rivets stained with specks of rust, the droplets of water that dripped from the uplifted oars, the leering, lupine grin on Skorri's face. The moment seemed to draw out, as if time itself had slowed. This strange battle-focus is something I have come to accept in the years since, but then, as the Norse warriors leapt over the side of their ships, splashing into the river and wading towards me, hefting axes and swords, donning helms and pulling shields from where they had rested within the bellies of their wave-steeds, this feeling was new to me. I wondered absently whether it meant that my fear had unmanned me and I would swoon, but I was not dizzy. And, I realised with detached bemusement, I was no longer frightened.

Gone was the fear of waiting. This is what we had planned for. I knew what I must do and I understood then, as the cool calm washed through me like the rain that fell from the sky with ever-increasing force, why Gwawrddur had chosen me over Cormac.

I glanced over my shoulder. Wulfwaru was running fast. I would give her as much time as I could. I watched as more Norsemen piled from their ships and amassed on the small beach by the river's edge.

I leaned my back against the gnarled trunk of the willow and offered up a prayer that my strength and speed would not desert me. The air was thick with the moist green smell of moss, rotting leaves and loam. The peace of the wood was gone. Despite their attempts at stealth, the Norsemen were loud. They spoke in hushed tones. Someone grunted. There was a rasping grinding as the ships were heaved onto the beach.

I stared through the trees towards Werceworthe. I could still see Wulfwaru. She had lifted her skirts to run faster and, though distant now, the pale skin of her legs flashed bright as she ran out from the gloom beneath the trees and into the dull afternoon light.

A shout from one of the Norsemen by the river. I understood the words he called to his companions: "Look there. A woman!" The moment had come when I must act.

I drew in a deep breath of the damp air. A murmur of chatter went through the men. The sound of excitement; the growl of a pack of wolves on scenting a fawn in the forest. I heard their footfalls leave the shingle and move onto the soft earth beneath the trees. They did not come at a run, nor at the shuffling pace of men expecting imminent danger. Someone said something I could not make out. Several of the others laughed. These were not men in fear for their lives. They had seen the beacons and still came upon us, convinced that they would stride onto our land and take whatever they wished.

A grim rage began to burn within me. They would know fear soon, I told myself, gripping the spear haft tightly and listening to their approach. This part of the plan relied on disorder and chaos. I allowed my anger to build, stoking the flames with thoughts of all of those who had been slaughtered on Lindisfarnae, the plumes of smoke from the scriptorium, the screams of the abused echoing in the early morning air. I thought of Aelfwyn, as I had last seen her. Her face a mask of terror and anguish.

I had not been able to save her and my heart ached for that loss. But I was no longer the boy I had been then. No longer a monk. My body was stronger and I knew what it was to take a life. God had made me his weapon and I welcomed the rushing fury that gripped me as I stepped out into the path of the Norsemen.

Forty-Six

I was just one man and there were dozens of Norse. They were killers, warriors all, bearers of iron and death and I was but a monk playing at being a fighter. And yet they were not holding their round shields aloft, their swords still rested in their scabbards. Eyes widened at my appearance from behind the willow. I grinned.

I fixed my gaze on a young man in the front rank. He walked close to Skorri, but a few steps before him, as if more eager than the older jarl to reach their destination and the target of their lust and avarice. The young man wore a fine, polished byrnie. His beard was thick and fair, like the gold they had stolen from the church on Lindisfarnae. He was half-turned, speaking over his shoulder to the men behind him. On noting my movement, he began to turn towards me.

Too late, he started to lift his shield.

God guide my hand, I prayed and, with a scream that unleashed some of the fury that threatened to rip from me, I flung my spear with all my strength.

My target was not far from me, no more than a few paces and the Lord answered my prayer. The spear shot forward and for the briefest of instants, I lost sight of it in the gloom. And then the young man was staggering back into his friends.

He was still in the process of raising his shield when the spear struck him, and the iron rim of the board cracked into the haft that now protruded from his throat. For a heartbeat I stood still, watching the mayhem that I had caused. Disorder and chaos was what was needed and my spear had certainly created that. The spear point had punched through the man's throat and jutted out the nape of his neck. Blood blossomed a brilliant red to match the colour of Skorri's cloak. The dying man flailed at the ash haft of the spear and collapsed to the loamy soil, taking a couple of his comrades with him as he slumped into their arms and they were unable to hold him upright.

Briefly, the man's eyes met mine. They were full of disbelief and shock, no time for anger or fear. He blinked and looked up at the men around him. I could see the life already ebbing from his gaze. He would be dead soon and I felt a tremor of pleasure that it was I who had struck the first blow against our foe.

But my satisfaction was short-lived. In the heat of the moment, I had forgotten myself. I stood rooted like a tree before the Norsemen, and now they were already recovering from their surprise at my attack. One of the warriors closest to the man I had slain, tugged a short axe from his belt and without hesitation, flung it at me.

I threw myself to one side and felt the rush of wind as the weapon spun past my face.

The man's throw seemed to have awakened the rest of them, and as one, several of them surged forward with a roar.

I needed no further reminder of what my role here was. I was not positioned close to the beach to stand and fight, I was here to sow dissent and confusion and then to run.

"You cowardly, raven-starving mares!" I screamed in the Norse tongue. Runolf had told me those words would enrage his people. I did not wait to see what reaction they caused. Spinning on my heels, I fled towards Werceworthe.

My feet pounded the mud of the track. Shouts of anger rose behind me; very close behind me. I pushed myself to run even faster, certain that at any moment I would feel the bite of steel in my spine. I chanced a glance over my shoulder and saw that only four men were chasing me. Better than nothing, I thought grimly. Hereward had been sure this part of the plan would fail, but if I could keep these four on my heels, then I felt it would be deemed a success. Further in the distance, the larger group, led by the red-cloaked Skorri were jogging forward.

Skorri was shouting for his men to return to him and, as I watched, the four who were following me, faltered, turning back at the sound of their jarl's command.

I had to do something. Cursing, I pretended to stumble, missing my footing and sprawling headlong into the mud. No sooner had I hit the ground than I leapt up and was sprinting again, low hanging branches and leaves whipping at me.

On seeing me fall, my pursuers cheered and pressed on after me. Grinning to myself, I ran on. I slowed slightly, not wishing them to believe there was no chance of catching me.

Something hit my left shoulder, knocking me off my stride momentarily. I staggered, regained my footing and continued on towards the houses of Werceworthe. As I ran, my shoulder throbbed. I reached up and winced as my fingers found a gash in the woollen fabric and a deep cut beneath. I looked down. My hand was slick with my blood. I was no longer grinning.

Flicking a look over my shoulder I saw that the four men were closer now, as if landing the blow to me had given them a spurt of speed. Gritting my teeth against the sting of the wound, I ran as fast as I was able for a time.

"Come back here," one of the Norse shouted. "We only want to hurt you."

The others laughed.

"We'll make you pay for what you did to Kætil," another called.

"You'll be his thrall in Valhöll soon," said the third warrior.

I didn't know if they believed I could understand their words, but I ignored them and pressed on. My breath was rasping in my throat now and my shoulder burnt with the agony of the movement pulling at the edges of the cut. The rain had already soaked my cloak and kirtle, but now my left side and arm were warm with my spilt blood. Hereward had been right, this was a foolish plan.

Something alerted me to a new attack, and without conscious thought I changed my direction, sidestepping to the right. God must have been watching over me, for a throwing axe whistled through the air where I would have been. It spun onward and plunged into the mud. I stooped as I ran and snatched it up. One less thing for them to throw at me.

A glance showed me they had lost ground. Perhaps they were tiring, encumbered as they were with armour and weapons, or maybe they had decided to allow me to escape and to await the arrival of their jarl and the others of the raiding party. Whatever the reason, we were too close now. I would not fail. I feigned another misstep. I skidded in the mud and rolled over, splashing through a puddle and then back onto my feet again in a spray of muddy water. My shoulder screamed in pain. The effect must have been convincing for my pursuers laughed and came on at a sprint.

I was at the first of the buildings now. A long barn. If I could just get them to follow me past that, my risk would not have been wasted. I slowed and looked back. The four Norsemen were mud-splattered from their run. Their eyes blazed and their mouths were agape, panting like hunting hounds. I allowed myself to let out a squeal of terror, hoping that this would lure them onward. It was not difficult to summon fear. I could see death in those grim faces and I knew that if they caught me, they would make me suffer for killing their friend.

I could not wait to see if they would follow. They were almost upon me and so I turned my back on them and dashed around the barn and onto the expanse of muddy earth between the buildings of the settlement. I heard their footfalls, the jangle of their buckles and belts, the panting gasps of their ragged breath and I knew they were still in pursuit.

There was nobody in sight. None of the usual activity you would expect in a thriving community such as Werceworthe. There were no animals in pens, no children shouting and no adults going about their business. Surely this was the moment when my pursuers would sense that something was amiss. Where was the sound of the inhabitants? Perhaps they were all huddled inside around their hearth fires against the rain. But where then was the haze of smoke that should hang over the village like a mist? Where there is fire there is smoke, and yet here the air was clear and silent, save for the squelching of my feet in the mud and the sounds of the Norse warriors only paces behind me.

Maybe their proximity to me, the target of the long chase, blinded them to the signs all about. Mayhap they did not notice the high wattle fences that had been erected between the buildings. Maybe they were simply young and headstrong, and sure of their own superiority. Or perhaps God again answered my prayers. However it came to pass, the Norsemen chased after me, seemingly oblivious or uncaring of possible danger.

I had a sudden moment of panic when I saw the place where I had to run. I had marked the spot with a small scattering of light-coloured flint pebbles, so I was certain I would not miss, but I was suddenly sure that one of my hunters would strike me down in plain sight of my destination. I changed my direction, stepping first to the left and then to the right, but this time, no weapon flew past or struck me. I still held the axe I had retrieved in my right hand and I thought about flinging it back at them, but I knew that would slow me enough for them to reach me. And then all would be lost.

I offered up a silent prayer to the Almighty, who, despite my abandoning of the *Regula* of the brethren, had not forsaken me. Springing forward with a last surge of energy, I rushed towards the scattered pebbles.

My feet hit the hidden boards with a hollow thump and the wood buckled and bounced as I passed. Surely now my attackers would halt. They would have seen or heard that the ground I trod upon was not firm and they would retreat to safety.

When we had prepared the trap, Hereward had scoffed. "It cannot work," he said. "No man is such a fool."

Runolf had smiled.

"Anything is possible," he had said. "Men see what they want to see."

I ran on and, as I heard the cracking and splintering behind me, followed by the first screams of shock and pain, the savage grin returned to my face.

Slowing, I turned, panting and gasping for breath, to see the mayhem I had left in my wake.

Forty-Seven

The first two unsuspecting Norsemen had run onto the insubstantial lattice of twigs and straw that was covered in a layer of mud and sand. The fragile covering gave way beneath them, snapping and splintering and sending them tumbling into the deep pit. At least one of them must have landed on a sharpened stake of wood that jutted at the foot of the hole, as pitiful screams of agony emanated from the depths. The long, exhausting days of digging suddenly seemed worth it, but I cannot deny that my guts clenched at the sounds of helpless torment of the men who had fallen and had surely been impaled on the spikes I had helped to place there. It is something to stand and fight with your enemies. There is honour in it, man against man, blade against blade. In an even fight you win by dint of skill and strength. All men know this, and it is understood and accepted. But when you fight a far superior foe, guile and trickery become an important factor in deciding the victor. I had felt clever when we had toiled in the heat of the late summer, digging the pit and preparing the other defences, but now, as the howling wails of pain echoed up from the pit, I felt nothing but an empty sadness. There was no honour in such killing.

The third of my pursuers teetered on the edge of the pit, off balance. As I turned to watch what was happening, the fourth man collided with him, sending him plunging into the trench on top of his comrades in a tangle of limbs. The screams were instantly silenced, to be replaced by cursing and fresh cries of pain.

The fourth warrior took in what had happened. His bearded face was red from the exertion of the chase and his eyes shone with a furious light as he looked up from the pit and his struggling friends. His gaze met mine and he drew the sword that hung at his side. Raising it, he pointed its tip at me.

"Now you die!" he shouted in Norse.

He glanced about him and quickly saw the thick planks that traversed the gap that had been uncovered when the others fell, pulling the thin cover of straw and mud down with them. He bared his teeth in a wolfish grin. One of the others started to climb from the pit, which was deep, but not so much that a man could not jump and scramble his way out.

I felt suddenly very exposed. The only weapons I had were the short axe I had scooped up from the path and the seax hanging sheathed from my belt. Panic rose within me like bile. Where were the defenders? They should have been here. The plan relied on them. Without them, I would be slain and Werceworthe lost. Had they fled? Was such a thing possible?

The Norseman swung his sword to loosen his muscles and stepped onto the planks. I hefted the axe, judging its weight. Would it be better to throw it or to keep it in my grasp and fight him, hoping that the Norse in the pit would not clamber out until I had bested this one?

He took another step onto the plank, which flexed beneath his bulk. I made a couple of practice cuts with the axe. It was well weighted and the stinging pain in my shoulder and the streaming blood staining my kirtle told me it was sharp. I would hold onto it, I decided. As I made the decision, so my adversary's eyes widened and he stopped walking. He was almost over the pit that ran the breadth of the land between two of the man-high wattle walls we had erected. He faltered, looking confused. It was then that I noticed a flash of white just above his collarbone. For a heartbeat I could not make sense of what I was seeing. He looked down, seemingly bemused, and a second splash of white appeared in his left eye. Feathers. The white goose feather fletchings of Wulfwaru's arrows. He toppled into the pit, dislodging the man who was trying to climb out. The first arrow had wounded him, the second had penetrated his eye, killing him instantly.

I let out a breath, only then comprehending the tension that had gripped me, standing against these four men alone.

The faces of Wulfwaru and her archers appeared over a couple of the high fences. There were timber platforms behind for them to stand on. From their raised vantage point, they could partially see into the ditch and as I watched several arrows flew down, thumping into flesh and mud.

"Halt your shooting," shouted Wulfwaru, her voice cracking and breathless from her headlong run from the river. "Do not waste your arrows."

I bent over, placing my hands on my knees and dragging in ragged breaths. I could hear a rushing in my ears, like a blizzard howling through a forest. My vision blurred and darkened. I was dimly aware of figures hurrying past me as I fought not to lose consciousness.

A half dozen villagers, armed with the fire-hardened spears, crowded the pit. They were led by Drosten, who held one of the few precious, iron-tipped spears, designed for hunting boar. A flurry of shouting and grunting, down-thrust spears wrenching screams from the throats of the remaining Norsemen. The sounds of death became hollow; echoed as if they were coming from the depths of a great cavern.

A hand on my right shoulder. I looked up, dazed and confused.

Gwawrddur.

"Breathe," he said. "You have done well." My sight began to clear and I shook my head. Spitting into the mud, I stood up straight. Gwawrddur scanned the activity by the pit. There was no longer any sound coming from the Norsemen, but the villagers continued to thrust their makeshift spears downward in a paroxysm of ecstatic bloodletting.

"Drosten," snapped Gwawrddur. "There is no time for that. Quickly, have the men strip them of weapons and armour. The rest of the raiders will be upon us in moments."

The Pict, boar spear slick with blood, nodded and began barking orders. The villagers were not trained warriors, but they knew well enough to obey, and they had put aside their spears and were scrambling down into the stake-filled trench and passing swords, seaxes, helms and byrnies up to their comrades.

I was breathing more easily now, and no longer feared that I would pass out. Gwawrddur glanced at my left shoulder.

"How bad is that?" he asked.

"It hurts," I said and shrugged, instantly regretting the movement.

"Wounds do that, Killer," he said with a wink. He peered at the rip in my kirtle, pulling the cloth apart to better see the cut beneath. "It is not too deep," he said. "We'll have one of the womenfolk stitch you up and bandage the wound as soon as we are able."

I wondered when that would be.

"That won't be for a while though," Gwawrddur growled, as if in answer to my thoughts. "Drosten," he called, an edge of tension in his voice, "there is no more time. Get out of there and move the men back." He was staring beyond the ditch, across the expanse of open ground to where the barn marked the beginning of Werceworthe. I followed his gaze and shivered. Lining up in the distance were the remainder of the Norse raiders.

The flash of Skorri's crimson cloak was bright in the gloomy afternoon drizzled haze. There were easily more than two score of them and they were arrayed as a warband, ready for battle. Their iron-bossed round shields were held high and ready. War axes and sword blades gleamed dully in the wet air. At a shouted command from their jarl they stamped forward and hammered their weapons into the willow boards of their shields. At the same time they let out a guttural roar of anger and defiance. The sound was huge and terrifying.

"I hope you are ready for some more action," Gwawrddur said to me with a humourless grin.

Skorri's band of warriors bellowed and stepped closer with another thunderous crash of steel on shields.

I swallowed the terror that threatened to engulf me. Nothing had prepared me for the sight of such an array of enemies. What had I been thinking when I had cast aside my calling and picked up the sword? My shoulder throbbed and I felt naked standing there in the mud before the tightly packed ranks of Norsemen who advanced towards us, as inexorable as wyrd.

Drosten and the villagers moved back from the pit. They had stripped as much as they were able from the corpses and had drawn back the planks that had covered the trap. The men's blackened spear-tips were blood-stained now; their faces pale. Drosten handed me a mud-splattered shield that I recognised as the one carried by the man who had almost crossed the pit on the planks. It was hide-covered and bore a red swirling symbol on a black field. I hefted it. My shoulder ached all the more, but I was glad of its protection.

I longed for the comfort of my sword. I had thought Gwawrddur would have brought it out for me, but it was nowhere to be seen. Too late to worry about that now. I clutched the hand axe and hoped it would be enough.

The Norse came on, step after step. Their shouted challenge as loud as thunder. Around me, the men quailed to see the might of those who attacked us. We had slain four of their number in the pit, and I had killed one in the wood, but still they outnumbered us and seemed undaunted by their losses.

"Hold, men," said Gwawrddur. "Stand strong. Anyone can shout loudly, but we have prepared well for this day. And you have bloodied your weapons."

The Norse war cry grew louder with each step.

"They shout to frighten you," he said.

"It is working," replied Wigmund, a thickset man who made up for his lack of spear-skill with his strength and wit. His eyes glistened with fear. Nobody laughed at his jest.

"Our plan is good," said Gwawrddur, "and we will send these bastards on their way soon enough."

The Norse shieldwall was still some way off, but the closer they got, the more fear gnawed at my guts. I glanced left and right. The men who stood with us looked as though they would flee or vomit at any moment. Perhaps both. My own stomach churned and I wondered if this was where I would find death, unready and unshriven.

"Stand fast," growled Gwawrddur, sensing the resolve of the men around us wavering. "They will not pass that ditch. Hold firm."

I looked at the gap from one side of the spike-filled ditch to the other, calculating the distance. It was easily large enough for an unsuspecting man to fall into, but now, with the covering removed, it seemed almost insignificant, no real obstacle for these Norse raiders.

Skorri bellowed out a command. It seemed he had surmised the same, for the first line of the Norse invaders broke into a sprint, screaming as they came.

They raved and yelled like demons unleashed from the bowels of hell. I grew cold and my skin crawled. My breath caught in my throat. They were going to leap over the pit.

Forty-Eight

The Norsemen snarled and rushed forward through the mud. They howled and screamed like wild beasts as they came. Involuntarily, the men around me shuffled back a pace. Drosten growled deep in the back of his throat and used the haft of his bloody boar spear to prod those closest to him back into line.

The first row of the Norse were well ahead of the rest of the raiders now. They were all tall men and strong. Their long strides quickly ate up the ground between them and the corpse-clogged pit. They had thrown aside their shields, but gripped axes or swords in their thick-fingered fists. They would jump over the ditch and be upon us in a heartbeat.

My mouth was dry. It was all I could do to stand where I was and not run screaming. I bit my lip and held my ground with difficulty. If only Hereward, Runolf and Cormac were with us, we might have stood a chance, but I knew they were positioned elsewhere. So be it. This was the life I had chosen for myself and I had known it would likely end in a bloody and painful death.

The instant before the Norse reached the gore-churned pit, Gwawrddur let out a piercing cry.

"Now!" he shouted.

Instantly, from either side of our position, the women archers rose above the wattle barriers and loosed arrows that must have already been nocked to their strings. The thrum of the bowstrings was followed a heartbeat later by the thud of arrows hitting flesh and iron byrnies.

Two men were brought up short with white-fletched arrows jutting from their bodies. The third man took an arrow through his opened mouth and I knew instinctively that it was Wulfwaru who had loosed that deadly dart. A fourth man was slowed by an arrow clattering from his iron-link shirt. Staggering, he lost his footing, to tumble into the pit atop his fallen comrades.

Of the six Norsemen who had charged at the ditch, only two made the jump and cleared the distance.

Their hatred washed off them like a stink. Their bellowing rage was like a physical thing, such was its power as they careened into our defensive line. I was dimly aware of more arrows flying through the rain-washed air, but all my focus was on the Norseman nearest to me. His eyes were crazed, wide and dark and bloodshot. Despite his bulk, the bearded warrior seemed to drift past the lowered spears like so much smoke. With prodigious strength, his great axe cracked into the skull of Wigmund, splitting it as easily as one might crack an egg. Warm blood and brains showered my face the instant before I raised my shield against the terrible onslaught of this madman. His axe hammered into the board and my shoulder screamed. I almost dropped the shield, but I knew that if I did, I would be dead an eye-blink later. Again the axe-head thudded into my board, this time splintering the willow wood, despite the blow seeming to be less powerful than the first. I staggered back, trying to make space for me to swing the small axe I gripped in my right hand. Though God alone knew how I could hope to best that brute with his massive reach and huge war axe.

I braced myself for another blow on my shield, but none came. Risking a look, I saw the Norseman on his knees. His throat had been slit from ear to ear and blood fountained and gushed down his byrnie and puddled in the mud before him. Gwawrddur's sword point was smeared red and the Welshman offered me a savage grin such as I had never seen on the dour swordsman's face before.

"A good thing only a couple of the whoresons crossed that ditch, eh?" he said.

I could not speak. Wigmund's opened head steamed at my feet, his corpse a tangle of lifeless limbs and meat enshrouded in a stained kirtle and breeches that until a moment before had clothed a man who lived and breathed and loved. The faces of his wife and his three children flickered in my mind's eye. My gorge rose and bile stung my throat.

Further along the line Drosten had fended off the second Norseman with his boar spear and the help of the spear-wielding villagers. As I watched, the tattooed Pict jabbed the iron point of his spear beneath the attacker's uplifted arm and into the soft flesh there. With a roar like a bull, Drosten shoved forward with all his great strength and the Norseman fell back, flailing into the mud. The villagers quickly finished him in a frenzy of thrusts with their crude weapons. The wooden shafts pierced his face and his neck. One pinned his outstretched hand to the muddy ground.

Gwawrddur raised his hand and shouted for the archers to cease their onslaught.

The other men who had tried to leap over the defence were all dead or dying. White feathers jutted obscenely bright and clean from mud-splattered, bloody flesh. A few arrows had fallen into the dark earth before the Norse shieldwall. Skorri had held the bulk of his force back, and it appeared that Wulfwaru and her archers had attempted to take some more prizes from their number. But the rain still came down and the bowstrings were damp, sapping the arrows of power, and the armoured men were distant. Nothing but the luckiest of shot would hurt them and so any arrow loosed was an arrow lost. There were still some two score warriors before us and we might well need those arrows yet.

I realised with a start that it was getting dark. The Norsemen had landed as the sun was lowering in the sky and now it must have fallen below the rain-drenched western horizon.

The Norse were not shouting now. They had halted their approach and stood glowering at us with undisguised loathing.

Gwawrddur stepped past the corpses of Wigmund and the Norse axeman. He beckoned for me to follow him. I hesitated. I felt faint. My shoulder throbbed and my head swam from the exertion and the horror I had witnessed. I had stood firm and done my duty, but now, with the lull in the fight, it seemed I had time to think of fear once more and it transfixed me as surely as if my feet had been nailed to the earth.

"Hunlaf," whispered Gwawrddur. "I need your voice."

I shook my head, still uncertain and unable to move.

"Hunlaf!" he snapped. "I must speak to their leader and you are the only one who can make their words clearly, without confusion. Now come here!"

I drew in a juddering breath. The air was dank and bitter with the metallic bite of blood. Gwawrddur was staring at me, willing me to obey him. I shook my head. All I wanted was to turn and flee. But with a great effort of will, I lifted first my left foot from the mire and then the right. Soon, I had closed the gap and stood trembling beside the lean Welsh swordsman.

He offered me a silent nod.

"Repeat my words," he hissed. "And loudly now. They must all hear them and you must not sound fearful."

I said nothing, but assented with a small nod. I was terrified.

"You cannot take from us that which you came for,"

Gwawrddur shouted. "We knew of your coming and have hidden all of our treasure."

I took a deep breath and repeated his words in the Norse tongue. My voice cracked at first and I had to pause to hawk and spit before continuing. On the second attempt my voice came out strongly enough and I pushed the thoughts of Wigmund and the fallen from my mind.

"We are ready for you," Gwawrddur continued, with me echoing his words in Norse. "We are no sheep for you to prey on like wolves. Begone back to the sea and find others to plunder. All that awaits you here is death. Like those we have already slain."

For a long while Skorri was silent. The men around him murmured and grumbled, but they were too far for me to hear any of their words. The rain began to fall more heavily, filling the darkening world with its hissing voice.

At last, Skorri, his crimson cloak sodden and dark, took a pace forward.

"You do not fight like the followers of the nailed god," he shouted. I translated his words. "But you are few. And we are many. I am Skorri, son of Ragnar, jarl of these raven-feeding warriors, and I do not flee from a battle with peasants and holy men."

"We are not holy men," replied Gwawrddur through me. "We too are warriors and we will soak the earth in your lifeblood and feed the raven and the wolf with your flesh if you do not return to your own land and leave us. There is no shame in leading your men to safety. Gold can profit you nothing, if you are dead."

"True," shouted back Skorri, "but battle-fame and renown live on forever, even after death."

Gwawrddur grinned at that and I wondered how different these two men really were.

"There will be no songs sung of what happens here," he said.

"We will kill all of you and I will see to it that your name is never repeated."

Skorri spat into the mud. He looked up at the dark sky, perhaps judging how long until full darkness fell.

"You have big words for such a thin man," Skorri shouted against the increasing roar of the rain. "It is getting dark. The night is no time for fighting. We shall continue this conversation on the morrow."

As I translated his words, Gwawrddur smiled.

"Until tomorrow," he shouted. Then, more quietly to me, "We shall see what fruits the night bears. I can imagine there will be those who speak for leaving us and moving on." We watched as the Norse turned and trudged away, back towards the woods and their ships. Gwawrddur waved to Drosten.

"Go and tell Hereward what has happened here," he said. "And tell him to be wary. That Norse whoreson might yet strike from a different place. It seems to me he has decided to retire too easily."

I looked into the bloody morass of the pit with its pile of gore-smeared pallid flesh and then back to where the two men who had leapt the trap lay, twisted and open-eyed, unseeing and staring up at the gloaming. Finally, my gaze rested on Wigmund's smashed skull.

If this struck Gwawrddur as an easy victory, I could barely begin to imagine what the future might hold if the Norse returned.

Forty-Nine

"You are certain there were three ships?" asked Gwawrddur, his voice a whisper that would not carry to those we watched. The sound of his murmured words would be lost in the constant sighing rustle of the trees. The rain still fell and we were soaked and shivering. It was dank and miserable in the night-time woods and my body ached. At least the murmur of the rainfall would mask any sound we'd made while approaching the Norse encampment.

"Yes," I hissed. "There were three." There was no doubt that Skorri had led three long ships to Werceworthe. Both Osfrith and I had seen them. But now, by the flickering light of the two small campfires that burnt on the shingle strand of the Cocueda, we could see clearly enough that only two ships were beached. What had happened to the third, we could not tell.

"Let us get a closer look," whispered Gwawrddur and his teeth flashed bright in the gloom. I wondered at the change in him and not for the first time questioned the decision to come here.

After the Norse had left, we had retreated to Werce's Hall. It was crowded and stifling, but it felt safe to be surrounded by so many friendly faces. My mind continually flew back to the horror and death of the dusk, and it was all I could do

397

not to weep and moan, such was the fear that now gripped me. I knew that safety was an illusion. We had survived the first attack, but when the Norse returned, it would be different. They would come prepared for our traps and defences, and surely they would sweep all before them. I looked about at the people of Werceworthe, the womenfolk, the children and the brothers from the minster. They should all flee, now, while they could.

I said as much to Hereward, but he shook his head.

"If they were going to run, they would have gone already. Now they are too scared that the Norsemen might be roaming the land. And they pray that we will protect them until more aid comes. No," he said, "all they can do now is remain here and trust that our plans will work and that men will come from Corebricg."

The moment we knew the Norse had come, Hereward had sent Ingild, a young man and a good rider, on our fastest horse to Corebricg. It would take time for Lord Gleadwine to gather men to come to our aid, and then they would have the rain-sodden walk back here. Of course, it could be that there would be no help from that quarter. We had heard that the conflict with Causantín's Picts still raged in the north so, like Uhtric, Gleadwine of Corebricg might well be far away with all of his fighting men.

We could not rely on salvation in the form of spear-men from Lord Gleadwine's men, but we knew the people of Werceworthe prayed for the swift arrival of a warband. We hoped God answered their prayers, but Hereward had emphasised that they might well not come at all, or come too late to save us. The defence of the settlement and the minster rested on our shoulders alone. At least for another day, for we could see no way that men could reach us from Corebricg before then.

"Who knows?" Hereward said with a glance at my blood-stained kirtle. "After your run today, perhaps our plans will work and we will see the Norse off before the need of any aid."

I knew he was saying this for the benefit of our morale, but still it pleased me to hear it. And Hereward had been genuinely surprised that we had managed to lure so many of the raiders to their deaths. He smiled grimly and nodded as Gwawrddur told the tale of it. Runolf and Cormac listened carefully. When the story was finished, Runolf slapped me on the right shoulder.

"You did well," he said. I beamed with pride at his words, but still the sensation of terror scratching at my insides did not abate.

"I wish that I had been there," said Cormac. "Perhaps we could have slain them all."

Hereward shook his head.

"We must stick to what we have agreed. We do not know where they might strike and therefore we need to watch other routes into the settlement. If we do not follow the plan, all will be lost."

"But we could have added our swords and killed more of the Norse bastards," Cormac said.

"If there is more fighting," said Hereward, keeping his voice low so that only we warriors could hear him, "you will have ample chance to wet your blade."

Cormac frowned.

"You think they may leave without further fighting?"

Hereward shrugged.

"As Runolf likes to say, anything is possible. It is what I pray for," he said. "That they have lost enough men, that they see this place as too costly a prize. Whatever happens, tomorrow will see the end of it. Skorri is no fool, I'm sure, and he will know that others will come to our aid soon. Time is on our side, which might make him decide to leave in the end. All we have to do is to hold them off on the morrow."

"Skorri will not run," Runolf rumbled. "He will return and seek vengeance now, as well as silver and slaves."

We fell silent at his grim prediction and the quiet weeping of Wigmund's wife rose above the general hubbub of the hall. When she had heard of her husband's death, her keening had cut through me like a seax. Now she was huddled with her children, and the other womenfolk brought them food and drink in an effort to distract the young ones. How many more widows would there be before the Norse left or were all slain?

Most of the able men were set to watch for possible night attacks, but Hereward had ordered me to sleep after my shoulder had been tended to. Hildegyth, one of the older women, took a bone needle, threaded it with horsehair and, after thoroughly cleaning the cut and washing the needle and thread in fresh urine, she had sewn the lips of the gash together. It had stung, and I flinched.

"Better it should hurt, Hunlaf. For only the dead feel no pain," Hildegyth said, patting my hand. "Your wound is not so bad." She bandaged it tightly and I moved my arm and was surprised that it was sore, but not agony. I thanked her and she smiled. "Rest now," she said. "I fear tomorrow will be a long day."

When I lay down I imagined the throb in my shoulder and the tumult of thoughts and fears that battered inside my mind would keep me from sleep, but no sooner had I wrapped myself in my cloak than I fell into a deep, dreamless slumber.

Gwawrddur had awoken me with a touch and a whisper. It was the darkest part of the night and most of those within the hall slept. I felt as though I had barely closed my eyes, but I was instantly alert. For a moment I wondered which of the offices I would need to pray. Were the brethren already waiting in the church? Then my memories of the previous day's bloodshed and terror flooded back like the tide at Lindisfarnae.

I had followed the Welshman out into the darkness, shivering against the rain and wind that blustered about the hill.

"What is it?" I asked. "Have they come back?"

"No," he whispered, "they have not."

"Is it my turn to watch?"

By way of answer, he handed me my belt, to which was attached my seax sheath and sword scabbard. I struggled with the leather and the weapons that dangled from it, but soon I had it buckled. My shoulder ached and I wondered if I had pulled any of the stitches out. Gwawrddur tugged on the sleeve of my kirtle, pulling me away from the hall. When we were some distance away, trudging down the slope, the wet grass soaking our shoes and leg wraps, I pulled Gwawrddur to a halt.

"Where are we going?" I asked.

"Knowledge is all important in battle, Hunlaf," he said. "You heard Hereward earlier. We need to split our meagre force because we do not know where they might strike. Let us see what they are planning." He walked on through the pouring rain and, after a moment's hesitation, I jogged after him to catch up.

"How are we going to do that?"

"That is the easy part," he said, grinning. "We are going to find their camp."

The idea had seemed madness then, but Gwawrddur was my mentor, my sword trainer and the man Hereward trusted most of all of us. And so, I had swallowed my fear and followed the Welshman down to the river's edge.

Now that we looked upon the flame-licked shapes of the sleek ships and the figures that crouched low beside the fires, sheltering from the worst of the storm with their backs to the beached hulls, I wondered again at the sanity of what we were doing.

Gwawrddur rose silent as a ghost and flitted between the boles of the trees, moving ever closer to the camp and the moored ships. I followed, terrified that the sound of our steps on the damp earth, the snagging of a branch on our clothing or the rustle of leaves brushing past, might alert the Norse sentries. But truly there was little chance of that. The night was loud with the falling rain and there was no sign of it easing.

Gwawrddur paused to peer at the fires on the beach and I halted behind him. Despite the rain and the night-chill that seeped through my sodden clothes I did not feel cold. I was on edge, as taut as a bowstring, my blood coursing through me like a hot torrent.

"Do you think we can take some of them?" asked Cormac, his voice louder than it should be in the gloom.

I shook my head, knowing he would not see the movement. This was madness indeed and it seemed that Cormac had been infected with the same crazed energy that had a grip on the usually sombre Gwawrddur.

Cormac had come upon us just as we were pushing the rowing boat into the black waters of the Cocueda. I had been startled at the crunch of his feet on the shingle, but Gwawrddur had seemed to know who it was without looking.

"Where are you off to?" the Hibernian asked.

"Scouting," Gwawrddur replied.

"I'll join you," Cormac said. "I don't want to miss all the excitement."

I bridled at his words, thinking again of the terror of the day and the feeling of Wigmund's hot brains slapping against my skin. I opened my mouth to snap a retort, but Gwawrddur spoke first.

"You are not needed on watch?"

There was the briefest of pauses.

"No more than you are," replied Cormac.

Gwawrddur contemplated Cormac's words, then nodded.

"Very well," he said, clambering over the side and into the boat. "You can row. Hunlaf's shoulder would trouble him and he will do better acting as our eyes. He knows this river better than us."

It was not just my shoulder that troubled me as we rowed quietly along the wide river. Nothing about this seemed right. I wished I had spoken up and said that we should talk to Hereward before slinking away from the settlement. I began to wonder whether our leader even knew of Gwawrddur's plan and I cursed myself silently for a fool. Ever since the fight that afternoon, the Welshman seemed almost to be another person. Gone was the thoughtful, careful man, who mulled over every decision until certain that it was the best one for all of us and the people we protected. He had been replaced by a warrior whose lust for battle burnt in his eyes. He had said that he wished to test himself, that his life was a quest to pit himself against the ultimate opponent. As we slipped along the river, the oar blades cutting into the water silently, the only sounds the wind and rain and the hushed creak of the tholes, I began to wonder if he had not brought me along as a witness to his bravery. For what could we hope to gain by seeing the Norsemen's camp?

Cormac, all bravado and vengeful desire, seemed more than happy to follow Gwawrddur wherever he led. All he wanted was to feel the bite of his blade in Norse flesh, to slay as many of them as he could. I wondered if he thought such a feat would make his piercing loss more bearable.

We rowed for some time along the river and I began to think we might reach the estuary and the sea beyond. Could it be that the Norse had actually fled, despite what Runolf had said? But my hopes were quickly dashed. The faint glimmer of campfires flickered through the trees and I signalled to Cormac to bring us in to the north bank. I knew where we were. The Norse had chosen a good spot, with a shallow beach wide enough for all of their ships to be moored and for them to sleep ashore if they wished. It was on the opposite side of the river from

Werceworthe and so they must also have thought it unlikely they would be disturbed by the defenders.

Willows overhung the swollen river and there was nowhere to pull our boat ashore, so we used the rope that lay in a puddle of rainwater in the boat's belly to tie it to a branch. We then pulled ourselves up, climbing into the enveloping darkness beneath the trees. I'd glanced up at the sky. The moon was a pale glow through the thick clouds. It would be dawn soon. We should not linger here.

We reached the edge of the trees without incident and it was then, when we had an unobscured view of the beach, that we saw that one of the Norse ships was missing.

The sound of a blade being drawn slowly from its scabbard made my breath catch.

"We should kill some," hissed Cormac and I realised it was he who had unsheathed his sword, Moralltach. I placed a restraining hand on his shoulder.

"No," I whispered. "We are here to look." I turned to Gwawrddur for support, but he was peering through the undergrowth. "We just want information," I muttered.

Gwawrddur had said he wanted me there as I knew the land and also, if we managed to capture or confront one of the raiders, I could understand the Norse tongue. This made sense, but I hoped we would not have to use my language skills that night. All I wanted was to move back stealthily to the boat and return unnoticed to Werce's Hall.

"We already know they have only two ships now," I said. "That is something. Let's go now."

"Kodran?" said a deep voice. It was very close to us and must have come from just behind one of the trees between our position and the campfires. It was all I could do not to cry out, such was my terror. Cormac, despite his brash shows of courage, also stood as if frozen. I could see the flame-light shimmer in his wide eyes. He looked as scared as I felt.

I sensed, more than heard, a movement, and a moment later, Gwawrddur slipped back behind the tree where we stood. In his grasp was a burly man, much broader than the Welshman, but nearly a head shorter. The dim light from the campfires glistened against the long seax blade pressed into the Norseman's throat. Gwawrddur's other hand was clamped over the man's bearded mouth. His eyes were wide and furious. He began to struggle and Gwawrddur held on tightly. Of the two of us, Cormac reacted first and hammered a punch hard into the Norse sentry's stomach. His eyes bulged. Cormac hit him again as hard as he could.

"Stop moving," I whispered in Norse, finally snapping out of my inaction.

Gwawrddur pressed the seax into his throat, cutting the skin.

"Do as he says," he hissed in the man's ear. The Norseman might not have understood the words, but he comprehended their meaning. He ceased struggling.

"Help me to get him away from their camp," said Gwawrddur.

A powerful gust of wind shook the trees and rain splattered down around us with renewed force. Taking the moment to cover the sound of our passage, we half-lifted the sentry and dragged him as quickly and quietly as we could through the woods.

Fifty

The Norseman's eyes glimmered in the darkness, wide and bright, with fear or defiance, I could not tell. Perhaps both. I had bound his hands behind his back with his own leg wraps, but even though he could not cause us any harm with his weapons or his obviously prodigious strength, he still held power over us. We were within earshot of the Norse camp and one shout from our captive would bring them sweeping down on us in moments. And yet, if we wanted to gain information, we could not gag him. Gwawrddur leaned over the man, his face as close as a lover's and the wicked blade of his seax still pressing down into the soft flesh of the Norse warrior's throat.

"Tell him," hissed Gwawrddur, "that if he calls out, I will kill him."

The Norseman's eyes flicked towards me as I translated Gwawrddur's words. He snorted.

"You will kill me anyway," he said, making no effort to lower his voice. "I am already dead."

Gwawrddur did not wait for me to speak the words in Englisc, the man's meaning was clear. Without warning, the Welshman shifted his weight, lifting the seax from the Norseman's throat. Then, as quick as a striking viper, he whipped the blade down to the man's groin. With a couple of quick sawing strokes of the blade, Gwawrddur cut through the man's breeches. The Norseman's eyes widened, and he began to struggle.

"Keep him quiet," Gwawrddur said, his voice as cold and sibilant as a blade being drawn from a scabbard.

Unsure what to do, I did not react. But Cormac clapped a hand over the man's mouth, pressing the sharp point of his short eating knife into the hollow beneath his greasy beard. The Norseman tried to shake him off, but Cormac growled and jabbed with the small knife to get his attention. A heartbeat later, the Norseman grew very still.

"Tell him I will do worse than kill him if he calls out," said Gwawrddur.

I looked down and was shocked by what I saw in the dim light of the moon beneath the trees. Gwawrddur had cut the man's breeches away from his waist to his upper thighs. Now, in his left fist, Gwawrddur held the man's balls, while the deadly blade of the seax that he grasped in his right, was pressed firmly against that soft flesh.

I swallowed, aghast at what I was witnessing. Gwawrddur squeezed and moved the knife blade fractionally. The Norseman whimpered beneath Cormac's hand.

"Tell him," Gwawrddur said.

I told him in Norse, though words hardly seemed necessary.

"Does he understand?" asked Gwawrddur.

I asked him and he grunted and tried to nod his head, which was difficult and dangerous with Cormac's hand clasped over his mouth and his blade jabbing into his throat. Gwawrddur seemed satisfied.

"Remove your hand, Cormac," he whispered.

Slowly, Cormac pulled his hand and knife away and moved back from the Norseman, giving Gwawrddur more space.

"Keep watch, Cormac," Gwawrddur said. "I don't want any of those Norse bastards creeping up on us."

Without a word, Cormac sheathed his eating knife and stepped into the darkness.

"Tell him," Gwawrddur said, his voice oddly calm, "that if he tries to call out for help, I will slice off his balls and shove them in his mouth before killing him." I could hear my blood rushing in my ears as my heart hammered against my ribs. A gust of wind rattled the trees and a sighing spray of rainwater fell through the canopy. I shivered. I could not utter the words.

"By Christ's bones, boy," whispered the Welshman. "You must speak my words. There is no time now for any of your monkish softness." His words stung, but still I was unable to say the words he asked of me. "Come on, boy," he growled. "Each warrior must use the skills he has for the good of the warband." I looked at him. His face was a shadowed mask in the gloom, but his eyes seemed to blaze from the darkness. "Do you not say that God placed you here for a reason? Then use the skills He has given you."

I sighed. He was right, of course. With a nod, I told the Norseman Gwawrddur's message. He glowered up at us from where he lay in the wet leaf mould, but after a moment's hesitation, he nodded.

"Ask him where the third ship has gone," Gwawrddur whispered.

The Norseman listened to my question. He seemed to ponder my words, perhaps wondering whether to answer or not. Gwawrddur gave the flesh in his left fist a tug and the sentry spoke in a rush.

"He says that the ship belonged to Øybiorn. Five of Øybiorn's men were slain today. He decided the gods were against him and he did not want to sacrifice more of his crew."

"But Skorri decided to stay?" Gwawrddur asked.

The Norseman nodded. He glared up at us and I could feel the hatred coming off him like waves buffeting a cliff.

"Skorri says we will take many thralls, silver and gold," he said. "These houses of the nailed god are rich and," he hesitated, "unguarded. Or so we thought. Øybiorn said that slaves and treasure are no use to dead men." The Norseman flicked his gaze down to where Gwawrddur clutched his delicate flesh against the cold steel of his seax blade. "I am beginning to see the wisdom of Øybiorn's words."

I translated his words and Gwawrddur chuckled. Something about the interaction between the two men shifted imperceptibly in that darkened, rain-washed glade. I wondered what had changed and then it struck me. There was now a grudging admiration between the two warriors. Gwawrddur for the Norseman's bravery in the face of torture and death, the Norseman for the courage of the defenders in inflicting losses on the raiders and perhaps our audacity in coming to their camp.

Perhaps Gwawrddur would let him live after all. The man was brave, of that there was no doubt, but the idea of this bearded brute, with his huge arms and their boulder-like muscles and savage scars, standing before me in combat threatened to turn my bowels to water.

"When will Skorri attack?" Gwawrddur asked.

The Norseman shrugged and offered the Welshman a thin smile.

"When there is enough light in the sky for us to see the faces of those we are killing." The Norseman's teeth flashed in the darkness. Here he was, bound and helpless, with his captor holding a knife to his manhood, and yet he was grinning and defiant still. By God, what manner of man was this? Is this what warriors were? I glanced at Gwawrddur's rigid posture, his gleaming eyes. He was like a hound on the hunt, eager and excited, scenting blood on the wind. The faint glow of the moon shone on his seax blade. Could I ever truly be like these men?

Another gust of wind shook the trees, but along with the

rustle of leaves, clatter of branches and shower of rain around us, came a new sound. One that filled me with dread. A voice bellowed out a warning in Norse. The loud shout was taken up by others and soon the night was echoing with the cries of angry men. Panicking, I looked to Gwawrddur for guidance. His eyes glimmered red and with a startled gasp I realised the night was no longer dark. Spinning about, I looked through the trees towards the Norse camp and the sounds of alarm. Great gouts of flame lit the sky. The boles of the alders and sallows were black against the bright conflagration.

A muted rasping cry pulled my attention back to the Norse sentry and Gwawrddur. As I watched, Gwawrddur pulled his blood-smeared blade from the man's throat. By the light of the fire that blazed back at the beach encampment, I saw at a glance that the Welshman had not gone through with his threat of emasculation. The Norseman shook and writhed as blood pumped and gushed from the deep slash across his neck. His beard was slick with his lifeblood and his eyes glared accusingly at Gwawrddur. But he made no sound loud enough to call his comrades to our location. Gwawrddur had hacked through his windpipe as well as his arteries. Bubbles formed in the blood that welled there and with a final gurgling sigh, the Norseman shuddered and lay still.

"Cormac," Gwawrddur hissed. He cast about us in search of the Hibernian. For a heartbeat, I could not pull my gaze away from the dead Norse sentry. Blood still pumped from the ruin of his throat, but his body was unmoving, his eyes unblinking and unseeing. Gone was the powerful hatred and defiance of moments before. He was nothing more than meat now; carrion for the animals of the forest.

"Cormac," Gwawrddur called out again, raising his voice slightly, but still not much above a whisper. The screams and shouts from the Norse camp were louder now and the flames brighter.

"Where is he?" asked Gwawrddur, his tone sharp and impatient.

I did not know. I scoured the dark, flame-licked forest. My mind span. What had happened? Had Cormac been captured somehow? What was burning? And then I spotted movement. Moments later this was followed by the crash of branches, as Cormac came bounding through the dense foliage towards us. Behind him the night was ablaze, as red and bright as a setting sun.

I pointed.

"There."

Gwawrddur looked and his eyes must have been sharper than mine, or his mind was less confused and addled by what was happening, for he instantly saw Cormac's pursuers. There were three of them, long hair and beards aglow in the firelight. Two carried axes, the third held a sword in his meaty fist.

"You take the left one," said Gwawrddur. Without another word, he slipped behind the thick trunk of a tree, drawing his sword from its scabbard as he did so.

For the briefest of moments, I stood there, watching Cormac running towards me. I did not know if he or the men on his heels had seen me, so I followed Gwawrddur's example and leapt to the side of the path that they would follow. I leaned my back against the rough bark of an alder and dragged my sword from its scabbard. It felt cold and heavier than ever before in my hand.

The night was filled with sound and light, but above the crackle and hiss of the fire, I could hear the approaching crash of Cormac and his hunters. The Norsemen shouted, telling him what they would do when they caught up with him. They would pull his entrails from his stomach and have him watch. They would tear his lungs from his back and drape them over his shoulders. I shuddered, in no doubt that they would offer me the same hospitality should I fall into their hands. I looked down at the bloody corpse of the Norse sentry. The night, like the day, was already filled with blood and death. There would be no chance of quarter here. We needed to slay the men who pursued Cormac and then flee. If we were captured, we would not only be killed, but we would be tortured and we would give up all the secrets of Werceworthe's defenders.

I took a deep breath. The damp, heavy verdant scent of the forest was tinged with the acrid bite of smoke. Cormac rushed past my position. The sword-wielding Norseman was just behind. A heartbeat later, the second pursuer ran past. Gwawrddur sprang out from his hiding place, scything his sword into the man's thighs. The Norseman screamed and tumbled to the earth in a scattering of leaves, twigs and mud.

At hearing the noise of fighting, Cormac spun around and faced the attacker closest to him. Their blades clashed and I pulled my gaze from the confrontation, waiting for the final pursuer.

But he did not come.

He must have been alerted by the fate of his comrades. Even though I had not run anywhere, my breath came in short gasps as I stood with my back to the alder. I clutched my sword and tried to listen for a sign of the third Norseman's position, but the night was a cacophony of yelling and distant snapping and crackle of blistering burning wood.

Cormac and his adversary exchanged blows. Gwawrddur had dropped onto the second warrior, plunging his sword into the man's back before he was able to rise.

My feet were as rooted to the ground as the alder. I could not move. Where was the third warrior? Had he gone back in search of help? Should I go to Cormac's aid?

Gwawrddur turned back from the man he had slain and looked in my direction. His eyes widened, red and aglow with the reflected firelight, like a fox's eyes in the night.

"Hunlaf!" he shouted.

His cry broke the spell that had fallen on me. He had no more time for a warning, but somehow, perhaps by the direction of his gaze, I knew with sudden terrible certainty that the third warrior had crept up on the other side of the tree I had hid behind. Without thought, I threw myself to my left and away from the trunk of the alder. Splinters of bark showered my face as the man's axe bit deep into the wood where my neck had been. Without Gwawrddur's warning, that axe would have taken my head from my shoulders. But now there was no time for thinking. The moment for fear and concern was gone and I rolled in the mud and came to my feet in one smooth motion. Absently, I felt a tugging sting in my shoulder as Hildegyth's stitches parted.

The Norseman roared at having his prey escape him at the last possible moment. He tugged his axe free from the tree and came towards me bellowing like a bull. He had no shield and neither did I. As Gwawrddur had taught me, I watched the man's eyes and his shoulders, rather than his blade. I was calm now, filled with the energy that washes through me when blades clang and blood flows in battle. Perhaps the man saw that I was not frightened of him, or maybe he became aware that his two comrades in arms had been killed, for Cormac had dispatched his enemy. But whatever the reason, my opponent hesitated for an eye-blink before deciding to attack. In that instant, his eyes showed me where he was going to aim his strike and when it came I rolled under his swing and buried my blade high in his chest. Such was the force of my lunge that I lifted the Norseman off his feet and we both tumbled into the muck. Gwawrddur ran forward and kicked the man's axe out of his hand. At this, my opponent's eyes widened and he groaned in abject terror, though he must have already known he was dying, with my sword jutting from between his ribs.

Gwawrddur grabbed hold of me and pulled me to my feet. I drew my sword from the dying man's body with an effort. The flesh sucked at the blade as if it wanted to keep hold of it even as the soul left its shell and headed to hell, for that is surely where this heathen would go.

Scooping up the axe, Gwawrddur tossed it to me. I caught it. Its smooth ash handle was still warm from the grasp of the man I had killed.

In the distance, there were more shouts as the flames grew ever more intense. What was burning? Was the forest itself alight? How could that be?

Gwawrddur did not pause. He lifted the axe from the man he had slain, and tugged a seax from the Norseman's belt and then he hurried towards Cormac.

"Take his sword," Gwawrddur snapped, nodding to the dead Norseman at Cormac's feet.

Cormac picked it up and grinned. How could he be happy, I wondered? But then I recalled the savage sense of joy that had filled me moments before as I took the life of the axeman. Who was I to judge the Hibernian?

"Come on," said Gwawrddur and, without waiting, he led the way through the dancing shadows of the forest back to where we had tethered our boat.

No more enemies loomed out of the darkness, and the sounds of chaos and the light and heat from the great blaze behind us, dimmed in the distance. We slid down the rain-slick bank and lowered ourselves into the boat. I untied the slimy rope and pushed us out into the river.

The glow from the far-off flames shone against the dark waters and lit Cormac's smiling features as he pulled at the oars.

"What have you done?" hissed Gwawrddur when we could no longer hear the shouts of the Norse in the night.

"I have evened the odds," Cormac said, his grin widening.

"How so?"

"Well, not only have we slain more of the heathen whoresons, but I have burnt their ships too! Those Norse bastards are going nowhere now!"

Fifty-One

"What have you done, you fool?" roared Hereward. He shook with fury. Spittle flew from his lips, flecking his beard. His fists were bunched and he raised them up before Cormac. I thought he would strike the Hibernian.

A baby started crying and the sound seemed to pull Hereward back from the brink of violence. He looked over to where Wulfwaru rocked her son soothingly. She shook her head sadly at Hereward. Her eyes were shadowed in the dim light of the tallow tapers that burnt and guttered with their foul-smelling smoke. Despite her face being veiled in the gloom of the hall, her disapproval was clear.

Hereward swallowed, and with an effort, lowered his fists. It was yet before dawn and most of the villagers had still been asleep until his outburst. Now people were sitting up, bleary-faced and frightened, perhaps believing that the raiders had attacked again in the pre-dawn darkness. The thought made me shudder. They would not wait long to exact their revenge for what we had done, I was sure. Hereward knew it too.

"What in the name of all that is holy were you thinking?" he asked, his voice lowered from a shout, but still tight and clipped with anger.

Cormac did his best not to quail before the Northumbrian thegn. He squared his shoulders and stood as tall as he was able.

"We killed more of our foe-men. That is a good thing, is it not?"

For a time, Hereward's rage engulfed him and he was unable to speak. His face reddened and the muscles of his neck bulged and bunched.

"But the ships," he said, letting his breath out with a sigh, as if his anger, like a summer squall, had dissipated as quickly as it had come, leaving nothing behind it but a gentle breeze.

"I saw a chance to even the odds and I took it," Cormac said, jutting out his chin defiantly.

Hereward looked about him as if in search of an ally, someone who would understand the reason for his rage. His eyes settled on me.

"Hunlaf," he said, "you are a clever lad. Certainly not such a fool as this Hibernian jester." I wanted to look away, but he held my gaze as a hawk that stares at a mouse in a field of scythed barley. I could sense everyone in the hall looking at me. "Do you think it was a good idea to put the Norse ships to the flame?"

I did not want to answer him. Not with all the people of Werceworthe listening. Hereward had impressed upon us the importance of morale, of not showing the people we were defending that we had any doubts in our ability to win against our adversaries. But now it was Hereward himself who was threatening to break the fragile hope we had managed to build in the villagers with our plans and the victory we had won the day before.

He was staring at me, his expression implacable.

"Well?" he asked, his tone sharp. "Perhaps you too are as foolish as Cormac. Do you believe he should have burnt their ships?"

I could not remain silent in the face of his ire.

"No," I mumbled, shaking my head.

"No," he said with a sigh. "And why not?"

The reason was clear to me. When Cormac had told us what he had done on the boat as we rowed back to the shingle beach on the southern side of the river, Gwawrddur and I had grown sombre. We had told Cormac what we thought of his actions but then, as now, he refused to accept any guilt and stood by his decision with resolute stubbornness.

"Speak, Hunlaf," Hereward said. "Explain to this dolt what he has done."

I swallowed. I flicked a glance at Cormac, but he was ignoring me, instead staring angrily at Hereward.

"He has taken from them any means to leave," I said.

"So what will the Norse do now?" he asked, his voice taking on the same tone Leofstan used when speaking to a particularly dim student.

"They will fight," I murmured.

"They will fight!" he exclaimed, slapping his hands together. The sharp sound startled Aethelwulf, who started crying again. Wulfwaru muttered a curse and turned her back. Some of the other children joined her son in weeping now, frightened by Hereward's anger.

"They were already going to fight," exclaimed Cormac. "All we have done is to lessen their chances by slaying more of them."

"The Norse you killed are not the problem here," snapped Hereward. "Even with those you have slain and the men who left on the third ship," he looked about him and lowered his voice now, as if suddenly aware that he could be heard by all the inhabitants of Werceworthe, who thronged the hall, "do you really believe we can defeat all those who remain?"

"It is my plan to kill all who come before me," said Cormac.

"By Christ's teeth," said Hereward, pushing both his hands over his head, his fingers entwined in his hair as if he planned to rip it out. "They will fight like trapped wolves," he hissed. "Our only hope of victory was that they would tire of being killed by us and that they would go elsewhere. Now they cannot flee."

Cormac bridled now.

"And where did you hope they would go to?" he spat. "To Gyruum or Uuiremutha south of here?" Hereward shrugged. "What?" continued Cormac, incredulous at Hereward's disinterest as to where the raiders might go. "You would be content for them to kill the unsuspecting nuns and monks there? Where is the honour in that?"

Hereward's jaw clenched and he spoke through his teeth.

"There is no honour in any of this," he said, stabbing the noisome air of the hall with his finger to accentuate his words. "Just survival. It is not the shepherd's task to see to the safety of the sheep from other farms, just his own. Where the Norse go from here, I care not. I am trying to save these people." He swept his arm about the place. Men and women were rising now. The monks were huddled in prayer at the far end of the hall. Children still cried in the gloom.

"There is honour in killing those heathen whoresons," snarled Cormac. "We must slay every last one of them. They are vermin. Violators of women and children, defilers, killers, animals!" His voice cracked with the strength of his emotions. I was glad that Runolf was on watch. Although he had sworn his oath to Æthelred, such words about his countrymen would be hard for him to stomach.

Gwawrddur stepped forward, raising his hands in a gesture aimed at placating both men.

"What is done is done," he said. "We cannot change the past and truly this day is no different than it would have been without Cormac's actions."

Hereward rounded on the Welshman. He was furious with Cormac, but the burning anger he directed at Gwawrddur seared as hot as a forge.

"None of this would have happened without your rash action, Gwawrddur," he said. "I thought you were a man to be trusted. A true shield-brother who knew when to attack and when to stand strong with his comrades."

"I am your shield-brother," replied Gwawrddur, his face and tone serious and calm, "and I will stand with you when the time comes. Have no doubt of that. I am no coward. You know this."

"It is not your bravery I am concerned with," spat Hereward. "It is your sanity. To lead these two," he indicated Cormac and me, "into the night and to strike the Norse at their camp was beyond folly. I fear your quest to test yourself has made you rash and foolhardy."

"We obtained useful information," replied Gwawrddur, keeping his voice cool, despite Hereward's insults. "We took more weapons we can use in the defence of the hall, and we killed four of their number."

"Six," said Cormac. They both turned to him. He shrugged. "I killed two more when I fired their ships." He had not told us this. How he had managed to burn both the ships was still unclear. With a flask of oil he had found and God's grace, he had said to me. I think he had set a fire in one of the vessels, only for the other one to catch light from the sparks and flames of the first. With the rain falling as it had, perhaps it was God's grace after all that had burnt the ships. I longed to make the sign of the cross then, but I held my arms at my sides. I was a warrior now. I had the wounds to prove it, and my wrist and forearm were yet sticky with the blood of the Norseman I had killed, despite having washed my hands in the river's cold water.

"So, we killed six of them," said Gwawrddur. "This is a good thing for us."

Hereward glared at him, apparently unable to think of words to refute Gwawrddur's statement.

At last he said, "You say that this day has not changed. How can you think that is so? Surely you can see how burning their ships has shifted things."

Gwawrddur scratched at his beard and shook his head.

"Come, let us speak outside." He beckoned to Hereward, Cormac and me, and began walking towards the door of the hall. With a scowl, Hereward followed and Cormac and I fell into step behind.

Outside it was still dark, but the eastern horizon was the dull grey of a sword blade. The rain had stopped momentarily, but the air was cold and damp. The sentry, grey-haired Gewis, was standing in the wind-shadow of the hall. He nodded as we stepped into the cool pre-dawn and he moved some distance away, sensing that we wished to speak without being overheard.

"So, Gwawrddur?" asked Hereward, keeping his voice low. "Tell me how this day has not changed." Gone was the anger in his voice, replaced by tired resignation.

Gwawrddur stepped in close and we huddled together so that we could speak in whispered tones. The Welshman's breath steamed in the air between us.

"The Norse were already going to attack today," he said, "and all we needed to do was to hold them off until Gleadwine's men arrive."

"They might have sailed away before then, if we bleed them enough," said Hereward.

"True enough, I suppose," answered Gwawrddur, "but it seems unlikely. This Skorri does not seem to be the kind of man to run from a fight." He shook his head and gazed out over the iron grey sky to the east. "No. We need to fight the Norse until the warriors arrive from Corebricg. With those extra men and by the grace of God," he flicked a glance at me, "we will be able to finish this once and for all."

"Today is going to get bloody," Hereward whispered. "Hunlaf, you had best ask the holy men to pray that Ingild is bringing reinforcements back with him and that they arrive soon. It seems that is now our only hope."

A light drew my attention. Down in the settlement below, a flower of flame blossomed. As I watched, it bloomed and grew, rising up into the dawn sky and reflecting on the broad river beyond. It was the church. Around it, the tiny shadow figures of distant men prowled about the settlement. They bore torches and soon more buildings were aflame. Sheets of fire shot up from the thatch of the refectory and then the scriptorium, and I remembered the horror of Lindisfarnae.

I became dimly aware of the people of Werceworthe amassing around us. Soon, everyone was there. Some of the women and children sobbed, but most of the villagers were silent, stunned by what they were witnessing. They gazed down at the destruction of their homes and the flame light lit their tear-streaked faces with its ruddy glow.

The Norse had returned and they would make us pay for burning their ships.

Hereward raised his voice so that all there could hear him.

"We can rebuild what is burnt," he said. Some of those gathered turned to look at him. Many could not pull their gaze away from the destruction taking place. "And as you saw yesterday, when we stand together, we can prevail against these heathens. God is on our side and all we must do is to follow the plans we have made. We are strong here. You know we have prepared for this." He scanned the faces of the men and women. "Do not lose heart. You know what you must do. Every one of you has a role to play. You have trained hard these last weeks and if you do what we have practised, we will be victorious."

"We cannot hope to defeat them all," said Garulf, the smith. "There are too many and we are not warriors."

"You are warriors," replied Hereward with force. "You are strong together. A single stick is easy to snap. If we stand together, like a faggot of twigs bound together, we will not break. And," he said, sweeping them all with his gaze, "we do not need to defeat them all. All we need to do is to hold them and by this afternoon, Gleadwine will come with his warriors. There is no way those Norse raiders can withstand the combined strength of us and his warband."

Gone was the defeatist and angry tone of moments before. This was the Hereward that Uhtric had sent to defend the settlement. I marvelled at the change in him, but looking at the flame-licked faces of the onlookers, I could see the strength they took from his words and his confidence. This was the true worth of a leader. To inspire those who followed to greater feats than they believed possible, to turn their fears of defeat and weakness into pride and power.

The thin wailing of a hunting horn echoed eerily in the dawn, making us all pause, listening to the sound. I thought it must have come from the Norse in the burning settlement. Then the horn sounded again and I realised it came from the other side of the hall.

"That is Eowils," said Hereward. "He is watching the south."

Eowils was Gewis' son, and the grey-haired man turned from the burning buildings and looked to the south. His face was pale and drawn.

For a third time, the horn blew its plaintive note in the chill morning air.

"Go, Gwawrddur," Hereward said, knowing that a lack of decision now would see the new resolve of the villagers unravel in moments. "Take Cormac and Hunlaf and five of the spear-men. It seems those fires are a distraction and Skorri has decided to send his men in from more than one direction."

Without hesitation, Gwawrddur began barking orders. Men obeyed, jostling to fall into line.

"Hunlaf," he snapped. "Cormac." We both turned to him, eager and anxious. "Take a byrnie each." He nodded towards the hall where the iron-knit shirts that had been stripped from the dead Norse were heaped by the door. "Get it over your heads and tighten your belt to take some of the weight." We hesitated. "Do it now!"

We hurried to obey, each helping the other to wriggle into the heavy shirts of iron. The weight pulled on my shoulders, making me wince at where it pressed against the stitched wound. But to wear the byrnie brought on another distinct change in me. As soon as the metal links enveloped my body, I felt bolder, as if only then did I wear the true skin of a warrior.

"Come on," shouted Gwawrddur.

Moments later I was running along with seven other men, including Gewis who had snatched up his spear and joined us. We ran through the wet grass towards the oak where Eowils was posted. The heft of the byrnie pushed down on my shoulders and soon the muscles in my legs burnt at the extra weight. I glanced over my shoulder and looked back at the hulking silhouette of Werce's Hall. The sky behind it was the colour of bronze, lit by the flying flames that consumed the minster and settlement that had been my home these past years. I could smell the smoke of its dying on the breeze.

We ran in silence and for a time the only sounds were those of the panting men around me and the thud of our feet on the damp earth. The horn's ululating note pierced the air once more and my mind was filled with the faces of the Norsemen we had fought and killed in the forest. So far we had slain them when they had been tricked or taken by surprise, but there was no doubt that these men of the north, with their plaited beards and deadly axes, were trained killers. How would we fare, fire-hardened spears against steel, when we needed to face them shield to shield?

We ran on as the sun crested the eastern horizon, its bright red fire lighting our way and turning the drops of rain on the blades of grass into jewels the colour of garnets. Or blood.

My shoulder throbbed from the axe wound and where the stitches had pulled free, and as we sprinted towards the towering oak, I wondered which of us would live to see the sunset.

Fifty-Two

We arrived at the oak with a clatter of weapons and the rasp of ragged breathing. Our breath steamed about us as if we were winded horses. Like animals, we were skittish too, eyes roving in search of enemies, sure that death awaited us on the shallow slope that fell away to the south. The Norse must have sent out men during the darkest part of the night to have been able to circle around and reach this point by dawn. Perhaps they had sent them even before sailing down the Cocueda to their riverside encampment.

We slowed as we approached the oak that dominated the skyline to the south of the hall. Gwawrddur held up his hand and we halted, listening for sounds of battle. The horn had not sounded again and now, apart from our laboured breathing, the land was eerily quiet. A golden plover burst forth from the grass in a welter of beating wings and angry chirping at being disturbed. I followed the bird's path with my gaze. It flew northward, towards the fire-glow of the burning settlement. Dark plumes of smoke roiled into the sky there, making me think of the funeral pyres of warriors of legend. The scops tell of how our forebears believed the smoke would carry the fallen to the hall of the gods. I wondered how many souls that black smoke would send on their way to the afterlife that day.

Gwawrddur beckoned for us to move forward slowly. He held his sword at his side and we followed him cautiously towards the oak. Eowils must have been slain, I thought, and shuddered, my heart twisting. I glanced at the boy's father. His face was the colour of ash. If the poor boy had been killed, where were the Norse? Were they lying in wait for us just beyond the tree where the land dropped away?

We took a few more tentative steps. Despite the cool of the morning, sweat trickled into my left eye and I blinked at its sting. We shuffled on and I was certain that at any moment, the trap would be sprung and the Norse would rise up from their hiding place with a bellowing battle cry.

Without warning, a figure stepped from behind the broad trunk of the oak. Cormac gasped and stiffened beside me. One of the spear-bearing villagers, Gewis, I think, let out a small cry of alarm. I clutched my sword's grip so tightly that my knuckles popped and cracked, but I was pleased that I did not show the fear I felt.

But this was no Norseman. By the light of the rising sun I recognised the slender form.

"Eowils," called out Gewis, his tone full of relief.

"You sounded your horn," said Gwawrddur cautiously, as if he expected a trap of some kind. Perhaps the Norse were yet huddled behind the tree and sought to use Eowils to lure us closer.

"I did not know what else to do," stammered Eowils, looking from his father to Gwawrddur. He was clearly nervous. His gaze flickered to the smoke-smeared northern horizon. "Have they attacked?"

"They have set the buildings afire," replied Gwawrddur. "But never mind that now. Hereward has that in hand. What caused you to call us here?"

As if in answer, another figure stepped from the shadow of the tree. We tensed. We all knew that Eowils had been posted here alone. He was too young and small to fight, but he had keen eyes and was nimble and fast. From the limbs of the tree, he could warn of the enemies' approach and then flee to safety.

The newcomer moved close to Eowils and for an instant I assumed he was threatening him, perhaps placing a blade against the boy's ribs. Gewis tensed and took a step forward. But then I saw that the figure staggered as if unwell, and he leaned on the boy for support.

"Ingild," hissed Gwawrddur, recognising the man at last. "You have returned so soon? Praise be to God. With Gleadwine's warriors we will soon send those Norse bastards to hell."

No wonder that the messenger was tired, he must have had precious little sleep to have ridden to Corebricg, mustered Gleadwine's warriors and then led them back here so soon. The Welshman stepped closer and we followed. We were still anxious, aware that the raiders were even then destroying our homes and might already be turning their attentions to the hall on the hill. Hereward would be hard-pressed to defend it with the few fighters available to him. The sight of Ingild did not dispel our trepidation, but it did lift our spirits to know that reinforcements had come so soon.

Our hopes of salvation were quickly dashed.

Gwawrddur cast about for signs of the warriors Ingild had brought with him. It was then that I noticed the pallor of the man's skin. He was the colour of curds and his face was sheened with sweat, his hair plastered to his scalp. His eyes were dark-rimmed with tiredness and something else: pain. Eowils shifted his position, causing Ingild to wince and groan. I noted the way his right arm dangled at his side, his shoulder dipped at an odd angle.

"Where are Gleadwine's men?" asked Gwawrddur.

Ingild attempted a shrug, moaned at the effort and thought better of it.

"In Corebricg, I would wager." Ingild was sombre and obviously suffering and yet a ghost of a smile played on his lips.

Gwawrddur's face clouded. He looked Ingild up and down and I could see the realisation of his injuries dawning on the Welshman.

"What happened?" he asked, his voice flat, devoid of emotion.

Ingild sighed.

"My mount fell," he said, his voice catching in his throat, "put its hoof in a badger sett, I think." He shook his head and frowned. "My fault. I should not have pushed her so hard in the rain. I could barely see where we were going, but I knew it was important that I reach Corebricg as soon as possible…" His voice trailed off. "Poor thing snapped its foreleg, just like a twig for kindling." He wiped sweat, or maybe tears, from his cheeks. "She did cry so," he said, taking a breath and letting it out in a juddering sigh. "It was the animal's screams that woke me. I'd been thrown from the path and hit a tree or a rock hard enough to do this." He indicated with his chin his right shoulder and arm. "I think the collar bone is snapped." He reached up to touch his chest on the right side and hissed through his teeth, almost seeming to laugh, as men do when they are gripped by agony. "A couple of ribs too, I'd say."

"What did you do?" Gwawrddur asked, though the answer was evident. Ingild was standing before us, so what he had done was clear.

"I put the poor mare out of her misery." His face darkened at the memory. "The pain was too much for me then and I must have hit my head during the fall, for I swooned. When I awoke, I knew I would not make it to Corebricg on foot, not like this. And so I made my way home." He glanced at the smoke billowing in the northern sky. "I am sorry."

Nobody spoke for a time. I could feel the disappointment in

the men around me. I felt it myself. Moments before we had believed that help was at hand, armed warriors were coming to bolster our numbers and to turn the tide of the fight that might already be underway at Werce's Hall. Now we knew that we were as alone as ever. I looked at Cormac. His face was as pallid as Ingild's. Perhaps the gravity of what he had done in the night was finally hitting home. There would be no reinforcements and we were doomed to stand against the Norsemen until we had slain all of them, or had died in defence of the minster and settlement.

Gwawrddur took a deep breath. He squared his shoulders, showing the rest of us how a warrior dealt with bad tidings.

"We cannot give up hope," he said, sweeping the gathered men with his glare. "To do so would be to see the monks, women and children of Werceworthe slaughtered or enslaved. They have only us to protect them now. And, Ingild," he said, turning to the injured man, "you are not at fault."

Ingild nodded his thanks, but it was clear that he did not truly believe the Welshman's words.

"You two," Gwawrddur pointed at a couple of the spear-men, "give your spears to others to carry and help Ingild back to the hall." The men hesitated. "This is no time to tarry," Gwawrddur snapped and they jumped to do his bidding. "All of you," he went on, "hurry back to the hall. If the fighting has not started already, it will soon, and Hereward will need all the spears and blades he can get. Eowils here will keep watch for us." He clapped the boy on the shoulder and a silent understanding passed between the Welshman and Gewis. The boy would be safer here, far from the fighting at the minster. Gewis nodded.

"Back up that tree with you, boy," he said.

"And, if you see any of those heathen whoresons," said Gwawrddur, "blow your horn as if Satan himself is risen from hell. And then run like the wind."

Eowils grinned, despite his obvious fear. His father ruffled his hair and pushed him towards the tree.

"I won't let you down," Eowils said and leapt for a low branch. He swung for a moment before pulling himself up and was soon high in the leafy canopy.

"Well," said Gwawrddur, turning to Cormac and me, "what are you waiting for?" The rest of the villagers were already making their way back up the rise towards the hall. Gewis looked back once and waved at his son. The sky was dark with smoke. Neither Cormac nor I had moved. "Your fine blades will be no use to anyone here," he said, falling into a loping run. We hurried to catch up with him.

And so, for the second time that ill-fated morning, with the sun's red disc barely over the horizon, I found myself running through the rain-soaked grass. When we had run towards the sounds of Eowils' horn, we had been filled with anxiety at what we might find. Would the Norse be awaiting us there, with swords and axes bared to hew our flesh? Now, as we headed back towards Werce's Hall and the smoke-leavened sky beyond it, there was no doubt in our minds of what we would face when we reached our destination. We had seen the Norse put their torches to the thatch and wattle of the buildings and watched as the flames leapt high, just as the ships' fires had burnt brightly in the darkest part of the night. Skorri's wolves were loose in the sheep pen and there was nowhere for them to turn.

Gwawrddur had told Eowils to sound his horn as if Satan was coming from his sulphurous realm should he see the Norsemen approaching. We were running towards a mass of those Norse demons and I could not shake the image of the flames licking the sky, as if hell itself had already opened up its fiery depths to spew forth pain and misery on God's children. The stink of smoke was thick in the morning air now. It burnt my throat and my eyes streamed.

I ran on, the weight of my byrnie encumbering me, but not slowing me unduly. I kept close to Cormac and Gwawrddur and we soon passed Ingild and the two men who were helping him up the rise. Not for the first time I wondered at the madness that had taken a hold of me back in that bloody dawn on Lindisfarnae. For was this not what I had wanted since then? To run towards danger instead of away from it? Whether I was chosen by the Almighty to bring the defenders to this place, or I had become moonstruck, or even, I thought with a stab of unease, if I had been touched by the Devil himself, there was no time now for second thoughts. For, as we grew closer to the hall and the knap of the hill, the clash of blade against blade and the screams of men fighting and dying reached us.

There was no more time for thought now. Blood and fire had come to Werceworthe and all I could do was to stand alongside my new shield-brothers and fight until we had vanquished or I could fight no more. It was in the Lord's hands now and I offered up a silent prayer to Him as we crested the hill to look down at the mayhem arrayed before us.

Fifty-Three

Catching my breath after running up to the hall, I looked down in horror. The land beyond the hill was wreathed in thick black smoke, obscuring the river and forest. Every now and then fire ripped through the black murk, rending the smoke with red claws of flame. Sparks showered into the darkened sky and beneath them, Werceworthe blazed.

Once more I thought of hell and the Devil. Perhaps there was truth to what Godwig and Eadgar had said on Lindisfarnae. Mayhap these Norse heathens had been sent to punish us for our sins.

The roof of the scriptorium, where I had spent so many hours copying texts onto stretched hides of vellum, collapsed. The growl and hollow groan of its demise reached me a heartbeat after it fell and in that instant, I was back in Lindisfarnae, witnessing the buildings there, the knowledge and learning, being destroyed as peaceful, God-fearing men and women were violated, butchered and enslaved. The aches of my body and the fear that had gripped me since the raiders had first torched the buildings vanished, burnt away in the flames of the savage destruction of my home.

Closer to my position I could see that the raiders had advanced on the steep incline. There they had found another of

our defences. I well remembered the gruelling labour of digging
the deep trench and then helping Drosten to drag the heaps
of brambles to fill them with their thorny tangle that would
claw and snag at anyone who attempted to pass. My arms and
hands still bore the scratched memories of those sharp thorns.
We had created the obstacle to slow down any attack, but the
Norse were no fools. They had fallen foul of the ditch in the
village and they would not be so easily tricked again.

They had brought planks and boards of timber they must
have taken from the buildings before setting them on fire.
These they had lain across the bramble-tangled trench, using
them as a bridge, just as we had done.

But they would not cross unimpeded.

Hereward and Drosten had led half a dozen spear-wielding
villagers to the edge of the ditch. And there, in the smoke-
swirled morning, they were holding back the score or more
Norse raiders. The Norse had formed a shieldwall to ward off
the thrusts of the crude spears and more than one of their hide-
covered boards bristled with white-fletched arrows. Some way
up the slope stood five of Wulfwaru's archers, though where she
was, I did not know. More arrows flew, flickering bright in the
morning sunlight that struggled to penetrate the gloom that had
enshrouded the settlement. None of the arrows found flesh. The
Norse seemed content to stand behind their shields, perhaps
waiting for the archers' meagre supply of arrows to be used up.

The Norse line parted and a tall warrior stepped forward,
right onto the lip of the trench, seemingly uncaring of the
spears that probed for him. His right arm swung and the dawn
light gleamed from a flying axe. With unerring accuracy, it spun
towards Drosten. I wanted to shout out a warning, but the
words caught in my throat. The axe flew true, and would have
buried itself in the Pictish warrior's head, if not for his uncanny
speed and instinct. Drosten must have noticed the movement
of the weapon out of the corner of his eye, for in the instant

before impact, he swayed to the left and the axe sped harmlessly past him. The villager beside him was Freothogar, the man who made the best honey cakes I have ever eaten. Freothogar was a wonderful baker, but he had neither Drosten's skill in battle, nor his luck. The axe-head buried itself deep in his throat. As I watched from the hilltop, Freothogar clawed at the axe, staggering backwards, before collapsing on the wet grass, to stare up sightlessly at the smoke that filled the sky. Perhaps his soul was even now flying with that hot smoke towards our Heavenly Father.

On the hill beside me Cormac growled. Gwawrddur's face was set and stern. Off to my right, I noticed Runolf. He had donned his byrnie and at his side he held his huge axe. The stark shadows from the light of the rising sun made him appear to be carved out of granite. Around him were gathered the last of the ceorl spear-men. Some of them also bore axes and swords stolen from the fallen Norse. Beside the giant Norseman, the villagers seemed like men in the shadow of a god of war stepped from a saga of old. His expression was resolute and bore no emotion. His beard jutted and I saw that he had brushed and oiled it so that it shone in the morning light. The peasants stared down at the battle below them, their faces aghast and pale, the only colour on their cheeks coming from the flames and the fire of the sun.

"What are you doing standing there?" I bellowed, suddenly unable to contain my fury. The men who had run with us to the oak had now reached the hill too and looked down with horror at the doom that was before them. "Come on!" I shouted. "Follow me. We must aid them."

I raised my sword and made to run down the hill, but Gwawrddur's hand gripped my shoulder, pulling me up short and making me wince against the pain of his fingers digging into the wound there.

"Wait," he said. I tried to shake him off, but he tightened his grip and the pain was excruciating, so I stopped struggling. Look-

434

ing over at Runolf, he shouted, "Do you plan to just watch?"

Runolf glanced over.

"Hereward ordered us to stay here," he said. "Protect hall."

Gwawrddur nodded. Below us, the Norse began to push forward, arranging their shields into a wedge that would allow them to be protected while they used their makeshift bridge to cross the ditch. Once they were over that obstacle, death would be upon us all. There was no way that the defenders there could hold against so many. Only Drosten and Hereward were true warriors, but they were but mortal. In moments, they would be overwhelmed, hacked down by Norse blades.

"You cowardly, Norse bastard," spat Cormac.

Runolf's face darkened.

"I no coward, Hibernian puppy," he said, his rumbling voice carrying over the tumult of the fighting and the roar of the flames from the burning settlement. "I follow orders. Not like you."

Cormac moved towards the huge Norseman. The men around us shifted nervously.

"Enough, Cormac!" snapped Gwawrddur, his voice cutting through the tension like a sharp sword blade. "Runolf was right to follow Hereward's command. And the hall must be protected. If Skorri has split his force and attacks the hall when none of us is here to stand against him, all we fight for will be lost." He rubbed a slender hand over his face. His eyes narrowed as he thought of our predicament. "But Hereward thought Skorri had attacked from the south," he went on. "We know that he hasn't and so I will give a new order. Runolf, stay here with those men in case some of the raiders come from the south after all. Cormac, Hunlaf, stay here too and save your anger for the enemy. If they break through, you must defend the hall." I longed to rush down the hill towards the fighting, to aid Hereward and Drosten and the others; to throw myself into the fray and feel the bite of my blade into the flesh of the heathens who had defiled our land. But

Gwawrddur squeezed my shoulder, making me wince. "Do not give in to your lust for battle, Hunlaf," he whispered, so that only I could hear him. Then, raising his voice again, he shouted, "Listen for Eowils' horn. The rest of you," he swept his gaze across the pale-faced spear-men who had run with us, "follow me!"

With that, the lean Welshman, sword in one hand and a short axe in the other, sprinted down the slope. The spear-men hesitated for a heartbeat. I wished to run after Gwawrddur, but they were terrified. And yet, he was right. Hereward had drilled into us over and over the importance of obeying commands in battle and so, despite the burning fury that threatened to overwhelm me, I held myself back.

"You heard him," I shouted, my own impotent rage lending my voice a savage edge, "do not just stand there. Do your duty! Do not forget what you are fighting for!"

Dudwine, a stocky man who I knew had three children under the age of four cowering in the hall, was the first to react. He nodded at me and set off after Gwawrddur. An instant later, the others followed and soon they were roaring their own battle cries and exhortations to God to give themselves courage and to drown out the rage-filled shouts of the Norse.

"Where is Wulfwaru?" asked Cormac.

"I know not," I replied. "I cannot spy her amongst the archers." Even as I spoke the words, the women on the slope loosed their last arrows and turned to hurry back up the hill, passing the shouting men with their black-tipped spears. As they reached within earshot, Cormac called out to them.

"Where is Wulfwaru?"

They carried on up the slope, but none of them replied.

When they reached the crest of the hill, Cormac grabbed hold of Mildrith. She tried to pull away. One of the men with Runolf shouted out angrily.

"That's my wife! Unhand her!"

Cormac ignored the man, instead focusing his glare on Mildrith. She was pale beneath the soot streaks on her face. Cormac would not relinquish his grasp on her. "Where is she?" he hissed.

Mildrith looked about her for support, but the other archers had hurried inside the hall and her husband was being held back by Runolf, who seemed interested to hear what she had to say. There was something in the demeanour of the women that demanded an answer.

"Tell him," I snapped, suddenly certain that there was a secret we needed to hear.

Without warning, Mildrith's shoulders slumped and she looked down at the churned mud before the entrance of the hall.

"She is doing what she must," she murmured.

"What do you mean?" said Cormac. "Speak clearly, woman!" He shook her, and her husband called out again.

"She is protecting our families," Mildrith said with resignation in her voice.

I could make no sense of her words. The heat of the fires that yet raged in the settlement reached us here on the hill, drying the sweat on my forehead. The acrid stink of the smoke that billowed and swirled from the conflagrations scratched in my throat and stung my eyes. The families of those defending the settlement were in the hall.

"Why has Wulfwaru remained inside with the monks, with the women and children?" I asked. "She is the best archer of you all."

Mildrith shook her head. Perhaps sorry for what she was going to say, or maybe bemused at my lack of ability to understand what she was telling me. I should have known. We all should have seen what would happen when the sword-song began, when the flames licked the sky and the raiders were so close we could hear the hatred in their shouts. I was young then, and naive, but I am surprised the older men did not comprehend what I have since witnessed countless times in my long life. For a mother will do anything to protect her children. She will lie and cheat and even sacrifice her own life, if she thinks she can save her loved ones.

Wulfwaru was no craven. She had not avoided the battle. But she had looked at the force arrayed against us and had decided we could not prevail.

"She is leading them away from here?" I asked, knowing the answer from her expression, even before she replied with a nod.

"She is leading them all to safety," she said.

I sighed. Of course. The attack had not come from the south as we had thought and so, after realising that the way was clear, and with the savage fighting at the ditch to the north holding the Norse at bay, Wulfwaru had made the hard choice to betray our trust and to disobey the orders Hereward had given us. She had broken her word, but I could not find it within me to be angry at her. Neither, it seemed, could Cormac, who was nodding.

"It is dangerous," he said. "She cannot have gone far. I must go with her."

I reached for him, holding him back.

"Wait. If you go too, we will have lost two of our best fighters. You will be dooming us all."

He glared at me, weighing the value of my words. I like to think he was going to stay with us, to stand shoulder to shoulder against the attacking Norse. But in that moment, everything changed, and he pulled free of my grip and sprinted away, quickly disappearing around the side of the hall.

For over the clash of battle and the hissing crackle of the fires, a scream had echoed on the morning air. It had come from the south, from behind the hall and it was some way off. It was a terrible scream of pain and anguish.

It was a woman's scream. And we all recognised the voice behind it.

Wulfwaru.

Fifty-Four

The southern slope beyond the hall was chaos. The great oak loomed in the distance, and I wondered for a heartbeat how Eowils had allowed the Norse to approach us without warning. A dozen or more warriors, led by the red-cloaked Skorri himself in the great helm I had first seen on the beach at Lindisfarnae, had swarmed up the shallow rise and met the fleeing villagers. If Wulfwaru had not been leading them away from the fray, we would have had no warning of this second group of attackers.

I cursed Eowils and then with a wrench of my stomach, I understood he must surely be dead. Skorri must have somehow sniffed out the boy hiding in the tree's branches and slain him before he was able to warn us. Either that or Eowils had fled the moment we had left him to watch the south.

The Norse had yet to reach the huddle of villagers, but they would be upon them in moments. They laboured up the incline, their faces grim; the steel of their swords, knives and axes bright in the morning sun. Most of the people from Werceworthe who were gathered there were frightened women and children. I saw none of the brethren who had been my brothers until so very recently, so it seemed Beonna had ordered them to remain in the hall, perhaps trusting to God's mercy. Watching the

439

oncoming Norse raiders, with their round shields, sharp blades and snarling grins, it would make little difference whether they were in the hall or not. Soon we would all be dead.

Wulfwaru sent an arrow flying and I lost sight of it as it shot towards the Norse. It hit its target though, and I saw its effect as one man halted, and fell to his knees, clutching at the shaft that now jutted from his throat. Blood bubbled up between his grasping fingers, smearing the white goose feather fletchings. Wulfwaru nocked another arrow and loosed seemingly without thought. The Norse were almost on the villagers now and she could not miss. But these were men of war, not straw targets, and having seen their comrade fall, they raised their shields as they ran. Even over the cacophony of shouts, and screams, and the clash and crash of battle and fire to the north, I heard the arrow strike Skorri's linden board. The arrow remained there, quivering, but the jarl did not slow, and a heartbeat later, the Norse were upon the villagers.

I was running now, sword in my right hand. Surely, the invaders would slaughter the defenceless people cowering there before I could reach them. Yet still I ran. Cormac was some way ahead of me, but I could see that even with his head start he would be too late. And then something unexpected happened.

Just before the Norse reached the terrified villagers, a small group stepped forward to intercept them. These were the old and the infirm and I saw that Ingild, broken collar bone and all, was amongst them. Aethelwig was at the centre of the small band that blocked the Norse warriors' path and I marvelled at the bravery of it. These greybeards and peasants stood no chance of halting the Norse attack and yet they threw themselves into their path in an effort to buy enough time for the women and children to escape.

"Flee!" came Aethelwig's hoarse shout to Wulfwaru and the others.

The women and children were pale-faced, sobbing and terrified, but Wulfwaru pushed and cajoled them into motion, moving back towards the hall and away from the Norse.

The tanner clutched a knife in his hand, nothing more. Some of the other men carried axes. One bore a hoe, another a rake. The Norse wore byrnies of burnished iron, their heads were covered in metal helms, their faces part-hidden by grim eye and nose guards. In their hands, these raiders wielded long swords and axes as if they had no heft at all. These were wolves meeting sheep and the outcome of the encounter was inevitable.

I let out a roar of rage and desperation as the first of the villagers was cut down and blood sprayed crimson. Another fell, head smashed and opened by a savage axe stroke.

"To me!" I shouted, remembering Runolf and the others who had been near me at the hall. "To me!" My breath tore at my throat and my shoulder screamed as I ran. I could feel hot blood soaking into my kirtle from the reopened wound.

Wulfwaru screamed and I saw that Aethelwig had fallen, battered under the force of the Norse charge. Skorri's red cloak fluttered and flapped about the tall Norse warlord as he fought, blending with the blood that misted the air.

The women and children were some distance from the fighting now, but I could see that Wulfwaru could no longer loose arrows without fear of striking the defenders and so, like me, she was forced to watch in impotent rage as the men were hacked down.

Like Cormac, who sprinted before me, I ran directly towards the bloodletting. My mind had gone blank and all I knew was that I had to defend these people; my people. I was as certain as I have ever been of anything before or since that it was my destiny to fight those Norse and that my presence would somehow make a difference, perhaps even turn the tide of the fight.

What pride, what hubris the young. To think that I, little more than a boy who was more monk than warrior, could stand before those men of battle! It was madness, and yet, as is so often the case, it is not the cautious warrior who lives to tell of his exploits, but the foolhardy and the mad. And it seemed I was not the only young man consumed with that madness on that blood-drenched morning, for with a bellowing scream that gave all those fighting a moment's pause, Cormac careened into the gap left by Aethelwig in the defensive line. The Hibernian sprang over the tanner's prostrate form and flung himself at the attackers. He fought with a frenzied savagery, smashing his sword into shields and using the momentum of his rushing run to push the Norse warriors back.

I could scarcely believe what I was seeing, but in that first hesitation, Cormac's blade found the neck of a broad-shouldered brute who had been swinging a great axe with abandon. Blood fountained and Cormac let out a cry like that of a beast. More animal than man then, Cormac scythed his blade into another warrior's chest, bursting the rings of his byrnie so that they flashed silver, like sparks in the rising sunlight.

The Norse were wary now. They took a pace backward and Cormac followed them, taunting and screaming. The few village men who remained on their feet faltered. They were not killers and they saw that Cormac might have gained them enough of a respite to flee back to their families. He had sped to their aid and now they deserted him and I could not blame them. But Cormac was my sword-brother and I would not allow him to fight alone. We were all doomed anyway and with that thought, I threw away all concerns. We would both die but we would die fighting. Even then I was sure that God had brought me to that moment. That it was my divine calling.

The first man Cormac had struck was on the ground, his blood turning the earth about him to mud. Without pause I kicked him square in the face. Blood sprayed from his ruined neck and he flopped back, unmoving. I scooped up his shield and lifted it just as one of the other Norse sent a vicious swiping blow of his sword at my chest. Despite the unfamiliar bulk of the byrnie, I was fast and the battle instinct was upon me. At such times it always seemed to me as though I could move faster than any opponent, and see them react almost before they knew it themselves. I can barely walk twenty paces now without losing my breath. I am slow and decrepit and it is many a year since I was quick and deadly. But then, as I hefted the shield taken from the dying Norseman's hand and felt the reassuring weight of the iron-ringed shirt upon my shoulders, I felt invincible. I caught the sword blow on the rim of the shield and turned the blade away. I was dimly aware of the pain in my shoulder as I positioned the shield, angling the board to deflect the blows that came thick and fast, but the real pain would come later. In that instant, with the blood coursing hot through my veins, I shrugged off the hurt. As in every fight since, I would not truly acknowledge the injuries my body has sustained until after the battle was over.

To my left, I saw that Cormac was battling against the huge leader of the Norse. Skorri laughed as the young Hibernian flung himself at him time and again. Each time, the jarl stepped away, using his shield to slide the attacks effortlessly away, or raising the blade of his sword to parry with a ringing clang that reminded me of Werceworthe's warning bell. From the briefest of glances, I could see that Cormac was struggling. Skorri was clearly not just large and strong, he was a master swordsman and Cormac's brutal onslaught had carried him as far as it would without more skill to back it up.

But there was no time for me to watch. I had my own Norse brute to contend with. The Norseman before me was raining stinging strikes on my shield. He was strong, massively muscled and powerful and with each hit splinters flew up from the linden board. His blows were so vigorous and relentless that I could not find an opening. I was skilled enough that I could soak up his attacks on the shield and my blade, but if I did not end this soon, one of his comrades might turn their attention to me, plunging a blade into my unprotected back or side. Failing that, the warrior, clumsy as he was, might still land a lucky blow.

Around us, the rest of the Norsemen, now no longer held in check by the greybeards and ceorls, headed towards the retreating men, women and children. There was nothing either Cormac or I could do to halt them. We were both locked in struggles to the death. I put the fate of Wulfwaru and the others from my mind and focused all of my attention on the man before me. His attacks followed a pattern and I quickly saw that he relied on his prodigious strength to defeat his opponents. Another strike splintered my shield and I felt the force of it rattling down my arm and into my shoulder. I remembered what Gwawrddur had taught us.

"You do not have to take your enemy in the neck, head or chest to win a fight," he said. "These are the blows all men seek to land, and most expect to defend against."

I saw another attack coming. I took it on my shield as I had all the previous strikes, but this time, instead of sending my own counterattack towards his midriff, where he too would easily block it with his shield, I dropped down and hacked my sword into his foremost foot. He wore stout leather boots, but the animal hide did nothing to stop my blade, which sliced through flesh, sinew and bone.

I wrenched the blade free and my assailant let out a shriek like that of a woman in childbirth. His face was a mask of agony and shock. Without hesitation, I sprang up from where I knelt and drove the point of my sword into his exposed throat. His cry was cut off and his body stiffened for the briefest of moments as my blade plunged further and further up into his head. I felt the tremor of the blade as it connected with bone and I heaved it upward, breaking through the skull. His life left him in a flash and instantly he grew limp and collapsed. My sword was embedded deeply in his brains and his dead bodyweight wrested the weapon from my grasp as he fell.

I staggered at the suddenness of his death and for a heartbeat I was standing alone. Behind me I could hear the sounds of combat, presumably as the Norse reached the fleeing men and their families once more. A woman screamed and the wailing cry of a baby rose above the tumult of the fighting. I should run to their aid. I was filled with the joyful ire of battle, blood-spattered and panting. Perhaps this is what God had intended for me all along; to singlehandedly defeat the Norse who, without my intervention, would rape and murder the weak and defenceless. But I could not rush to help the people of Werceworthe. I did not even turn to witness how the fight was going. For to my left, Skorri seemed to have tired of fighting the wild Hibernian who still beat at his shield with abandon.

As I watched, aghast, the red-cloaked jarl pushed an over-reaching lunge away with the iron boss of his shield and in the same instant he sent a savage riposte slicing into Cormac's side. It was a terrible blow, swung with great force. I noticed the sparkling flash of iron rings shattered and flying. Cormac's face drained of colour and he stumbled. His sword tumbled from his grip and he fell to his knees in the wet grass. Blood sheeted down his side.

Skorri turned away from Cormac, certain of his victory. Our eyes met and I had never known such fear before. The jarl's eyes were not those of a man, they were devoid of feeling, like the cold, killer eyes of a pike that lurks deep beneath the surface of gloomy waters. I could see Cormac moving from the edge of my vision, but I could not pull my gaze away from those eyes. Cormac gasped and whimpered, lifting his hands to try to prevent his gut rope from spilling out. The vivid red of his blood was spreading out, reminiscent of the way that Skorri's cloak was draped over his shoulder. I stared into Skorri's animal eyes and all I saw was death.

"Do not falter, Hunlaf," rasped Cormac with a great effort.

His voice spurred me to action. I had stared into the face of death, and knew that it might well claim me that day, but I would claw and fight against its cold embrace until I could no longer draw breath. I darted forward and grasped my sword. Its grip was blood-soaked; warm and sticky. I tugged it hard, but the man's brains and skull would not relinquish their death-grip easily. Skorri swung his sword with a flourish and stepped forward.

He chuckled.

"By Óðinn, is it only the boys who fight in this land?" he said. His tone was bemused and he clearly spoke to himself, not expecting me to understand his tongue.

Shaking his helmeted head, as if saddened by what he witnessed, Skorri raised his sword. The blade was smeared with Cormac's blood. I heaved at my weapon, almost losing my hold on it. In a heartbeat, he would strike me down and all would be for nought. Was this what God had intended for me?

"Jesu, give me strength," I screamed.

With a sucking pop the sword came free of its fleshy prison and I swung it up to parry Skorri's downward stroke. The swords rang out and the shock of the man's strength shook me. My hand throbbed from the blow and I knew then that I could not beat him. Cormac fell onto his side in the blood-stained grass and I leapt back, making space for me to be able to use the footwork Gwawrddur had spent so long teaching. I might not be able to win, but I would not die easily.

"I am no boy," I said in Norse, spitting the words at Skorri. His eyes widened behind the face mask of his great helm. "And neither is he." I pointed with my blade at Cormac's fallen form.

"Well, what have we here?" said Skorri, his voice amused and as relaxed as if we were chatting over a horn of mead in a feast. "A boy who fights and knows my tongue. You are intriguing indeed. But, alas there is no time to talk and I doubt I will ever know your story." He raised his shield and sword and lowered himself into a fighting stance. "For the dead do not talk."

"I will not die so easily," I said with a bravado I did not believe.

"We shall see," he said. "You will die soon enough, unless you can fight better than your friend there."

And with that, he jumped forward with incredible speed and power, and the skill of a warrior seasoned in countless combats.

Fifty-Five

I raised my shield, barely able to deflect the blow and too off balance to counter. I staggered backwards.

Skorri came on, slashing and hacking his sword remorselessly into my shield. Such was the speed and ferocity of his attacks that I could barely defend against them. I allowed him to drive me back, but I knew that soon, he would seek to alter his attack, hoping to catch me off guard. A heartbeat later he turned an overarm swing into a feint, changing the direction of his strike in an effort to slice into my sword arm.

This was what I had been waiting for. I could not beat him strength for strength and so I must use my speed and guile if I was to have any chance of success. Gwawrddur would be pleased to know I had been listening on all those long, hot days of endless repetition.

I twisted my body, pulling back my arm so that Skorri's blade slashed past harmlessly. Seizing the opportunity, I cut upward. If I could have made the same blow in a downward motion, with my weight behind it, I would surely have severed Skorri's hand, but as it was, my attack lacked power. Still, it was a hit and I felt my blade snag on the jarl's clothing as he snatched his hand away with a sharp intake of breath. Blood bloomed and his sleeve was soon red and wet with it. It was not a deep wound, and I could see that it would not impair his ability to swing his weapon. And yet still it was a victory and I grinned in savage delight at having claimed first blood.

"So," he said, glancing down at his blood-soaked sleeve, "the boy has teeth." His eyes narrowed. "It was you who came to our camp last night, wasn't it?"

"I was not alone," I replied, flicking a glance at Cormac's still form.

Skorri laughed.

"Well, you are alone now," he said. "Every man is alone when death comes for him."

His words filled me with a sudden fear and again I was staggering back, parrying and blocking his flurrying attacks. This time, his speed, strength and skill got the better of me. Using his shield to block mine with a bone-rattling crash, he dragged his sword across my left shoulder. The byrnie stopped the blade for an instant, before it slid from the iron rings and cut into the flesh between my neck and shoulder. I screamed, feeling the hot blood stream down my back and chest, mingling with the blood already oozing from the axe wound.

I flicked a wild swipe at his face, catching the side of his helm with a sonorous, hollow clang. He pulled back and I let him go, glad of the respite.

Skorri shook his head and fumbled at his helm. Perhaps I should have slain him then, but I was too concerned with my own wounds. My shoulder was a burning agony. I tried to raise the shield, but even though I was able to push away much of the pain, I was not sure I would be able to move the linden board with enough speed to make it useful against such a powerful enemy.

Casting his helm aside, Skorri shook his head like a dog leaving a river. He roared and the sound of his fury chilled my blood.

Behind me I could hear cries of pain and the splintering of

sundered shields. Skorri looked in the direction of the fight, but I dared not turn away from him for an instant. If there is one thing I have learnt over the years it is that you do not turn your back on a killer, any more than you would pet a wolf. Skorri frowned.

"By Óðinn, boy," he snarled, "this has gone on long enough. Now you die."

I had struggled before to defend against him. Now, he was injured and fury-filled, and my shield shattered under the brunt of his attacks. Soon, I had little left in my hand save the iron boss, splinters of linden and tatters of hide. He hammered another blow at me and I somehow managed to deflect it with the shield boss. The sound was like that of a smith at his anvil, and as if at the forge, sparks flew. I groaned at the impact and the toll on my shoulder.

I aimed a lunge at Skorri's unprotected face, but he took the attack easily on his shield. I felt a jolt to my left leg and Skorri laughed.

"Time to die!" he jeered.

I stumbled back. Looking down, I saw crimson soaking my breeches. Skorri's blade had clanged off my shield boss and buried itself in the flesh of my thigh, a hand's breadth beneath the protection of my byrnie. He strode towards me and I tried to adopt the warrior stance, legs bent, ready to leap backward or forward. My left leg gave way and I sprawled to the earth.

"It is almost a pity I will not learn of your tale, boy," Skorri said, stepping close. I swung my sword at him, but he clattered the rim of his shield into my wrist and the weapon fell from my numb fingers. He kicked the blade out of my reach. I squirmed, trying to slide away. If I could gain some distance from him, I could regain my footing. I yet had the seax in my belt. I could still fight. As if he could see the thought in my eyes, without warning he jumped forward and placed a booted foot on my waist. His foot covered the seax, preventing me from pulling it from its sheath.

"Pray to whichever god you worship, boy," Skorri said, turning his sword so that the blade pointed downward towards me. I realised then that I was already mumbling the words of the paternoster under my breath. I did not know when I had started to pray, but I hoped that the Almighty would hear my supplication for mercy and welcome my unshriven soul into His kingdom upon my death. For I could no longer deny it. Death was upon me. There were no more words, no more feints or attacks I could use to prolong the fight. Skorri stood over me and he would plunge his sword into my flesh. Cormac's blood, still slick on the blade, would mingle with mine and I would die. I wondered if I would meet Cormac in heaven.

Was this truly the end? God had not intervened. He would allow me to die just like all the others at Lindisfarnae. Perhaps this was a punishment for our sins after all. In that moment, I hated God. I closed my eyes, not wishing to see the descent of the blade or the triumph on Skorri's bearded face. I stopped praying, instead I shouted a curse at the Almighty. Was this how He treated his faithful? Allowing them to be brutalised and slain? Curse Him then, I thought, and readied myself for death.

I have often pondered what happened next. Was it God's way of showing his forgiveness to me, that even when I had forsaken Him and railed against His divine plan, He should choose to save me? Or was it perchance God's sense of the absurd that He should grant me salvation at the very moment when I had ceased to expect it, or even ask for it? I will never know, but before Skorri's sword blade cut into me to take my life, a rumbling voice cut through the noises of fighting, my panting breath and the roaring of my blood.

"Brother!" screamed the voice. It spoke in the tongue of the Norse and I recognised the speaker.

Runolf.

I opened my eyes to see what fresh insanity that morning of madness had brought.

Fifty-Six

Skorri lifted his foot before shoving against my chest with the sole of his boot. Sprawling onto my back in the wet grass, I let out a stifled cry as my shoulder connected with the ground. The Norse jarl turned away from me, disdainful of the threat I posed.

He spun to face Runolf, who was striding towards him. In his wake, Runolf left dying and injured men. It appeared that with his spear-men and his own formidable prowess and bulk, the men of Werceworthe had shattered the Norse line. Runolf's great axe dripped with gore and his face and beard were blood-spattered and begrimed. His eyes gleamed from the dark mask of blood and muck.

"You!" said Skorri. "I cannot believe you yet live."

"No thanks to you," spat Runolf. "Why did you leave me there? I have asked myself that these last months. My own brother…"

They were close now, each tense and ready for combat. They glowered at each other and now that I saw them together, the familial similarity was obvious. Both men were huge and muscled, though Skorri was perhaps slightly taller. Both had the same deep-set eyes, jutting jaw hidden behind a thatch of red beard. And each had a bloodied weapon in his hand. I shuddered at the sight of them there, bristling with ire, exuding power and danger.

"I would have killed you in an eye-blink," Skorri said. "I had grown tired of your morose nature. We sons of Ragnar Olafsson are wolves, not sheep to bleat about our loss and sorrow."

"Then why did you not do it?" shouted Runolf, in a sudden outburst of fury, like lightning from a darkening sky. "I would be free of the burden I carry."

"Your burden?" Skorri sneered. "By Óðinn, man! We have all lost loved ones. Death is the stuff of life itself."

For a moment, there was a tenderness between the two men. Skorri's shoulders slumped and a sorrow entered Runolf's eyes.

"I told Estrid it would be kinder to kill you," said Skorri. He shook his head. "But she made me swear not to slay you."

"Estrid?" said Runolf, his voice hollow and bleak.

"She is my woman now," replied Skorri, a thin smile playing on his lips. "She was always too good for you. It was her destiny to be the wife of the jarl, not his brother."

Runolf's eyes glistened beneath his heavy brows.

"So the betrayal is complete," he said.

"Estrid hates you," said Skorri, his voice almost gentle. "You know this. But she is a soft woman. Soft of heart, like you. I can see why she loved you. Once." The jarl glanced at me. I was yet prostrate on the ground, and for a fleeting moment I imagined he was going to come back to finish what he had left with a quick stroke of his blade. Just as he had slain Tidraed on Lindisfarnae. But his gaze did not linger on me. Instead he indicated me and Cormac with a nod of his shaggy head. The instant he looked away, I pushed myself to my feet with a grunt of pain. I would face what was to come on my feet. Like a warrior.

"I see you are still sending boys to fight in your stead." Skorri sneered.

Runolf grew very still. His face darkened like a thunderhead before a storm. A breeze shivered the branches of the alders off to the west. The first fat drops of rain splattered from the grey sky and a chill fell over Werceworthe.

"And I see you still talk too much," Runolf said, his words clipped and as sharp as shards of ice.

They stared at each other, neither moving. Such hatred flickered between them and something else, a sadness and disappointment that things should end this way, perhaps. I thought then of my brother and the frequent enmity that burnt between us. What would need to occur to drive us to seek the other's death?

I shuddered and, as if my slightest of movements had shattered the moment of calm before the storm, the Norse brothers sprang at each other. Runolf's axe clattered into Skorri's shield with the sound of a clap of thunder. The tempest had begun and the huge warriors hammered blows, parrying and dodging with a nimbleness that belied their size.

My head spun at what I was seeing. I had lost a lot of blood. My kirtle was soaked and plastered to my skin. The rain fell more heavily and its cold touch kept my mind sharp, focused. I knew that I should turn and flee, taking advantage of the distraction. I knew not what was happening on the north side of the hall, but it seemed that here, on the south, the Norse had been subdued or slain. All except Skorri, and I did not doubt that Runolf would deal with him. I should go to Hereward's aid at the bramble-filled trench. And yet I could not bring myself to leave. The strength and skill of the fighting men wove a spell over me, and I could not drag my gaze away. Each man was like a warrior of legend or a Norse god of battle; hugely muscled, tall and as fast as a cat. And each of them burnt with a loathing, the flames of which had been fanned over years of resentment.

A proud man such as Runolf would seek vengeance for what Skorri had done. Abandoning his brother and taking his wife for his own. But there was something else that fuelled their hatred, something more despicable, it seemed to me. Darker and deeper.

The rain seethed down, drenching the fighting men. Their feet churned the earth into a quagmire as they danced with death.

They fought on, clashing together like waves striking cliffs and then retreating. Steel flashed in the morning sunlight and I squinted at the bright flourishes. With a start I saw that the sun was yet low in the sky and it pierced beneath the clouds like a well-struck blade beneath a shield. A rainbow glowed in the sky and, unbidden, I thought of God. He had promised Noah that He would deliver his family from the great flood that He had sent. Surely this was the Almighty's sign to me that He would grant us victory over these pagans.

My body ached and trembled with exhaustion. It felt as though most of a day might have passed and yet it was only a matter of moments since the sun had risen above the horizon. So much death and destruction in such a short amount of time. And there would be more before the end, of that I was certain. I stooped to retrieve my sword from where Skorri had kicked it into the grass. Its grip was wet and cold against my hot palm.

Pulling apart, the brothers circled, wary and breathing heavily.

"You are a nithing," spat Runolf.

"A nithing with a warband," replied Skorri. "What do you have here? Christ monks, old men and children?"

"I have my honour."

Skorri laughed.

"Honour?" he said, turning his head this way and that to loosen the muscles in his neck. "You lost your honour when you lost your son. You have nothing now!"

Runolf's scowl deepened.

"You are right that Osvif's death will always weigh upon me. Perhaps neither of the sons of Ragnar have any honour. By Óðinn, we are both fools. And it seems there is little to separate us. We are both in a strange land, with no ships to carry us home."

"Death will separate us soon enough," snarled Skorri.

He flew at Runolf and I have seldom in all my years since witnessed two stronger warriors locked in combat. Their weapons sliced and hacked, parried and countered. Each man was drenched with sweat, mud, blood and rain. Their breath steamed in the rain-cooled air as they panted and grunted, lunging, blocking, twisting and swaying. They were both huge men, but they moved with the grace of dancers and I wondered how many times as they were growing up they had practised together. They appeared to know what the other would do before he acted and it seemed that neither of them would ever tire.

But such ferocity can never last, and no battle rages forever without a conclusion. Like many fights I have witnessed or fought in over the long decades since that early autumn day at Werceworthe, the epic duel between Runolf and Skorri was decided by luck. My Christian brethren would say there is no such thing as chance; that God's hand intercedes, and perhaps they are right. But I have seen too many good men fall to believe God wanted all of them dead. And yet, who am I to question the way of the Lord? In His divine wisdom perhaps every blow and movement of warriors in a battle is preordained according to His design.

On that rain-sodden morning, the acrid tang of the smoke from the minster buildings in my throat, I watched as Runolf sprang forward to deliver what was surely a killing blow. Skorri was overstretched and off balance and his brother's axe would crunch into his exposed shoulder, ending the fight with a victory for my Norse friend. The rainbow gleamed in the dark sky, a reminder of God's promise of salvation. My heart swelled with pride in Runolf's triumph and I rejoiced.

But Runolf did not deliver death to Skorri.

As he jumped towards his brother, Runolf stepped on Skorri's great helm. The ornate helmet lay in the long grass where the jarl had discarded it, and now, unseen, it saved him from certain defeat. Runolf's ankle turned and he stumbled awkwardly to the side. With uncanny agility and the speed I had marvelled at, Skorri seized his chance and surged up. He had almost fallen moments before, and he had only prevented himself from tumbling to the earth by holding himself up with his sword hand, his fist against the earth while his sword was still in his grip. So it was that he could not bring his sword to bear instantly. Instead, he pushed himself up and slammed into Runolf with his shield.

Already staggering, Runolf toppled to the ground. His axe flew from his grasp. Skorri was upon him in a heartbeat.

"Goodbye, Runolf," he said, bringing his sword scything down. Runolf tried to roll away, but the blade struck him. However, instead of slicing deep into his neck, Skorri's sword smashed into his brother's shoulder. Runolf grunted from the force of the blow, which had surely broken bones. But the iron rings of his byrnie protected him from the worst of it.

"Time to die now, brother," Skorri said, grinning. "I will tell Estrid you died at my feet, as it should be."

He raised his sword for another strike. Runolf seemed resigned to his death now. He glowered up at his brother.

"You can tell that whore whatever you want, if you meet in the afterlife." Runolf spat the words. "For you will never leave these shores."

Skorri seemed about to reply, then he tightened his grip on his sword and plunged it down towards Runolf's defenceless form.

Fifty-Seven

"No!" I screamed.

As if woken from a nightmare, I rushed forward, stumbling towards Skorri. The rain came down in sheets now and my feet threw up great splashes of muddy water.

Skorri's sword flashed downward and I knew I would not reach him in time. But the jarl's killing blow never landed. Skorri pulled up, his mouth and eyes gaping in shock. A white-fletched arrow quivered from his unarmoured thigh. He looked down at the projectile jutting from his flesh and growled. Raising his sword once more, he readied himself to kill his kin.

Directly beyond Skorri, I saw Wulfwaru draw back her bow again. The rain tumbled in a torrent from the leaden skies. Her bow string must have been wet, with much less power than if dry. And the rain and wind must have made the shot almost impossible from that distance. As I ran I realised that if her aim was not true, she was as likely to strike me as to hit Skorri. I did not hesitate. I trusted in her skill and, perhaps, I trusted in the promise in that rainbow too, though with a wrenching in my guts, I saw that the coloured arc was no longer visible in the sky.

I ran on, screaming defiance at Skorri, in an effort to distract him. He turned slightly at the sound of my voice as Wulfwaru let fly another arrow through the wet air. It found its mark, burying itself in the jarl's neck. He arched his back, roaring at the sudden pain. Without thought, I sliced my sword down with all my strength. I barely felt resistance as my blade hacked cleanly through Skorri's wrist. His sword fell, as useless to him now as his severed hand that flopped beside the weapon, fingers splayed out like one of the starfish I would find in the rock pools by the mouth of the Cocueda.

"I told you you talk too much," said Runolf, heaving himself up with a groan. His left arm hung at his side and blood stained the links of his byrnie.

Skorri spat. He glared first at his brother and then at me. His eyes narrowed.

"Gods! Defeated by a boy."

The second arrow twitched as he spoke. It was not a deep wound, the power of the arrow having been sapped by the rain and the damp bowstring.

"And a woman," said Wulfwaru, who had approached us. She still held her bow and had a new arrow nocked, ready for whatever might come to pass.

Skorri spat again and then laughed.

"Women!" he said. "They are always the undoing of men." His eyes flicked and roved, looking about him perhaps for a way to escape, for it is not in man's nature to admit he has been defeated. Blood was pumping from the stump of his sword arm which he clutched to his chest. A thin trickle of blood oozed from the arrow wound in his neck and his breeches were stained red where the first arrow jutted from his thigh. His face was pale and I knew that death would claim him soon. His gaze settled once more on me and his eyes widened in recognition.

"You were there, weren't you?" he asked, his voice weaker now than it had been only moments before. Absently, I noticed Runolf stoop to retrieve his great axe.

"Where?" I asked. My mouth was dry and my voice rasped.

"At the island of the Christ men," he said, and my blood ran cold. He had seen me? Remembered me? "You wore the robes of a holy man. Your head was shaven, but I saw you."

I said nothing. I could not speak.

"You tried to save the girl. Killed Sigfast. By Óðinn," he chuckled and the sound filled me with horror, "I bet that didn't go down well with the priests of the nailed god." He groaned then, unable to hide the agony he was surely feeling. The flow of blood from his wrist was slower now, his face deathly pale. He fell to his knees, glowering up at us in his humiliation and defeat. "And so you became a warrior. For a woman."

At last I found my voice. I wanted to say that I was a warrior of Christ. That it was I who had assembled the defenders to this place. That, by the grace of God, I had defeated him and his raiders. But I said none of those things.

"She was my kin," I said. "Your men killed her." I wanted to be as stoic and strong as Runolf and Skorri, but tears mingled with the rain on my cheeks and my voice cracked. "You destroyed so much... killed so many of my friends..." I could find no words to explain what had happened to me that day on Lindisfarnae, and what explanation did I owe this dying man? This Norse jarl who had turned my world upside down and changed the path of my life forever? I owed him nothing. I longed to spit into his face as I was sure he would have done if our positions had been reversed, and yet all I could feel now, as I looked down at his curds-white face, was pity.

"We did not kill that one," he said with a sigh. "Aelfwyn." He closed his eyes, perhaps remembering her face, or maybe allowing death to claim him.

I felt faint and my vision swam with tears and rain blurring my sight.

"Aelfwyn is alive?"

Skorri opened his eyes slowly, as if it was a great effort.

"Much too pretty to kill, that one," he said with a weak smile. "Fetched me half a pound of silver."

"Where is she now?" My voice was urgent. If Aelfwyn yet lived, I must rescue her. The thought of her, abused and used by pagan Norsemen in some far-off land of mountains and rivers, filled me with dread and a sudden, powerful renewed purpose.

Skorri's eyes had closed again and he swayed on his knees.

"Where is she?" I shouted, reaching for his shoulder to shake him. He could not die yet. I must learn of her whereabouts. But before I was able to lay my hand on him, a figure crashed into Skorri, tumbling them both to the muddy, blood-churned earth.

Cormac, covered in gore, screamed as he landed atop the Norse jarl. His blade rose and fell, hacking into Skorri. Blood sprayed in the air and was quickly washed into the grass and mud by the driving rain.

Wulfwaru staggered back from the sudden violence. Runolf did not move. His face was grim, his mouth a thin line in his beard.

I looked on in dismay as Cormac slashed and hewed at Skorri's already dead body until he finally collapsed atop it, panting and gasping for breath.

My mind roiled.

Cormac was not dead. I should have been overjoyed at seeing my friend alive, and yet my heart sank as I saw Skorri's lifeblood soaking into the earth. Vanishing with it, I imagined, was my chance of learning where Aelfwyn had been taken. I wanted to scream at Cormac. I would never find out where my cousin was now, and it was all his fault.

I opened my mouth, ready for a torrent of furious expletives, when Wulfwaru rushed past me and threw herself down beside the Hibernian. My words died on my lips as I saw how pallid he was. His sundered byrnie and the torn kirtle beneath it were both dark with blood, and his face was as grey as Skorri's. Wulfwaru glanced up at me with tears in her eyes. Her hands were smeared in Cormac's blood. Beneath her fingers I caught a glimpse of the gaping wound and the obscene jumble of innards within. I understood then that Cormac was not somehow less severely injured than I had at first thought. The wound he had sustained was mortal and he would die all too soon. My anger vanished, like the blood being washed away from Skorri's cooling cheeks by the downpour. I knelt in the mud beside them. Wulfwaru was cradling Cormac's head, smoothing his hair.

"Wulfwaru," he whispered and a small smile played on his blue lips. "Did we win?"

"We won, Cormac," said Runolf sombrely. Reaching down, he turned over his brother's body. Skorri's left hand was revealed. In it, he yet grasped in death a slender knife that he must have pulled from his boot. Runolf nodded and caught my gaze. Perhaps Skorri had meant to attack us one final time with that knife, or maybe he wished to be holding a weapon when death claimed him.

"Look, Cormac," I said, my mouth dry. "Skorri had a knife. You saved me."

He did not answer. I stared down at him. His eyes were unseeing. Drops of rain splattered into them and he did not blink. Water pooled on his face.

Sorrow filled me and I pushed myself to my feet. There was so much death there. So much suffering. I staggered through the injured and dead, hurrying now to the north of the hall. The time had come to finish this; to avenge Cormac and all the other fallen.

"With me!" I shouted, and the few remaining spear-men of Werceworthe fell into step behind me.

I left Wulfwaru weeping over Cormac, her tears falling onto the Hibernian's upturned face, where they were intermingled with the blood and rain.

Fifty-Eight

The rain had made the smoke from the fires darker and denser. The land before the hall was thick with the fug of the burning buildings. Fighting yet raged near the trench. Several bodies were strewn about the pit and many more lay tangled and bloody within the thorny grasp of the brambles.

The Norse had crossed the obstacle and the defenders had been pushed slowly backwards. But despite their inferior numbers and most of the spear-men being untrained ceorls, Hereward's small force had acquitted itself well. The Norse dead were heaped before the shieldwall and as we ran down the slope I could see Hereward, Drosten and Gwawrddur yet stood. Only three of the villagers fought on and my heart sank to think of the great losses of the people of Werceworthe.

As I watched, Drosten, a great axe in his hands, hacked into a shield. Using his prodigious strength he pulled the hide-covered willow board down, exposing the raider behind. Hereward roared, slicing his blood-drenched sword into the Norseman's unprotected face. Beside Hereward, Gwawrddur carried no shield. Instead in each hand he held a sword. He parried a savage stroke with his right blade and, dropping to his knee in a fluid motion, thrust his left sword beneath his attacker's shield and deep into his thigh. The Norse fell back from the vicious onslaught, a couple of the remaining villagers menacing them with their spears.

But the third villager was not wielding a spear. The dark-garbed man bore a shield and a gore-slick sword. As the Norse line took a step back, this swordsman sprang forward and cut into the foot of one of the retreating warriors. With a gasp as if I had been struck, I recognised the figure. It was Leofstan!

My mind reeled. How could this be? And yet there was no denying what my eyes beheld. My old master was fighting in the shieldwall, and judging from the speed with which he had attacked and then jumped back into position, he was no newcomer to battle.

I shook my head. There was no time to think on this; no time to hesitate, as Leofstan had told me. Fewer than a dozen Norse remained. We would end this now.

Flanked by the spear-men who had already blooded themselves against Skorri's warband to the south, I staggered down the hill, brandishing my sword. I had no shield now, my shoulder screamed and my left leg throbbed with the effort of running. But I would not stand by while my friends fought. Together with the ceorls of Werceworthe, we could turn the tide and overcome the Norse once and for all.

As we neared the fighting, I heard Runolf's bellowing cry from atop the hill behind me.

"Your jarl is dead!" he screamed in his native tongue. "Skorri Ragnarsson is dead!"

Turning, I saw he held his brother's severed head by his mane of red hair. Gore dripped from the ragged neck.

The Norse hesitated. Their morale, already weakened by the terrible losses they had suffered, threatened to leave them completely at the sight of their leader's disembodied head.

Hereward and the defenders paused too, taking a few steps backward to distance themselves from the attackers. Hereward could see me approaching with more men and was glad of the respite and reinforcements. His teeth flashed in a savage grin. He could scent victory now where not too long before he must have been sure all he would reap from this bloody harvest was the bitter fruit of defeat.

With a shock, I saw that one figure had not pulled back with the other men of Werceworthe. Gwawrddur sprang forward into the gap between the two lines of fighters. His blades flickered as he hacked and lunged. What was he doing? Was he mad? And then I understood.

While Drosten, Leofstan and Hereward had been distracted by Runolf's gory prize, the Norse had quickly renewed their attack. As quickly as their morale had weakened, so their rage flared into a searing flame of fury and they came on again, blood-soaked blades dripping, intent on vengeance for their jarl and their fallen comrades.

Alone, Gwawrddur had seen the danger and he rushed to meet it. I screamed out a warning, but it was lost in the noise and distance.

The slim Welsh swordsman, his two blades flashing, leapt high, climbing the shield of the central man in a move that I would not have believed possible, if I had not witnessed it with my own eyes. His blades sliced down and he took the man's head from his shoulders. Blood spouted high into the air. Leaping from the dying man's shield, Gwawrddur spun towards the man on his right, his long sword flicking out and piercing the second enemy's eye.

Gwawrddur cut into the forearm of a third man, who stumbled away from the Welshman's glimmering blades. This was the stuff of legends. Scops would sing of Gwawrddur's sword-skill in halls throughout the land. Such was his speed and prowess that for a heartbeat it looked to me as though he would slay all the remaining raiders unaided.

But alas, this was no bard's song and Gwawrddur was but mortal. No man can tempt his fate forever. As Gwawrddur turned to face the fourth warrior, another slammed a short axe into the Welshman's back. Gwawrddur spun around, slashing the sword in his right hand across the axeman's eyes. He advanced on the remaining Norsemen. But his wound was deep and streamed blood. His strength would wane quickly. Even a warrior with his skill and bravery could not hope to be victorious standing alone against such odds.

But Gwawrddur was not alone.

Drosten let out a Pictish war cry and jumped forward, with Hereward and Leofstan on either side. A moment later, I reached them and together, with the spear-men of Werceworthe, we dispatched the last of the Norse warriors in a welter of slicing sword cuts, hacking axe blows and piercing thrusts of wood-tipped spears.

Gwawrddur had collapsed to the ground in the final assault and for a terrible instant I believed he had been slain. Then, with a groan, the Welshman began to push himself to his feet. Drosten stepped forward and helped him up.

"You are a selfish man, Gwawrddur," said Hereward, removing his helm and running a bloody hand through his sweat-drenched hair.

Gwawrddur gave Hereward a twisted smile.

"How so?"

"Did you think to leave none of the bastards for the rest of us?"

Gwawrddur winced with the pain from the cut to his back.

"Well, I had seen how slow you were, Northumbrian," he said, his face expressionless. "You needed all the help you could get."

Hereward grinned and Drosten laughed. But I could not bring myself to smile as I gazed about me at the destruction and death.

We had won, but at what cost? Was this victory worth what we all had lost? So many had died and the minster and houses yet burnt, coughing out thick belches of black smoke into the rain-hazed morning.

I panted, dragging in deep breaths of air. The smoke stung my throat. I stared about me at the blood-smeared corpses of men I had known as peaceful farmers. There was Freothogar, who was always cheery and baked mouth-watering cakes. There was Garulf, the smith. Their corpses now were twisted and broken where they had been slain. They were barely recognisable as the men I had known.

The defeat of the attacking raiders awoke a lust for blood in the remaining villagers, and they now hammered blows down on their enemies over and over until the Norse dead were more meat than men. I stepped back, allowing them their vengeance for they had lost many loved ones that day.

My hands shook and I wondered whether I was still the man I had been. Turning away from the death all about me, I knew I was not. I never would be that man again. Not truly. I was a warrior now, but I wanted no more of this killing. Not then. My heart quailed at the thought of fighting again. And yet, even if I were to cast aside my sword and eschew combat and return to the life of the brethren, the Hunlaf of before was as dead as the corpses scattered about Werceworthe.

I knew that to be the truth, but I pushed the thought aside. For all the while another thought whirled and fluttered in my mind, making me giddy.

Aelfwyn yet lived.

My sweet cousin lived!

But where she might be I would never know. Her where-abouts had been lost with the last Norse breath.

A voice cut through my thoughts. A man cried out in the Norse tongue, terrified and pleading. The villagers had not yet killed all their enemies it seemed. One man whimpered and wept as they kicked and hacked at him.

"For the love of Christ, stop this!" Leofstan's stern voice sliced through the villagers' ire, making them pause and look to him. The sight of his tonsured head and kindly face soot-smeared and splattered with blood filled me with dismay. I looked down to the blood-covered sword in his hand. As if noticing it was there for the first time, Leofstan shuddered and dropped the blade to the earth. My mind was full of questions, but I could not put words to them. I just stared at my old teacher, my mouth agape.

Runolf strode past us and into the midst of the villagers. I thought he meant to lay about him with his great axe, for it was clutched in his fist where his brother's hair had been a short time before. But he merely shouldered and shoved the villagers aside.

"Leave him," he snarled, his voice thick and deep.

The men of Werceworthe, blinking as if awoken from a dark dream, staggered back, pale-faced and frightened at what they had become. Runolf knelt beside the fallen raider. He whispered something to the man. The injured warrior shook his head and spat. Runolf put down his axe and then dug his fingers savagely into a deep gash in the Norseman's stomach. The raider screamed in agony. Runolf whispered something else and the man groaned a reply that I could not hear. Runolf stood, retrieving his axe as he did so.

Looking about the corpse-strewn battlefield Runolf pointed to a discarded axe, smaller than his own, but deadly enough. Its iron head was smothered in blood. I wondered if it was Freothogar's, or Garulf's. Or maybe even Gwawrddur's.

"Bring me the axe," said Runolf.

In my confused state it took me a moment to realise he was speaking to me. I stumbled over to it, picked it up in my left hand, gritting my teeth against the pain in my back and shoulder, and went to the giant axeman.

"Place it in his hand," he said, looking down at the stricken warrior. I could see his fresh, dark blood, wet on Runolf's fingers where he had probed the man's wound.

"But…" I said, unsure what words to utter, and yet certain I did not want to arm the last of the Norsemen.

"Do it," Runolf growled. "He does not have long and I gave him my word."

The man stared up at me, pleading with his eyes. He must have been a man of some standing, for his arms were encircled in silver warrior rings and a gold necklace gleamed at his throat. His body was full of deep wounds from spear, knife and axe. Perhaps God had spared him so that he could speak to us, for it must have been a miracle that he was not dead already.

Stooping, I placed the haft of the axe in his left hand. He gripped it feebly and a slight smile played on his features. His eyes took on a look of peace. I stood, pulling away from him and gasped as Runolf's axe took the man's head cleanly from his shoulders. The dead man's legs danced, his feet further churning the earth. His hand convulsed on the axe, twitching the blade and making me start.

Blood began to pump out of his neck and into the rain-soaked earth. My stomach clenched, bile rising in my throat and I turned away. My eyes met Runolf's.

"Now I will never know where Aelfwyn is," I said.

Runolf had left his axe in the earth after cutting the head from the Norseman. Now he placed his right hand on my shoulder. His left hung at his side.

"I know where she is, Hunlaf," he said. He glanced down at the decapitated corpse. "Haki told me."

I felt a wave of hope.

"Where? Where is she?"

"She is far from here. Across the sea. In the land of my people. But Haki told me who Skorri sold her to. I know the man and where his steading is." His face grew hard. "I too have a kinswoman I need to see again. She is not far from where your Aelfwyn is."

"We must rescue her," I said, my voice cracking. "To think of her there…" I chose not to dwell on the fate awaiting the other woman Runolf spoke of.

Leofstan stepped past me, stooped and tugged the ornate necklace free from the headless corpse. The metal gleamed, despite dripping with Haki's blood.

"Looting the dead now, brother?" said Hereward. "I have to say, you fight like a warrior. It seems you plunder like one too." He let out a barking laugh. Leofstan's face clouded as he raised the necklace to the light. Ignoring Hereward, he turned to me.

"How?" I asked, still unable to form the question I wanted to ask.

Seeming to understand, Leofstan placed his left hand on my shoulder.

"I was not always a monk," he said. "It takes a long time for some men to find their true calling." Our eyes met and he handed me the necklace. I looked down. What I had first taken for the crimson of blood was in fact a dark red gemstone. It glittered in the early morning light. The jewel was held within an intricate nest of fine golden threads attached to a solid band of gold that had formed a torc around Haki's neck.

"There is more than your cousin we must seek, Hunlaf," Leofstan said, his voice hoarse with emotion.

I gazed at the trinket in my hands and my stomach lurched. This was from the cover of *The Treasure of Life*. There could be no doubt. Such a thing was unique, the work of a master craftsman.

"They took the book?" I asked in a quiet voice.

"If they did, we must find it. If this evil has descended upon the land because of that book…" His voice trailed off.

"It is just words, you said." I stared into his face and saw the terrible confusion and grief there. "Just learning."

"And if I am wrong?" he whispered. "I could not bear it." He swallowed and rubbed a bloody hand across his face. "Perhaps there is no evil in the tome, but it must not be lost. We must find it."

"But how?" I asked, a sense of despair threatening to overcome me. "Even if Haki told the truth," I waved a hand at the body, not wishing to look at the accusing eyes that stared back from the severed head, "the ships are gone. Even if we had a crew to man them, we have no way to get to Runolf's homeland."

Runolf grinned then and the sight of his white teeth, glinting from within his beard like the maw of a great bear, made me shiver.

"I never told you what I was known for back in my homeland, did I, Hunlaf?" he said.

His words meant nothing to me. I shook my head.

"No," I replied, "but why speak of it now?"

His smile broadened and again I shuddered at his apparent merriment in the midst of so much death and pain.

"Trades run in families, do they not?" he asked.

"Indeed," I said, wondering where he was going with this and wanting nothing more than to be far from the stink of blood and spilt bowels. "Often a son will follow in his father's footsteps." I thought then of my own father. He tilled the land, sowing seeds and harvesting his crops. Such was an honest occupation. I looked down again at the faces of Garulf and Freothogar. I was sure that their fathers had worked the land just like them. Gazing down at my own hand, I saw that it was caked in mud and blood and my sword nestled in my grasp as naturally as a plough is yoked to an ox. Some men it seemed strayed far from their father's shadow.

"So it is with my family," said Runolf. "My father was the best shipbuilder in all of Rygjafylki."

At last I understood.

"And you have inherited your father's skill?"

"No."

Confused again, I found myself growing angry.

"Then why speak of it, man? Now is not the time for riddles."

He laughed and the sound scratched at my nerves.

"I am not as good a shipbuilder as my father," Runolf said and clapped me on the shoulder, making me wince at the pain. "I am better! Better than any shipwright who has come before me." I stared at him. He had never spoken of this before. I recalled his duel with Skorri and the things they had said to each other. He had not told me he was Skorri's brother either. I wondered how many other secrets the giant Norseman was guarding behind his piercing eyes.

"What are you saying, Runolf?" I asked, tired of the conversation. Exhaustion and sorrow threatened to overcome me.

He smiled and I wanted to punch him, but his words filled me with a surge of hope and excitement.

"If you wish to find Aelfwyn and this book you and Leofstan speak of," he said in his rumbling voice like distant thunder, "I can build you a ship. I will leave finding the crew to you."

Fifty-Nine

I am tired now. I have struggled to write these last lines and have been seeking a suitable place where I can pause and set aside my quill without leaving the tale in a state that would prove unsatisfactory for a reader. I may well not live to tell the rest, so I thought I should at least write to the end of the battle for Werceworthe.

I can scarcely believe how many days I have spent scratching away at these lamb hides. Foolishly, I had thought I would be able to tell the whole saga of my life in a matter of days. But the weeks have gone by and each day I have come here to this damp room as soon as there is light in the sky. Here, with my eyesight failing as much as my health and my strength, I have hunched over my writing desk, dipped my pen into the ink and the words have poured from me as I have looked back through the veil of time.

I have smiled to myself when thinking of friends I have not seen for many years, and I am not ashamed to say that I have wept too. That year, when the Norse first came to our lands and descended upon the minsters of the coast like so many savage wolves rampaging through flocks of sheep, was filled with darkness and despair. And yet there were flashes of light. As I have recounted the events of that blood-soaked time, when I lost so much and also, perhaps, found so much more, I have become lost in the very telling. With each passing day I have felt some of the burden of my sins and the crimes I have committed lifting from me. Perhaps this very account is serving as a confession of sorts; a confession of things I have never been able to put into words before.

To think that I began to write this when snow was yet on the ground and now midsummer has been and gone. If truth be told I am surprised that I yet live. I sometimes wonder if perchance God has spared me from the death I was certain would come back in the harsh bitter cold of winter so that I could finish this tale. But I know that is pride, which has been one of my many sins ever since I was that young man who became a warrior all those years ago.

And yet, perhaps it is the Lord's wish that I complete the account of my time on this earth. I am filled with pride, I do not contest that, but I am no fool. I know that I am merely mortal, despite surviving many battles. I will die, as all men do. Sometimes, without warning, my guts remind me that death is waiting for me. My stomach twists with pain all of a sudden, causing me to gasp and pant like a dog. At those times, I am racked with a terrible biting agony and I cannot write for some time. And yet, the pain is more bearable than I imagined it would be. I sought out an old cunning woman in the village and she gave me a potion made of woundwort, mugwort, wormwood and honey. When I drink the foul liquid, the pain becomes dull, like a blunted sword pressed into my flesh, but the memories and dreams of my distant past become vivid and bright. They are so real and clear it is almost as if I could reach out and caress Aelfwyn's cheek, or once again feel the heft of the sword I took from the dead man by the stream.

When I am not writing, my mind has often turned to the reason I yet live. I think back to Anstan, the old man on Cocwaedesae, and how, when he was given a purpose, his strength returned to him and he was able to remain strong enough to light the beacon that warned us of the approaching Norse. Like him, I have come to believe that the purpose of writing the history of my life has kept death at bay. I had thought I would be dead in days when I started to pen this, and yet I still live, clinging to this life as a limpet clings to a wave-washed rock.

Once again my thoughts smack of pride, for surely it must be God's will, and His alone, that has allowed my heart to keep beating; for my mind to remain sharp enough and my hand steady, so that I have been able to fill these sheets of vellum with my increasingly crabbed penmanship. It must also be the Almighty who has kept Abbot Criba away from my cell. Not once has he been to check on the progress of the hagiography of Saint Wilfrid. Even when I sent Coenric, one of the young monks, for more copperas and oak apples, so that I could make more encaustum, the abbot did not question what I have been doing. I sent the lad for another stack of the expensive sheets of vellum, and still the abbot has not come to enquire as to my purpose for the materials. Criba must surely suspect that I have not followed his instructions, and I feel every now and then a slight pang of guilt at the thought of using valuable resources of the monastery for my own selfish ends. And yet, does not the monastery owe me a debt which could easily be valued at more than some calfskins and ink galls. Surely lives are worth more than the goose feathers I use for my pens. Without my intervention, all of the inhabitants of Werceworthe would surely have been slain or enslaved all those years ago. I've often wondered, in my darkest moments, when the light of Christ's love has seemed as far away as the chill stars in a winter sky, whether I caused more deaths than I saved. Could it be that if I had not brought Hereward, Gwawrddur, Drosten and the others to the minster, that the Norse would have come and taken gold and silver and enslaved some of the younger people, but not have killed as many of the inhabitants who died defending the place?

Leofstan thought as much, I was sure. After the battle his eyes were bleak and I could sense his disapproval. He brooded with a simmering fury, as angry at himself as much as with me. More so, probably. He refused to speak of his past life, but it was clear that we shared more than a love of books and learning. I had witnessed how easily he rode a horse, how natural it had been for him to sit and riddle with bawdy warriors. And yet I had never imagined he might have once been anything other than the old monk I knew. That the events had forced him to once more take up a sword and shed blood filled him with dismay and I wondered whether he too, like me, felt a rushing joy when fighting. Was that sense of exhilaration something he had thought himself rid of forever? Whatever his past, he would say nothing on the subject, preferring his own counsel. But he did not hide his despair at the violence that had ripped the minster apart. He never said as much, but I believed he held me responsible, and blamed me for the lapse of his vows of peace. And yet he cleaned and bound my cuts with tenderness and skill, his actions speaking of his affection for me more eloquently than any words.

I remember all too well the smell of the land in the days after the fighting had ended. The lingering acrid stench of the smoke and charred timbers mingling with the metallic salty tang of slaughter and the sweet, sickening aroma as the bodies began to bloat and putrefy. For in the days following the battle, we gave good Christian burials to those of the defenders who had fallen. We had no time of the Norse dead, and we piled them together away from Werce's Hall. Eventually, we buried them in a large pit, far from sacred ground. But not before they began to rot. Grief and sadness hung over the place like a cold dark shroud and it was in nobody's mind to see to the corpses of the raiders who had brought so much sorrow to us all. It was only when the rain blew over and the days were hot once more, as summer had its final burst of warmth and light before the long, dark days of winter, that the smell of the dead drove us to dig, our faces covered by rags. When the pit was deep enough, we heaved the flyblown tangled mass of the dead into their final resting place. We gagged and puked at the stench and the sound of the gas and ichor oozing from their corrupting flesh. I sometimes dream of it to this day and awake drenched in sweat and shivering with the remembered horror.

There was so much death and boundless sorrow in those last bitter throes of summer.

I recall how I wept in those days for all I had lost. I cried for the young innocent monk I had ceased to be, and for all those who had given their life in the defence of the villagers and the brethren.

I can still see clearly the slender form of Eowils' linen-wrapped corpse, being lowered into the earth. We'd found the boy's body, slumped beneath the great oak, his head split with a single slash of a Norse axe. Hereward had mumbled that he would have felt no pain from such a blow, but such words meant nothing to Eowils' father and I can still hear in my memory Gewis's shuddering sobs as he watched the earth shovelled onto his son.

My own tears fell without cease as we buried my friend, Cormac. I was glad that in his last moments he had known that his death was not in vain. He had sacrificed himself for his friends and it was a good death, but I still grieve when I think of what might have been, if he had lived. And yet such is the life of warriors. Death is ever lurking in their shadows, hounding their steps. But Cormac was young, like me, and his end, along with that of Eowils, made me confront the reality that even young men, and those with a talent for wielding a sword, are not immortal.

And I was further saddened that Cormac did not see that Aethelwig had survived. This was one of the only happy moments of those dreadful days. When the smoke cleared, Wulfwaru had found her husband was insensate and bleeding, but not dead. She nursed him to health and they lived happily together for many more years. They had three more children. A daughter and two sons. The first son they named Cormac. The second, Hunlaf. And for that I still feel a sliver of pride. I do not recall what they called their daughter. And for that I am ashamed.

Gwawrddur too recovered from his wound. He always complained thereafter that his shoulder was stiff on cold days and that he had lost some of the lightning speed in his right arm. I could never notice any difference, and he was as deadly as ever for the rest of his days. Gwawrddur went on to send many other enemies to their graves before he finally met his end. It would take more than a Norse axe to slay the Welshman, but I will not recount that sad story here.

My tale has barely begun. But I will rest now, setting aside quill and ink for a day or two. The pangs in my gut have grown stronger of late. Perhaps it is enough that I have told of how we fought against the Norse, or maybe the good Lord will spare me a while longer and I will find the strength to tell of what came next. How Runolf built a ship the like of which no Englisc man had ever voyaged in before. And how together we sailed the Whale Road in search of something that perchance was already lost forever. With God's grace, I will live long enough to write of the search for Aelfwyn and *The Treasure of Life*, and to tell the tales of other deeds that should never be forgotten. Adventures that took me to lands so far to the north that the sea is ice and the winter is one long night. And to distant southern deserts where the sand burns so hot you cannot bear to touch it, and your skin sears beneath the scorching sun.

If it is in the Almighty's plan, I will live to write of these things and more, but for now I will close this book here. And yet, there is the matter of the title of this tome. It is not a hagiography, as I am no saint. No, I will call it an annal of my life. But what name should I use for myself, for I have gone by many names in many places.

The Türkmen clans of the Oguz il called me *Ölümügut*, the Merchant of Death. A band of Nubian pirates off the coast of Ifriqiya knew me as the White-Faced Killer, in their impenetrable tongue. In Vestfold, the men of Halfdan the Mild gave me the moniker of *Skjaldarhleypr*, Shield Leaper, and in the realms of the Lombards and the Franks, I was known simply as the Warrior Monk. I have answered to all of these names and more, and yet, I think it would be seemly if I used the name that would be recognised by the brethren amongst whom I have lived the autumn years of my long life. Yes, it shall be so.

And thus ends the first volume of the Annals of the life of Hunlaf of Ubbanford.

Author's Note

Like many stories, *A Time for Swords* started off as a "what if" question. What if the monks of Lindisfarne had fought back against the Vikings on that fateful day of 793 that is considered the beginning of the Viking Age? I have read tales which have warriors becoming monks in their old age, and my initial question then led me to ask "what if a monk became a warrior?"

My next thought was that if I had the monks fight and win, it would make the book fantasy. We know the outcome of the attack on Lindisfarne, and of the subsequent raids on monasteries around the coastline of Britain at the end of the eighth and beginning of the ninth centuries. I quickly decided that I did not wish to write a fantasy, or a story set in an alternate reality. I wanted to keep the novel grounded in historical fact, even if I needed to take some artistic licence. And so I asked myself how I could tell a gripping story about a group of monks defending a monastery against a vicious Viking attack without altering what we know of the period.

I'm a huge fan of westerns, many of which owe a massive debt to that master of film-making, Akira Kurosawa. Perhaps the most notable of these westerns is *The Magnificent Seven*, which is based on Kurosawa's masterpiece, *Seven Samurai*.

Another inspiration for me was David Gemmell, whose seminal novel *Legend*, features the ageing axeman, Druss, organising a terribly outnumbered force's defence of a seemingly doomed castle against hordes of invaders.

And so the seeds of the idea for this book were planted many years ago when I first watched *Seven Samurai* and when I first read Gemmell's *Legend*. I knew what I needed to do. I would create a motley bunch of warriors, who would stand against overwhelming odds to defend a monastery.

But if I wanted to keep it historically true, or at least not alter the known history, where would I set the novel? It could not be Lindisfarne, or Monkwearmouth or Jarrow. Those monasteries were attacked, but there is no record of any spirited defence, only of destruction and death. And so I began to cast around for a suitable location for a fictional monastery, a site that would match the secluded spots chosen by the abbots and priors of the time. I soon found out that Warkworth in Northumberland, now the site of a village and an imposing Norman castle, was gifted to the Church by Ceolwulf, the king of Northumbria. In 737, Ceolwulf resigned his crown to join the community of Lindisfarne, and bestowed many properties on the monastery to mark the event. There is no evidence that a monastery or priory was ever situated at Warkworth, but with that piece of information, I had the link I needed to Lindisfarne, and the location is suitable for a monastery. Surrounded on three sides by the waters of the River Coquet, the tongue of land is the perfect setting for the novel.

As soon as I had the inkling of the idea for this story, I began to write, having done no real research. This is often the way with me, and the first few pages flowed easily until I suddenly realised I had to slow down and make sure the story I wanted to tell fit within the historical and geographical context. In those initial pages of the first draft, the Vikings attacked on a cold January day. I had read that the raid took place on 8 January, but I struggled to understand how and why the Norsemen would put to sea at such a time and risk the danger of sailing in the winter across the perilous North Sea. But the *Anglo-Saxon Chronicle* said January, so January it was.

And yet the more I wrote, the stranger that date seemed to me. Eventually I dug a little further and reached out to historian Matt Bunker and fellow historical fiction author Tim Hodkinson, both of whom know a lot more about the period than I do. It turns out I was right to be sceptical of the date. They both informed me that the attack actually took place in June and that it is widely accepted that the January date in two versions (D and E) of the *Anglo-Saxon Chronicle* are in fact a scribal error! Apparently, the June date is recorded in the *Annals of Lindisfarne*, and the brethren there should surely have known the correct date.

Throughout the novel, a running theme is Hunlaf worrying about his motivation and also why God has allowed the atrocious attack to take place. Other monks mention that perhaps it is a punishment for the sins of Northumbria. This idea was voiced by the most famous ecclesiastical figure of the time, Alcuin of York, who was then residing in the kingdom of the Franks, serving in the court of Charlemagne. Alcuin was worried about why God had allowed that most holy of places, Lindisfarne, to suffer so. He advised Hygebald to examine his conscience to see if there was any reason why God might have allowed such a terrible disaster to happen. "Is this the outcome of the sins of those who live there?" he asked in his letters. "It has not happened by chance, but is the sign of some great guilt."

It seems Alcuin thought he knew why God's wrath had been visited upon Northumbria. The Anglo-Saxon chroniclers suggest that he perhaps had recent events in mind. The burial of Sicga on the island might have been one of the reasons for Alcuin's belief that God was exacting a punishment on the brethren and the kingdom. Sicga was a rather unsavoury character who, in 788 had led a group of conspirators who murdered King Ælfwald of Northumbria. After his death in February 793, Sicga, who had supposedly committed suicide, was buried on Lindisfarne on 23 April, only a couple of months before the Viking raid.

This was not the only event that Alcuin would have seen as sinful and worthy of punishment from God. The king of Northumbria, Æthelred, had been involved in several plots and many of his rivals had died prematurely, probably on the king's orders. Like many of the kings of the period, Æthelred seems to be little more than a gangster. The exiled king of Northumbria, Osred, attempted to regain the throne from Æthelred in 792, but he was defeated, captured and killed. That took place in September and so it was less than a year later when Lindisfarne was sacked by the Norsemen. Alcuin's letters to Æthelred clearly pointed the blame for this on the sins of the king and his nobility.

The *Anglo-Saxon Chronicle* mentions the signs and storms of God's displeasure in the months before the attack on Lindisfarne and a great famine in the same year. There is probably an element of artistic licence in that, and most certainly not a little hindsight, but tales of whirlwinds, famine and even fiery dragons in the sky, give an indication of the terrible impact the first Viking raid had on the people of Britain.

Throughout the book I have used the term "minster" and "monastery" interchangeably. Such places did not necessarily only house one gender at this time in history and there are female names recorded in the graveyard of Lindisfarne Priory. It was also usual for there to be a settlement of lay people attached to each minster. The people in such settlements would have helped provide necessary labour and certain goods for the minster, while the monks and nuns would provide for their spiritual wellbeing and also lend their own services, farming, healing, brewing and so forth.

The layout of Warkworth is based on the disposition of minster buildings of the time. The monastery buildings would be separated from those of the lay people by a vallum, or ditch, that encircled the minster. This was symbolic of the separation from the worldly of the brethren within. The later thirteenth-century castle at Warkworth looms high above the village on a motte. But there is evidence that this man-made hill was created on top of an older earthwork. There is also what looks like a defensive ditch to the south that predates the castle and even the Anglo-Saxon period. So I have chosen to have Werce's Hall, situated on this lower, but still significant, elevation in the south portion of the piece of land that is almost surrounded by the river.

Monastic hours and the names of the offices have changed over time, but it seems likely that at this time in history Lauds was not celebrated, rather the dawn prayer was Matins. There would also have been a series of Vigils, or Nocturns, during the night.

The books that are mentioned in the scriptoria are all real and would be volumes that a monk at the end of the eighth century might well have read or worked on. The exception is *The Treasure of Life*. It is unlikely a Northumbrian monk would have stumbled on a copy, but that book too is based on reality. The title is one of the books written in the third century by an Iranian named Mani. His works and teachings went on to spawn Manichaeism, a major religion that spread quickly across the known world and in many regions vied for supremacy with Christianity, Buddhism and Islam. Manichaeism is a dualist religion, in which God is not omnipotent and the earth and humans are a battleground between the light goodness of God and the evil darkness of the Devil. Mani believed that the teachings of Buddha, Zoroaster and Jesus were incomplete, and that his revelations, which he called the "Religion of Light", were for the entire world. The Manichaean religion was repressed and persecuted, and copies of Mani's teachings were destroyed as heretical. However, it was still practised as late as the fourteenth century in parts of China. In Europe, later religions, deemed to be heretical and persecuted by the Inquisition, such as the Cathar church, were collectively known as "Manichaean" and were clearly influenced by the teachings of Mani.

Mani's writings would originally have been in Syriac Aramaic, so a book of his teachings in Latin would have been a marvel for a scholar and theologian such as Leofstan.

The covers of early medieval books were often decorated with incredible craftsmanship, adding the value of gold and gems to the almost priceless contents of learning and knowledge within them. I have largely based the description of the cover of *The Treasure of Life* on the lower cover of the *Lindau Gospels* that dates from the eighth century.

Paulinus founded St Peter's School and York Minster in 627. I have assumed that the town would pay special attention to the feast day of St Peter as a result of their church's dedication to that saint. The feast is on 29 June and again I have made an assumption that for several days prior to the actual feast day, festivities would take place in the city. Incidentally, St Peter's School in York is still going strong and is the fourth oldest school in the world. The aforementioned Alcuin was also one of its headmasters for a time before heading to the continent to teach Charlemagne's children.

As far as I am aware there is no evidence for an immersion baptismal font in St Peter's Church in York. But as the capital of Northumbria and the episcopal see, it seemed possible that such a font might exist, despite the abundance of water nearby where baptisms could be performed. Royalty and nobility usually prefer to be baptised in comfort. The cruciform shape of the font, with the three steps leading down into it, is based on early medieval fonts found throughout Christendom.

A quick note about the use of the word "Christendom". It is an Anglo-Saxon term, probably invented in the ninth century by a scribe somewhere in southern England (quite possibly at the court of King Alfred the Great of Wessex). The scribe in question was translating *History Against the Pagans* by Paulus Orosius. Needing a word to express the concept of the universal culture focused on Jesus Christ, the scribe coined the term "Christendom". At that time the word was akin to the modern word "Christianity". It has since evolved and I have used it in its modern context of meaning the "Christian World".

Coquet Island was owned by the Lindisfarne community and there is evidence of a monk's cell there. So it is not much of a stretch to imagine a solitary monk living there in isolation following the most ascetic monastic lifestyle.

The Anglo-Saxons loved to riddle. The rather obscene riddles told by Hereward during the feast when the warriors first arrive at Warkworth are taken directly from the *Exeter Book*. Also known as the *Codex Exoniensis*, the *Exeter Book* is a tenth-century anthology of Anglo-Saxon poetry. In fact, it is the largest known existing collection of Old English literature.

At the end of *A Time for Swords*, Hunlaf has put down his quill to rest, perhaps for death to claim him. But if he manages to stay alive for a few more weeks or months, hopefully he will take up pen and ink once more and tell the tales he has only hinted at so far. Tales of his journeys across the known world, to places most men of the early medieval period would never even have heard of, let alone dreamt of visiting. It is clear that by the twilight of his life Hunlaf had seen many wondrous things and I hope he managed to get more of them down onto vellum before he succumbed to whatever illness ailed him in his old age.

But whatever other tales he will tell, they will be for another day. And other books.

Acknowledgements

As always, thank you, dear reader, for taking the time to read this book. The modern world is a hectic place and I know how difficult it can be to find the time to read a book. I hope you have found this one to be worth the effort. If you have enjoyed it, please spread the word to others who haven't yet discovered my writing. And if you have a moment, please consider leaving a short review on your online store of choice. Reviews really do help new readers find books and decide on one they might otherwise not take a chance on.

Extra special thanks to Jon McAfee, Anna Bucci, Roger Dyer, Robert Vicky McGuire, Emma Stone, Holly Smith and Mary Faulkner for their generous patronage. To find out more about becoming a patron, and what rewards you can receive for doing so, please go to www.matthewharffy.com.

Thanks to my test readers, Gareth Jones, Alex Forbes, Clive Harffy, Shane Smart and Simon Blunsdon. Their input into the early draft was invaluable in improving the manuscript.

I must extend my gratitude to Tim Hodkinson and Matt Bunker, both of whom were quick to help me pinpoint the correct date of the first Viking attack on Lindisfarne and to explain to me how the confusion with the date arose.

Special thanks to Dr Kate Wiles for her advice on the Old English and to Phil Lavender for help with one of the trickier Old Norse terms. Any linguistic errors in the final text are my own.

No book reaches publication without a lot of help, so thank you to my editor, Nicolas Cheetham, and all of the wonderful team at Head of Zeus. With every book they produce I am in awe of the quality. I do my best with the writing, but the wonderful professionals at Head of Zeus are responsible for creating the beautiful books that end up on bookshelves and in your hands.

Thanks to the incredibly supportive online community of historical fiction authors and readers who connect with me regularly on Facebook, Twitter and Instagram. My writing career would be a lot more isolated without the ability to connect with like-minded people via the Internet.

And finally, but of course not least, my undying thanks and love to my family. To my daughters for putting up with me and keeping me grounded, and to my gorgeous wife, Maite (Maria to her work colleagues), for her endless support, wise counsel and, of course, love.

Matthew Harffy
Wiltshire, May 2020

NORTHERN BRITAIN

N

Ubbanford ○

Magilros ✝

R. Tuede

The Wall

HIBERNIAN SEA

0 ⸻ 25 miles

0 ⸻ 50 km